Praise

In Wonder in the Waves, *Jennifer Collins takes us along as Larissa and her son set out to find her first child, an infant she was forced to place for adoption when she was only sixteen. Though there are references to events that occurred in Collins's first book,* Comfort in the Wings, *this story also stands on its own. Readers will be hooked as the search leads Larissa in multiple directions, while she continues to come to terms with other relationships in her life. Throughout, she is inspired by signs of encouragement from her daughter, Emma, who passed less than a year earlier.*

A compelling read, this book will appeal especially to those who have lost children or others they love, to those who have been separated through adoption, and to those who find inspiration in stories of learning to find, within the space of not knowing, joy beside grief. Collins, who has experienced multiple losses in her own life, has a message for us all: We remain connected, even after death, and as life goes on for those who remain, we learn to celebrate those we love. —Casey Mulligan Walsh, author of *The Full Catastrophe: A Love Story* and Host of The Personal Element Podcast.

A tale of deep and enduring love, Wonders in the Waves *touched my heart as it drew me into the most intimate of journeys. Collins masterfully paints a portrait of loss and life. In a rhythm all their own, waves of grief crash, beautifully and intricately interwoven with waves of wonder and possibility. Out of the depths, fresh hope and new life arise. Readers will cheer Larissa on as she answers the incessant call to live, discovering abundant miracles even within the depths of unimaginable loss and pain. This book is an invaluable gift for those who live with grief and those who love them.* —Barb Klein, author of *111 Invitations: Step into the Full Richness of Life* and founder of Inspired Possibility

A beautifully written story about a woman living her life after profound loss. Yet this is not a maudlin tale. Wonder in the Waves *transports Larissa and the reader to the seaside where the beauty of the ocean and the whisper of the waves are warm, healing balm. The characters come alive and it's here that the random threads of life begin to form a tapestry for Larissa that will keep you turning the pages and wishing Larissa was your friend.* —Linda Mazur, co-author of *Emilee: The Story of a Girl and Her Family Hijacked by Anorexia*

The natural wonders of our ocean and coastal waters connect us with a universal spirit. This connection provides peace, healing, and a sense of guidance for the lives in Wonders in the Waves. *This moving novel reminds us to renew our connection and restore our spirit.* —Mark Perry, Executive Director & CEO, Florida Oceanographic Society

Jennifer Collins is a compelling story teller. Collins's first book, Comfort in the Wings, *tugged powerfully at my heart with each turn of the page, and I was truly left longing for more.* Wonder in the Waves *offers new and different ways to honor and celebrate the ever-changing landscape of life. It is one of the first books I have read that successfully travels from the devastation felt by a parent who loses a child to a place where that same parent can emerge from the depths of despair to a life where hope can live and healing becomes possible.* —Kelly A. Reed, President & CEO, Huther Doyle Memorial Institute

Also by Jennifer Collins

Comfort in the Wings

With striking clarity of prose and a feeling for surprising human connections, Collins, in her debut, reveals the inner life of a woman facing grief, uncertainty, and the possibility of restoring severed relationships.... From the first page, Collins demonstrates rare acuity and precision in pinning down Larissa's complex, shifting emotions.... This detailed, immersive novel of a woman facing grief offers wisdom and surprise connections. —BookLife Reviews

Wonders in the Waves

Jennifer Collins

A Novel Inspired by Love That Does Not Die

Words in the Wings Press
New York

Published by: Words in the Wings Press, Inc.
2366 Turk Hill Rd.
Victor, NY 14564
wordsinthewingspress2021@gmail.com

Copyright © 2022 Jennifer Collins

All rights reserved. No part of this book may be reproduced or transmitted in any form or by any electronic or mechanical means, including information storage and retrieval systems, without permission in writing from the publisher.

978-1-7376766-4-5 Hardcover
978-1-7376766-5-2 Softcover
978-1-7376766-6-9 Electronic Book
Library of Congress Control Number: 2022914673

Publisher's Cataloging-in-Publication data

Names: Collins, Jennifer E., author.

Title: Wonders in the waves / Jennifer Collins.

Description: Victor, NY: Words in the Wings Press, Inc., 2022.

Identifiers: 978-1-7376766-4-5 (hardcover) | 978-7376766-5-2 (paperback) | 978-1-73-76-766-6-9 (ebook)

Subjects: LCSH Motherhood--Fiction. | Mother and child--Fiction. | Mothers and sons--Fiction. | Adoption--Fiction. | Florida--Fiction. | BISAC FICTION / General | FICTION / Women | FICTION / Family Life / General

Classification: LCC PS3603.O454255 W66 2022 | DDC 813.6--dc23

Author photos, back cover and interior: Photography by Anna

Cover design and artwork: Sarah Maxwell, BlueViewsStudio.com

Interior design: Mary Neighbour, MediaNeighbours.com

First Edition, Printed in the USA

Although portions of the content of this book, including but not limited to events, people, or entities, were inspired by real life encounters, they have been adjusted or woven together in entirely new ways to create a story that is fiction.

*To my pillars,
my family and friends who are beside me every step of way,
cheering me on, bolstering my confidence,
and inspiring me to keep on keeping on.
I love you dearly.*

Acknowledgments

Almost exactly a year ago, I finished writing my first novel, *Comfort in the Wings*. I never could have imagined the number of inspiring and fulfilling connections that I have made with people in the last year as a result of sharing the story of Larissa and her loved ones. Emails, phone calls, and responses on social media have come from so many who shared their feelings openly after reading the book. These connections are true gifts, and for those, I am grateful. Now I can only hope that with the release of *Wonders in the Waves*, many more readers will reach out to me, share the book with others, and find it to be a meaningful story.

Continuing the theme of connection, I am again indebted to Mary Neighbour. Her expertise and experience are invaluable, and her firm but gentle guidance made this path to publishing so much richer.

Also, a new connection arose during the writing of *Wonders in the Waves*. A friend on Hutchinson Island, Sarah, collaborated with me on the cover art for this book. Learning about the art and creativity of another person has been a gift.

And finally, I value connections to water. In both books, Larissa finds herself near water as she navigates her journey of grief and healing. The settings I chose, the Finger Lakes and the Indian River Lagoon, are special because of their unique geographical qualities and their importance in my own life. I want to recognize the people who work tirelessly to protect our precious waterways and ecosystems. These dedicated stewards are essential to preserving the integrity of our varied bodies of water, regionally and nationally. Not only does this ensure the survival of intricate ecosystems, it also continues to bring the healing characteristics of water to those who seek it. I learned in a personal, profound way that being near water may be an essential part of restoring depleted energy and providing a respite from stress and trauma. Whether it is the beautiful, undulating terrain around gently rippling lakes, the rolling of rivers, or the ever-changing waves of the ocean, all are truly wonders. Each contributed to my own ability to find gratitude and contentment during some of the worst moments of my life. We need the committed, knowledgeable individuals who make water preservation a priority—they bring a heightened quality to our existence that all living things deserve. Thank you.

"Waves are the voices of the tides. Tides are life."
TAMORA PIERCE

1

There are losses that rearrange the world. Deaths that change the way you see everything, grief that tears everything down. Pain that transports you to an entirely different universe, even while everyone else thinks nothing has really changed.

MEGAN DEVINE

Everything about this moment, this scene, is warm and cozy. As I watch the kids, my hands encircle my treasured mug filled with my favorite coffee. The mug is special because it is emblazoned with a photo collage of the three of them. And the coffee, because it's one of those freshly ground, indulgent flavors with a seasonal name like "White Frosty Morning."

I'm wearing well-worn, red-and-green striped, flannel pajama pants that are snug around my legs, which are tightly crossed under me to keep ever-frozen toes toasty. Beyond those beloved heads of hair is an evergreen tree carefully chosen by all of us, with its soft pastel lights almost perfectly spaced to create the heartwarming holiday backdrop. A large window reveals soft flakes settling on outdoor surfaces, giving us a gift of the serene, quintessential white ... *wait a minute*. My eyes flit back to those heads—my three kids surrounded by crumpled, shiny paper, all looking at one electronic device in Emma's hands. The age gap between them is irrelevant as all three stare at the screen and excitedly encourage her to keep pressing the buttons to get to the next option. *Three*! What the bleeping hell?

Just then, I notice my partially numb hand under my pillow, semi-crushed by my head, and am jolted awake by the cruelty of my own brain. This precious scene, this warm glow that every mother, every parent, every grandparent cherishes on one morning a year, is a blasted dream?

The sheer torture of this realization is more than I can bear. I curse a few more times, feel the tears soaking the pillow, and ask once again that ever-present question—why? Again and again, why? Listening to countless people, every darn place I go, wishing one another "Merry Christmas" for the last four weeks has not been hard enough? Dreading my, no our, first major holiday without Emma has not been brutal enough for Eric and me? Now my unconscious, or subconscious, or semi-conscious brain waves bring me this dream, this vivid image three days before December 25th? What will happen on the actual day? They say the first time you experience a holiday, a birthday, or God-forbid, the one-year date since you lost your child is the hardest. Who are "they" anyway? The anticipation has been awful—I can't fathom what the real thing is going to be like.

By some merciful stroke of luck, I must have fallen back asleep for a while, because the next thing I know, it is light, and I need to take a few minutes to sort out real world from dream world. My heart sinks, then totally collapses, as I grudgingly acknowledge the whole Christmas-glow thing was a dream. Can I even force myself to engage in my now well-learned ritual of writing the dream down quickly so I don't forget it?

As the words tumble from my pen onto the nubby, cream-colored pages of the third journal I've filled with dreams since Eric left and Emma died, my eyes rest on the corner of the page. Each page has a tiny image of an animal or a plant or some other representation of nature; that's why I chose this journal when the last one was nearly full. This particular page has a cardinal on the bottom corner. A cardinal—the bird that represents lost loved ones and assures those of us left to actually write in journals that they are looking over us. A tiny little bit of that warm glow from the dream envelops me once again. So, yes, it felt very cruel to wake up to the reality that my three children are not together for Christmas.

In fact, they never were all together—Everett somewhere out in the world, lost to me since his adoption well before Eric and Emma came along. But is the presence of the cardinal on this particular page some kind of sign? Maybe it's a sign that Eric and I will actually find Everett soon. A sign that we will feel Emma's presence on Christmas morning? Is this dream some sort of metaphor created by my imagination? As I recall the dream in writing, it occurs to me that although we all are not physically together, perhaps our efforts to find Everett and to honor Emma unite us in a way we mortals can't possibly understand. I decide to stop the contemplation of signs and metaphors and focus on the details of the dream while they are fresh. I can ponder and put mental puzzle pieces together later—on my walk or when I finally get my butt to a counselor again. Wow! Won't she have a field day with this dream stuff?

A few days after Christmas, I finally make an appointment with a counselor. Over the last several months, I made promises to myself and my best friends, Renee and Isabel, to make an appointment. After my previous experience with a counselor, who told me I should be happy to be able to get out of bed each morning after all I'd endured, making an appointment to try therapy again kept falling to the bottom of my to-do list. It rose to the top occasionally, but the dream about all three kids in front of a Christmas tree pushed me to stop procrastinating and make the appointment. She had a last-minute cancellation and squeezed me into her schedule far more quickly than I'd expected. It's past time to share all the repetitive thoughts I've had with an objective listener.

No more solitary thinking about holidays or how I will manage Emma's birthday in a few months; or worse, the date marking when she passed away. Some grieving parents call it the "angel-versary," but somehow, I cannot bring myself to utter that strange-sounding word. And I actually need to slog my way through two of those "versaries"—one for Emma and one for my first pregnancy, many years prior. What does one call the day your child is ripped out of your arms to go to adoptive parents, against your will?

Such dates are unsettling. On a birthday, do I celebrate that my child once lived, or do I cry that I can no longer hold him? Do both? I haven't gotten there yet for the first birthday since Emma passed on, but I've always felt dramatically mixed emotions on Everett's birthday—my son who was born when I was practically a child myself. Those extremes made me almost schizophrenic for years, until I learned to play the mind games in my twenties to try to forget him. That was no solution; it just caused more guilt. Now that we're searching to find Everett, his birthday this year didn't hold quite as much pain. When his birthday was shortly followed by that dream and then Christmas, I made up my mind it was time to just do it, time to try counseling yet again. The anxiety, the "what-ifs" lingering in the background and jumping out at me far too often, drove me to action. It's about time; it's way past time.

Paul, a grief-group acquaintance turned friend, recommended this counselor. He suggested I read her bio online, study up on the approaches she uses, and then decide for myself. There was something unique about the way Marie described her beliefs about counseling, about life, about grief, and most of all, about motherhood and parenting. She drew me in with her well-chosen words that revealed an obvious passion about her work and compassion for her clients.

As she greets me for the first time, I'm amazed that her smile is as endearing in person as it was on her website. Most of them don't smile—I guess they think a smile is not the professional image they wish to portray? Well, it worked for me, and here I sit.

Marie repeats herself, "Larissa, I need help from you. Can you prioritize how you wish to use your time during this first appointment? Your online registration form indicated you are in need of help with grief, losing a child. Yet, the first thing you mentioned a few moments ago is your search for a child who was adopted. You are dealing with grief around him not being in your life, while trying to find him?"

It's just too much to try to explain. Mine is a messy story, tangled up like a ball of yarn that takes hours to unravel after a cat has played with it. "I guess I did jump around, didn't I? My motivation to be here, to seek help, has many facets. Let's just say it's, uh, complicated. A chronology of my journey here is probably easiest, but not much chance I'll get to it all before the time is up."

"I want you to decide how to use your time. For a first appointment, I schedule a longer than usual session, so please feel free to start the ninety minutes anyway you choose. I'll only interrupt if I get lost and need clarification, or think it's important to do so," Marie explains patiently.

Although I suggest a chronological order, I almost immediately lose that focus and begin jumping all around. I start with Emma's unexpected death nearly a year ago, and relate the gut-wrenching facts quite clinically. Somehow, I've come up with this mechanical, concise version that I can deliver quite unemotionally. It took practice—it was a survival tactic to develop a version I can tell without breaking down in tears. Doesn't mean a tearful rendition is far off, just that I try to get through the facts before I'm assaulted by their meaning.

"Emma was barely twenty-one when I found her in her room, um, unresponsive. After waiting months that seemed like years, the envelope arrived in my mailbox from the medical examiner. It listed a concoction of substances in her system as the cause of death. Most were medications prescribed by her psychiatrist and primary care physician at various times over the last couple of years, like tramadol, Xanax, and gabapentin."

I pause. Even with practice, this part still does not roll off my tongue easily. "Then, fentanyl was thrown in. No one expected fentanyl—she was adamant she would never go near any illegal drugs after her rehabilitation stay. The only logical explanation that I've been able to come up with is that she had no idea she was taking it. Maybe she got a pill that looked like one of those other medications but had fentanyl mixed in? I read every day about that happening to people. If so—then it's murder—that's the only word to describe it.

"At least the medical examiner didn't call it *overdose*, although it seems everyone else, the press, the politicians call it that. How can you overdose on something you didn't know you were taking? After a few days of calling and begging, the medical examiner agreed to speak with me. She told me it was *fentanyl poisoning*. I've actually read recently about families pressing charges and arrests being made related to fentanyl. No one let me know that was an option." My voice trickles away to nothing. I drop my chin to my chest for a few seconds, take a deep breath and change subjects.

I jump from Emma to the almost-as-awful months before that when Eric was first missing, whereabouts unknown. I remember to recount my mostly happy reunion with him three months ago, but confuse Marie momentarily when I go back in time to my pregnancy loss, then further back to my teenage pregnancy that resulted in Everett being taken from me at birth—yet another loss.

"I need to interrupt, Larissa. You're correct—there's a lot to talk about here. Before we go any further, your story is so very sad. I admire your courage and your ability to state all of those events so factually. How did it feel to relate all of that to me?"

I'm struck by the calm, compassionate way she interrupted to reassure me, and then encouraged me to articulate my feelings. It frees me to be very honest, some might say blunt. "It feels shitty. It hurts more than anything ever hurt before."

Her response is intriguing and reassuring. "Larissa, that's because it was traumatic. Grief over the kind of experience you had with Emma is not anything mothers should ever have to endure. That's why we may want to approach this more like post-traumatic stress than grief. I'll tell you more about how we might do that with a treatment called EMDR—Eye Movement Desensitization and Reprocessing—later, but believe me, you have been through the unthinkable. Things that comprise trauma may call for trying something more than cognitive behavioral therapy, if you think you want to."

By the time I walk out of Marie's office, it's almost two hours later. Either she had more time on her hands than I thought, or she unobtrusively notified someone else to come later while I sobbed. I'm exhausted.

I drive to a nearby park and sit in silence for a while. I successfully kept the details of my life factual and to the point until she asked me how it *felt* to do so. That's when the weeping started. I hadn't cried uncontrollably in a long while. In fact, I'd reached the conclusion I was cried out, but apparently, not. Something about being so well rehearsed that I can usually tell it all without feeling, made the feelings more intense when Marie prodded me to describe them. Bogged down by the sadness, I didn't get the chance to tell her about coming to believe in signs from birds and butterflies that bring me messages from loved ones, or of communicating with them through the psychic medium. I guess I can save all that for next time.

I wish I had time to tell her those things, because sadness is only part of the story. Memories are also bittersweet, and more recently, I've even had a few happy moments. But then there are the dreams—a mix of bitter and happy. To her credit, I didn't sense her hurrying me or leaping to conclusions, as happened with previous counselors. This time, I actually *want* to return and look forward to the opportunity to share more with her. I also want to do some research on my own about EMDR before the next appointment.

My phone vibrates in my pocket—Eric. I quickly pick up. "What's going on? Are you home or still with Steven?"

I marvel at how easily, after so long apart, we fall back into multiple, casual conversations a day. The difference for me is, my heart flutters a bit every time I see his name on the screen, and I almost can't respond fast enough. That flutter is a combination of worry for his safety and relief that he's connecting. I'm so grateful for our connection, our reconnection. I cherish every interaction.

"I'm going to hang out here a while longer. Steven is helping me polish up my résumé some more. When we finish, want to join us for dinner? We made a little progress on adoption research and want to fill you in before he goes back to New York. Nothing monumental, but progress." We agree on dinner details for later.

I promised to meet Renee for coffee after counseling, so I text and arrange to see her at our favorite place. She's encouraged me to contact Marie for weeks and wants to hear about the appointment.

The heavy wood door to the coffee shop opens to a little hideaway where we often find ourselves when we need to catch up. Many aspects of our lives have been debated and analyzed sitting in its high-backed window booth. I see her waiting, order my coffee, and walk into her warm hug. She immediately starts an animated invitation to "spill my guts" about how counseling went.

"How was she? Did you like her? Was she easy to talk to?"

When she finally stops her barrage of questions long enough to come up for air, I fill her in on Marie and my ease speaking with her. Renee is glad I plan to go see Marie again.

"Yup, I'll go back. There's a lot I didn't get to share yet. And she described an approach I've never heard of that treats profound grief like trauma. I want to investigate."

"What a great distinction. Sounds promising. And what about Eric and Steven?"

"They continue to enjoy spending time together. What's the expression—'thick as thieves'? He's helping Eric write his résumé and they're continuing to research finding people who were adopted."

"Steven's really stepped into the dad role, hey?"

Reconnecting with Steven (my first ex-husband) over a work project led to the unexpected revelation that he was likely Eric's biological father. Not without a little trepidation, we decided to tell Eric and seek his input into whether to confirm by DNA or not. While I had no clue what my twenty-six-year-old son would think, he didn't hold back his excitement for one minute. Ever since the results confirmed the blood relationship, Eric and Steven spend time together as often as possible, building the emotional bond. It's a ray of happiness for Eric after our loss of Emma. For that and many other reasons, I am grateful. They're also enthusiastic partners in assisting me in the search for Everett. Renee, as I suspected, is interested in hearing about the search.

"So, what's up with the adoption stuff? What have you discovered?"

I explain our approach to go slowly and gather as much background information as possible before making specific inquiries. I find myself being protective of the young man who came into, then out of, my life more than thirty years ago. We don't know if he's even interested in finding me; or should I say, us.

"We've researched the legalities around adoption at that time, thirty-five years ago, and found it was kinda different. It also varies quite a bit by state, and whether it was a private adoption or agency-directed. So, there's all that to sort out. Then, the online search options seem endless! There are forums for people searching for biological parents or children, and agencies who help as well. There's even people who call themselves *search angels*—volunteers who help adoptees looking for families. Who knew? I sent a request through one website for someone to contact me and explain more about how they work. Or, if we can figure out what agency my family used, I'll contact the agency and sign a waiver allowing my confidential and personal contact information to be shared with anyone who might be searching. Just before I came in here, Eric told me they have more information to share later this evening, so the story's ongoing."

Renee appears interested, then jumps to another question. "So, back to Steven and Eric. It's terrific to hear they're spending so much time together. But what's the deal with Steven still being here? Doesn't he need to get back to his job, his brother, his life in upstate New York? Georgia is a long way from the Finger Lakes!"

"Yeah, well, funny you should ask—I wondered the same thing when he came back down to visit this time. Apparently, Steven has an amazingly competent assistant, so they conference call every morning and figure out a way for him to fulfill most, if not all, of his work responsibilities from a distance, at least for the short term. As for his brother, Jimmy, he's doing much better at the moment. He was discharged from the hospital and is in his apartment with his two roommates and their care providers. Steven video chats with him every day, and Eric's started chatting with them as well. I think they're planning for Eric to visit New York and, hopefully, meet Jimmy. If we make progress on the adoption inquiries, I may coordinate anything I need to do in person and go along. It's a lot to get used to, but I keep reminding myself how positive it is for Eric."

Something is still on Renee's mind. Her eyes flit downward and back up again. "Do you, um, think maybe, um, Steven is around so much for another reason? Like maybe he wants to rekindle what you guys once had? Be like a family? Or whatever?" She's smiling in the same goofy way she did when she was with me in New York and first heard Steven and I had talked about our shared past, including Eric.

Slightly annoyed, I know I need to be circumspect about my response. I don't want to overdo the denial and have her quote the old Shakespeare line about protesting too much. "Well, if that's what he's got in mind, he certainly hasn't told me about it."

"What about you? Would you like to start up where you left off? Or start over? Maybe for Eric's sake?"

Wonders in the Waves 11

"Uh, in a word, no. I'm not into a, uh, romantic relationship with any man right now. There are far too many pulls on my emotions, way too many feelings to sort through. Just too complicated. I told you and Isabel at the lake—I'm emotionally worn out, totally spent, just trying to put one foot in front of the other. Christmastime almost did me in, and I haven't even gotten through a year without Emma, and I, well, I ..."

The tears just start flowing. Sometimes, the pain of it all comes crashing back down on me, in waves. Right now, it's more like a tsunami. Every day on this journey of mine is full of peaks and valleys, including landmines. I can be ecstatic one moment to see Eric at the breakfast counter again or hear the excitement in his voice as we talk about searching for Everett, his brother; then devastated the next when I look at the date and count how many days, weeks, or months have gone by without my sweet Emma at the same counter. The idea of a romantic relationship right now is the furthest thing from my mind. Is Renee out of *her* mind?

2

*In the end,
We only regret the chances we didn't take.
The relationships we were afraid to have,
And the decisions we waited too long to make.*
　　　　　　LEWIS CARROLL

After I leave Renee, I check in with Eric again. He and Steven are stopping for takeout and bringing dinner over to the house. Relief—I am too damn tired after counseling and coffee to think about making anything to eat. Even driving over to the short-term rental house where Steven is staying would have been too much effort for me. My energy has been pulled in a dozen different directions today.

　　Although Eric and Steven have been doing research on how to find a person who has been adopted, I began to explore some aspects of this alone. For one thing, I had to figure out where we should even be looking. I retrieved a map to look up the cities along the New York border with Vermont. My aunt's home, where I was sent when pregnant at fifteen, was in a very small town somewhere along that border. The name of the city or town or whatever it was didn't come back to me until I looked at the map. Right away, I recognized the names *Whitehall, Port Henry, Rouses Point*—small places. I was hopeful I could narrow down what hospital I was taken to, or what the closest adoption agency may have been in the early eighties.

At the time, though, the adults were in charge and sure didn't share much information with me. I had been in no state of mind to ask many questions, either. First, it was the shame and guilt at being sent away. Then, the emptiness after the birth left me listless, with no drive to do anything other than survive, and to figure out how get back to my life as a teenager. A teenager who had been hijacked into pregnant adulthood for a few months, then expected to return to normal—whatever normal was.

So, decades later when we decided to embark on the project of finding my son, I let Steven and Eric look into the practical aspects of searching while I tried to wrack my brain and recall anything at all, any small detail that might help direct our efforts. After searching these towns, the nearest hospitals could have easily been in either New York or Vermont, making our work a little more complex. Same for the adoption agencies—if an agency was even used. Oh, how I wish I'd asked my mother this stuff before she died. Why was I so hesitant to look for him before now? By not getting information from her, did I lose my best chances at finding him? These questions are swirling in my head when I hear two male voices and then the loud clomping of their feet up the front steps. Dinner has arrived!

As Eric walks through the door followed by Steven, the inevitable yell for me echoes through the house, "Mom, Mom, are you here?"

I wonder to myself if he ever actually looks before he yells. "Uh, yeah, it's me hiding here behind this mountain of laundry. Makes it look like I'm doing something, but actually, I just got here and put my feet up for a few minutes. What's up with you guys?"

Eric drops the take-out bags on the counter, bolts towards me, nearly knocking all the laundry off the bench, and reaches out for a hug. Oh, dear God, does anything feel better than your kid, your adult son, coming in the door and making a beeline to connect? I can vouch, after months of no kid around to even talk to, there is no better feeling on this planet.

I look over his shoulder and my eyes meet Steven's. A slow smile comes over his face as he greets me a bit more calmly, "Hey, Larissa, we got some of your favorites, according to Eric. Hope you have an appetite!"

Not much later, I survey the empty bags and take-out containers with nothing more than crumbs left in them, and offer, "Guess I was hungrier than I thought. Thanks for grabbing dinner. I too worn out after my counseling appointment to feel like cooking. Tell me about your research today."

Steven begins to clean up and assumes a business-like tone. "It's definitely interesting to try to dig up this information. Eric and I were talking about it in the car on the way over. Maybe we just need to try as many different ways of looking for Everett as we can and see what happens. It seems like the first step no matter what, is for you to let it be known that you are willing to be contacted, that you want to connect. You can go to online forums as a place to start."

Eric chimes in quickly, as if he wants to head off any protest or cautionary statement I might express, "Yeah, Mom, let's just start somewhere. Can't you at least start with a DNA test at one of those online places? I don't want to lose any more time."

This sense of urgency has been Eric's modus operandi ever since the idea of finding Everett came up. His enthusiasm and drive to find his brother are both heartwarming and concerning. Heartwarming—because what mom doesn't want her sons to be together, to enjoy one another, even become friends once they finally meet? Concerning—because this mom is also worried he may be using the search to hide or deny his grief over the death of his little sister. I'm no psychologist, but I know he shouldn't be trying to replace one with the other. On the other hand, maybe I'm making trouble where there isn't any. Maybe it's a helpful coping mechanism for now. Put that on my list to ask Marie.

"Mom, are you even listening? You're staring off into space as if there is no one in this room right now except you. Please listen to me and say we can get started on an action plan—let's just do something while we keep on researching. I'm no good at waiting around."

No good at waiting around is an understatement. Eric has never been patient, and his immersion in this project keeps growing.

"I don't want to wait around either. I sent in a form for someone from one of those search groups to contact me. If I like the sound of how they go about this, I'll fill in the documents about my willingness to be contacted. I promise I will dedicate tomorrow morning to serious searching of agencies that were in operation in 1982; thirty-five years has brought a lot of changes in everything from record-keeping to procedures. I made a little progress in remembering the towns near Aunt Mary's house, and my guess is that they were too small for their own agencies, so maybe they used a place in Albany or even Bennington, Vermont. Maybe the search angel people even have historical information that will point me in the right direction. Good enough for you right now?"

Eric strides across the room with great purpose to give me a hug that almost takes my breath away. "Yeah, Mom, that's an awesome start. Maybe we can work on that together tomorrow?"

3

Don't ever make decisions based on fear.
Make decisions based on hope and possibility.
Make decisions based on what should happen,
Not what shouldn't.
MICHELLE OBAMA

When my eyes flutter open in the morning, unless I have a dream to write about, I typically jump right up to get my coffee and read emails or online newspapers. I don't want to lie there in bed, giving my thoughts time to wander to sad places so soon in the day. I don't want to rush around either—I just want to try to embrace the day before my brain pulls me into the myriad of thoughts about Emma and the bleak days since she has been gone.

I'm on my second cup, engrossed in someone's post on social media, when I hear Eric rummaging around in the kitchen. I call out, "Hello in there—whatcha looking for?"

I hear some mumbled profanities before he finally responds with, "Just an old mug that I always liked. It's ..." He comes out on the porch and spots what he's looking for in my hands. "Oh, I guess you got it. When did she make that anyway?"

He's asking about a mug that Emma made in school. Or rather, she made the drawing of sunshine and purple flowers surrounded by musical notes, and some dedicated teacher saw to it that every family received a mug and some kitchen magnets with their child's artwork on display for all to see. Who could have predicted how special that mug became?

"I think it was first or second grade. It's a treasure, isn't it?"

"Yeah—I got dibs on that one tomorrow morning, OK?" He returns to the kitchen and comes back with some nondescript mug from a convenience store. "So, can we get started or what?"

At first I have no clue what he is talking about, and it must have shown on my face.

Slapping the center of his forehead he exclaims, "Geez, Mom, how many times I gotta ask you? Can we do something about finding my freaking brother?"

Eric looks incredibly annoyed and impatient with me. My concerns for his intensity about the search bubble back up. I want to find Everett as much as anyone, but he is obsessing over this. Trying to broach this carefully, I offer, "Yes, honey, I'm ready to get started today. But can you just take a deep breath? You've only known about him a few weeks, from the tiny little bit of information that I can recall. It's not like you knew him all your life and were then separated. I, well, I'm worried you're trying to use him to replace Emma, or to distract you from facing the loss of Emma, or something else like that?" I realize my voice got squeaky at the end of my statement and made it into a question of sorts. The effort to keep my voice from quivering resulted in more emotion than I'd intended.

Eric stares at me for several seconds, then gets up and starts pacing. Since he was a little kid, he seemed to have an easier time expressing his thoughts while in motion. And the more challenging his thoughts and feelings, the faster he paced.

He is going at a pretty good clip when he sputters out, "I grew up being someone's brother, sharing life with another kid. It's who I am. Don't you get that? No one can ever, ever replace Emma. But I'm not cut out to go it alone. Sure—I have friends, and you, and now Steven, but that's all different. I like being a brother. I didn't always show it, I suppose, but I do. If we find Everett, maybe I can feel like a brother again. I know it could be weird, but it could also be good, right?"

I hear so much in his words. Just like I have clung to my identity as a mother as my most cherished role in life, it sounds like he feels the same about his identity being ripped away from him. I also hear, and feel this myself, that there is no guarantee about anything coming out of this adoptee search. It could be wonderful, awful, anything in between, or absolutely nothing. I'm going to give it my all, but I don't want his hopes and energy to be so totally wrapped up in the search.

"Eric, thank you for telling me about your feelings as a brother. I think I do get it—at least somewhat. I felt pretty alone after my parents and your Uncle Jeff passed away. I knew my parents would eventually die as part of the 'circle of life' or whatever, but I sure didn't want to stop being a sister when Jeff got sick. You know, maybe there is a sibling loss support group around here you could try, or--"

He cuts me off. "Yeah, maybe, but I've been thinking about it. You know how you went to a psychic or medium or whatever and felt like you talked with Emma and Gamma? I'm thinking I'd like to do that too. It freaked me out when that woman spoke to me while I was in Colorado, cuz I'd never even heard of a medium before she talked to me in the mountains. Monica scared me, but also totally drew me in with her comments about the butterfly and Emma. I almost felt enchanted by her and the things she said. Then, once I heard you talk about your experience in a similar way, I wanted to try going to a medium. I want to connect with Emma. Just like I want to find Everett. I want them both."

I look at my sweet, crazy, impulsive, and caring son and reply, "Yeah, so do I." My eyes rest on his most recent tattoo, one he got while in Colorado. "While we're talking about stuff we want to do, what does it feel like, really, to get a tattoo? I've been thinking I want one."

Eric let out a gasp. "What the fu--?" He took a deep breath and burst out laughing. "Are you freaking kidding me? When I got my tattoo, you cried, Mom. You said I was ruining my beautiful, healthy body. Every time you walked by me for a week, you asked me what was I thinking. Then when your little girl got one on her hip bone, you went nuts all over again. I know a lot has happened to you in a short time, but maybe you need to calm down a little. Simmer down, Mom."

It's my turn to burst out laughing. The look on his face as he spewed all that out was priceless. "Well, whether I 'simmer down' or not is my business. I'm fifty-one years old, not like you at seventeen and Emma at sixteen! Anyway, I'm pretty serious and guess I'd like you to go with me for moral support. Are you up for that? Maybe hold my hand or something if it hurts? Say yes, and then we will get started on that search you've been bugging me about."

"Hell, yes! I'll go with you—not to get you to do the search, but just because. And I don't know, I might want you to be there when I do the medium thing. Deal?"

Our eyes connect and for a few seconds all feels right in our world. I stand to walk into the office so we can boot up and start our search, and Eric stops me once again.

"I know you're having dinner with Renee and Isabel, so I'm going to go see Dad, Steven, uh wow, that's confusing. Anyway, can we talk later about maybe getting away from here for a while? It's hard to keep thinking I'm going to see Emma every time I walk downstairs or out into the yard. You know how she loved to sit out here on the porch in the dark and listen to music? I swear I've seen the outline of her head and heard a few bars of that one Grateful Dead song she played all the time. It's kinda cool, but I think I need a break. What about going to the beach or something? A beach we haven't been to before?"

"Wow, Eric, we have a lot to do! Search for Everett, see a medium, get a tattoo, and go to the beach. I thought you were going to New York with Steven, and I have to figure out what I'm going to do about work. But right now, I'm not ruling anything out. Let's just start and put one foot in front of the other. A beach retreat might be good for us both."

"Beach vacations were always the best, Mom. You remember, don't you? We'd always find the coolest things."

Do I ever remember! I'm instantly transported back and see Eric and Emma running far ahead of me. This is what I love about the beach: they can run far ahead and I can still see them. Then, their little legs tire out and they plop down in the sand and wait for me.

I love to make it a time to search for special things like shells, sand dollars, and other treasures. I remember the day vividly when I told them about trying to find heart-shaped rocks. "So, Gamma's best friend—my godmother, Holly—always told me she liked to look for stones that are heart shaped. She told me they were gifts from the sea; that with each wave that came in on the shore, there was another chance that the ocean would give me a present of a heart-shaped stone. If I found one, she always told me it was because someone in heaven loved me very much. So, you guys want to start looking for your presents?"

They started off running, but realized they had to slow down if they were really going to spot a heart-shaped stone. Of course, they got discouraged fast and Emma started whimpering, "It's too hard, Mommy. I can't find any shaped like hearts. No present for me, I can't." We sat in the sand and I reminded Emma and Eric of one of their favorite books, the one about the little fire engine that no one thought could make it up a hill until it started to repeat over and over, "I think I can." Pretty soon, they were back at their search. Several yards ahead of me, I heard first Eric, then Emma reciting the motto over and over. Then, a shriek of delight burst out of Emma's mouth as she found her first heart-shaped stone. Every beach trip after that, even in their teens, they had a competition to see who found the first one, and who found the most. Eric's right about one thing for sure—beach vacations were good for our souls.

"Yes, they were the best, Eric."

Eric smiles and grabs my hand so we can go to the office and start our project for the day.

4

*You will never forget a person who came to you
with a torch in the dark.*

M. ROSE

few hours later my shoulders are rounded forward, my back aches, and my eyes are exhausted from the computer research about adoptees and birth parents' options for finding one another. Who knew there was so much information out there? Eric and I jumped from the search angel site to links for various genealogy services to state maps depicting adoption laws, and finally, to adoptee blogs about their feelings during the search process. The personal accounts were sometimes gut-wrenching and sometimes heartwarming. I also remember that Katrina, a woman I met on the plane when I traveled to New York, had offered to help us if and when we got around to this, so I send her an email as well. I'm tired, both physically and emotionally, but we accomplished quite a bit for our first earnest effort at this complicated task.

Eric's phone pings with a text at almost the same time as mine. Steven is checking in on him, and Isabel is asking me if I can stop at the store on my way to her house and grab olive oil and something for dessert. These messages bring us back from our research and send us both upstairs to get ready to go eat with our respective dinner dates. We decide I'll drop him off at Steven's and then pick him up on my way back. He'll text if he decides to do something different.

One of Eric's buddies from back in high school also texted him, but he's not sure what he feels like doing. It strikes me that he's experiencing something that plagued me for the first few months after Emma died—the uncertainty about who I wanted to be with, and when. Sometimes, I thought I really wanted to be around people, only to discover five minutes into a social encounter that I was ready to be back home. Social settings are still like landmines to me. I'm living in the moment, talking to friends or acquaintances, and some seemingly innocuous comment or question makes my barely stifled emotions explode with the force of a hidden bomb.

Nothing like an emotional blast to keep you from accepting the next invitation. That's how my social contacts became whittled down to Renee and Isabel. True friends—those who can be gentle in the presence of grief and handle outbursts with grace, and not a shred of judgement. I'm grateful for them every day. Eric is not sure how any of his friends will be with him in his grief. Probably tougher for a twenty-six-year-old to figure out than for me with lifelong friends.

I give the front door of Isabel's house the half knock that only an old friend can get away with, just as Renee whips it open to greet me with her effervescent, "Hooray, you're here!" And from the kitchen, comes the restrained voice of Isabel, "In here, love, come on back. And I hope you have that olive oil with you." Their greetings are of such disparate styles, yet both are music to my ears. Although it's only been a day since I saw

Renee and a few since Isabel, it feels like more—busy days will do that, I guess.

Isabel gestures toward the counter and says, "I have one more ingredient to add to the sauce. Please pour yourselves some wine, go sit on the patio, and I'll join you in just a minute." Her house is older than mine, decorated in a homey, cozy style. It's like a warm hug when you need it most. Renee has my glass filled before I can do it. I pick my favorite high-backed wicker chair and curl up into the plush cushions to the wonderful sensation of all my muscles loosening up at the same time.

Once Renee and Isabel join me, each catches me up on the happenings in their lives. Renee always has an entertaining anecdote or two about her work colleagues, and inevitably gets us laughing. Isabel relates a story of the never-ending juggling that comprises her life. As a single mother of two and a professional in the IT world, her schedule is rarely her own. She gets the occasional break when her ex is in town and spends time with the kids at a local hotel, using the pool and other facilities to keep them entertained.

As Isabel's talking about the kids, I'm thinking it's too quiet in the house—*where is Valentino?* She sort of adopted Emma's dog after she died because I could not face that silly little dog and his demands. Besides, her kids had always loved him. I ask her, "Hey, where's Valentino? He didn't come running to the door like usual."

"You will not believe it. Hank actually agreed to let the kids bring Valentino along to the hotel—I guess he knuckled under to their begging and found a dog-friendly place this time. It does make it strangely quiet around here, doesn't it?" I think to myself that a quiet house is a blessing in small doses, but it can be torture when it's thrust upon you without any warning.

During dinner, we continue small talk. But with dessert and coffee, Renee dives into all the topics she has obviously been resisting the urge to ask about.

"Did you guys find out any more about searching for Everett? What's going on? That whole 'search angel' thing you talked about sounded like just what you need to get started."

I begin with telling them about that website. We found a free service, all volunteer, that helps adoptees and birth parents search, based on whatever information you can provide them. There are other, faster-paced or more in-depth search options for a fee. I report that I completed the form and agreed to one of the paid levels of searching.

"It made me sad, though, how many details I couldn't fill in. Of course, I had all my family information, but in the boxes for the father, the only ones I could fill in were his name and the country he came from. I think I know the date of Everett's birth, but not where, or if it was an agency or private adoption. I was able to save the information and submit what I know now. Thankfully, you can go back in and amend it if you find out any other details. I did, at Eric's urging, include Everett as the baby's name, but who knows if the nurse put that down or if the adoptive family kept it? I don't know which is worse—possibly incorrect guesses or blank spaces."

As I pause to sip my hot coffee, Renee prods me along. "OK, what else did you find out?"

"So, they also work with three main DNA testing services and recommend using all of them when you are trying to match someone unknown because they do not exchange information with one another. Of course, the success with that depends on if the adopted child also uses the service. It's not like I'm looking for just any relation, like a long-lost cousin or something. In that case, we might get connected by a shared grandparent to another cousin. We decided that Eric and I are both going to do all three services. He said maybe an adoptee would feel more comfortable contacting a sibling than a parent, who knows? I set up an online consult in a couple of days to get more of my questions answered. I need to go back through all of my mother's belongings for any clues about whether this may have happened in New York or Vermont. New York has unrestricted access to adoption records, meaning that an adult adoptee can get access to an original birth certificate if it wasn't provided to them any other way. That's not the case in Vermont and a bunch of other states. I'm hoping it was New York. Like I told you, my aunt lived in a small town near the Vermont border, and for that matter, not even very far from the Canadian border. I can't imagine them going over the border, but then, I can't imagine half of what's happened to me! I just have to try anything that seems legitimate—leave no stone unturned."

"How was Eric with all of this?"

"Totally, entirely wrapped up in every aspect. It's good in one way, because when I get down on myself for not having done this sooner, he is an absolute cheerleader and motivates me to continue. It's a little like I'm going to be leaving a trail of breadcrumbs in every place I possibly can. But his drive is almost an obsession, and it scares me a little. When I told him that, his response was pretty interesting. Sad, but interesting."

I can hear him saying he doesn't want to be an only child and my heart weeps. I'm not sure I can get the words out to tell them about that part of our conversation, so I start with the rest of what we spoke about.

"Before we started our research this morning, he told me he wants to try going to a medium. Between Danielle, the one from out west who called to tell me she didn't think Eric was dead; Monica, who pointed butterflies out to him in Colorado; and the story of Paulette in upstate New York, he thinks it would help him to see a medium and try to connect with Emma. He, uh, said he wants to connect with her and he wants to find

Wonders in the Waves 27

Everett for the same reason. Says he needs to be a brother, it's who he is."

Isabel reaches over and puts her hand gently on my knee, "Oh, Larissa, honey, that is so sweet. Did you sob?"

Wow, I swear, Isabel is the most empathetic person on the planet. She connects with every emotion. Renee is my action-taker friend, and Isabel is the feeler. What a duo they are, what endearing companions.

"Yeah, maybe not ugly sob, but there were certainly tears pooling in my eyes—maybe his as well. But I surprised him then by saying if he's going to see a medium, I'm going to get a tattoo! That sure made the whole conversation shift gears." All three of us start laughing and telling tattoo stories, and then begin looking up mediums in the area, since none of us had seen anyone here. The searching and speculating about possibilities lightens the mood for a little while.

Renee asks, "Seriously, Larissa, what kind of tattoo are you thinking about?"

"Lots of ideas swirling around in my head. I've thought about replicating some of the school-age art of Emma's, I've also thought about her signature—a lot of moms who've lost kids have posted those images online, or maybe even three intertwined hearts with the letter E in each? One for each kid? But does that leave out the baby I lost when I was pregnant? Steven reminded me I'd wanted to give her an E name also—Elizabeth—so, four hearts? I don't know yet, that's a lot of ink for a first timer; it's a huge decision. Then, there's the decision of where to have it. Do I want it visible to only me or where I can show it off? Don't think I should do this till I'm pretty darn sure. Changing your mind isn't so easy!"

I'm not sure that Renee has heard all my questions; she's still scrolling through tattoo images on her phone. Isabel is picking up our dessert plates and coffee cups, asking if anyone wants a refill.

"I'll just have half a cup. I need to text Eric and see if he wants a ride home or if he's doing something else with Steven or his buddy that offered to take him out for a beer later."

I send the text off and hope that it doesn't take him long to answer. I'm still not over the anxiety that inevitably starts my insides rolling over and over if I don't hear back from him as soon as I expect to. One of the hardest aftereffects (other than the ever-present grief) of losing a child is that you're always waiting for the other shoe to drop.

I can't say that out loud to him; it's a heavy burden for a young man to carry. He wants his independence, as he should, but it doesn't take much of a silence from him to start this mother on a roller coaster of worry, while continuously reminding myself that every time he is silent does not necessarily mean it's the worst-case scenario. Only a parent who has lost a child knows this kind of utter and complete terror.

Eric texts me back that Arnie picked him up from Steven's, and they're at his apartment playing cards and listening to music. Arnie will bring him home. I text back a thumbs-up emoji, although my heart sinks. I wanted to pick him up and go home together. I know that's not realistic, and I should be happy that he's reconnecting with friends. But what my head knows and what my heart feels are vastly far apart.

I thank Isabel for the coffee and fill them in on one more thing, "He also says he wants to go to the beach. Not a beach we've visited before, someplace new. Thinks we could both use a change of scenery. It made me remember a place my parents raved about many years ago, some barrier island on the east coast of Florida. They went fishing there a few years, even urged us to come along back when Jeff and I were in high school, but it sounded boring to us. Eric might be right, but I also need to figure out my work situation before I go taking off to be a beach bum."

Suddenly, as the front door bursts open, Renee and I both shriek as the noise startles us from our calm conversation. Isabel recognizes the voices first and hollers at her kids, "What the heck is going on?" No response is heard because dog barking adds to the confusion. After starting in the door at break-neck speed, Valentino has turned around and is barking—maybe at someone else coming in? Then, my own mother radar kicks in as I hear Eric's voice soft and soothing, quite a contrast to all of the others contributing to the chaos say, "Oh, Valentino, how are you, you little rug rat?"

The commotion settles down a bit within a few minutes and everyone in the room is looking for an explanation. Valentino is the only content one, settling into Eric's upper arms like the old friends that they are.

Isabel's eldest, twelve-year-old Lisa, often described as wise beyond her years, starts with, "Well, Valentino wasn't too happy at the hotel, so then Daddy wasn't too happy with the arrangement, so we're back home!" As she finishes her proclamation, a quick *toot-toot* of a car horn tells us all that Hank must have dropped them off without coming in. My fleeting thoughts about describing Hank, next time I speak of him, as a low-life chicken are interrupted by Bobby, Isabel's eight-year-old.

"Yeah, Valentino barfed on the chair and the rug at the hotel. Dad said I shouldn't have fed him the hotdog I didn't want. It smelled so weird that I almost barfed. Anyway, now look at him, he's all cuddled into Uncle Eric's arms like he's missed him. We all kinda missed you, Uncle Eric, where you been?"

Isabel's kids started calling him *uncle* years ago. Lisa and Bobby were so much younger than Eric, that when they started the uncle thing, it just stuck. There was a time when it bugged Eric, but he looks pretty happy at the moment. He gives Bobby a half smile and keeps on cuddling with Valentino.

"Hey, you're not going to take him back are you? He came to stay with us when you and, uh, Emmie were, uh, well, he's been living here for a while now."

Eric asked me about Valentino when he first came back from Colorado. He and Valentino were not always the best of pals, probably because Eric often ended up taking him out when Emma wasn't home or was just sick of walking her dog. But he was surprised when I said I'd let Isabel's kids take him, maybe even disappointed by the looks of things now. Did I make a mistake in being relieved when the dog wasn't around to remind me of Emma every second? Eric sure looks like the dog is working some kind of magic on whatever strange mood he was in when he walked in here.

"I know he's been here, Bobby. Thanks for taking good care of him. It's just good to see an old friend. My night with another old friend didn't go the way I thought."

Lisa jumps into the conversation, "If you want to borrow Valentino sometimes, Uncle Eric, that's OK. Right, Bobby? Or maybe watch him when we have to go somewhere? Maybe like the next time we go with our dad or whatever?" Lisa the peacemaker; what a sweet, thoughtful thing to offer. She's as sensitive and caring as her mom.

Bobby looks at his mom, then his sister, and says, "I guess, yeah. I really like having Valentino around, but we could share. And Lisa's right, Dad was not cool with us bringing Valentino."

The thought of shared custody of the dog makes me relieved at my guilt for giving him away, and also makes me laugh. When Lisa and Bobby are being shared with their parents, Valentino can be shared as well.

"I'm glad you guys got that all figured out! It's gotten late, and I'm thinking Eric and I should head home. Thank you, Isabel, for the lovely dinner and good company. I'm sure you want to get things straightened out here so you can all get to bed."

Eric puts the dog down on the floor, but Valentino stays by his feet, and with a little whimper curls up in a ball on top of his sneakers. Eric looks confused about what he should do next.

Renee blurts out, "Oh, how sweet, he doesn't want Eric to go--"

Lisa interrupts with, "Bobby, I think since Uncle Eric's night didn't work out, maybe we can let him take Valentino tonight."

Bobby looks toward his mom as if to get her support in this arrangement, but Isabel nods her head and says, "I think so too. Plus, we have to get your beds made before you can get to sleep. I left everything in the dryer because I wasn't expecting you back, uh, quite this soon. We can get him tomorrow after we figure out our schedule for the day. I have to rearrange a few things."

I know tomorrow was supposed to be her day to herself. She had a nail appointment and had asked if anyone wanted to go to yoga with her.

Eric scoops Valentino back up as I hug my friends goodbye, and we loosely plan to get together for lunch in a few days.

After I back out of the driveway, I ask the obvious question, "What's up? I didn't expect to see you till later on."

"Yeah, well, I thought I'd be gone a while, too, but the vibe at Arnie's was lousy. At least once two other guys came over."

After a minute or two of heavy silence, I try again, "Want to talk about it?"

"Can we just get home first?"

Once inside, I make myself a cup of tea and Eric and Valentino go into the living room. As I come in, Valentino is sniffing every inch of the room. I guess he needs to get himself reacquainted with this space.

Eric watches him and shakes his head. "Has it been like this for you, Mom? Since Emma died? Do people say things that just make you want to scream? Or punch a wall? Or worse, punch them?"

I'm mulling over what I can possibly say that will be helpful. Honesty is all that's going to work here. Sugar-coating the experience could only cause mistrust between us or make Eric think his feelings are in some way wrong.

"It is like that for me sometimes, Eric. At first, some comments hit me as outright audacious or insensitive. Others were from well-meaning people who simply didn't know what to say, and their discomfort inadvertently brought out clichés that were simply wrong for the situation. So, what happened tonight? What was said that made you want to punch someone or something?"

"Things were really good with Arnie and me. He started to shake my hand when he first saw me, then pulled me in for a big ol' hug and said, 'What happened with Emma really sucks, Eric. I feel for you and your Mom.' Right away, it felt like old times. We talked a little more about Emma and me being gone so long, but he didn't push it. We started playing poker and catching up on other stuff—like I'd just been gone a little while. After about an hour, these other guys from his work came in that I didn't know. Arnie told them my name and this one guy said, 'Oh, yeah, you're the guy whose kid sister just died one day, right? Did they ever figure out what the heck happened?' Mom, I didn't know what to say. I was mad, I was sad, I felt dizzy, I just wanted to get outta there."

"I've had those times, Eric. I'd be pretending if I said I've figured out how to handle them well. It kinda depends on who it is and if I care at all about them. For someone I don't care much about, I'll usually say something like, 'It's not clear what happened, and it doesn't change the hurt for my family anyway.' I guess I hope maybe that will stop the questions and make them think a little next time, but I don't know. Did you or Arnie say anything?"

"No—I just shook my head and told Arnie I'd catch up with him later. Then, I walked to Isabel's—I needed the fresh air to clear my head. I thought about going back to Steven's, but I just wanted to get in my own bed."

Just then, Valentino jumps into his lap and does the same curling up he'd done on his feet at Isabel's. Absentmindedly rubbing Valentino's head, he says, "What the heck are we going to do, Mom? When is it going to feel any better?"

"I don't know. You need to give yourself some time, Eric. You've only really had this whole story for a short while. I'm not going to say anything dumb about time healing all wounds, but I do know you need to process your feelings more than you've been able to so far. Maybe you'd like to talk to someone other than me about this?"

"I did talk to Arnie, and it felt almost normal. But I don't want to be dumping my stuff on him either."

"Maybe counseling or a sibling group or something would be helpful." I offer gently.

"Do they have those? Sibling groups, I mean? I've heard of grief groups, but I thought they were for like, well, older people, widows and that kind of stuff."

I think of Paul and some of my other friends I've made at a group specifically for parents who have lost children. Some of them must know about services for siblings. "I know a few people from my group, who may have connections that will help us. I have a meeting tomorrow and I'll ask."

"You can ask, I suppose—not sure if I'll go. I'm not too keen on talking in front of strangers, but maybe, sometime, I guess."

Neither one of us feels much like talking anymore. Eric is flipping through TV channels, but I'm exhausted. Heading toward the stairs, I call over my shoulder, "Love you, Eric. Get some sleep."

"Love you, too, Mom."

Those four words make my trek up the steps just a little bit easier.

5

There are souls that you just can't forget.
They might fade off into the distance,
But they will always find their way back to you.
Maybe through a dream,
An old love letter or a song,
Some souls are never truly gone.
Kristin Kory

I'm startled awake. Valentino's barking, Emma's overslept again. I'm happy to go let him out. Swinging my legs out of bed to rescue him, confusion hits me. Did I dream, have a nightmare, that Emma passed away? If so, then the dog never left to go stay at Isabel's. How can this be? The fleeting moment of happiness fades as my thoughts begin to untangle what's real and what's a dream. We were at Isabel's last night, and there was all this chaos...

"Geez, really? Do you have to get up this early? Now I remember why I thought you were always such a pain in the neck. Come on, little dude." Eric's tone of voice starts out about as grumbly as a voice can get, then shifts to thinly-veiled affection.

It also confirms that I really was mixed up a few moments ago. Our Emma is not here to attend to her dog, and Eric has stepped up. Bittersweet, again.

A little while later, I'm on my way to see Marie. I did look up the treatment she suggested, EMDR, and read the explanation. I have some questions for her but am relieved to be going to see her again. Every day presents constant challenges to my emotions and my decision-making. The effort to keep on track with helping Eric readjust to living at home, as well as trying to find Everett, while my emotions are all over the place is really exhausting. I have trouble falling asleep, then have trouble coming out of the dream state in the morning. If I've been dreaming of happy times in the past, or of a family member connecting, it's hard to let go of the images just because it happens to be morning. More often than not, I seem befuddled when I wake up. I read somewhere that people call this "grief brain." The sources that describe it do not exactly have solid statistical evidence, but people who are in grief describe the fogginess or inability to concentrate pretty vividly. I'm going to ask Marie what she thinks.

Marie starts off with the usual niceties, asking how I've been since I saw her last.

"I'm not exactly sure how to answer that question. I'm busy—Eric and I are trying to figure out how to find the son that was taken away from me when I was sixteen and given to who knows who? Besides that, I need to make a decision about whether to return to full-time work anytime soon. Part of me doesn't know if I'll ever be able to go back to a daily commitment. Facing people, dealing with their questions, their insensitive comments, feels like imposing torture on myself. Yet, it's a little soon to think that my retirement and savings can last from now till, well, as long as I need it." I can't utter the words *till I die*. It's scary to think of what that would do to Eric. I'm healthy and might be around a very long time still, but one thing I've learned is that there are no guarantees.

"Larissa, you kind of trailed off there. What came into your mind? Please share with me."

I take a deep, shaky breath and tell her, "It just struck me that if something happens to me, what would that do to Eric? He'd have nobody. Well, I guess he'd have Steven, but he's only known about Steven for a short time. What would my son do with another damn loss? He's dealt with too much already for someone his age. He told me the other day that he can't stand not being a brother anymore. He's so driven to find Everett, to be a brother again. The what-ifs are exhausting me. What if something happens to Eric and I lose another child? I feel panic attacks if he doesn't respond to my texts right after I send them. The other night, he went out with a friend, and I was a wreck until he came home. Of course he wants his independence, and I want that for him, except it's scary. Once you're taught the cruel lesson that it's possible to have your child die, you have looked into a deep darkness that cannot be forgotten. The naivete of thinking we can all watch our children grow into adulthood, see them get married, be part of them having a family, has vanished—literally gone in the moment you accept that your child has died. So, what if he goes, too? Could I survive this all yet again? What if I get sick and can't be here for him? What if we never find Everett so Eric remains the lone child?"

Marie has let me go on and on without interruption. She doesn't jump right in and try to respond to my questions. She's quiet and entirely focused on me. When she finally speaks up, she says, "That's a lot." The silence is deafening, but calming.

"Do you think I'm crazy? I'm not sure what to do with my thoughts sometimes. Who wants to hear this crap? I'm every parent's worst nightmare."

"You've lived through more than anyone should have to, Larissa; had a profound loss. As a mother, all we want to do is protect our children. If we can't, we beat ourselves up and wonder what other horrible things are going to happen. I'm not surprised at anything you've said. You're not crazy, you're grieving the greatest, most unimaginable loss a parent can experience. It's out of the natural order of things. I'd be surprised if you didn't have thoughts that keep you awake, or that you're hesitant to share with others."

"One more thing, it's getting close to Emma's birthday. On February nineteenth, she would have been turning twenty-two. I'm beginning to be obsessed by thinking about the weeks leading up to when she was born. I almost feel her heartbeat in my belly. I start replaying the first signs of labor, the chaos getting to the hospital, and the first time I held her. It repeats over and over in my mind when I try to fall asleep, like a never-ending tape. Even before she died, I always thought of those days leading up to her birth with great joy at the memories and at the beautiful young woman she'd become. It's different now; all I can think of are the things she didn't get the chance to do yet. I'm dreading that date with all my heart."

Marie offers, "Isn't a birthday a celebration of a person? A time to rejoice in the person's special place in your family? Could it still be that?"

"I don't know, maybe? Like the phrase a 'celebration of life'? Yes, I'd like to celebrate Emma and that she was here and she is still important. I just don't know how to do that without her at the table, so to speak. And I'm worried how Eric would take a celebration."

"I need to give you two things to contemplate, Larissa. You've told me that you see signs from Emma. Like a cardinal or the story of the butterfly that landed on your knee—she was with you then, right? And when you went to the medium, you said you heard her laughter and felt she was right there in the room with you. So, maybe she is with you, and will be on February nineteenth. I'm not telling you what to do or feel, but I think you have told me that you really believe she is nearby sometimes. Why wouldn't she be? Why wouldn't she come if you celebrated her?"

Tears trickle down my face. They are tears of appreciation. Tears of relief—relief that Marie has listened closely enough to offer me just the encouragement I need right now.

She waits for me to dab at the tears and be ready to pay attention. I remember she said she had two things to say.

"Second, of course you're worried about how Eric will feel that day, how he'll react to what you choose to do. That's the protective mother thing again. But we all cope with the curveballs of life in our own way. Larissa, sometimes we need to tend our own fire. Maybe one of your friends prefers a fire with slow burning embers that last all night long, so she doesn't choose to get up and stir those coals once they're at a comfortable level of warmth. For her, that sameness over a length of time creates a serene place. On the other hand, you may stoke your fire because you want it burning bright; maybe that makes your friend back away, because the heat is too much for her to bear. You and Eric, or you and anyone else, aren't going to tend your fires in the same way all the time, maybe not ever. You can, and should consider Eric and his feelings, but you can't tend his fire, only your own."

I drive away from Marie's thinking about tending my own fire. I've heard a similar message before—like when people talk about needing to do self-care. But this imagery is more intriguing to me. There are many times in my life when I stirred up the red-hot coals and many times when I enjoyed watching the smoldering, gray, ashy edges of the fire from a distance. I guess the question is whether to stick around when the fire is not as you like it or whether to simply take a walk and wait it out.

I make a stop to walk in the park before the grief group I'm attending later. As I turn off the car, my mind wanders to Marie's first point: why wouldn't Emma come, indeed? Lost in those thoughts, I head toward one of my favorite trails. At the end, there is a white, wooden archway covered with wisteria—those lovely, pale-lavender blossoms cascading from above, enveloping walkers with a musky-sweet aroma. I reach to pick one of several waterfall-like blooms gently draping across my shoulder. Three butterflies immediately swirl around my arm. I stop moving and hold my breath, so as not to interrupt their flight pattern. *Three—hmm. Oops, now four.*

One lands on the bench under the arch, one on the blossom in my hand, the other two keep gently circling. I silently beg them to stay as long as possible. I'm hypnotized by their graceful dance. Individually, they steer off to other flowering shrubs nearby, except for one. It's as if she's teasing me by starting to dart away, but then coming back within inches of my hand. It's so tempting to try to touch her, yet I know she is untouchable. To touch her would break the connection. I drop my head and close my eyes to silently release her, but only for right now. I'm overcome by certainty that I will see her again. When I look back up, she is gone from the wisteria, but I catch a glimpse of her orange wings contrasting with the blue sky, waving at me.

6

People talk about caterpillars becoming butterflies as though they just go into a cocoon, slap on wings, and are good to go. Caterpillars have to dissolve into a disgusting pile of goo to become butterflies. So, if you're a mess wrapped up in blankets right now, keep going.
Jennifer Wright

After my park encounter, I have about an hour until the group meets. I do a couple of errands and then drive to the lot adjacent to the church that invites the grief group to use its space. I keep a journal in the car for when a lot is on my mind and I have time to spare. I begin to write about my appointment with Marie and the fire tending, then move on to the butterflies. Engrossed in my writing, I'm startled at a rap on my car window. Stifling a scream, I drop my pen and look up.

I immediately see that Paul is the window-rapper this time. Such a kind, caring guy—ran into him a few times at these meetings, sad first encounters that no one really wants to have. From the dozens of people I've met, he's become a friend after exchanging thoughts most of us are afraid to share with people closest to us. We don't want to scare our family members off—but we learn that the attendees here are not so easily driven away. The pull of someone actually understanding the myriad of emotions without judging is what brings me back, and I'm guessing it's the same for many others.

"Paul! How are things? Sorry I didn't see you at first."

"No, it's me that's sorry, Larissa. I'm sorry I startled you. Well, anyway, I'm OK. The meeting's about to start, want to head in? Or not so sure?"

"I'm never sure, Paul, about much of anything anymore. But I'm here, you're here, let's do it."

As we cross the parking lot, I ask him if he knows anything about a sibling group and he tells me both his daughter and her closest cousin went after his son David died. "They said they felt a little weird at first; it's an awkward way for people their age to meet up. But after a few times, it was helpful. Just like us, I guess, right?" We catch one another's eyes fleetingly and respond with a little laugh that sounds more like a moan than anything to do with a funny remark.

Everyone is already seated, so we go opposite ways to find empty seats. It's a pretty full house. Sad—maybe a commentary on people trying to wrap their arms around the idea of a new year without their beloved children? Or just to support one another on having gotten through another round of holidays they couldn't share with some of their loved ones?

A timid-looking woman walks up to the table in front and a couple of others join her. The conveners of the group decided that when there are too many of us to form a circle, a table will be set up in front with several chairs, so no one has to stand up in front alone. The idea is to help make people a little more likely to talk than if they were solo. As she starts to speak, I'm reminded that looks can be deceiving. There is nothing timid about her.

"Hi, everyone. I've been coming a while but haven't spoken up. My name is Janet, and I'm just amazed at all of you when you talk about your kids. I'm a schoolteacher, and I've never had trouble talking in front of groups. That is, until here. After my daughter crossed over, no way I could talk about her or anything related to her—no thanks. But then, I just got so mad over the holidays that I've got to get it out—somewhere. My family doesn't want me talking about her anymore. They didn't want to let me have an empty chair at our dining room table for Christmas dinner—said it was too creepy. And if one more person said 'Happy New Year' to me, I may have slapped them silly, or maybe just melted in a puddle like the witch in *Wizard of Oz*. Violent anger or total meltdown—that's me lately." Lots of heads nod in agreement and a few people clap.

Janet is not ready to stop. "I've listened to a bunch of you talk about, at various times, the ways you dealt with your kids' birthdays. Now I got that coming up too. I'm teetering on the edge of something—I'm not sure what—a gaping hole in the center of the earth? A sky-high bridge that I can't be trusted to cross without falling, or, or jumping?"

One of the other parents at the table rises and goes over and holds Janet's hand. Once she does, Janet turns into the woman's arms, and allows herself to be led back to a chair. She thanks the woman then haltingly tries to apologize to the group.

My heart is drawn to Janet's, and like a magnet, I am pulled forward and hear my own voice begin, "You don't need to apologize, Janet. You're among friends. You're among many willing partners who can walk beside you. Thank you for saying what so many of us were feeling over the last few weeks. These holidays full of family events only serve to make our already empty homes all the more solitary. Not that every day isn't tough, but the last month has been full of immense torment for most of us, I'm certain of it. I know it has been for me. In our hearts and heads the calendar should have just stopped after our kids' heartbeats did. The realization that seasons are going to change, holidays are going to come around again, comes on like a cataclysm this time of year. Congratulate yourself, though. You got through it, you got to this meeting, and now you can figure out how to continue to exist in a place where you can't see your daughter."

Now I want to offer Janet something—some fragment of a rope to hang onto. "I don't know about anyone else, but at my lowest moments, when I've had something happen that breaks my heart all over again, if I settle down and tell myself Emma is out there somewhere, I can usually feel her. And when I feel her, if I stop and pay attention, then I can often begin to focus on good memories or ways to honor her. Not always, but often enough to keep me going." Then I describe the butterfly encounter just this morning, and continue, "I'm not sure what the message was from the butterflies, maybe more will come to me later, but at that moment, it felt like the message was that even when it seems like she's flying away, she will come back. I will see her again. That was enough to help me pull myself together after a tumultuous counseling session and get myself here. And maybe, Janet, you speaking helped me to make sense of the message. Thank you."

Someone suggests we take a break for coffee and reconvene in fifteen minutes. The coffee breaks seem to let people say things to one or two other people without the stress of talking to the whole group. Whoever set up this meeting structure, whenever they started, did a good job. Or maybe it's evolved over time with the input from those participating. I need to remember to email the coordinator sometime and see if he is interested in the ideas that I got from the group in New York when I was traveling, like organizing hikes or kayaking or dinners out for people to socialize, but with people who understand what they are experiencing. I thought it sounded good when I heard it, but who knows? Each group is different.

After the break, several people speak about how they dealt with their child's birthdays. Some avoided the day all together, some retreated alone, but many came up with meaningful, touching ways to honor their children. A lot like what Marie had suggested earlier today: figure out a way to celebrate that is comfortable, tend your own fire.

At the end of the meeting, I run back into Paul. As we approach the cars, he says, "Want to go get coffee, Larissa?"

I hesitate, look at my watch, wonder what Eric's doing. Then I realize I need to be better about giving him some space. "Sure, Paul, that sounds nice. I need to get decaf or I'll be up all night—I don't need anything else that might interrupt my sleep."

He smiles and suggests a place I've not been before. We agree that I'll follow him there.

"I can see why you like this place. It's small and cozy but not so small that you can't find a table to be able to talk privately. Catch me up on what's going on with you, Paul."

He tells me more about how his daughter's doing. It's been a couple of years since David passed, and she's gotten back into college after taking a break for a couple of semesters. "I'm happy she's doing well—dare I say, kind of normal, whatever normal is? It makes me relieved when Hilary acts like her old self. I'm still traveling quite a bit for work, so I'm less worried about her being alone now that she's got schoolwork and new friends to keep her busy. How's Eric? How's the search—any progress?"

I fill him in on the search, and my conversations with Eric. I find myself pouring out my concerns about Eric, my fear of something happening to him, and my recent realization that I also worry about him if something should happen to me.

"I totally get it, Larissa. I don't think either of us, or any parent, can get over worrying, being terrified, about our kids who are still here with us. Stop beating yourself up about it. I'd think you were weird if you didn't worry."

"Hell, I don't want you thinking I'm weird!" We simultaneously burst out in laugher. It's a welcome relief to laugh with someone who understands how quickly the pendulum swings from being suffocated by sadness to the freeing effect of laughter.

"I'm coming up on Emma's birthday—just like Janet at the meeting. I was dreading it, but both my counselor and the comments from other parents today have gotten me thinking, maybe I can plan something that feels like a celebration after all. She loved to make tie-dye clothing. Maybe I'll have a tie-dye party for anyone willing to come. How do you feel about tie-dye?"

We laugh again as Paul describes the last time he'd worn anything tie-dye. "Go for it, Larissa. Make it a colorful, joyous gathering, at least if you think you want to. There are plenty of times when we can't make the sadness go away. If a tie-dye party makes you think of Emma with happiness, then put it on the calendar. And sure, I'll come—maybe even bring Hilary along to meet you and Eric."

I tell him I'll let him know if I decide to go through with it. We finish our coffees and head out to our respective commitments. "I had a nice time, Paul. Thanks for the coffee!"

7

Love is not written on paper, for paper can be erased.
Nor is it etched on stone, for a stone can be broken.
But it is inscribed on a heart
and there it shall remain forever.
                              RUMI

A few days later, I see a subject line in an email from Terry, the woman I'd spoken to at the volunteer adoptee search organization, that makes my heart race a bit. She was kind and helpful on our first phone call, but in the name of transparency, made me aware this might be a challenging search. Cautious in her encouragement, she suggested that I investigate my mother's belongings more carefully and put rush orders on our DNA tests. She also had agreed with my investment in the faster-paced search option, recognizing the urgency in my voice.

Rereading the subject line, the words *follow-up to phone call* start my fingers trembling as I move the mouse to click on it. Once I finish the email, I call Eric and Steven in from outdoors. They have been working on some secret project, only revealing that I will be able to see it "when the time is right."

"So, you guys, I just got an email back from Terry. They matched her up with me because she's located in New York and has worked with several families before us, particularly in areas outside of New York City—she said in the phone call that New York City is like a whole other world. Anyway, she says that babies, unless home birthed, weren't delivered in the small towns like Whitehall or Port Henry, so that it's more likely, presuming it was a hospital delivery, that it was in Albany, Schenectady, or Saratoga. She's made contact with three adoption agencies that were in the area at that time. She sent along permission forms to notify each of them that I agree to be contacted by any adoptee who may fit with the information I've provided. She also urged me again to go back through my mother's personal effects to see if there are any other bits of information that might help. If we can narrow things any—like agency versus private or hospital versus home, it would be easier. So, I filled out the forms and returned them already, and now I'm heading up into the attic. I have a bunch of large trunks full of Mom's stuff that I haven't looked at in a long time. I figured you'd want to know where to find me."

"Wow, Larissa, the first sign of progress. I'm so happy for you guys. Do you want help up in that attic, or want to do it yourself?" Steven's smile shows he's genuinely pleased and wants to help without intruding. His sensitivity during trying times is welcome—few people in my life have struck that balance.

"How about if you guys drag the trunks down for me? It's stuffy up there and too dark to try to read through things for any decent period of time. If you get them down here for me to sort through, you can go back to your cloak and dagger work out back."

After a couple of hours, I realize it's very different looking through her personal things with a specific purpose. The last time

I did it, the household cleanup was done and the house sold, so I was mostly looking for which items would be donated, thrown away, or kept. Without reading anything carefully, I'd wrapped all of her correspondence in rubber bands sorted according to letters, cards, or official looking documents. Clearly, I need a better system now and want to get these organized chronologically, but it's taking a lot of time. I keep getting sidetracked because when a letter reminds me of the sender, my thoughts wander. The pile of cards addressed to Gamma from Eric and Emma on various holidays keeps taking me on a sentimental journey of sorts, so I set those aside and vow to read them another time. There won't be any hints in those about the decisions she and Dad and Aunt Mary and whoever else made about me and my "situation" in 1982.

    I wasn't all that organized when I did this. It would have been nice if all of the correspondence was in one trunk, all of the clothes in another, but no such luck. There are bundles of documents wrapped with dried rubber bands (barely able to do their jobs any longer), interspersed between scarves and shawls and cardboard jewelry boxes (also held together with fraying rubber bands), as well as a few hand-crocheted doilies that apparently were important to me at the time. This assortment is scattered among the trunks, so I spend the first hour just collecting all of the correspondence into one big pile.

    Just when I think I've gotten all the papers out, I tug on some bright, tropical-print blouses, and several colorful postcards with palm trees and beach umbrellas fall out. The postcards are all addressed to my mother, from small towns in Florida that sound vaguely familiar to me: Stuart, Jensen Beach, Hobe Sound, Fort Pierce. Hmm—they're all from a woman named Harriett, with short messages like, "All is well—wish you were here" or "If you ever come back this way, we sure would like to see you again."

Once or twice she refers to Harold, who I assume is her husband, and Junior, who must be a son. As I reread them, I see that the dates are from when my parents used to go to Florida. My dad loved the fishing in an area he called the "Treasure Coast." They said it was way quieter than that "Crazy Miami tourist scene." That's the area I thought of earlier when Eric asked about going to a beach we'd never been to. I'll have to look it up, or better yet, let him do the research and see if he likes the sound of it. If there's still fishing there, it just might be the place!

I shove those to the side to show him later and start with the letters. There are some from her cousin who moved to Montana and some from college friends. They were all dated well before Everett was born, so I'm able to move through them pretty quickly. I look at the clock and decide to give myself one more hour. My hips are hurting from sitting cross-legged for so long, and my eyes are getting blurry.

I find a couple of letters from Aunt Mary that perk me up a bit. But in reading them, I eventually get discouraged, not only because they don't say much of anything or reveal whatever it is I'm hoping for, but also because my Aunt Mary always insisted on her own version of my name.

My mother loved the proper name of Larissa, as well as its shortened version, Lara. She read the book *Dr. Zhivago* during college and thought the main character's name was the loveliest she'd ever heard. My earliest memory of the story of my name is her telling me that she was so happy to give me two pretty names because I was the prettiest baby she'd ever seen. Later, I realized all mothers think their babies are the prettiest, but at the time, it made me glow with pride.

But Aunt Mary could never get the short version right—she always referred to me as sweet little Laura. Yuk, Laura was just too typical for someone who had the glorious name that I did.

There were also about three Lauras in every class I had in elementary school, so I liked being the one and only Larissa much better. In one letter, she wrote, "Just when are you going to bring my darling niece Laura and nephew to visit? It's been way too long, and I want them to see this pretty part of New York again soon." Nice that she wanted us to visit, just aggravating she couldn't get my name right.

Anyway, I put that letter and a couple of others from her in a pile of their own, in case I find more. The postmark is from Whitehall—aha!—I wasn't just imagining that the town sounded familiar when I perused the map a couple of weeks ago. Doesn't mean she lived in Whitehall or that's where I was sent in my pregnant state, but it must be in the general area. I set this aside and keep rifling through one letter at a time. Another from Aunt Mary again encouraged us to visit, and one expressed her willingness to help my mother. I'm not sure what my mother might have needed help with, unless, wait, could this be leading up to when I was sent there? In her practically perfect cursive script, it said:

I'm so sorry you have to go through this, my dear little sister. You sounded frustrated with me before you got off the phone the other night. I know these things happen, but I never expected to have to say this to you. You must do something so it doesn't ruin lives. I am here, I can help, I know a lot of people in these parts, and it's far enough away so that you can all go back home, pick up the pieces later, and no one will know any better. Call me soon and let's figure this out.

It's a bit cryptic, but the dates might be right for when my mother found out I was pregnant. By the sounds of this letter, I'd almost think my aunt wanted me to sneak off and get an abortion. Were they actually contemplating that? I can't even imagine, but I was so oblivious back then, so scared. I hated being shipped off to Aunt Mary as it did play out, but who knows what other options they'd discussed before that one? OK, another letter to put in the pile of possible clues.

Just then, Eric, with Valentino trailing behind him, comes in. "Anything interesting in here? Man, that stuff is dusty looking. How old is it anyway? What are all these postcards?"

He sure has a way of taking over when he comes in a room! And Valentino hasn't left his side since he came over to visit—how many days ago? "Those, my dear, are a bunch of postcards from people in Florida that your grandparents met when they used to go there—Papa loved to fish in that part of the state. Why don't you look it up? You said you wanted to go to a new beach—maybe we should go check it out, I mean, if you're still interested."

He was shuffling the postcards like playing cards, making note of the cities. "Yeah, sure, so you mean it? You'd agree to go? Let me check them out." He grabs the cards and his phone and starts scrolling, looking for tidbits of information and reciting from webpages whenever he finds something that he thinks will convince me to go.

He's not going to have to work very hard to convince me. I've been thinking that once we get past Emma's birthday, and then her, uh, passing, I will be ready for an escape. My memories of our beach vacations the other day made me think about how peaceful, almost rehabilitative, the sound of the ocean can be. The sound of waves can wash away the most unsettling of feelings. And then, the idea of it being a new place for us, but familiar to people we love, has an intriguing appeal.

I just need to figure out what to do about work. I have a phone meeting with my boss later this week to see if we can negotiate a part-time or a remote solution for me to continue working, but also to have the time I need to spend with Eric, to search for my other son, and to continue to stumble along this path of figuring out life with someone important missing. Working full time in an office or with extensive travel demands, as I used to, is not compatible with my other priorities any longer.

As Eric wanders outside, continuing his beach research, Steven appears. "Find anything?"

"Yeah, some correspondence between my mother and her Florida pals that has Eric occupied right now, looking up a coastal town that offers both beaches and fishing. Then there were some between my aunt and my mother. This one is kind of interesting."

I hand him the last letter I was looking at and wait for his response. "Yeah, you can kinda read between the lines that maybe this is about you and yours, as they might have called it. The dates are about right, aren't they?"

I agree with him and also tell him about the postmarks. It's not a lot, but I can write back to Terry later and see what she thinks. "Like I told Renee and Isabel the other day, I feel like I'm following breadcrumbs from my mother and aunt, as well as being the one leaving breadcrumbs for the search angels or Everett, or whoever. Let's just hope someone can make these meager trails lead somewhere interesting."

"What else can I be doing to help, Larissa? Eric and I were talking about your plans to do a little celebration of sorts for Emma's birthday. I know he was kinda silent when you first broached the subject, but while we were out there working just now, he said he really likes the idea of us all making tie-dye in honor of Emma. I told him I'd wait to go back to New York until after the party. He also said he wants to see a medium before then. I told him I'd be happy to go along with him, if he wants someone else to go."

"You know, Steven, it might be really good for you to go with him—better than if I do. I think if I go, maybe I'd be a distraction if Emma comes through to connect. Does that make any sense? If he goes on his own or with you nearby for support, it will be all his own time with the medium to, hopefully, communicate with Emma. I appreciate you thinking of that. And yes, certainly stick around until the party. I have no idea how Eric and I will be that day or what we'll need. What I do know is, I think we need our close friends and family around."

"Larissa, it's my pleasure to do whatever I can to help you and Eric. Whether we expected it or not, we're a family now. Maybe not the typical one, but I think typical might be overrated. I like being part of all of this in whatever way makes you comfortable. Like I told you before, I have no intention of taking over with Eric or butting in where I'm not wanted. I just figure that anything I can do to help you slog through this quagmire of figuring out what comes next, is what I want to do. For Eric, but also for you."

I take a minute to gather my thoughts. "You're right—nothing about this is typical. I appreciate any support I can get at this point. You, Renee, Isabel, Paul from my grief group, my new counselor, Katrina that I met on the plane, Eric's friend Arnie, are all helping us to keep putting one foot in front of the other. I do want Eric to get connected to a sibling support group. I got some info about one from Paul. Maybe you can encourage Eric after I give him the information. He sounds interested, but hesitant."

"Yes, of course. Let me know when you tell him, and I'll do what I can."

"I was about to throw something together for dinner. Want to join us, and we can bring it up then?"

Steven chuckles. "Like double-team him?"

Just then, Eric walks back in. "Double-team who?"

Realizing there is no easy way out of this now, I take the lead and explain to Eric about Paul's daughter and her experience at a sibling group. He's listening, but I can't really read his expression.

Then he offers, "Yeah, I looked them up, too. One sounded really religious. Not like there's anything wrong with that, I just don't think it's for me. But another one that meets once a week at the recreation center sounded like something I might try."

Once we compared my notes from Paul and the one Eric found, it looks like they're the same one. "Paul said you could call Hilary if you want to get more of the scoop on it, or to see if maybe you want to go at the same time?"

"I don't even know her, Mom. I'm not gonna call her out of the blue and start talking about this stuff. I'll try a meeting soon."

After a few seconds, Steven says, "Eric, no one's pushing you. Let me know if you want to make an appointment with a medium, and maybe try this group. Worst case scenario with either one, is that you don't like it and you don't go back. Best case, well, would be anything better than that."

"Got it—change of topic. Mom, that Treasure Coast looks pretty cool. There's a lot of good fishing—both river and ocean. I found a fishing forum on social media where people post all the time about what fish are biting and on what. It also has links to a bunch of decent-looking places to stay. I think we should do it. How about you, you want to go too?" As Eric asks the question, he glances toward Steven, who looks caught off guard, and as surprised as I am, to say the least. In my mind, we're some semblance of family, but we sure haven't gotten to the place where we are talking about taking vacations together. I was envisioning just Eric and me—maybe that's selfish, but definitely my hope.

Not ruffled by Eric's spontaneity, Steven responds, "Whoa, there's a lot to be tackled before this trip, right? Like Emma's birthday, your mom's work deal, and I gotta go back to New York after that. We didn't even figure out if you're going to New York with me, right? Let's take it one step at a time. It does sound like a nice getaway, though. Worth planning at some point."

I make a classic mom move and offer up dinner to get through the awkward part of the conversation. For the rest of the evening, we mostly stick to small talk and then my next steps with Terry. Finally, I bring up the idea of Emma's birthday again.

"I want to go ahead and plan a birthday celebration. Let's invite our friends and suggest everyone bring at least one item of clothing they want to tie-dye. I'll get the dye, rubber bands, all that stuff. We can set up tables in the backyard to work on, and then have a clothesline for the projects to dry. We'll do that first, then have pizza and cake. What do you think?"

"I'm in, Mom. At first it seemed weird to me to have a party, but I think the only way to get rid of the constant sad is to let a few moments of happy in. I liked what you said about birthdays being the date we celebrate someone being born—whether she's still with us on this earth or not, that dang little Emma was special. The best way to be sure she's not forgotten is to celebrate who she is. Can I invite Arnie and his girlfriend? They've been easy to chill with ever since that weird time over at his house. I think he'd like to see you, too—it's been a while."

"Of course, Arnie can come. He was pretty sweet to me when Emma passed on. It was hard for me to see him because you were gone, and I didn't know anything about where. But he showed up—even sent purple flowers—the day of Emma's memorial service. He's been a good friend." What I didn't share with Eric was that I initially had such mixed feelings about seeing any of their friends while Eric was gone and when Emma died. It was painful at that time to see kids their age happy, healthy, and carefree while mine were gone; and yet, they brought an innocence to the whole experience that was endearing. Especially

Wonders in the Waves

when Arnie showed up with flowers. As they say, showing up is half the battle, right?

But then, he made the day for me, gave me a special gift. So, I share it with Eric, "Arnie even stuck around until only a small handful of people were still at the service. He waited until I was pretty much alone, except for Isabel, and shyly asked me, 'Can I tell you something, Ms. Whitcomb? I don't want to make you more sad, but you might want to know.' Of course, I doubted that anything could make me more sad, so I encouraged him to go ahead.

"He said, 'Well, one day, I was eating at the café where Emma worked, kinda in a back booth. When she came into work, she stopped at two different tables where older ladies were having coffee. At each one, she talked to them a few minutes, set down her coat and purse, and went right over to refill their cups. She hadn't even clocked in, and she was taking care of them. It seemed like maybe they were regulars or something. And when she brought their coffee and they asked for their checks, she shook her head no and said, "Happy Monday, ladies." I never forgot that, Ms. Whitcomb. It was really something. She was a good person, you know.' Then, he could hardly get any more words out of his mouth, hugged me, and walked out the door."

"That's awesome, Mom. Makes me even more happy that Arnie and I have reconnected. Thanks for telling me. When she wasn't being a pain in the you-know-what, Emma was a good kid. Damn, it doesn't make any sense, does it?"

"No, honey, it sure as hell doesn't."

The rest of the evening is spent planning the party details and making a to-do list. So much is going on between our search for Everett, our quest to celebrate Emma, and our desire for a getaway, that my head is spinning. First on the agenda is designing invitations with rainbows or birds or some pretty image that reminds me of Emma and sending them out tomorrow. Turning the date into something to look forward to now feels right. I'm not going to question it anymore, just going with it. After that, maybe the rest will fall into place.

8

*Now is no time to think of what you do not have.
Think of what you can do with what there is.*
ERNEST HEMINGWAY

My work meeting goes as well as I'd hoped for. My boss has always allowed me to schedule my time independently. He doesn't hover or micromanage. But I wasn't sure how he'd take my proposal to work only part time for some, as yet undetermined, period. When he asks how long I thought it "would take to get back to normal," I pause to check my reaction. *Normal?* No sense in giving him a lecture about there never being anything close to normal in my life again; that would only get me more emotional than I want to be for this conversation, and probably just make him uncomfortable. To get myself back on track, my eyes scan my desk area and I focus on a photo I'd taken a few months ago of two bird feathers, lying closely side by side. Those feathers reminded me of Eric and Emma at a time when I was convinced that I would never recover. This conversation is important not to recovery, but to learning how to live life a different way. So, I choose my words carefully so as not to blow this chance.

"I'd be lying, just making up a story, if I tell you I know when I might be ready for full-time work. Honestly, it may be never or it may be a couple of months. All I can tell you is that right now, my energy is pulled in a dozen different directions. If I can make my own work schedule to keep providing my established clients with excellent service for the time being, it'll give me a chance to accomplish the most important goals for me and my family. We can check in as often as you want to reevaluate, or I can target next year at budget time to come up with a more specific plan. We know the business I can generate with those accounts for now, for the rest of this cycle."

By the end of the meeting, he had agreed to my plan, at least for the next six months, with a few caveats. If my clients complain, or if I miss deadlines for reporting, we'll revisit the schedule. He finishes with, "Honestly, Larissa, I was worried you'd flat out quit. And I wouldn't have blamed you. My wife tells me about three times a week that the events in your life keep her up at night with worry. She says she never thought about how vulnerable life, the lives of our kids, really is until you went through this. You've always been a top sales person—I know you'll do what others do in about half the time. Let's talk in a couple of weeks."

That's one huge checkmark off my list. Maybe I can get a better night's sleep tonight. Last night was nothing but tossing and turning, one weird dream after another. Maybe I'll tell Marie about them. Sometimes, though, the jumbled-up characters and events in my dreams take us off on such a sidetrack, I end up regretting the topic of dreams all together. If she just didn't start almost every session with a question about how well I am sleeping! Then again, she seems to think that's an indicator of how well I'm doing otherwise. I'll see how I feel at my appointment.

I do have a call with Terry shortly, and I'm fidgety just thinking about it. Her email this morning said that she had some news—a couple of leads on people who might "know something." Not exactly clear what that means—about my son? About the search process? The speculation is making my stomach jump around as if it's full of grasshoppers breaking free from their eggs. I make some tea and sit in front of the computer to wait for the phone call. I want to be able to immediately look up places or agencies or whatever else she may be bringing up during the call.

Although I'm waiting expectantly, the ring of the phone makes me startle and I spill my tea. Valentino comes running in to check out the commotion, and I'm shouting, "Shit!" right into the phone as we connect. Terry replies, a bit timidly, "Larissa? Is that you?"

"Oh, geez, Terry, I'm so sorry. I tipped over my mug full of tea right when you called. Give me one sec to grab something to clean it up."

What a disruptive start! All I want to do is listen to what she has to say, but I'm delaying it with being a total klutz. I need to remind Eric to take the dog back over to Isabel's—those kids are going to be missing him.

I take a few deep breaths and gather myself to try again. "OK, Terry. I'm here."

"Larissa, there are a couple of possible leads to discuss. Not definitive, but interesting and worth follow-up, I think. Are you good to talk now?"

I assure her that I am and encourage her to go on.

"So, I convinced my contacts at two of the three agencies to go back into the records for 1982. Between the two of them, there were seven babies born in the two weeks on either side of November 28, the date you believe is the day you gave birth. I did two weeks on either side as a starting place, because it sounded like you weren't one hundred percent sure that the date you remember is correct. It doesn't necessarily mean that they handled the adoptions, it just means they were notified by hospitals that there were potential adoptees. Now they're going to try to match up any adoptee requests for information through various databases to see if the dates match, if the name Everett is amongst them, if your name is on any of the birth certificates provided to adoptees, or anything else they can get from their records."

I feel my heartbeat pounding in my ears. I squeeze my eyes tightly shut to try to clear my thoughts. Instead of attaining the clarity I need to ask her a halfway intelligent question, I see what I think I saw on that date: a baby, semi-lying across my bare breast. It is "semi" because the kind nurse, who warned me she was not supposed to let me see my baby at all, set him against me, but kept her hands protectively around him—I suppose to prevent me from grabbing him. The contact was brief, so no one would know, but long enough for the image of his tiny profile to be ingrained in my memory, my heart, forever.

"Larissa, are you still there?"

I shake my head to achieve what the eye squeezing did not, and answer, "Yes, yes, sorry. Um, so what does that really mean? Seven doesn't seem like too many to investigate."

"It doesn't, but it all depends on if there's any information that matches up. Plus, there is the possibility that an agency wasn't used at all. It could have been a private adoption. If that's the case, then finding him is going to be more challenging, more dependent on hospital records and DNA testing. You guys sent in the DNA testing, right?"

"Yes, both Eric and I did the DNA stuff—it should be back in a few weeks. My racing heart sinks down into my chest as it hits me how long that sounds. Then I ask, "What about the third agency? What's up with contacting them?"

"I've left messages, but no one has gotten back to me yet. It's a small, religiously affiliated group, and they're often shorthanded. They'll get back to me; I just don't know when."

"So, what's next? What else can I do at this point?"

"We need to wait a bit for people to catch up with tracking down details. Have you been back through your mother's records to see if you have any other clues?"

I fill her in on my aunt's correspondence with my mother. "It seems like they were talking about my pregnancy in a couple of letters I found. She was encouraging my mother to let her help, and said she knew a lot of people where she lived that might be able to assist. It almost sounded like she was hinting at abortion, but I'm not sure. I got tired of her always getting my name wrong in the letters, and the idea of abortion really shook me up, so I haven't gotten back to the letter pile in a few days."

"Hmm. Knowing a lot of people that could help could also imply someone who could help with a private adoption—like an attorney, or even that she knew a couple that wanted to have a child and couldn't. Keep looking through that stuff. You might find something about an attorney or a doctor who would deliver a baby privately and then have a lawyer or family lined up. What is your aunt's name again? I'd like to have that in my records."

"Unfortunately, it's a really common name—Mary Miller. Everyone called her Millie. Except me—if she was always going to call me Laura instead of Larissa or Lara, I started calling her Aunt Mary."

Laughing a little, Terry comments, "OK, then, nothing like making things more difficult because none of you could call people by their actual names! Get back into those letters and let me know if you come across anything—even an attorney's invoice. It probably wouldn't come right out and specify the nature of the business, just be a bill for a certain number of hours or something like that. Just like the old saying about the needle in a haystack—be persistent and save everything that could possibly be helpful. I'll get back to you when I hear something."

"Thanks, Terry. You've got me revved up and ready to get back to those dusty bins of letters. Keep in touch!"

I've only been off the phone for a minute or two when it rings again. I see Renee's name on the caller ID, so pick up.

Before I say hello, she blurts out, "Hey, I just opened that beautiful electronic invitation. I'm so excited you're doing a party for Emma's birthday! And tie-dye—what a blast! What can I do to help? How about I get the birthday cake? The shop down the street does a beautiful job and will replicate a photo on the cake. Have a favorite photo of Emma you want me to use?"

The characteristic enthusiasm practically blasts through the phone line. She tires me out, but I'm grateful for her ever-present support. "Renee, whoa, I just got off the phone with Terry. My head is stuck back in 1982, trying to remember more details for her, and now you've yanked me back into the present!"

She slows down and asks about Terry. After I fill her in on as much as I know, I get back to her reason for calling. "Yes, I'd love it if you ordered a cake. The challenge will be a favorite photo. I must have five hundred favorites!"

Knowing this is true, and trying not to lose momentum for getting the cake done, Renee suggests, "OK, well, why don't you narrow it to five to ten, and then let me pick which will look the best? I can talk to the people at the bakery if there are some photo features that are better for the cake top."

Wonders in the Waves

As we are talking, I look down at my watch and suddenly blurt out, "Holy crap, Renee, I need to get to my appointment with Marie. I'll call you later." I throw a decent-looking sweater over my ratty-looking tee shirt, grab my keys, and head out the door. I hate being late for an appointment—it just means less time with Marie, which I've come to realize is really valuable. I want every minute I can get—for my money and my sanity.

9

Seeker, empty the boat, lighten the load,
Be free of craving and judgement and hatred and
feel the joy of the way.
GAUTAMA BUDDHA

I respectfully ask Marie to skip anything about dreams for now. I have so many other things I want, actually need, to talk about before we get into dissecting dreams.

"OK, sure, it's your time. I like to check in on sleep, though, because it's a big part of returning to some semblance of coping, if you can actually get a good night's sleep. Interrupted sleep and disturbing dreams were also among, as we like to say in health care, your 'chief complaints' when you first came in."

"I don't want to be argumentative, Marie, but sleep and dreams are not my chief complaints at all. Those are sadness, anxiety, confused identity about my role as a mother, and ..." I stop myself. I hear this from her perspective, and it actually does sound argumentative—almost like an attack. "Yeah, OK, sometimes I'm angry at the world, other times I'm sad, other times

I'm all consumed by trying to be sure Eric is doing OK, and oh, yeah, there's the trying like hell to see if we can find Everett."

She nods her head in agreement and asks if there is one of those that has been most challenging this week.

"I'm worried a lot about being sure Eric is OK. It's difficult enough dealing with my own roller-coaster feelings, but I can't help thinking about him all the time too. I have failed so many times already at being a good mother, I don't want to, I can't, freakin' fail him. Not now, while I have a chance."

"Tell me more about how you failed as a mother."

"How *didn't* I? My first child was gone before I knew him—I never even mothered him. Then, I denied his existence for so long, that now there is no one around who was there at the time who can help me find him. I left Steven before Eric was born, so they spent twenty-six years not knowing each other. I ignored the facts that would have told me I was lying to myself and to Eric about his father. I married Roger—who never really knew how to love a child unconditionally, not Eric, nor even his own daughter, Emma. I didn't get my daughter the help she needed to feel better about herself, to maybe have the chance to grow into her amazing potential. I can barely look at myself in the mirror some days." Man, where did all of that come from? I'm shaking from spilling that out. At the same time, I'm aware that my shoulders have relaxed, lowered from their typical tightened position, and my teeth have unclenched.

"Larissa, I may now be the one to risk sounding argumentative, but there's another side to all of those stories. Shall I share those, or can you figure out the other side with me?"

She starts with the adoption and points out that when pregnant while I was fifteen to sixteen years old, I had few choices but to go along with my parents' wishes and guidance. My parents had not led me astray before then, so why wouldn't I do as they directed? She also points out that I was told, again by trusted adults, to forget about the baby boy and go back to being a teenager. Told that was the kinder, more loving thing to do, so that he had a good set of parents who could care for him.

"And let's talk about your claim that you denied Eric his father for twenty-six years. Was that your intent?"

I look at her blankly, and then blurt out, "No, of course not. I really thought that his father was a guy I'd just dated a few times. A guy that wanted nothing to do with kids."

"Correct—so, you did what you knew at the time to be the responsible, the most loving way to take care of your son. We both know that a father who doesn't want a child can be very harmful. You didn't subject Eric to that, you were a protective, devoted mother. When you met Roger, he presented himself as someone who did, in fact, want a child. He wanted to marry you and adopt Eric. Larissa, of course looking back now, with the wisdom and experience of two more decades of living, you're critiquing decisions you made along the way. At the time, though, with the information you had at hand, you made caring, motherly decisions. See if you can do it, now. See if you can tell us both the other side of your claims about Emma."

I listed the myriad physicians and other practitioners that Emma went to over the course of her life. I had taken her to every mainstream clinician and every alternative therapy that I could think of. I also brought her along on many of my work trips; I thought she might benefit from getting away from her environment and learning about the world. She had been to the Caribbean, Europe, even India, with me. For a young woman her age, she was well traveled and loved different cultures, different foods, and she danced to music from all those countries.

As I'm describing all of this, a smile comes over my face. I get what Marie is saying. The outcome for all of my mothering efforts wasn't always as I hoped, but it wasn't for lack of trying.

"Hence where we get the phrase, 'hindsight is twenty-twenty.' It's an oversimplification, like so many phrases, but it's true. Looking back from this place you are in now, you can tear yourself apart, accuse yourself of being a lousy mother, but I wonder if that helps you or Eric, or even Everett in any way?"

I mumble, "And it sure doesn't change a damn thing for Emma. I hear you. I told my boss the other day that I'm pulled in a dozen different directions. Maybe I can let go of the pull to hold on to all of this guilt."

"Your load is heavy enough. You don't need to add to that huge satchel full of burdens every minute of every day. Some of them just need to be put away. Store them somewhere. You're not discarding people who are important to you, you're not ignoring their feelings, you're not neglecting them. You can, however, just put the weighty load down in a safe place now and then. Lighten up on the self-blame so you can pay attention to what matters the most now. Tell me a few things that are important right now. Let's make room for them."

I tell her about plans for the party, about Eric wanting to go to the beach for a getaway, about the little bit of progress with the adoption mystery.

"The birthday celebration sounds lovely, Larissa. What a beautiful tribute for your beautiful daughter. Inviting friends of Eric's will help with one of the things you're so worried about. He'll have his own support system, outside of you and Steven, to enjoy the moments of sharing about Emma. Those friends will be better able to help him if they observe the ways you and Eric are moving forward with your attempts at honoring her. Young people take their cues from us when we don't even realize it."

The remaining minutes of the session are taken up with her giving me the name of a counselor that might be a good fit for Eric, if I think he will be amenable, and then affirming the idea of a support group for him as well. She also urges me to set a date for travel. "If there is at least a date on the calendar, Eric will know you've heard his desire to go. The specifics of who goes along with the two of you, if anyone, or exact location, can be solidified later. Dates can even be changed."

She's right. So many times, I've been weighed down by the process of making a decision, by the back and forth of what's right and what's wrong. Once the decision is made, the burden is lifted. I guess the theme for today is finding ways to lighten the burdens. When I say as much, Marie replies, "Ah, a minor success! The relief that comes with lightening the load can be freeing. Today, you freed yourself up to accomplish things that will buoy you up rather than drag you down."

My drive home seemed to last only a minute. I can sense some energy returning and can't wait to dive back into the trunks full of old letters. I'm also going to look up the websites Eric shared about the beach, calculate a target date for travel, and finalize the appointment I tentatively made with the tattoo artist. I've not mentioned it again to anyone since I let it slip with Eric that day, and then to Renee and Isabel, but I've been going back and forth with the guy to refine the design. I never had a clue how much artistry goes into coming up with the kind of tattoo I'm looking for!

Sitting cross-legged with most of Mom's letters, now in four distinct piles and only a few still scattered around me, the back door slams and years of conditioning prepare me to hear Eric yell my name immediately. When that doesn't happen, I look up in time to see him holding the door open, and a slender young woman come in behind him. She is a tiny thing, walking very quietly as if she does not want to disturb anyone, dressed in her generation's version of something you might call *business casual*—khakis and a button-down shirt—and clearly waiting for a cue from Eric. He waves her in and then turns to see me sprawled on the floor.

"Oh, hi, Mom, didn't know you were home. I, uh, did it. I went to a group, for, um, siblings, of you know . . ." he trails off.

The young woman walks forward and confidently says, "Hello! I'm pretty sure you might know my father, Paul. I'm Hilary, he told me about you. So, at the meeting we just came from, when I talked to Eric afterwards, his description of what happened to his sister sounded familiar." Walking closer, she sticks out her hand and offers, "Nice to meet you."

As she started talking, I was confused, then totally startled that Eric actually took it upon himself to venture to a meeting, unannounced. And he's still standing there, looking rather cowardly, or sheepish, or some other version of not-too-sure what else to say.

Giving him a moment, and pleasantly impressed by Hilary's introduction and explanation, I shake her hand. "Yes, I do know your father. I guess you know that my name is Larissa. Your dad and I bumped into one another at the airport a while back—we were both struggling with repeated flight cancellations, when he reminded me that we'd been at a couple of parents' meetings together. Since then, our paths seem to keep crossing. He told me about you—I heard you're back at college and doing well."

"Not sure about 'well,' Mrs.-- or is Larissa OK?" I nod, so she continues, "Not sure that *well* is the word, but I'm hanging in there. That's what I was trying to tell Eric after the meeting, on the ride home. I know my brother would have kicked my ass, uh, sorry, butt, if I had not finished my degree. That's really what got me going. If he can see me from somewhere, wherever he is, I know he'd tell me it's lame to lie around and do nothing with myself just because he didn't make it. David was pretty blunt about telling me what he thought I should do."

"Sounds familiar, right Eric? A little like you and Emma?" He looks like he's watching a ping-pong ball go back and forth between two players as his head swivels from one of us to the other as we speak.

"Yeah, right. She needed some butt kicking now and then, if you ask me." A lop-sided grin emerges from his confused face. "Hilary, want some ice tea or something?"

Watching them head into the kitchen, my thoughts go where every mom's thoughts go. I wonder what he said at the meeting, if anything? I wonder how he felt? If he'd come home without her, I'd have to resist the temptation to ask a dozen questions. Guess it's a good thing she came with him—they can debrief on their own. As I watch them go out on the porch, I then wonder, *Hmm, could this be a different kind of relationship? Whoa, Larissa, slow down. They just walked through the door from a grief meeting—hardly a set up for a romantic encounter.* Laughing at myself, I finish sorting the piles and tackle the one of business correspondence.

Nearly to the bottom of the pile, I unfold one, then another, then another business letter from a heading with several names—an attorney's office? Looking closer, sure enough. Amazing they can use so many words and charge so much money and still give very little information about the nature of the services. The letters list activities such as interviews, background search, correspondence with other attorneys, and 'other professional fees.' Honestly, that could be anything, right? Real estate? Planning a will? Or even, adoption? Maybe Terry can help me decipher this.

Just then, the two young folks come back in the house and announce they are going out to dinner. Trying to sound as nonchalant as they are acting, I look up briefly and respond, "Great—have fun." I purse my lips slightly to resist asking where they are going, when they'll be back, or who's driving. More impressively, I say nothing about being safe or not driving if they have cocktails. My progress on this is slow, but I can pat myself on the back for that small accomplishment.

10

*It is not impermanence that makes us suffer.
What makes us suffer is wanting things to be
permanent when they are not.*
Thich Nhat Hanh

After a quick dinner of leftovers, I call Renee back, since I'd cut her off earlier to get to my appointment with Marie. I give her a quick version of counseling, the scoop on Eric and Hilary, ask if she got the photos I sent her to potentially use for the cake, and then start describing the letters I found.

Ever the enthusiastic sleuth, she jumps on the attorney invoice. "Does it say what the heck your parents were up to?"

We venture some guesses, and after a few silent moments, she says, "Can you tell if there was an agency? Why don't you see if that law firm is still around? Or, if not, it seems like an awful lot of attorneys keep practices in their families, so there might even be old records in a practice with some of the same names. Probably the one who was doing all these activities signed the letter, right? What's that name?"

Although she can sometimes tire me out with the way her brain bounces all over the place, I gotta admit that she comes up with some interesting ideas. I find the letter and invoice, read her name, and she's already scrolling on her laptop on the other end of the phone. "What town did you say your aunt lived in? There's a law practice with two of those names in some city named Schenectady." (She totally butchers that city name, but I know better than to criticize her when she's on a roll.) "There's another with exactly the same names in Saratoga. Does that make any sense?"

"Yeah, it does—her town was pretty small. Those are bigger cities that are within driving distance. When Terry was looking for adoption agencies and hospitals, she also came up with the Albany/Schenectady area and then Saratoga. They're bigger than my aunt's town. And they all had hospitals back then—still do."

We hash over a bunch of possibilities, but it does seem like these invoices could be related to arranging an adoption. Beyond that, we're both pretty clueless about what goes into making such an arrangement, or how the lawyer's role differs between a private and an agency adoption. More questions for Terry.

Renee and I chat a while longer, but I end the call when I find myself yawning repeatedly. We agree to talk more tomorrow about the party. It can wait another day.

This particular day has been a long one. I so want to be casually watching television when Eric comes home, to be able to chat with him, but I'm just too tired. I need to decompress. Maybe a mindless book will help me drift off to sleep. Something tells me I'll be jolted awake the minute I hear him come in the door, but I vow to stay in my room and let him be.

Rolling over to glance at the clock, I'm aware that it's light outside. What? I slept through the night? It's a little after 7:00 a.m.!

Surprised, actually elated and damn proud of myself, I reach for my phone. Please don't tell me that some emergency happened with Eric and he never came home? How else could I have missed hearing him come in the door? Sure enough, I see a text from Eric—my heart stops while I search for my reading glasses, trying not to knock over the glass of water ever present on my nightstand. I read it, let out my tightly held breath and smile, "Mom, I'm home. Thought I heard you snoring through the door so didn't wake you," followed by a blowing-kiss emoji.

Wow, OK, not only proud of myself for sleeping through his return, also damn proud of him for being considerate enough to let me know. I lay in bed a few more minutes, relishing a contentment and sense of well-being that I have not felt in a very long time. I can't even remember when, but I'll sure take it now.

I turn on the coffeemaker and proceed straight to my laptop. I email Terry to tell her to please call me as soon as possible. It's probably well before she's in her office, but you never know—some people like to get an early start. I want to be first on her call list. With coffee in hand, I return to the pile of my mother's correspondence, looking for something I may have missed. The postcards on top of the pile, depicting waves in every shade of blue-green imaginable, remind me of my vow to look up possible Florida accommodations. I find a few little beachside communities that look particularly attractive and click on several houses for rent. Maybe if we go soon after the anniversary of Emma passing? I enter the dates and find three with availability. When Eric gets up, I'll let him know he can choose among them. I made sure they have at least three bedrooms, in case he's jumped the gun and talked more to Steven about coming along.

Bolstered by the energy that a good night of sleep has delivered to me, I scribble a note to Eric that I'll be back soon and head out to buy supplies for the birthday celebration. As I turn into a parking spot, a song comes on the radio that convinces me I'm doing the right thing with this party. This band was performing at the very first concert Emma and I went to together, and this song was the opener. Its lyrics about the sun and its upbeat tempo lighten my step as I walk in to buy tie-dye supplies, decorations, and frames for the photos of Emma that I printed to display. The first display in the store is the perfect theme—rainbows, birds, but also palm trees and shells. Shells—another thing that Eric, Emma, and I used to collect at the beach. All these signs and reminiscences energize my efforts.

As I'm making my selections, I reach for an assortment of balloons, but then pull back. No way—Emma would have had a fit if we bought balloons that animals could choke on. The sea turtles along the coast are known to mistake deflated balloons for jellyfish and be harmed by eating them. But as I pull away, I see a notice—it definitely should be bigger—proclaiming that all of the items in this display are fully biodegradable. Aha—hence, the nature theme! I can buy this stuff, including balloons, after all. I can't wait to show Eric. I realize it's only a few days till the party, and I'm feeling pretty good about doing this. It's such a lift to my spirit to be acknowledging Emma rather than hesitating to speak her name out loud. If only I hear something good from Terry, or Katrina calls me back, this day might actually prompt me to say I'm doing well.

I walk in the house and start wondering where Eric is, when a text answers the question. He's stopping at Isabel's house to visit the dog, meeting Steven for lunch, then going on a job interview (*Wow!*). I also have an alert that emails are waiting and scroll to see that Terry has answered me. OK, I'm on a definite roll here.

A few hours later, I walk out onto the back porch to sit and reflect. I'm cautiously optimistic about the information from Terry. And I'm looking forward to the party, although I recognize that could be temporary. Another text from Eric that he'll be home later has my curiosity heightened, but I'm not riddled with anxiety about what he's doing or feeling. I even had time to check in with a couple of my best customers today and arrange periodic communication with them regarding their priorities over the next few months. This all brings me a modicum of serenity compared to how things have generally been the last few weeks. Pinch me—can this be real?

Later in the evening, when Eric comes home, we have a chance to catch up. He tells me a few more details about going to the grief group, connecting with Hilary, and very casually says, "I think I might go again tomorrow and meet her there—we'll see. Oh, and I think something might work out with that job. It'd just start out as a part-time internship type of thing, but that's fine with me. Not sure we're, I mean I'm, ready for more than that yet."

I let his little slip about "we" go—it's actually kind of sweet that he's worried about me, or the time he spends with me.

When I show him the party supplies, he shakes his head and asks, "You're really OK with this, Mom?" I share the details, the timing of the song, the biodegradable decorations, and he smiles. "OK, let's do it, then! You're right, it should be good."

Finally, I fill him in on the emails with Terry, and her follow-up phone call.

"Terry thinks the information I found in Gamma's old correspondence sounds like a private adoption. Although lawyers are used either way, their involvement is pretty perfunctory when it's done through an agency. She looked up the attorney's names I found and it seems like they, or others who took over their practice, are still in business. She left a message with the records office to see what it might take to get more details of what exactly their office did for Gamma. As next of kin, I probably have to sign some documents to gain access, but hopefully, that's all it will take."

He starts to ask more questions, but I continue on, "Wait, there's more! It seems like she found someone in the database that, uh, matches some of the information I gave her."

"Like what, what do you mean matches 'some'?"

"There's an adoptee on one of her lists who was born in the two-week time period I gave her, in the general area of New York we're talking about."

"Holy shit! What else? Is there any more than that, like what kind of list?"

"Yes. So, he put his name into some kind of registry to be contacted and for information to be released if a birth parent is looking for him. That's the good news. Possibly not so good is that he put the form in three years ago and hasn't checked back in for quite some time. She said that usually when someone is interested, they check back frequently, like every couple of months. Also, she can't give me his name until she hears back from him as to whether his search is still active. She shared that his last name isn't Whitcomb, though."

"Mom, this is exciting but scary at the same time. What do you think? Think it could be him?"

"I'm afraid to get my hopes up. I guess he uploaded a photo copy of his birth certificate in the database. In New York, an adult adoptee can get access to a copy of his or her original birth certificate. Terry did share the parents' names on the certificate. The mother's name on it is Laura Miller, the father is "unknown" for the first name, but also, Miller for the last name. It could be coincidence, but it's just so freaky that Aunt Mary always insisted on calling me Laura. It makes me wonder. And then, Miller? It's like the most common name on the planet. But it was my Aunt Mary's last name. Did my Aunt make up the mother's name for the birth certificate? Did someone, like the lawyer or whoever delivered him, just fill it in, or could it be there was really a Laura Miller and her husband who had to give the baby up? It's no wonder the information using my actual name didn't turn up any matches!"

"So what next? What do we do now?"

"We wait to see what Terry finds out from the lawyer's office or if she can connect with this guy to confirm if he wants to make contact." His face drops, until I add, "By the way, I looked into those Florida towns, put in some possible dates, and narrowed it down to three places I think would be fun to explore. Maybe a week or two after the anniversary of Emma, uh, passing?" My earlier joy withers a bit as I address the much harder date that's coming up in the not-so-distant future. Talk about a roller coaster!

"OK, awesome, I'll look at them. Yeah, we need to plan something to get us through April 8. I can't believe that shitty date is coming up already, and that it's been more than a damn year since I walked out of here, Mom."

I get a flashing image of the day Eric was so frustrated with Emma and I arguing yet again about her late nights with people she barely knew, that he left. Left and didn't contact me for months. Cut off all contact. With not a word until the police called to say they thought he was dead. But before I let my mind wander to a dark place I don't want to confront right now, I walk over and hug him. "We're going to get through this, Eric. There is no choice. It's definitely been a damn year, a shitty year, a year that defies words to describe it. But you know what? We also have each other again, we're figuring out a way to honor your sister, and we might be onto something with your brother. No one has happy days every day in this life, Eric. There's more sadness than most of us like to admit. Like you said the other day, we need to find the good moments and make them be enough. Make them be what gets us through the sad moments and everything in between. It's the only decent choice, really."

He returns the hug, and holds on just a bit longer. Long enough to let me know we're definitely in this together, without using actual words. It's enough.

11

We cannot all do great things,
but we can do small things with great love.
MOTHER TERESA

I'm nervous and excited as I look for a parking spot close to "Moving On," the tattoo parlor that's my secret destination. Eric and Steven have their secret project, and I have mine! I thought about asking one of them or Renee or Isabel to come along, but decided to do this all on my own. It's between Emma and me; oh, and I guess this guy whose pen name is Fin. I'm not too sure why these guys all have one syllable names, but it's not my place to question. I just know that he was recommended by another mother in the grief group, and I really liked the renderings he came up with based on the pictures and images I sent him.

All of the paperwork, permissions, and disclaimers do not exactly help much with my nervousness about the whole thing. I'm happy they're being informative and careful, but whoa, this is serious stuff. It also makes me wonder about the places Eric and Emma went for theirs—behind my back. Who knows if they even read those disclaimers—doubt it.

Of course, tattoos have gotten way more mainstream than the days when my uncle proclaimed that only "sailors and prisoners" got them, or even just five years ago, but I am definitely the only middle-class mom sitting in this waiting area today.

A dark-haired, burly man, probably in his late twenties or early thirties, walks in the waiting area, carrying sketches in front of him. His arms are, unsurprisingly, covered in tattoos. What's called "full sleeve," for obvious reasons. He looks up at me and politely asks, "Are you, uh, Larissa? Ms. Whitcomb?"

"Yes, Larissa is fine. Are you Fin?"

"The one and only, mama," and puts out his hand to shake mine. There is something oddly endearing about the way he says *mama*. It's respectful in an unexpected way. "Let's go back here where we have some privacy and talk over your ideas."

He leads me into a well-lit, colorful room, with privacy barriers evenly spaced, so that there looks to be four or five individual places for the tattoo artists to work with their clients. I don't know why I expected something dark or dingy, but I'm super glad my preconceived notions are wrong. It's much more comfortable than I'd envisioned.

After we review everything I'd sent him, he remarks, "Yes, this is going to look real nice. You said on the inside of your wrist?"

"I think so. I want to be able to see it. If it's on my back or my upper arm, it's kinda like its purpose is for everyone else, right? I want this to be for me. I can look at it when I need to—I can even hold my arm against my heart and, well, like I told you in the email, this is for my daughter. In honor of her, I mean. Tomorrow is her first birthday since she's been gone ..." my voice trails off.

Fin speaks quietly, "You know, mama, almost everyone who comes in here has a special story to tell. Most people don't put random stuff all over their bodies—a few, maybe, but not most. You can cry all you want. You can even blame the tears on me or the needle or whatever, though I promise you, I'm pretty gentle— they call it *a soft hand*. Anyway, I think, actually I know, that right now, your girl is honored. She sees you, mama, she knows you're doing this. And she is honored."

With that proclamation, he explains the details of the process, helps me get in a position that puts my arm right where he needs it, and offers several ways to make me more comfortable once he starts. He says he can give me breaks whenever I need them, but just asks that I let him know before I need to move, so that he can adjust accordingly. It's all new to me, but clearly, he knows how to make this go smoothly.

"All set? I'm ready when you are."

I give him a nod and I hear the tool start up. At first it reminds me of the electric clippers I used when giving Eric a buzz cut when he was a little guy. Before long the sound, so repetitive, is purely background noise. I close my eyes, and while far from sleep, I find it to be an almost meditative experience. Once when he asks if I need a break, it takes me a minute to even form my words. As my eyes flutter open, I see the image on my arm starting to take form and am in awe. This is really happening. There is really an intricate design including a butterfly, a rainbow, a flower, a heart, a bird, and a replica of Emma's signature with OXOX after her name. He hasn't filled the colors in yet, but that's next.

A few times, the needle causes pain, but it is so odd. I'm not sure I could describe the sensation to anyone even if I tried. It is painful, yet calming, it is sharp, yet dull. It is annoying but I don't want it to stop. I'm not sure how much time has lapsed—he had predicted it would be about two hours—when he says, "OK, what do you think?"

Is this real? Have these ideas I had for a tattoo actually been emblazoned on my body? My eyes glaze over, and I start to pull my right forearm to my chest, I want that signature over my heart.

"No, no, not yet, mama. Let me cover this and tell you how to take care of it over the next few days. Soon enough, you can cuddle that 'Emma' all you want. Just not right this minute."

Fin carefully covers his masterpiece with plastic wrap, tells me how to care for it, and prints off instructions as well. Then he says, "I hope this meets your expectations—I know a lot went into this, and it's my honor to help you honor Emma."

Once again, tender words from this tough-looking guy touch my heart. This is a day I won't soon forget. Like many days, but this one warms my heart, comforts my soul. An early Emma birthday present for myself.

The morning of the party, Renee bursts into the back door of the house, arms full, yelling, "Don't come in here, don't look. I want to surprise you guys." As she rustles around in the refrigerator, Isabel arrives close behind, also loaded down with tote bags full of who knows what, and her kids straggling behind, whipping tee shirts around over their heads, singing some made up rhyme about "tie-dye, why-oh-why," and something else I can't decipher. Oh, for the days when you can make songs about anything!

Isabel scoots them out the back door into the yard and calls out to me, "What can I do to help you set up? I see you put up the folding tables, where's everything else?"

I grab the supplies for our project, the decorations, and suggest she come help me on the porch. It's a beautiful day, considering it's February, but that's the beauty of where we live—being able to do things outside almost all year round.

As I reach into the bag to pull things out, I push up my sleeves because it's getting warm out already. Too late, I realize that the artful addition to my arm is likely to show. I wanted to wait until later to show anyone. As I quickly try to pull it back down, Isabel hasn't missed a thing. "Whoa, stop, what the heck?" She turns my arm over to see my inner wrist and lets out a quick gasp. "Are you kidding? Larissa, oh, wow . . ." As she looks at it more closely, she pulls me over to a chair, and says, "Wow, you actually did it! It is beautiful, Larissa. Just beautiful." Tears are welling up in her eyes as she stares into mine. "When?"

"I just did it yesterday. I can't believe it either. When I woke up this morning and looked at my arm, I was startled to see it—I'm not quite used to it, but I love it. I just didn't want to show anyone yet. I'd thought maybe later, as part of a little tribute to Emma, but hadn't really decided. Can you just keep it to yourself for now?"

"Keep what to herself? What's going on?"

I look up and realize keeping this between Isabel and me is hopeless. Renee caught that last phrase, and I see that Eric and Steven are close behind her. Time for the big reveal!

Each person has an exclamation of disbelief to offer. I guess no one thought I'd really do this—even though I'd shared some of my deliberations. Each expression of disbelief is followed by words of support for doing it at all, and then remarks about its beauty. Although I'd thought about including more in the tattoo, I'd settled on memorializing Emma for now. There's always my other arm for more tributes some other time! Eric, of course, has additional commentary about clean lines and other observations that seemingly attest to Fin's skill—high compliments from him.

"Enough of the distraction my new addition has caused. We have things to do to get ready for our guests. Steven, can you help me unload a few things from the car? And Eric, can you finish with the music playlist you were doing and get it going? I think we'd all work better and get in the mood with some of Emma's favorites."

Out of the earshot of everyone else, Steven half whispers, "That's really amazing, Larissa. Eric said you were thinking about getting a tattoo, but I didn't think you'd really do it. How'd you do? One of us could have gone along. Hold your hand or something?"

"I'm proud, and maybe as surprised as you are, that I didn't feel like I needed anyone. I know I would've had several volunteers, but it was something I wanted to try to do on my own."

"Well, it's not the first, nor I'm gonna guess, the last time you've done something all on your own!" We both laugh, pick up the shopping bags, and head back to join the others.

By the time our other guests arrive—everyone who we invited has shown up, with garments in hand—the house and the yard are brightly festooned with decorations, flowers are in bouquets on almost every surface, and the smell of pizza is wafting around us. Everyone who comes in blesses us with their hugs, then asks about getting started with the tie-dye. I'd also decided to get out the basket of heart-shaped stones and invite everyone to paint those rocks if they like. Emma had painted many with me years ago, and her samples are definitely gifts to all of us from somewhere beyond.

Renee directs guests to the drinks and snacks, and Isabel helps everyone get oriented to how to do the various tie-dye designs. She made samples of several options and hung them around the table for inspiration—some using rubber bands for circular patterns, or clothespins for others. She even found two tank tops among Emma's things and hung them between two of the photos I'd suggested to Renee for the cake. As I look at everyone working diligently on their clothing and stones, and see Emma's photos and shirts around us, I'm struck by the immense support all of these dear friends have offered. I was going to wait to say a few words later when we'd eaten and were ready for cake, but the time is right to do it now.

"Hey, everyone, I just want to say something. Don't stop what you're doing, I'm sure you can listen and do your birthday projects at the same time. I just, we just, well, Eric and I want to thank you all for being here today. It may have seemed a little weird to get an invitation to a birthday party for Emma, but thank you for not saying or acting like it's weird. Thank you for showing up, for bringing something along to keep with the theme, thank you for helping us all remember our sweet girl, young woman. We were blessed to have her." With this, my voice gets shaky, and I need to wipe a tear away.

Before I know what has happened, Eric and Steven come out of the garage wheeling something on carts. What the . . .?

"And when you're done with your shirts or stones or whatever, there's another station here," announces Eric. "Steven and I will help you get started with one more special project for the day—birdhouses. Most of you know that we've seen so many signs from Emma, many of them birds. We want everyone to share in how much joy it brings when a cardinal stops by to say hello. Mom, Steven and I already did three for you to hang around the yard while everyone else decorates one to take home. What do you think?" He's absolutely beaming.

I don't know whether to laugh at finally figuring out what they've been doing in the garage or cry at the sweet thoughts that went into adding this to our day. The houses are decorated with symbols from nature, much like the party decorations. Each one different, but each one consistent with the theme—so beautiful. Eric comes to help me hang them while Steven helps guests start painting their own.

A few hours later, when almost everyone is gone, I ask Renee and Isabel to sit and have a glass of wine with me. Eric and Hilary have taken Isabel's kids home. Eric said he wanted to have Hilary meet Valentino, but I think he was really just giving me a chance to hang with my friends, while also spending more time with Hilary. I'm struck again by how considerate he's becoming.

Sitting on the porch chairs, I glance over at one of the birdhouses we had hung earlier. Just as I'm about to remark to my friends about how pretty they look in my yard, Isabel puts her finger to her lips to indicate we should be quiet. She points with her other hand at the house closest to us, and sitting on the branch right above it is a cardinal. The cardinal is quiet at first, then starts its distinctive trill. We sit, mesmerized, as the sounds continue for a few minutes.

When it stops, all I can say is, "I think Emma approves of our birthday gathering, don't you?"

12

Because at the end of the day,
The right people fight for you,
The right people show up.
The right people care,
Not only when life is convenient,
but when it is difficult
And messy, and it aches all over.
BIANCA SPARACINO

Eric and Hilary have come back and join those of us left—Renee, Isabel, Steven, and Paul—for a late-night chat with tea. When cleanup is finished and we all finally settle down, I see that Terry called during the party. Damn—it's probably too late to call her now. I'm so curious about what she has to say that I call her number anyway. Of course, I get her recording. I impatiently wait for the beep and leave a message, "It's Larissa. I'm sorry I didn't get your call. Call me back anytime—even if it's late tonight or early in the morning. I'm definitely interested in hearing what you've found out."

Just as I finish speaking the message, I hear Terry's voice. "Larissa, is that you? Sorry it went to voicemail—I didn't hear it ring. Do you have a minute? I have something to share."

"Is it news? Yes, what is it? Did you hear from my son, the guy, Everett, whoever?"

Everyone stops talking in the background. They hear me say *my son* and immediately go silent.

"Please, Larissa, slow down. I did hear back from the young man. But I don't think you're going to be too happy. He confirmed he did put the request in, and at the time he did it, he wanted to find his biological family."

Terry pauses, and I interject, "OK, so that's good."

"Yes, it was good news *at the time* he completed the forms, but now he's hesitant. He has a family member who's very ill, and he's helping care for whoever that is—I'm not sure. He said he doubts he can handle anything else emotional right now. Says he and his family are really stressed out. So, right now, no, he's not ready to let me release his last name or contact information to you. I'm so sorry."

Tears stream down my face as she utters the last three words. I can't believe this. Another setback, all because I couldn't face it before and waited too long. If I'd tried this three years ago, if I hadn't been so wrapped up in whatever the hell I was wrapped up in. "So, like, we just drop it? Terry, can I write him a letter? Just let him know I'm here whenever he's ready? I need to do something. I can't just sit around waiting for something to change in his life. Please?"

"I don't know, Larissa. Remember, we don't even know if it's your son. It's somebody born around the same time, who three years ago was looking for his family. That's not exactly a certainty. Maybe, well, I suppose you can send a letter to me, and I can forward it along. He seemed pretty sure this is not a good time, but I guess he can choose to open it or not. Better let me check with my supervisor on this, I don't know. I'm sorry, I'll get back to you tomorrow. Take care, Larissa." The phone goes silent. It's a chilling, lonely sound—or lack of sound, I should say.

I slowly set my phone down on the table. She says *we don't even know*. Well, I *know*, I feel it deep inside every cell of my body. Ever since she told me about the names on the birth certificate he provided. The minute she said *Laura* and the last name *Miller*, I had a visceral reaction. I stuffed that reaction down and tried to act nonchalant, so as not to get my hopes up, but no way those names are coincidence. My silly aunt, overly conscious of what people will think, just had to get in the middle of this whole thing and try to manage it her way. Now, my chance to finally see him, to try to make things right, to help Eric be a brother again is all going down the tubes. I can't let this happen. I'm not letting go of him—not again.

Everyone is looking at me, clearly waiting for me to say something. I start to walk away, not able to formulate any words. I'm afraid if I open my mouth, I will lose all the pizza, cake, and wine I've consumed over the last several hours. Or I'll explode. The party was so much better than I ever expected, so sweet, and now this. One more damn disappointment, one more way that I'm knocked back down into the quicksand, just when I thought I was crawling out. I can't stand it.

That's what comes out. "I can't stand this anymore! I just cannot fucking stand it! That stupid phrase about 'God doesn't give you more than you can handle'? Who the hell came up with that shit? I cannot handle another version of a child being gone. If that's a 'God thing' to show me what I can handle, count me out. I want nothing to do with any of it—nothing. I'm done! Eric, you want to go to the beach, let's go. Tomorrow—I'm out. I'm getting the hell away from here. In fact, you can all come, or no one can come."

With that, I stomp upstairs to my room, slam the door, and throw myself on the bed. Tears erupt as abruptly as those words had, and stop just as suddenly. I mutter to myself, "Where the hell is my laptop? I'm reserving a house on the beach and I'm writing that letter for Terry to send along, then I'm outta here."

As soon as I finish booking the biggest house of the three possibilities I'd saved earlier, I open up a new blank document and start writing:

Dear Everett (Everett—the name I secretly gave you):

I'm told that at one time a few years back, you were interested in finding your biological family, your mother. Things are different in your life now, and I respect that. You need to do what's best for you and for those you love. I'm presuming you have a family that you love because Terry shared that you're caring for someone close to you who is ill. That sounds like an act of love to me. I'm sure that person is blessed to have you in his or her life.

That's kind of what this letter is about—the people who are blessings in our lives. I believe you are a blessing in my life that I've not yet had the privilege of meeting. I'm sure that sounds weird, but if I've learned anything at all, it's that life truly IS weird. It's a lot of things, good and bad, but definitely weird.

I became pregnant when I was fifteen. To say I didn't know any better is an understatement. The adults in my life swooped in and made decisions that I'm still trying to sort out by piecing together old letters and invoices from lawyers. They were adamant that I shouldn't even see my baby. But a caring young nurse—I don't know her name or even where we were—I think she did let me see my son, did let his skin come in contact with mine, ever so briefly. At least, that's what I remember; she told me never to tell anyone she did that. In that moment, I told her I wanted the baby's name to be Everett.

Before I even told anyone that I was pregnant, I went to the library and looked up the meaning of names. I found out that Everett means "brave." I didn't know much of what was going on or being planned for my baby and me, but one thing I knew was that we both needed to be brave. I wasn't so sure I was going to be able to fulfill that, but some part of me felt that if the baby had that name, it might help, it might help him with whatever was to come in his future. The nurse told me she thought that was a beautiful, important name, and that I should never forget that I gave that to my baby.

If I continued to tell you everything that happened between then and now, this letter would be as long as a dissertation. I don't think this is the time. However, I hope and pray that there will be a time.

I think you are Everett. I hope you've had a happy life so far. I hope you've been loved and cherished by the family that has raised you. Again, it sounds weird, but I love and cherish you. That love is actually what kept me from trying to contact you for so long. I did not want to complicate your life; I did not want you to be placed in the position of making difficult decisions. I wanted to spare you any pain that I possibly could.

But things have changed, because of my other children, your siblings (I know I'm supposed to say "half" siblings, but I don't think people can be half of that kind of special title, special relationship). Eric and Emma. I'll get right to it. Emma died unexpectedly almost a year ago, when she was twenty-one. It has been a heartbreaking, gut-wrenching, horrific experience for all who loved her. Eric, her older brother, your younger, is struggling. He says he wasn't raised to be an only child. He says he wants to be a brother again. He wants to find you—desperately.

So, while I would have probably endured the rest of my life without interfering in yours (not because that was what my heart wanted, but because my brain kept telling me to let you live your life without interference), Eric wants and needs his brother. Maybe in making him happy, you will be happy too. I don't know if you are already a brother, but maybe it would be good for you as well. I can only hope.

Anyway, Terry said she can't tell me anymore about you than what's on the birth certificate you uploaded (with your name blacked out), because you have put a hold on any permissions you'd previously given. The only reason she agreed to let me write this letter to you is that she figured you can choose to open it or not, choose to contact me or not, choose to release your information or not.

I have to take the chance that this will be the time we can actually connect. I couldn't see myself being content to wait until the day when you might contact her again and say you are ready. I have to try to convey to you that Eric and I would love the chance to be part of your life, to include you in ours—such as it is.

I'm listing all of my contact information, as well as Eric's, at the bottom of this letter. We are going away for a little while, but that doesn't matter. Our phones and our email are there for you. Any time you want to make contact, we are here.

By the way, you may have noticed that both their names start with E, as does the name I chose for you. My dear friend Steven also reminded me that a baby I had hoped to deliver, but could not, was also given an E-name in my mind before I lost her. And although I highly doubt you are called Everett, maybe your name also starts with an E. I don't know, but I just don't think that there are coincidences like that. I think it's a sign that we are all meant to be together.

Loads and loads of love,

Larissa/Mom/whatever you want to call me, I'll answer.

And PS, it wouldn't surprise me that the mother's name on your birth certificate is listed as something else—maybe Laura—a long story about my aunt that you don't need to hear unless you want to. She's one of our family's well intended, but a little overbearing, members. I'm guessing every family has some of those!

As I hit the last keystroke, I realize someone is standing at my door.

"Lissa, if you hit those keys any harder, I think that laptop is going to crumble from the impact." Lissa? I haven't heard that nickname in decades. I look up as Steven takes a hesitant step into the room, and I'm momentarily disoriented.

"Are you OK? I mean, we're worried about you. The way you ran away. You seemed like you wanted to be alone, but maybe you shouldn't be. Want to talk?" I can't tell if his look is one of fear that I'll blow up again, or if it's concern that he's expressing from everyone downstairs.

After summarizing my phone call with Terry, I tell him, "So, like I said a while ago, I'm sick of sitting around here. It's making me stir-crazy. I thought I'd want to stay until the anniversary of the day Emma died, but that's a lousy reason to put my life, Eric's life, on hold. We need a break—he's said it several times—I finally agree. It's time to make it happen. I reserved a house on Hutchinson Island, Florida, in a town called Stuart. The owner said the house is available because she wasn't sure when some interior work was going to be finished, and she hadn't found anyone willing to deal with uncertain availability dates. She has no one now until late fall. I guess no one wants to go to Florida when it's too hot. I can come in and rent month to month, unless someone contacts her for a long-term stay. So, I'm going for it. I'm sick of being here in this house. I'm tired of waiting around to see if the puzzle pieces fit together with Everett. I want to spend time with my son, and honestly, with any one of the rest of you who wants to come along, or come visit. You're our people. We're not always great company, but it looks like the setting is beautiful, the house is big enough, so it's open door. I've done what I can to reach out to Everett. I'm going to send this to Terry, and then we might as well wait in a place where Eric can fish, and I can get a little salt-water, salty-air therapy." I hand him the laptop with the letter I'd just finished and let him read.

With tears in his eyes, Steven responds, "I don't know how you do it, Lissa. The letter is beautiful. And while pretty much everyone else downstairs was dumbstruck when you stomped up the stairs, I practically jumped off my chair to cheer you on. And Eric quietly said, 'You go, Madre.' You've held it together for everyone else long enough. A good door slam now and then is soothing to the soul; you needed to blow off some steam, and I'm happy for you that you did. It totally sucks that the young man doesn't want to connect right now, but he might want to tomorrow, or next month, or next year. There's no way of knowing. But what he will know, is that you and Eric are somewhere in the world waiting for him, hoping to be connected. You can wait for him anywhere. It doesn't need to be this house—life, as we well know, is too short—go to the damn beach!" We grab each other for a much-needed hug.

"Hey, Steven? What's with the 'Lissa'? I'm not criticizing, just surprised."

"I'm, uh, surprised, too. Not sure—it just popped out. Old habits die hard, right?"

"Whose bad habits you guys talking about?" Eric asks as he throws the door open further. "Better not be me!"

I pat the bed next to me and put my arms around him. "No, not you. No bad habits at all. Just Steven and I talking about old times and old habits. What do you think? Are you ready to hit the road tomorrow? Ready to pack your bags for some time in the sun and sand?"

"You were serious? That wasn't just pissed-off talk? That's pretty sudden, isn't it? Thought you didn't want to go till--"

I cut him off. "I'm serious, I want to go sooner than later, and I found a house to rent. You and I can go tomorrow, and anyone else can come—my friends, your friends, Steven, whoever—there's a bunch of bedrooms. All I know is I'm going. Are you?"

Looking startled at first, he then breaks into a grin and says, "Yup, I'm on it. I'll go pack right now. Shorts, flipflops, and a tee shirt or two."

13

*In life, it is not where you go,
it's who you travel with.*
CHARLES SCHULTZ

Morning comes quickly. I talked a big game last night about leaving right away, but I didn't pack a thing. I just fell into bed, a case of pure exhaustion, from the phone call, from the party, hell, from the whole last year. I think Steven was correct—that door slamming, stomping exhibition got a lot of crap out of my system, and I crashed into a deep sleep.

I jump out of bed, eager to pack, eager to get Eric going. I need to just be active and do something! As I'm throwing things in the suitcase, it dawns on me that I may want to grab those postcards that were sent to my parents from Florida. Maybe we can look those people up. Or if they're gone, at least try to see some of the sights that they shared with my parents. I'm sure they didn't just pick random scenes to send to Mom and Dad—probably places they'd visited. Who knows?

Eric finds me pulling the postcards and tropical shirts out of the trunk and asks, "So, uh, I guess you really meant it, huh? We're going? Today? You didn't change your mind?"

"I absolutely did not! I'm game if you are; gotta get my things together, but we can leave whenever we're ready and figure out the rest once we're on our way. You?"

"Yeah, sure, I'll be ready soon. I wrote an email to the guy who offered me the internship, and he said I can put it on hold for a few weeks. I can even do the orientation virtually, because they have it all online anyway. Hey, did you mean the rest of it? When you said others can come? Like Dad?" He's not even hesitating now when he refers to Steven as his Dad. I'm touched it is working out like that; it could have been very different.

Before I reply, he adds, "And I don't know, I'm not even sure if I will want to ask her, but if she wants, how would you feel about Hilary maybe joining us? Not right away—I want to just figure out the place we're going, but like, if we end up staying a while? Just wondering what you'd think."

"I meant it, Eric. It didn't really occur to me to include Hilary, but I'm realizing how important our friends really are to us figuring out how to go on with our lives. If she's someone that makes you feel comfortable and supported, then yes. But I agree: let's get settled and see if it's a place we really want to stay at for a while, and then, sure, invite the people who make you feel happy, or content, or whatever."

"And just one more thing, Mom. I hope you don't think this is weird, but, well, can we bring this?"

He holds out one of the small urns that contains Emma's precious ashes—they call it an "heirloom" urn. I ordered a couple after Emma died, never knowing if anyone other than me would want one. I had given him the one he's holding a few weeks after he returned. I waited to be sure he didn't seem he'd be disturbed or creeped out by the presence of ashes; some people are. But he was happy to have them and kept the urn near his bed ever since.

"I want, to, uh--"

"Take Emma with us? Oh, Eric, yes. If you hadn't remembered, I would have been really sad. Where we go, she goes, right?"

"And can we sprinkle some of her ashes in the water? I think, well, I know, she'd like that."

I'm so touched that he thought of this, annoyed with myself that I'd not thought of it, but pleased to know Emma is along for the ride. She loved road trips! That makes it official: time to pack up the car and be on our way.

Renee stops over with a tote bag full of snacks to wish us safe travels, and Steven drops by to wish us well and help around the house. Seeing as we are not sure how long we'll be gone, he offered to stay at the house. It saves him money on accommodations and is a comfort to me to have someone occupying the house.

As we're finishing up, Steven asks Eric, "Hey, pal, aren't you taking your fishing poles? I thought this was a big fishing place."

"Yeah, it is. Maybe I'll take one, but the fishing is different than what I've done before. I'm going to need to find out from someone who knows, a local, who can tell me what I really need as far as rods and tackle and all that stuff." His eyes widen like a signal of the proverbial light bulb going off, and he turns to me, "Wait! Mom, weren't those people who sent the postcards the ones Gamma and Papa visited? And Papa got help for fishing? Like charter captains or fishing guides or something?"

He's right, they were. I confirm his question and add, "Yeah. The thing is, I have no idea the name of the guy's business, how old he was when my parents met him, or anything else about them except their first names, Harriett and Harold. The postmarks on the cards they sent are somewhat useful. I've stuck them in my purse, and we certainly can try to find these folks, do a little detective work while we're there."

The next few minutes are absorbed by hugs, words about faring well (no one says *goodbye*), and assurances that we will see one another soon. No specific promises or arrangements for getting together, but I know the sentiment is heartfelt. We all just need to see where this goes. Maybe we will stay, maybe we will want to come back for that damn "angel-versary," or maybe our friends actually will join us. There is something that feels right about a non-agenda.

Before long, we're rolling down the highway, chatting about what tunes to play next, searching for special songs, and occasionally checking the GPS. We've decided to drive due east. I remember having stayed several years ago at St. Simon's Island on the Georgia coast. As I describe it to Eric, he likes the sound of it, so we make it our destination for this partial day of driving. Since we didn't start out very early, and we have no set schedule, neither of us feels the need to drive straight through to the rented house. He drives, while I make reservations online and read articles to him from travel sites about the history of St. Simon's Island, its legendary lighthouse, and its status as one of the Golden Isles.

This reminds me of the old days, except we did it all on paper—not our phones. Days when we would call up the automobile travel agency and have them do a map of where we were traveling. Attached to the map were little bits of geographical trivia and notes about interesting landmarks. I would enthusiastically read them aloud to the kids. I think they listened to only a small fraction of what I read, but inevitably they'd pick up some little tidbit and repeat it all day.

"Hey, Eric. Remember when we were driving on vacation one time, and I read one of those tour guides to you about the old oak? When I said oak tree neither one of you was too impressed, but when I said it was the kind of tree that drops acorns on the ground, you immediately got interested. You then kept saying,

'Emma, we're going to see a three-hundred-year-old oak-a-nut tree.' Everyone laughed at your made-up word, *oak-a-nut*, so you just kept saying it to get the laughs."

We both start laughing at the story, and I add, "It was somewhere near Charleston. We were visiting my old friend from college there. I can't remember the name of the tree, but I can see it in my mind, and I know we have photos somewhere of you and Emma climbing it, and running around underneath, gathering acorns, or should I say oak-a-nuts?"

We laugh some more, and then Eric's face becomes more serious as he remembers, "It's called *Angel Oak*, Mom. That's the name of that tree—angel. What made you think of it right now? It's not near where we're going, right?"

I'm stunned, then strangely comforted. "I don't know what made me think of it. I was thinking of previous road trips, of you and Emma in the back seat while I read trivia to you about where we were heading, and that's what came into my mind. See what I mean? I can't help but marvel at the feeling that overcomes me when something like this happens that just cannot possibly be a coincidence. I think it's a sign that Emma, *our* angel, is with us on this trip. Her spirit, her living energy, has not vanished. That energy finds us, nudges us along when we need a little help, lifts us a tiny bit when we are weighed down. It's said that energy never goes away, it re-forms itself. I believe her energy breaks through when we need it, permeates barriers to believing, and gives us the energy we need to keep going, to keep making new memories, to keep honoring her, maybe to find Everett or to help others find joy in some way. The energy and will to survive in spite of what we must endure to do so."

I'm looking straight ahead, yet out of the corner of my eye, I see Eric nodding in agreement. No words necessary. What is it about a car ride that sometimes makes the silences more comfortable, or other times, encourages conversation? There must be something about the constrained, shared space that changes how we communicate.

After a few more miles of the comfortable quiet, Eric speaks up. "Mom, tell me more about that day, the day Emma died--no, I agree with that energy stuff. Tell me about the day she passed over, when her energy changed, whatever."

Exactly my point about communicating in cars. He hadn't asked me for more details since the first few times we spoke about Emma. I decided back then that, probably just like most everyone else, he really cannot handle the details, and so they'd remain between Emma and me, heartbreaking and strangely intimate. Has the contemplation of angels and spiritual energy changed his mind?

Now, he's asked, so I'll give it a try. "We'd had a really nice day. We'd walked in the park with Valentino, she'd met up with a few friends in the late afternoon, then came home for dinner. We ate together, watched a movie, and planned to go out to breakfast the next day. You know how much Emma liked to go out for breakfast." I see his head nodding again. I'm weighing my words carefully; this isn't easy, not anything I've practiced. I've not said this all to anyone except Renee and Isabel, not even either counselor I've encountered.

"When I went to wake her up to go to breakfast, I knew right away something was wrong. After her rehab stay and all those healthy months after, I'd finally stopped dreading going in to wake her up. I had confidence in her recovery work and really thought that things were going well. I knew right away this was different. I can't describe how the room felt except, well, maybe it's like what we said a few minutes ago. It never struck me before now, maybe what felt different was there wasn't energy in the room. It was bereft of energy. She was there, but her energy, well, it wasn't."

I'm semi-conscious that Eric has pulled the car off the highway while I'm speaking. I'm not ready to stop. "In spite of that emptiness, I tried anything I knew to save her. One part of me knew it was too late, one part of me had to try anyway. At some point, I grabbed Valentino, ran out of the room to get my phone, called 911, and the rest you know."

"Mom, you had to be so freaking scared, so alone, I'm sorry."

"I was alone, Eric, totally alone. In a way, looking back, I'm glad you weren't home, glad you were away. It's too much for anyone to bear, and I'm thankful you were spared. That time, which I realize now was very brief, felt very long. Being alone, and waiting near her, by her side, was intimate. There was a sanctity about that space. As you know, I'm not very religious, but there was a holiness between Emma and me. In a way, it was similar to when she was born. While there are people around, there's a moment when it still really is just the child and the mother whose lives are intricately linked. I was the first one to touch her and feel her, and the last. In an indescribable way, it was an honor to be the one there, with her alone. I hate, hate, hate it, but I honor it. If it had to happen, if anyone was to be there, I'm grateful it was me."

We sit in silence, each lost in our thoughts. I've been breathing heavily throughout my response to his question and am trying to return those gasps of air to a more rhythmic, slower cadence.

"I suppose that's more than you really asked for, honey."

"I had no clue what I was asking for, Mom. Thanks for just answering, for not freaking out. It has to be hard to think about, no less put into words. Want to get out and walk for a few minutes?"

The peaceful space between us continues as we walk around the rest stop. It hadn't registered to me until now that he'd pulled into an actual parking area. I'm glad. Once the story started coming out, we needed to be parked in a safe place—not anywhere near the speeding cars all around us.

"Where the heck was Roger during that time? Did he show up?"

Interesting that although Roger adopted him shortly after we got married, and was Emma's biological father, Eric never called him *Dad*. He's comfortably using that name for Steven after only a few months. I'm not going to point it out, it's just interesting, very telling.

"You probably remember he hadn't been in any kind of regular communication in a while. He'd occasionally text Emma, but it was perfunctory, at best. I know it hurt her, but she always tried to make light of it or make excuses about the intensity of his work schedule. Afterwards, he didn't help with any arrangements, or seem all that interested in the dozens of decisions you have to make with the funeral home. Beyond making an appearance at the small service we held, nope, nothing. And I haven't heard from him since. I'm relieved, actually—I didn't need his self-centered bullshit on top of everything else."

Eric laughs and throws his arm around me, "Ha, Mom, come on. Let's get back on the road. Let's find this cool lighthouse you read about online."

14

*Don't let the waves of others drown out
your own ocean song.
Hold your heart as though it was a seashell.
And listen to it. Listen to its music.
To the whispers of your ocean within.
And then swim.*
S.C. Lourie

As the waitress brings our plates of eggs and pancakes to us on the hotel's outdoor patio the next morning, Eric and I compare notes about how we'd slept and start trying to decide if we want to do any sightseeing on St. Simon's or continue right away to Florida.

"I've been here before, Eric, so it's really up to you if you want to poke around at some of the sights. What I do want, though, either way, is to take a beach walk after we finish eating. That water looks inviting: no huge rolling waves, just gentle ripples. It's low tide—a perfect time to walk, maybe even find some beach treasures."

"Yeah, sure, let's do it."

Before long, I'm enjoying the wet sand between my toes. We stride along the beach, our feet kicking up just a bit of the calm ocean with each step. When the sand is firm like this, I want to walk indefinitely, letting all my heavy thoughts float away into the deep water, as far away from me as possible, making room for the inspiring, creative ideas that replace them. The ebb and flow of the waves is never-ending, eternal, and it brings comfort, with a kind of wonder that I've rarely felt anywhere else. It was a good decision to come to the beach again.

At almost exactly the same time, Eric and I bend down. I'd seen the circular pattern, barely beneath the sand that suggests a sand dollar right in front of me; Eric sees one as well. But as soon as I turn it over, I immediately put it down. "It's purply-brown, Eric, this one is still alive, don't pick it up or we might hurt it. Watch for ones that are white—white ones are actually skeletons and fine to collect."

"Wasn't there some sand dollar legend, a kind of religious thing?"

"Yeah, many people say it's a symbol of the story of Christ. The pattern on top has five long ovals that make it look like the star of Bethlehem. But what I always found enchanting is that, if the sand dollar breaks open even just a little bit, five little pieces that look just like doves will fall out. Whether you believe the story of Christ or not, the doves are a beautiful symbol of peace and love."

"Didn't you and Emma do some crafts using sand dollars?"

"Wow, yes, Eric. We made little pictures by gluing those doves into patterns on colored paper, and then one time, we'd collected enough whole sand dollars to make a wreath out of them at Christmastime. It's not often you find so many that aren't broken. They're pretty fragile. And if you do find them whole, the next challenge is transporting them without breaking them en route.

Once we got them home unbroken, they were so beautiful; lined up side by side to create something new."

"Hold that thought, Mom," Eric says, while digging around in his backpack. He pulls out the small urn he'd brought to be sure Emma is with us on our journey. "I think what you just said about the sand dollars being fragile, and quite beautiful side by side might kind of apply to people—to Emma. Let's sprinkle some of these here, OK?"

"It's more than OK, Eric, it's perfect. Memories of Emma, sand dollars, and the tiny doves that hide inside the sand dollars, are all little treasures brought to us by waves. It all somehow fits together right here, right now." We each take a pinch of ashes between our fingers and swirl our fingertips around to send Emma gently into the rippling ocean. The ashes make circular, smoky-looking patterns in the water, then slowly dissipate to become one with nature.

In silent agreement, we walk slowly to the hotel, not saying a word, not needing to. Once back, we empty our pockets out on the counter—not a bad array of treasures from the sea. We did each find a sand dollar, Eric found some shells he thought were different than any he'd found before, and I found two heart-shaped stones. I suggest we wrap the sand dollars carefully in our tee shirts before packing them up, and Eric makes a decision about the rest of our day.

"I vote for getting back on the road. It looks like it's only a little more than five hours from here to the beach house. I say let's get there and check it out. If we get going, we can get there before dark so we can see some of the area around the place and get our bearings. This walk was good, but the lighthouse has been here more than a hundred years, it'll be here another time."

"I'm good with that. You drove most of yesterday, so I volunteer to drive. If I get tired, you can take over. In the meantime, you can read to me like a tour guide, or relax. Whatever you feel like."

Before we check out, I scroll quickly through my email to see if there is anything from Terry. I'm disappointed, but not surprised that there are no new emails other than advertisements. There are two texts on my phone: one from Steven saying all is well, that I should give him a call when I have a chance, but it's nothing urgent. The other is from Renee, reminding me to let her know when we make it safely to the rental house. I feel a quick smile cross my face to know that people are checking in on us. It's a good feeling.

The fifteen miles or so before we get to the interstate are mostly wooded, with lots of live oak, evergreens, and a few palm trees. Road signs are urging us to stop for Georgia peaches and pecans, but we're now on a mission to our destination. Since it's middle of the day in the middle of the week, the traffic is sparse, and before we know it, we're crossing the state line to Florida. The GPS says we have about four hours to our temporary home away from home. I'm hoping it's as pleasant as it looked in the photos. Information about the area used a lot of descriptors that made me look up the topography to try to grasp why it is considered such a unique waterway that forms Hutchinson Island on the one side, with the ocean on the other. Maybe Eric can help me figure it out.

"Hey, Eric, can you look up where we're going? It said the house is on Hutchinson Island, an island along the intracoastal. The house faces the intracoastal, but supposedly, it's just a short walk over to the ocean."

"Ok, yeah. Weird, for some reason I thought it was right on the beach."

"The way it looked to me is that the house backs up onto the intracoastal and there is a small sandy area with kayaks and paddleboards and all that stuff, and then the beach on the ocean side is just across the street."

"You're right, Mom. According to this description of the Indian River Lagoon, it's part of the intracoastal, and not really a river at all. They say it's unique because it's an estuary, whatever that is. Oh, here it says that's where salt water from the ocean mixes with freshwater, so it's called *brackish*. Then it says it's the most biologically diverse estuary in North America. That's why there are so many animal species, especially birds, fish, and even manatees. I guess they all go to the lagoon because it's kind of a protection for them. Definitely sounds cool. And I can see why Papa wanted to fish there. I'm stoked."

As he finishes talking, I'm trying to remember anything I can that my parents told me about going there. I think they went to the same town each time and stayed at the same place. I can't remember exactly how many times; I think once when I was in high school, and a few times after that. Now I wish I'd paid attention to my parents and their travels, for so many reasons.

"Eric, the address where we are staying on Hutchinson is Stuart. Can you read off some of the other names? I want to see if they sound familiar from Papa's stories."

"So, let's see—Fort Pierce, Jensen Beach, Port Salerno, Hobe Sound, Tequesta, then it's all the way to Jupiter. I don't think that's it, right?"

"No, not Jupiter. Maybe they sound familiar from my searches or the postcards, but that Port Salerno and Jensen Beach ring a bell. I do know that Papa had pictures of fish he caught out on a dock as well as times he went out in a good-sized boat with a guide. I guess we'll just try to figure it out when we get there."

Before long, the GPS estimates our arrival in forty minutes, and we are crossing a bridge over what looks like a river. We can see the ocean in the distance.

"Wow, this is cool, Mom. I'm opening the windows to get fresh air in here. It totally smells like the ocean."

Boats seem to be moored in every direction that we look, before we go through traffic roundabouts and start heading straight south. We occasionally catch glimpses of the ocean on our left, then there's a long stretch of river, or lagoon, I guess, on the right. The lagoon is very close to the road; I wonder if it ever floods over the banks here? Eric's right, it's very cool. It's pristine and way different than any other beach areas we've traveled to. Once again, I'm struck by how right it feels to be traveling with him now.

We turn down a private drive, and it looks like we are headed straight into the lagoon. There are a few houses along the drive, best described as eclectic in style. Some look very new, with modern rooflines, some look like small bungalows that may have been here for decades. All are brightly painted shades of vibrant beachy colors, like turquoise, lime green, and blue, with yard and porch ornaments that would be kitschy anywhere else, but for some reason, they look fitting in this setting. The message "You have reached your destination" broadcasts into the car and we just stare at the place. The front of the property is relatively nondescript, but as we curve into our parking spot, the side and back views are spectacular. The house is likely one of the older ones but has been updated and well kept, and its porch looks like the place we'll want to spend all of our time. It is situated with a clear view of the water, with a long dock jutting out into the lagoon. Since it faces west, we'll have a magnificent sunset to enjoy on clear evenings.

Although we were both pretty groggy only a few minutes ago from driving, the excitement of arrival is energizing. We practically trip over one another trying to get to the front door to check out our accommodations. The front door motif matches the lawn ornaments, displaying a pelican etched in glass to greet us. The kitchen, the living area, and two of the downstairs bedrooms have a water view. As we climb the stairs, I gasp as the vaulted ceiling of the master suite reveals yet another wonderful vista to enjoy. The others don't have the expansive water view but are brightly painted with more beach-themed accessories.

We go back downstairs to scope out the porch. It's furnished with comfortable-looking rattan chairs, a dining table, several smaller tables, and an outdoor mini-kitchen for grilling and serving. Beyond that is an in-ground pool, further beyond, the lagoon. Just as the website stated, it's stocked with water toys, paddleboards, and kayaks.

"Wow, just wow. This place is mint! It's pretty big for just us, Mom. Better think about inviting some other people, right?"

"It sure seems like that would be a good idea, Eric. Let's unload, get settled, maybe order some food, and see if we can do it all in time to sit and watch the sunset with a cocktail in our hands."

I claim the master suite, and Eric takes one of the downstairs bedrooms with a water view. After hauling our suitcases and some plastic bins with other supplies and some snack foods, we are happy to find that the owners thoughtfully left some menus on the desk with recommendations of their personal favorites. Although a couple are pretty close by, we unanimously agree that delivery is the way to go. We want to settle on that porch before any more time lapses.

Changed into comfortable lounging clothes, I carry our drinks while Eric carries out the tray of snacks I'd thrown together to sustain us until our meals are delivered. After arranging the furniture so we can both reach the tray, both have a good view, and be able to see one another as we enjoy our first of, hopefully many, peaceful sunsets, we both plop down in our chairs. I don't know whose whoosh of air escapes first, but obviously, we both enjoy a sense of relief at being settled in.

The sky does not disappoint. As the sun begins its descent toward the river, the changing colors swirl around the clouds and the sun, making new patterns every few minutes. The sun's rays glisten as they reach the river, enhancing the light show. With each change one of us exclaims, "Look at it now!" or "Do you see that?" If there was a painting in a gallery with this many colors, one might accuse the artist of exaggerating the beauty of the sky. And while the sun meanders slowly downward for a while, all of a sudden, it seems to plummet more quickly, as if it's pulled by some powerful force out of the sky into the depths of the river. By now, it is too breathtaking to even utter a word about how it looks. It's a time to ponder and appreciate nature's glory in silence.

Just when I think it can't possibly get any better, Eric shouts out, "Holy shit, Mom, look over there! I think it's a dolphin!"

Sure enough, there are dolphins repeatedly coming up out of the water, turning, and going back down just as quickly. There are at least three, maybe more. It's difficult to count because they come up, let us catch a glimpse of their glimmering gray, and then smoothly, almost without rippling the water, go right back under. They're putting on a show, right in front of us. Their movements are mesmerizing. Playful, yet graceful. Moving through the water rapidly, yet seemingly without effort. Neither one of us has spoken for several minutes when the doorbell loudly startles us, apparently announcing something of importance to take our attention away from the living artwork in front of us.

It takes a moment for the meaning of the doorbell to sink in, to break through the hypnotic spell that the sky and the dolphins have placed us under.

"Uh, guess we better get that. Probably the food?"

I slowly nod my head, not totally willing to transition away from the moment of wonder we just experienced.

15

Let perseverance be your engine and hope your fuel.
H. Jackson Brown Jr.

When we finish eating, Eric tries to capture his feelings since we arrived. "Mom, this is more than I'd expected. I'm kinda overwhelmed. I haven't felt this, I don't know, speechless since, well, uh ..." He trails off, picks up our dinner dishes, and walks into the kitchen. I hear the banging and clanging of him putting things in the dishwasher and am thankful for this time together. Quite a difference from before he took off last year. Back then, he would rarely eat with us, and when he did, he ate and ran—almost literally—out the door as soon as we finished. He didn't have a lot of patience with Emma and me just before he decided he needed a road trip, a getaway for himself, a heartache for me.

He returns to the porch from kitchen duty, asking if I want anything else to drink. I accept the wine bottle he's offering and say, "Yes, thanks. And when? When did you feel as speechless as during that sunset?"

"Well, I meant to tell you, but there just hasn't been the right time."

Ugh! Speechless could have meant anything, but *waiting for the right time*—this does not sound good. It sounds like something I don't want to hear, but that he wants to get off his chest. He's been waiting for the right time, when we've been in the car for the last two days? Hmm.

"I did it, Mom. I went to the psychic medium, a couple of days before Emma's birthday. I went, and yeah, I was speechless. I'm still not sure I can describe it."

Not at all what I was expecting, but not so bad, at least it doesn't sound like it so far. "OK, well, I thought you wanted me to go with you, or someone. Must've changed your mind, cuz I know I didn't go along." I was trying to make light of it, but my attempt sort of sunk like a lead balloon.

"I did want someone, and I know you offered, but then so did Dad, and that was what ended up happening. He and I were talking about it, and then, just made the appointment for the following day, and it happened."

So, after we talked, Steven must have just gone ahead and offered to go with Eric. I thought Steven would tell me if something came of it, but does that really matter? Neither of us has really gotten used to the whole idea of sharing Eric as our son yet. *Put these thoughts away, Larissa and listen to your son. He wants to tell you about--*

Eric interrupts my silly self-talk. "Yeah, well we went. And it blew my mind. When we first went in her, I guess you'd say office, but it was more like a living room, I gotta admit I had my doubts. The décor, well, it was a little out there, you know? Like all stars and angel wings? I should have expected that, I guess. After you told me about when you went in New York, and Dad told me,

I should have guessed what it would be like. Now I know why you had a hard time describing it to me. Anyway, what made me speechless tonight is that it was just like something that happened during the session, the reading, whatever it's called."

I hear him struggling with all of the same things I did after going to a medium. The language for how to describe the whole experience is so different than with anything I ever tried to share with anyone before. Before I went myself, I was pretty skeptical, thinking maybe the medium would just make up generic stuff that could apply to anyone. But not so, not at all. Once I was there, once I experienced the amazingly reassuring connection with my daughter and mother who had passed over, I wanted to represent it accurately to other people. I wanted to be believable by others, because it was the most real connection that I could have ever imagined. They communicated things to me through the medium that only they would know. I don't have to understand how it works, I just know it does.

"So, I went to this medium, Justine, and Emma appeared to me. She talked about you and me together by water and the things we've seen already on this trip—like sand dollars and dolphins. Emma talked about the whole idea of gifts coming to us from the ocean waves, that we should pay attention to them because she would be sending us signs. Emma told me that you already know about butterflies and birds and pennies as signs, but that there is so much more that I should watch. That whenever there is something beautiful from nature that just shows up, I shouldn't shrug it off as coincidence; I should know it's her telling me she's around.

"Mom, we sat here tonight watching that sun go down over the lagoon. It was beautiful. Then, just as we were about to stop looking because we thought the show was over, those dolphins came swimming by. And they didn't just appear and go away—they played right in front of us, rolling in the gentle waves like they were saying 'Look, here we are!' It's kinda like a message, right? Just when you think something beautiful is about to end, there is more? Is that Emma's message? If we think she's gone, she will always send us something more?"

Now it's me who's speechless. When he went with Steven to this Justine a few days before Emma's birthday, we hadn't even made a solid plan to come here. And although we had visited oceanside places when Emma was living, we'd never witnessed dolphins playing in front of us before.

"Do you want to tell me the rest? Any other parts of your time with her you'd like to share, or was it more private? Did Steven come into the session with you or wait outside?"

"He came in, Mom. Like you and I talked about, I wasn't sure I could do it on my own. I wasn't exactly scared, but I'd be lying if I said I didn't have some real nervous thoughts and feelings on the way there. He came in, but sat off to the side. It was like it was just us, just Emma and me. I mean, Justine started the whole thing off with a prayer and a little about how spirits come to her. She asked me to verify that who she was seeing was someone I actually wanted to talk about. Right off the bat, she said, 'Do you have a young woman in the spirit world? Someone really close to you, like a sister or a cousin?' When I told her yes, she described a slender young woman with long, wavy hair who was wearing flowing, filmy clothes. She described the clothes as being a cross between hippie style and something ethereal. I'm like, what? How can this be? Then, she said the young woman wanted to speak through her to me, and asked if that was OK with me. Before one more word was said, I felt like I was in another world. I was spellbound."

"I remember that feeling, Eric. Afterward, I was so glad Renee had been there, because I couldn't figure out if everything that happened was real or not. She and I both took notes, and that helped me later to keep track of what was said."

"Yeah, I couldn't write—I hate taking notes, but Steven did, and get this—Justine records it and sends you the file of the whole thing. Maybe you want to hear it some time? I don't know—some parts were hard. Like Emma said that it was all accidental. She said that anyone who thinks she did this on purpose is crazy—way wrong. She said she was doing good, trying to get stuff together, and that her passing over to the other side was a mistake. Nothing anyone could have done. She did kinda call me out on leaving when you both needed me, said I deserved to be slapped for that, but then said she got it. She knew all her mess ups were hard on us and that she's sorry. She's sorry, Mom." With that, tears leak down his cheeks. He tries to swipe them away quickly, as if he doesn't want me to see, but that's futile.

That remark about the slap. Really? When I went to the medium, Emma said she was going to find Eric, get him a message, but slap him first for leaving me to handle all this alone. I never told Eric that part when we talked about the medium—another confirmation, to my way of thinking, about the authenticity of the communication with those in spirit. I pull my chair closer to Eric and rest my hand on his knee. I want to make contact, but want to give him space if he's going to continue. A silence settles over us, as if to suspend time. It's not an awkward silence; in fact, it's quite soothing.

"She also said it was peaceful. She didn't want to go, but then something happened. When she saw Gamma reach for her, she felt caressed and gently lifted away. I never believed this stuff, Mom, but there are just too many details, too many specifics that no one else could know except Emma."

"That's how I felt, too, Eric. It's challenging to wrap your arms around all this, but too many people have shared the same type of experience for me to deny it anymore. I'm convinced, and I'm comforted by the connection, by the signs we receive, and I choose to let it all sustain me. I think there will always be dark days, but there will always be these moments of joy and connection, if we're open to them."

I look up at the sky. Because we are so far from any ambient light source, the sky appears totally black except for the generous sprinkling of twinkling stars. I'm reminded of a meme I'd seen many times that has two small characters looking up at just such a sky, and one wonders, "What if they are not just stars but rather openings for our loved ones to look down on us?" It seems fitting to share that thought with Eric.

"Yeah, no doubt, that would be cool. I know this: whenever I look up at the sky, I think about Emma and wonder if she can see us. I wonder about what coulda been; it's tough. But since that day with Justine, I also wonder, almost constantly, about what Emma said. She said one more thing that I need to tell you. I'm not exactly sure what it means, but it's gotta mean something important, cuz she said it more than once.

"She said, 'Just don't give up, Eric. Anything worth having is worth a struggle. Keep going—it will be worth it.' I asked Justine to ask her to tell me more, but Justine said that she herself was tired from the connection, and that it was time to stop or she might not be accurate anymore. She said sometimes that's because the spirit is fading, or sometimes it's her own fatigue; she couldn't tell. So, we had to let it end. I didn't want to, though. I was tired, too, when we got outside. I told Dad I needed to just sit for a while, I was wiped out. I'd do it again in a nanosecond, though. I want to talk with Emma again and again."

I nod. "So do I. And her message to keep at it, not give up, could mean a lot of things. Maybe it's a message about life in general that she's learned by her own experiences and wants you to learn from?"

Without hesitation he says, "I think she meant looking for Everett. Sure, it could be more general, but it didn't seem that way. Especially because it came up twice. It seemed almost urgent."

"Well, I'm not ready to give up, Eric. It's just harder than I ever thought it would be. Now that we're here, I'll call Terry again tomorrow and see what's become of the letter I wrote."

Looking at my watch, I see it's gotten late. Maybe it's time to figure out what we want to do first with our precious island time.

"So, not to totally change the subject, but I'm going to. What do you want to do tomorrow, Eric? What's on your wish list?"

"I'm open to whatever, Mom. I'd kinda like to go to one of the bait and tackle places to find out the best places to fish, what to use for equipment, all that stuff. Not sure they'll tell me, not sure locals want to share their best fishing spots, but they do make money off people liking it here, so maybe I can find out something."

"Sounds like you need to explore a little on your own. How about if I go get us groceries whenever I wake up—it's usually pretty early. Then, you can take the car and check out some places. While you're doing that, I'll catch up on calls to Renee, Isabel, and Steven, and try to get some information out of Terry. Later in the day, we can figure out a dinner plan. Maybe while you're poking around, you can get some restaurant recommendations as well?"

Eric goes in the house to get ready for bed, and I pause one more time to ponder the sky, the messages, and then this river, lagoon, whatever it is. The lapping of the water against the rocks and beach is so gentle; it rolls just enough to make a barely audible lullaby. I'm going to leave the sliding doors open and hope it will perform its magic on my sleep cycle.

Before I climb the stairs, I sit at the kitchen counter to send off some quick texts to my dear friends, wondering if we made it here. I let Renee, Isabel, and Steven know that we arrived and that the place is way better than our expectations. The ladies answer back with quick, loving emojis. Steven's message comes back, "I hope you and Eric have had some peaceful moments to connect, to talk." I give him a thumbs-up and heart emoji. No way I'm going to get into a conversation about what Eric and I have shared so far. That can wait for a face-to-face conversation.

As I walk toward the huge bed, centered under the impressive windows, ensuring a view of the water, I remember to open the door. As soon as I do, the quiet murmur, only a few yards away, gives me hope for a peaceful night ahead.

16

*The heart of a man is very much like the sea.
It has its own storms, it has its tides,
and in its depths, it has its pearls, too.*
Vincent van Gogh

*I*t feels like I've been asleep a long time. No dreams popping into my head, confusing me with their convoluted story lines or the need to try to determine what is real and what is something my brain concocted during sleep. The room is still quite dark. Looking at the clock beside the bed, it's close to sunrise, but not quite. After a few lazy moments contemplating this rested feeling, the sound outside the sliding door almost lulls me back to sleep. Then I'm struck by the realization that just across the street, the sun is about to break over the horizon on the ocean. Scrambling in the suitcase for stretchy yoga pants I'd not yet unpacked, I hurry to dress and get over to the other side; I don't want to miss the sunrise. I hastily scribble a note to Eric telling him I went to the beach and to go ahead on his exploration—I can grocery shop anytime.

Again, I am enthralled by our location. It takes me only five minutes to traverse our private drive, cross the street, and find the private beach access designated for residents. Stepping onto sand, it's cool at first, in the shaded area. As soon as I step out from under the trees, the sand temperature rises and caresses my feet, like a foot massage; what a glorious, grounding feeling.

The sensory inputs from my surroundings explode! The sand, the heat, the humidity, and the breeze provide an array of tactile stimuli that one never feels anywhere but at the ocean. The smells of the salty water and air add to that undeniable awareness of being seaside. The visual impact of the peachy-yellow sphere poking through white and gray cloud formations is spellbinding. And the sounds—the cacophony of birds and the crashing of waves—are overwhelming. The ocean is wild today, tumultuous. The crests are high and white, the troughs pull back deeply into a dark blue, the same midnight blue that formed a canopy over us last night.

After only a few feet, I plop down in the sand to take it all in, to let it all wash over me. Except the water; it is too wild this morning to immerse myself in it. I need to back away from its roiling rhythm in order to appreciate it. A little distance allows me to appreciate its beauty without experiencing its roughness.

I breathe in deeply, then slowly let the warm air out. I call upon my yoga practice to assist me in being still. As I assume a cross-legged pose, I close my eyes, rest my hands on my knees and turn them upward. I want, I need, to be open to letting it all in.

With no awareness of how much time has passed, I slowly open my eyes while flexing and extending my fingers. I don't want to change position too quickly. I need to re-enter consciousness in a slow and steady manner or I'll lose the whole experience. It will blow away with the wind or wash away with the waves. I'm compelled to hold the feeling as long as possible. I slowly stand and put one foot in front of the other, gradually resuming a typical breathing pattern and an arm-swing that moves me along.

Slowly, I start to appreciate individual aspects of the environment. I laugh at the sandpipers scurrying around to avoid the crashing waves while in search of little critters in the sand. The squadron of pelicans overhead dive-bomb the water in their aggressive, yet graceful quest for fish. And the beach is strewn with shells. I see pretty, pinkish-and-purple-colored scallop shells and remember that my mother collected pink ones like these and brought them back to me in a pale, green decorative jar. I'd not seen them anywhere else we traveled, until of course, now. *Hmm. A sign from Mom? I remember she called them "wonders from the waves."* I cannot resist picking up an assortment of sizes and shades of them to add to our growing collection of sea treasures.

As the sun rises, I feel it hot on my shoulders and realize I should probably turn back. Time has vanished during this walk, and I've no idea how long it will take me to get back to the house.

I see the car is gone, but as I walk in, I smell the unmistakably comforting smell of coffee. Bless you, Eric. Thank you for this considerate gesture. And although he hates to write notes, would much rather text, I see he responded to mine, telling me he's gone to the store for more coffee and a few other things, but since I still wasn't here when he got back, he'd headed out to look for a bait shop. I'm touched because he added, "Please text me when you're back so I know you haven't floated out to sea" with a smiley face.

Coffee in hand, I stroll out to the porch to enjoy the water on our side of the road. I let Eric know I'm back and slowly sip, making a mental list of who I want to contact, whenever I'm finally ready to get going for the day. I realize I've already come to expect the sounds of seagulls and other water birds, when I'm rather startled by a songbird—a cardinal here? Immediately surrounding me, palm trees prevail, and I can't see a cardinal anywhere. But I know that unmistakable sound. I stand up, walk around the front of the house, and sure enough, between the house and the driveway is a bright-red cardinal atop a utility wire. As it calls out, I spot another in a live oak at the house across the street. They are talking, or singing, or whatever, to one another repeatedly. I watch them a moment, tilt my head upward, breathe deeply, and whisper to those in another place, the spirit world, and to myself, "Thank you for the signs this morning. I appreciate them, and I love you."

It takes a bit of time to boot up my laptop, connect it to the internet, and scroll through the myriad of messages, mostly advertising, cluttering up my inbox. I'm looking for something from Terry, but get distracted by a notification about a blog. It's one I've followed for quite a while. I've even written in it about some of my reactions to well-meaning people after Emma died. It was several weeks—no, I guess months ago—that I'd done that. I scroll through, stopping frequently because the entries are replete with genuine feelings. Eventually, as I go back further, I see responses to my post, and I'm sucked into them. Before I know it, I'm commenting again:

Months ago, I wrote of water, of the resilience of water. Today, as I find myself on a peaceful barrier island, I'm once again inspired to share my thoughts about water. Before the trauma of last year, a year when one of my children was missing and the other had died, I always thought of the beach, the place where the ocean meets the sand, as a place of peace and solitude. A place where I could retreat and recharge my energy. Yet during that time, for some reason I couldn't understand, I didn't run to the beach.

Instead, I traveled to an area near the home I grew up in, aside a calm, cold, freshwater lake. Old friends joined to sit with me, listen to me, sometimes comfort me, and it was what I needed. As my counselor recently suggested, it was what I needed to "tend my fire." In retrospect, I think I needed steady, quiet, reliable friends and environment to begin to tiptoe my way back into a life I didn't choose, a life I did not want. My fire was fizzling, and the people and the place gently added tiny bits of kindling until I could start to judge how much tending my fire required to keep going.

Fast forward, and last night I arrived, with my son, on an island. On one side is a body of water whose official name is the Indian River, but it's actually a lagoon—Indian River Lagoon. I had to look that one up: a lagoon is different from a river in many ways. What struck me is that rivers flow, typically from north to south, while the water in a lagoon is influenced by the wind. A river is freshwater, while the lagoon is a mix of fresh and salt, resulting in something completely different called brackish water. Then, just across the street, is the ocean. The ocean whose waves can be extreme, emotional, roiled up and foaming, or occasionally, almost flat. You never know what you'll find on the ocean from day to day. Maybe this is why I was hesitant to come to the ocean when my grief was raw, like a gaping wound. Maybe I couldn't stand the thought of something unpredictably crashing up against me. Maybe I thought the salt water would sting the open wounds.

This place, this mishmash of environments, is already captivating me. It is tending my fire in yet another way. In the evening, I can listen to the quietest whisper of water outside my window. When the sun emerges, I can venture to the ocean to investigate what mystery it holds for the new day. It's much like my own mixed-up emotions: one day I'm overcome with gratitude for what I do have—my son, my friends, perhaps a long-lost son—another day or another hour, I'm still vulnerable to grief engulfing me in its unwelcome power to derail every ounce of resilience I've built up.

I'm still trying to figure it out, but now, today, those highs and lows represented by the crests and troughs of the ocean waves and the ripples of the river, along with the stinging yet healing salt of the ocean and the somewhat diluted quality of the lagoon are the characteristics that are helping me figure out just how to tend my fire, just how to find the parts of life that will refuel me, replenish lost sparks.

And what led me here? How did I find it? Old postcards. Yup, old postcards sent to my parents by people they had met along the way, in their travels. People who clearly meant enough to stay in touch for years after they spent time together. I was led here by someone reaching out to my parents years ago. By searching in an old trunk for clues to where my lost child, long ago adopted, might be. By my son, Eric, begging me to get away, to get out of the house that screams, "Emma's not here . . . oh, but she is." And probably by some force I do not understand pulling me here, urging me along. I think the force is communication and love. I think it is communication from the spirits of beloved people who have passed on. My parents, who found this island years ago, and my precious daughter, the beach lover. Eric and I knew we had to get to the beach at some point, bring Emma's ashes here, and spend time together. We got past her first birthday since she died, and started here the next day.

All of these forces from the universe, from our angels, are working together to help me tend my fire. My message to all of you is to watch for the signs, heed the messages, tune in to your intuition, and figure out what tends your fire. One day it might be the calm, predictability of a lake, another day the raging emotions of the ocean, and another, a crazy mix of both. Do what you need to keep your fire warm, steady, and welcoming. It's important.

Holy shit! I've been pounding the keys on my laptop almost as aggressively as the night Steven interrupted my letter to Everett. Where did that all come from? I'd better reread this, because whatever just flowed out of me was anything but conscious -over eight hundred words, and I didn't anticipate even one of them! No, I'm not going to reread it. I'm hitting *send* right now, and what will be, will be.

Water. All of this writing about water. I need water to drink, right now, to come out of this writing spell and return to my to-do list. I have to push myself slowly up off the counter stool as slowly as I pushed myself up off the sand earlier. The act of finding a cup, getting ice, and filling the cup help me shake off the hypnotic state that predominated for the last twenty or thirty minutes. At least, that's how much time I think it was. Who knows?

So, getting back to the inbox, my original mission was to look for anything from Terry. Huh—actually it just came in about five minutes ago, while I was still composing the extensive essay meant to be a blog.

I skim her email once and don't know whether to sob or cheer. One more example of mixed-up, roiled-up emotions. I scroll back up to the top, noting that my finger is trembling on the mouse. Just as I finish reading it more carefully, Eric bursts through the door with his newly rediscovered exuberance, "Mom, Madre, it's so cool here. You gotta come for a ride with me! This island and all around it is mad cool."

Although I'm still contemplating the email from Terry, I definitely recognize that "mad cool" is quite the high compliment from Eric, right up there with "mint" and more heartfelt than "awesome." All of his encounters and observations of the last few hours tumble out of him, it seems, without him taking a breath. Definitely mad cool!

He finally notices I've said nothing and asks, "Well, what do you think? Go for a ride? How was the beach? Wait--you're pretty quiet. What's going on?"

I tell him a little about the beach, about the cardinals (also mad cool), and then tell him I just got an email from Terry and wonder if he wants to hear it.

"Yeah, of course, I want to hear it. Read it to me, or give me the highlights!"

"I'll give you the highlights, then let you read it yourself. Basically, there's two bits of news. First, a little tough to take, but she says that Everett let her know that he read my letter, but doesn't feel ready. He didn't shut the idea down, but he needs more time—said the same thing he told her before, that he's taking care of an ill relative. He doesn't say who the relative is. I'm pretty bummed by all that, but I get it, and I respect that he wants to focus on whoever is ill.

"But here's what's really interesting. You know how I found the lawyer's invoices, and Terry said she'd follow up on the practices with similar names as on the letterhead? When Terry made the calls, one of the offices had recently received a letter trying to reach anyone that had knowledge of an adoption from 1982. Office staff have been trying to find the old records from their storage area. Of course, everything was in paper files, so it was a slow process. Anyway, it seems the letter is from a woman who says she adopted a boy in 1982. She had information about the lawyer's office from back then and now she wants to make contact with his biological family, specifically, his mother if possible. Terry didn't say anything about what comes next, or how things might proceed, but maybe this is encouraging? It's something. I have no idea if the lawyer's office can even release such information, presuming they are able to locate what she's looking for. Terry just says she'll keep me posted."

"That's kind of leaving you hanging, don't you think? Are you gonna answer her? Ask her what's legal and what isn't?"

"I will—I literally just opened this before you walked in. By the way, that reminds me: have you checked your own email lately? Like, to see if you've gotten anything back on the DNA tests? You keep checking up on me and what I've done, but how about you?"

I get up to refill my water, not really expecting him to reply.

"Oh, yeah. Actually, I forgot to tell you that I did get something last night from one of the three places. It was confusing as all get out. It starts going into all the percentages of DNA and how much is shared if the two people being compared have both parents the same, or how it's different if only one of the parents is the same. When it's only one, like same mother with different fathers, for example, then the amount of shared DNA is similar to nieces or nephews, sometimes even first cousins. It goes on to say that there is an average of percent shared DNA, but also ranges. By the time I tried to figure that all out, I was falling asleep and didn't get any further."

"Well, why do you think they sent that? Was it saying they found relations of yours that could be cousins, or even half-siblings?" I'm startled that he didn't think this important enough to share. Of course, we kind of went our separate ways this morning, and both got distracted by our enticing environment.

"Geez, I don't know, Mom. Let's open it and see if you can help me figure it out, OK? You're better at science stuff than I am. Of course, almost anybody is better at it than me, right?" He says this jokingly, but it's always been a sticking point for Eric. He never felt as strong academically as Emma, or almost anyone, for that matter. So little confidence in himself for so long.

As he opens his inbox, I see a logo that looks familiar, and I remember seeing something similar in my own email. I thought it was junk and skipped right over it. I'll look at his first and then go back to mine. So much for giving him a hard time for not paying attention to the whole email!

I start reading the email out loud for both of us. He's right; it is a lot of information to process. I guess the website has to be educational to try to help users figure out some of this on their own. Otherwise, they'd have more questions than they could ever handle. I scroll to the frequently asked questions and find the chart with percent of shared DNA for the various relationships. If I had a printer here, I'd print it out for reference, but I scribble them down on a notepad instead. Then I click on a tab labeled "Your results."

"Hey, I didn't see that one before. What does it say, Mom?"

Trying to process the information as I read it out loud, I recite, "Uh, oh boy, Eric, it says there are two relatives for you in their database. According to their algorithm, the most likely relationship to you is a half-brother and a half-sister, or possibly, because the percentages are at the lower end of the matching range, cousins—what the . . .?" I trail off as my mind goes into a tailspin. *Two* possible matches?

Before I can find any words to even begin to make sense of this, Eric exclaims, "Is this for real? Wait, cousins? Did Uncle Jeff have kids, Mom? I don't ever remember that, but I wasn't that old when he died. So, I've got two cousins or half-siblings? I thought I was looking for one guy in his 30s, but there's also a female? Did you have another kid with some other guy, Mom? Sorry, that sounded bad, but what the heck do we do now?"

As he's expressing the exact same confusion that I'm feeling, I see there are more instructions for what to do next with this information. The next steps are to fill in any additional information that you may have to clarify relationships, or if you want to, you can click on the icon for the relation they have

Wonders in the Waves 133

found. This reveals if the relation wants to be contacted, and a contact form.

"Mom, shall I do this contact thing?"

I remember my email and tell him to stop for a minute, that I might have a similar email we should check. Opening it, I also have two relations identified. Both sons. Ok, so obviously, one is Eric, since we already know he's in this database, but there's another. Someone's out there, for sure, related to me. His DNA is a 53% match with mine. This is real now. The lead through Terry and the one at the lawyer have been intriguing speculation. We don't know if that guy is really Everett, or if I've just been wishing it to be true. But, this. This is real.

I turn to Eric and open my arms for a hug. I'm crying and laughing at the same time. "He's really out there somewhere, Eric. My other boy, well, he's a man. My other son is out there and is in this database somewhere. Do we both do the contact thing? Is that too much? The instructions suggest making the first contact factual and brief. It says people do searches for different reasons, and until you actually connect, you have no clue what reason could be motivating them. It could be as straight forward as curiosity, or it could be some type of medical problem that's spurring someone on to investigate their relatives."

"Right, I get that. Maybe just one of us should do the contact button. But what about this girl, this female? What do you think, Mom?" The look on his face can only be described as dumbfounded. Just exactly how I feel—dumbfounded.

In the excitement of receiving my own email connection, the other relation in Eric's had already slipped my mind. Granted, I never knew every detail of my brother Jeff's life, but we were pretty close. I think if there was a child of his out there, he'd have let me know. That is, if he was aware of the child. I guess that's the other possibility. I knew someone at work whose husband had a child he'd never known about contact him because of one of these DNA searches. Could Jeff have been in a relationship that resulted in a pregnancy that the woman never shared with him? After all, I was not exactly forthcoming with my own early relationships. It's not that far-fetched. But then again, thinking about all of that, there is another answer for this newly discovered relationship. Steven. Actually, it must be the answer. There's no mention of a niece relationship in my email, which there would be if the female in Eric's is a cousin.

Eric interrupts my churning brain with another question. "Wait, Mom. One answer is Uncle Jeff, but um, well, weird question, awkward, but what about, um, Dad?"

Good question, what about Steven? Does he have a child out there? Does he know, or is this another secret?

17

*Relinquish your attachment to the known,
step into the unknown, and you will
step into the field of all possibilities.*
Deepak Chopra

After many more speculative questions, a few ideas of how to communicate with these newly discovered relations, and a lot of pacing around the room, we decide that we'd better contact Steven. Awkward or not, he is part of this family now, he has wanted to be involved and help in any way he can, and now, this may be more his problem than any of us anticipated. Somehow, I think if he knows he has another child, he would have said something by now. We've had enough heart-to-heart talks, and he was involved in one specific DNA test earlier to verify he and Eric as father and son. That's precedent for a conversation about another child, isn't it? I may be uncomfortable with the idea, but the dialogue needs to happen. Before calling him, we also decide that Eric will contact the young man. Maybe the brother connection is less intimidating than mother. I'd written to the guy we knew about already, so if this is the same person, maybe a different approach would be more successful. If it's not him, then the sooner we find out, the sooner we can leave the guy alone to pursue his ancestry another way, live his life. I still don't believe that's the case, but this is turning out to be such a tangled web—we need to be open to all the potential *maybes*.

"So, uh, who's going to call Dad? Do we do rock-paper-scissors for this one or what?"

I smile at the old game to try to escape doing something he doesn't want to do. I don't blame him one bit; it's not an easy topic to broach with anyone, especially someone you've only known to be your father for a handful of months. Conversely, I don't exactly relish the idea of talking to my ex-husband, father of my child, about some other child, conceived who-knows-when? Before, during, after our relationship? I sure didn't see this coming when we started down the road to find my son.

Assuming my typical role to make life as easy as possible for Eric, I offer to initiate the call. After all, I'm the mature adult here and have had to do a lot of tougher things than this; let me make the list!

Starting to enter Steven's number, Eric reaches to stop me. "No, Mom, it came up on my DNA report. I'm the one that's related to this girl, I've got the most at stake, well, maybe other than him, but you know what I mean. I want to contact her as soon as I possibly can. It's just a courtesy to see what, if anything, he knows. Regardless of what he says, I'm making the contact. So, I need to be the one to call him."

"OK, then, you sound sure of yourself, like your mind is made up. Do you want me here, or do you want to do this in private?"

Eric pauses for a moment, looking like he wants the moral support for the phone call. Then, with a look of confident resolve, he suggests, "Why don't you go for a walk, Mom? No offense, but I think it just needs to be Dad and me."

"Your wish is my command, then." I grab a flavored seltzer water and head out the door to explore in another direction—maybe walk toward the bridge a couple of miles down the road for a new view of the island.

What a day it's been so far! Started on the beach in an almost meditative state, then accelerated to a somewhat startling discovery, nothing like I'd anticipated last night when planning the day. What's that saying about plans? *Man makes plans and God laughs*—isn't that the truth?

Not far down the road, I spot interesting places we ought to visit. The Florida Oceanographic Coastal Center is situated along the lagoon. Its signs promoting educational programs to preserve the regional ecosystem encourage me to come visit soon. And right across the street, the Elliott Museum, featuring local history, beckons me as well. Put these on my "must-do" list for later this week.

It seems like no time at all before I reach the bridge. The idea of being up over the lagoon beckons me. Without a moment's hesitation, I'm striding up the bridge walkway. At the peak, there are benches strategically placed to take advantage of the panorama that overlooks both sides of the lagoon. Boats, even yachts, are streaming along the channel. Who knows how many people are out enjoying this glorious day? Close to shore, paddleboarders and kayakers are ducking into little coves, sometimes almost totally obscured by the mangrove clusters. That's on my list for tomorrow, for sure. Watching the paddlers more closely, they morph into an image of Emma paddling, in a bright-purple bikini, with Valentino behind her on her board. Not on this lagoon, of course, but on Seneca Lake, back in New York, on vacation a few years ago. I'd totally forgotten that she paddleboarded while we were there—now it seems like only moments ago that I heard her reflect wistfully on the experience, "I've never felt as peaceful as right now, Mom. Just floating on this lake, with Valentino, it seems like all the hard stuff, the hassles of life, fade away. Ever since we got here, it feels like the universe is aligned, and that I'm the healthiest girl alive." I was both stunned and comforted at her words then, as I am again now as they waft across time and the water. How can a moment long forgotten return and be so real, so poignant?

I'm reluctant to break the spell, yet awareness of the surroundings creeps back. Checking the time on my phone, the walk has taken me farther than anticipated. I contemplate continuing to the other side of the bridge, but both my tired legs from this second walk of the day, and my curiosity about how the phone call is going, convince me to turn around and go back to the house.

As I walk back, I pass many walkers, a few runners, even a skateboarder or two. Almost everyone smiles, a few wave, then one person catches my eye. First, it's her body and her stride, so much like Emma that I nearly stumble. Probably in her twenties, she's keeping up a fast walk, in spite of the heat. When Emma was feeling healthy, she loved to kind of walk/jog to test herself, to see if she could run in spite of her asthma. Second, it's her bright-yellow tee shirt, emblazoned with a large heart that says "I LOVE FLX." FLX—the catchy abbreviation for the Finger Lakes region of upstate New York. The beautiful place that had just come to mind when remembering Emma a few moments ago and the place I retreated to after she died. Is Emma haunting me? *Haunt* is absolutely the wrong word. It's that her presence is all around me. As the medium told Eric, she will be with us, we need to watch and be open to her presence. And is she sending the message we need to hear right now? The one she repeated to Eric: the message that it's worth it to keep going, even when it's tough? It must be.

As the young woman gets closer, I comment on her shirt. Without breaking stride, she answers, "Yup, it's a great place. I have family there." She keeps walking, clearly does not want to stop and chitchat in the middle of her walk. Crazy, though. All this way from New York, I see someone with a connection to Emma, to my former home. It truly is a small world, a small universe that keeps us all connected. In one day, such a multitude of signs suggesting we're meant to be here. I'm not really sure why that's so, or when I'll figure it out, but this is our place for right now.

Back at the house, I tiptoe in so as not to interrupt if Eric and Steven are still talking. I don't see him anywhere in the house, so look out back. Sure enough, Eric's walking the length of the dock, phone in hand, staring out at the water for a moment as he reaches the end, then turning and walking back. The pace of someone deeply absorbed in conversation. With no clue if they've been talking the whole time I was gone, or if Eric needed to leave a message for Steven to call back, I decide to go take a shower. The day is nearly done, and I've not had a chance to get cleaned up.

Someone put serious thought into the layout of this main suite. Almost everywhere I stand, including the entry to the shower, I catch glimpses of the water. This perspective on the world is really growing on me.

Once dressed, I glance out at the water. I see that Eric's no longer on the phone, but he's sitting on the end of the dock, legs dangling off the side, propped with his hands behind him, looking upward. The mother in me wants to run right out to hear about the call and be sure he's OK. But some force holds me back, tells me he needs time. That force, or intuition, wins, and I stay in my room to unpack and get things arranged. We're staying a while, and the room invites me to settle in. Getting to the bottom of my suitcase, the old postcards tumble out. I'd almost forgotten about them! I need to get better oriented to where these towns are situated. The owner had left a local map, maybe these towns and tourist sights will suggest places to look for the old friends of my parents.

I stack the postcards in order of the dates. They start in 1980, shortly after my parents first came down here, when I was a teenager. Too old for a babysitter, too young to stay alone. Jeff and I had to stay with my grandparents because the trip was during the school year; probably Dad heard that was the best time of year for fishing. There are half a dozen cards, and then they stop in the mid-'80s. Interesting that they kept in touch with Mom and Dad for a while, and then stopped. Of course, I guess it doesn't mean they stopped keeping in touch, just this stack of postcards only goes that far.

The one from 1980 is postmarked Port Salerno. The photo is of calm water, every size and configuration of boat imaginable, and the description in italics at the top corner says "Home to World-Class Fishing Tournaments." One more testimony to why Dad picked this area.

The handwritten note is short and not too informative, "It was nice to meet you both—glad we got some time to talk. Do you guys plan to come back soon? Truly, Harriett and Harold." I notice a rubber stamp under the signature. I'd not seen it before, presumably the name of Harold's business: *Harold's Bait and Tackle*, where everything is fishy! OK, well, that slogan is pretty funny. Let's see if the place is still in business. Looking online, they do have a listing, but under the hours, the notation is *Temporarily Closed*. Interesting; maybe Eric and I need to drive over there and see if it looks like it's been closed a long time, or if there is some other notice on the shop itself. It would be fun to meet these people, if they're still alive or still in the area. I have no idea if they were my parents age, older, or younger.

The next one is dated almost three years later. It has an interesting structure on the front with a sunrise emerging over the rough ocean—just like it looked this morning. This time, the top corner reads, "House of Refuge, Stuart, Florida," and Harriett's writing shares a little news, "Everything is pretty well settled here. We took Junior over to this pretty place on Hutchinson Island last week. He loved playing in the sand. You're welcome to come back down anytime." It's signed the same way, including the catchy phrase about fish. Huh. Since it's on the island in Stuart, this place must be right close to where we are staying. If I keep going with these postcards, ol' Harriett will provide our whole itinerary.

In the midst of musing about the irony of these old friends of my parents and their impact on Eric and me, his voice calls up the stairs, "Mom, are you back?"

I call down, "Come on up if you want. I just finished unpacking and am shuffling through these postcards. They're giving me ideas of places we can go."

Eric doesn't reply, but I hear his feet slowly climbing up the stairs. He comes in the bedroom and throws himself down on the bed. "Well, that was something else, not like any other call I've ever had, that's for sure!"

After narrating almost every word that was said between them, Eric tries to summarize, "So, basically, after getting through the shock of the DNA website and re-capping all the emails, Dad said it's possible. He wasn't about to deny that he could have had a relationship that resulted in a pregnancy. No surprise. I mean, it's not like he was a monk or anything his whole life, right? It depends on what other stuff we find out, like how old she is, where she was born, if she'll share information about her mother or anything else that would help put the pieces together."

"So, you guys agreed that you should contact her through the website? See what you can find out? Or, is he going to do the DNA sampling for the same site before you make any other contact to see if something comes up for him?"

"Yeah, yeah, I'm going to send her something. He's going to do the sample, but we already know that will take a few weeks. Plus, he's preoccupied. It was a hard call for another reason. He hadn't had a chance to call to tell you yet, but he needs to go back to New York sooner than he'd planned. I guess Jimmy—uh, Uncle Jimmy, is sick again. Dad is sad and scared because they're saying there's a chance he might need a kidney transplant. He's being evaluated in a couple of days. And as if that doesn't suck enough, listen to this. I guess, I actually don't know anything about this, or get it at all, but because he has a disability, Down syndrome, Dad says sometimes that counts against people as far as getting a transplant, like they aren't a priority or something. What's up with that? Did you know that?"

"I didn't know that precisely, Eric, but I'm not really surprised. It's been a while since I was directly working with people with intellectual disabilities, but there's a long history of the medical community being, let's say, less aggressive with treating them because of bias about their quality of life. Basically, not to sound crass, it's all about if they think it's worth it to treat someone. Or, as shitty as this is, whether one person's life is more worth saving, more worth expending resources, than another person's. Maybe since Steven is someone who's directly involved in the field of disability services, maybe Jimmy's case will be strongly considered."

"I don't know. Dad sounded discouraged as well as sad. I guess he has a meeting with the team of people who make decisions about Jimmy's care. He's also hoping that if Jimmy really does need it, maybe someone who's related could be a donor. Says he'd do it himself in a minute if they let him, if he's compatible, or whatever. That kinda scares me, too, Mom. I just found my Dad. It's scary to think of him having a big surgery. Or wait a minute, maybe me? I'm a blood relative, too. And I'm younger, maybe that's better. Or what about this girl? Well, not gonna hit her with that right off the bat, but, man, this is crazy!"

"Eric, slow down, honey. You're getting way ahead of yourself. You can't jump in and solve this problem. It sounds like they need a lot more information before they even determine if a transplant is what Jimmy needs. And I'm sure Dad doesn't want you to communicate any of this to the young woman before we even know if her information lines up as an actual match. We need to tread slowly and softly when the matters are this sensitive. No sense in rushing these relationships. If they've been there this long, a few more days, even weeks is not going to change anything."

"I know your *go slow* thing, Mom. We still don't know anything about my brother—all this *go slowly* stuff stresses me out. Don't you just want to know?" His fist punches the pillow with each word of the last sentence, and then he flops back down, this time face first into the pillow.

How to answer? Of course, I want to know. I want to know so many things. I want to know why I had a pregnancy loss when married to Steven. I want to know where my son, Everett, is. I want to know what his life has been like and if he will ever forgive me for not raising him. I want to know why Emma couldn't have lived a long, happy, healthy life. I want to know if Emma really can see us, love us, and accompany us on this journey from afar. And as of today, I want to know if Eric has another sister, half-sister, somewhere out there. It seems like every day of my life there is more that I want to know, but in reality, I *know* less and less.

Maybe knowing is not the point. Maybe wondering and pondering possibility is what truly opens our minds as humans. Is the lesson here that very little in life is a certainty? When we think we know how, why, and when things will be, maybe we become too self-assured, too complacent, and take the wonder of life for granted? It's hard not knowing, yet an all-knowing, complacent, half-hearted existence might be worse, might be one that disregards the need to be humble, sensitive, and aware.

I try to abbreviate all that into, "Yes, Eric, I do want to know. I'm just not sure we're supposed to know. All I know is that I don't know. I don't have the answers." Feeling as worn out as he looks, I flop down on the bed next to him. Turning oneself over to the unknown is exhausting.

18

> *Memory is the treasury and guardian of all things.*
> CICERO

Not only exhausting. Turning oneself over to the unknown must also be a release, an unloading. Fatigue and unburdening had overtaken both of us. At some point, Eric made his way to his own room, and I must have crawled under the covers, totally unaware of time and place.

The next morning, Eric starts by writing an email to the young woman on the DNA website. Over coffee, we decide to spend the day together. With postcards, the local map to augment our GPS, fishing poles, and a cooler full of drinks and snacks, we head out to explore the island and its surrounding area.

The House of Refuge pictured on the postcard is only a couple of miles from our rental property. It has a charming reception area with local books and memorabilia, staffed by volunteers. Today, the elderly gentleman who welcomes us is a fount of knowledge about the House of Refuge as well as the whole area.

Each time we ask a question, he answers and then embellishes with another story. Basically, the house has been here for almost one hundred and fifty years. It was one of ten along the coast of Florida, the only one still standing. The houses, they kind of look like small inns next to lighthouses, were places that people who were shipwrecked could literally come for refuge until they were able to return to their own homes.

There was a keeper and his family on duty at all times to watch for anyone who became stranded by storms. The substantial number of ships, filled with treasure, that went down in this area earned the region's nickname as the Treasure Coast. The little museum features items typical of a household in the late 1800s, as well as photos of ships and the keepers' families. There is still at least one shipwreck only a hundred yards off shore.

After this mini history lesson, we set off for Port Salerno. We drive along twisty roads with small bridges over canals to the lagoon, and then through a whole group of huge banyan trees with branches that form a tunnel over the road. Around another turn and we see why it's called a port. There are docks and marinas all around us, and lots of seafood restaurants nestled waterside. We decide to stop at one to get lunch, then poke around to see if we can find out anything about Harold's Bait and Tackle. Eric almost laughed himself to the ground when he read the silly slogan on the postcard this morning. "Really? Where everything is fishy? Pretty *catchy*, huh?"

As we finish up a lunch of delicious fresh-caught fish, the server sees us looking at the little local map and asks helpfully, "Are you looking for something? I'm from around here; maybe I can help you find what you're looking for."

Eric replies quickly, "Yeah, well, maybe. We don't even know if this place is still here; my grandparents visited a long time ago.

They used a fishing guide who ran a shop called "Harold's Bait and Tackle." It seems like they made friends with the guy and his wife, because they sent them postcards after their visits."

"Hell, yeah. Everybody around here knew Harold. He and my grandpa were good friends. We were all sad when he passed, I think maybe a year ago. His kids run the shop now, but I heard they weren't sure if they were gonna keep on doing it. It's not exactly an easy living. It's just down the road a little bit from here—you can't miss it."

"The website said 'temporarily closed' when we looked it up yesterday. Do you know anything about that?" I ask.

"Uh, no, not really. I think they kinda make up the hours as they go. I'm not too sure, cuz I'm not a big fisherman. Did you try calling them?"

"Yeah, but the recording is almost like it's in code for people who know more about fishing than we do. Something like, 'No more live shrimp or pilchards today, try tomorrow before 10' was all it said."

The server picked up our payment, shook his head and gave a quick laugh as he walked away. Guess it didn't mean much to him either.

Driving over to the address we found online, the streets are lined with small, ranch-style homes—more of the old Florida bungalows. They do look like they've been here a long time, but the little yards are well maintained, most with outdoor chairs scattered among lawn ornaments. How funny that all the way down here, outdoor chairs that are plastic versions of the classic Adirondack style I grew up with in New York, are so popular.

Harold's Bait and Tackle is on a side street, with the water just a few steps across the narrow road. There's a short, well-worn dock that also has a faded "Harold's" sign on it, with two boats tied up. Eric points out, "On the map, the water here is called Manatee Pocket. So many different ways of referring to bodies of water; not sure I'll ever be able to keep it straight in my head; guess I'll never sound like a local."

A young woman in faded jeans and a pastel tank top strolls up next to us as we are looking at the dock and says, "Well, being local is over-rated. Don't you worry 'bout how you sound. What can I help you with, Mr. Not-So-Local?" Startled at first, I need to stifle my laugh because her shirt logo reads "Harold's—Where Everything is Fishy." I'm not sure Eric notices the slogan because she keeps right on talking. "Listen, we're closed right now. What can I help you with? Make it quick, though, cuz I gotta get back inside. My mama's been asking for an hour about this snack she wanted me to pick up. Can't keep her waiting much longer."

"Well, uh, I'm interested in learning more about the best bait to use for . . ."

Before he can finish she says, "Look, I'd love to give you a fishing lesson—I mean it. But there's a lot to it. All depends on if you're dock fishing, or out in the flats, or going through the channel. How long you here? Maybe come back next week, when my brother's back. He had to go out of town, so I'm the only one around left trying to take care of my mom and getting the bait fish in here early morning so all the guys, the regulars, get what they need and my suppliers get paid. He knows this stuff better than me, and loves to talk fish, so he's your guy."

Although I know Eric's interested in the fishing details, I don't want to lose a chance at the main reason we came over here, or at least why I came. "Uh, Miss, can I just ask you one question, not about fishing? Maybe go ahead and deliver the snack, I can wait."

"Name's Kristy, and yeah, sure, give me a minute. I'll be right back out. You got me curious why you'd ask me anything that's not about fish. Doesn't happen too often." She smiles as she walks away with the takeout container.

In a couple of minutes, she's back out and gestures to the Adirondack chairs in the front lawn of the house next to the bait shop. "I've only got a few minutes. When she's done eating, she needs help to get up out of her recliner. So, what can I tell you?"

I'm getting a kick out of her direct, to the point manner. Although the words are almost abrupt, her easy smile and direct eye contact make it clear she's more than willing to chat, even if her time is limited. "I have a question that might seem out of the blue, but since you're on a tight time frame, I'm going to get right to it. I have these postcards from when my mom and dad visited here many years ago. They're signed by Harriett and refer to Harold and Junior. Are you related? The server in the restaurant said Harold had passed, but are you or your mother related to him?"

The lips of her effervescent smile quickly become a straight line, and then purse. It's clear she is affected by my question. She reaches for the postcards, reads each one, and shakes her head before beginning to quietly cry. "Um, wow, well you sure surprised me with that one. Didn't see it coming at all. Thought you guys were just some curious sightseers, traveling during the off season. Yeah, well, Harold is, was, uh, my dad. He died, uh passed on, about a year, no actually who am I kidding, one year, two months, and two weeks ago. My mama ain't been the same since. It's been tough. My brother and I are trying to take care of her, see to the shop, and he's still got other stuff going on. So, yeah, short answer to your question, I'm related all right."

I'm stymied at what to say next. I want to offer sympathy, I want to find out more, I want to be considerate and let her get back inside to her mother. Starting at what's most important, I offer, "Oh, Kristy, it's so hard to lose someone you care about.

I can tell by your reaction that you must miss your father a great deal. I'm sorry if my question startled you."

"Wow, thank you."

"Why are you thanking me?"

"For not saying something fake like 'my condolences.' I hate those damn words."

"Well, me too, Kristy. I've lost some people I care about, too, and I try to think carefully before I speak, about what I've been told that is helpful and hurtful."

"I do miss him an awful lot. And I'm not complaining at all, I love this place, I love my mother, and the business, while tough, is what we've done as a family my whole life. It's just a lot to juggle. My brother is trying to help whenever he can, but, well, he's just got a lot going on and can't be here as much as I'd like, or he'd like. I'd better get back inside, but yes, those cards are from my parents to yours. Tell you what, maybe I can get my mother's friend to come sit with her sometime soon and we could meet out for a drink? Compare notes or something? You'd actually be doing me a favor—a reason to get a little break. How long you here?"

"That would be great. We're not totally sure how long we're staying, but at least a couple of weeks. Can I give you my contact info and you can get me a message if you can work it out with the friend?"

"Sure, and here's mine. What's your name?"

"I'm Larissa, and this is my son, Eric."

She looks up at me quickly when I give her our names, but then looks down and types them in her phone.

"I have one other question, Kristy. Not to stick my nose in, but is your mother, I mean, might she recognize these postcards or my parents' names if you were to ask her for me?"

"I don't know, ma'am. It depends. Day to day she is different. One day she is alert and almost peppy. The next, she will sit in that dang chair all day long and act confused about the living room she's sat in the last thirty years. I can try, but, well, no guarantees."

"Well, whatever you think. But I'd love to get together. Please keep in touch."

Kristy gives us a swift wave and saunters into the house.

Eric breaks the silence with, "Want to walk around a bit or head back to the island?"

"I saw a park on our way here. Want to go sit in the park for a few minutes and watch the boats go by?"

The park is less than a mile away. When we passed it earlier, there were kids on every piece of playground equipment with watchful parents huddled around them; now it's almost empty. I grab a blanket from the back of the car and some of the drinks we toted along, and head toward the water. Eric is a few steps behind, looking at his phone.

When he reaches the spot I've selected he says, "Well, that was interesting, huh? I mean, she was interesting. Did she like talking to us or were we a pain in her butt?"

I shake my head and respond, "I'm not too sure. She seems to have her hands full, and even though she wanted to talk, I think we certainly surprised her with the postcards."

"But she did suggest meeting up, so maybe it was the sudden mention of her father that took her off guard, shook her up. We know what that's like."

"Well, let's hope she follows up and gives us a call. I'd really like to know if her mother remembers my parents, but in the long run, it's not a big deal. Just another opportunity to wander down memory lane. More for me, than her. Seems like a nice person, though."

After we sit a few more minutes, my phone rings. I anxiously pick it up and say, "Hello, Terry, what's up? Any more news?"

"Not really, Larissa. The lawyer's receptionist says they haven't found the records yet and won't tell me what they plan to do if and when they find them. How about with you?"

"Actually, I did get a notice from the DNA registry that there's a match, likely a son, with my DNA. And Eric got similar news. Since there was no response when I wrote the letter to the guy you found, we thought it better for Eric to contact the person through the registry email. If it's the same person, maybe he'd rather hear from a sibling. Who knows? Listen, can you do anything else with the lawyer's office, or can I contact them?"

"Larissa, I don't think there's much else I can do with the lawyer's office. I don't want to let you down, but I also have limited time and don't want to keep bugging them. We have to be considerate when doing this work and not step on toes. A lot of this search stuff depends on careful relationship building. As far as you contacting them, I can't stop you. Let me know if you hear anything else, and I'll do the same."

I feel like she's kinda getting sick of me, but I can't help it, I need to figure this out.

"Let's head back to the beach house, Eric. I want to make a couple of calls before it's the end of business hours, and then maybe make contact with Renee and Isabel later, what do you think?"

"OK by me. I got a couple of calls to make, too."

"I was wondering, have you talked to Hilary since you've been here?" They had seemed to be getting close before we left. He'd even casually mentioned inviting her down here. I can't help but ask.

"Uh, yeah, actually, just yesterday, and I told her I'd call her again tonight. She's good to talk to, Mom."

"I'm glad for that, Eric. We all need people willing to listen."

His head nod says it all.

19

Normal day, let me be aware of the treasure you are.
Let me learn from you, love you,
savor your ideas before you depart.
Let me not pass you by in quest
of some rare and perfect tomorrow.
　　　　　　Mary Jean Irion

*B*ack at our beach house, I'm ready to call the people who'll listen to me. More than listen. They listen and they care and they respond. While Isabel listens to every detail of the correspondence we'd had with the DNA site and our interesting visit with Kristy at Harold's shop, she is mostly interested in how much Eric and I seem to be connecting to the location. More than once, she says, "Larissa, you sound almost content for the first time that I can remember in a long time. The coastal life agrees with you."

When I suggest that she's welcome to come visit, she's appreciative but realistic. "I have the kids the next couple of weekends because their father is traveling, and oh, there's this little guy, Valentino, who needs watching, remember?" I feel a pang of guilt that she is once again caring for the dog, but before I say anything about the guilt, she adds, "He's so sweet. I can't lie—Bobby is not one bit sorry that you and Eric left town for a while. That dog hardly leaves his side." OK, so not so much guilt, after all.

Renee focuses on everything Isabel did not. She goes a bit, well, *batshit crazy* over the possibility of Steven having a daughter. I find myself using Eric's phrase about we didn't exactly expect that Steven "was a monk," did we? She barely listens to my retelling of finding the bait shop and meeting with Kristy, and quickly leaps on the letter showing up at the lawyer's office from an adoptive mother whose information dates back to 1982. "That cannot be, it is absolutely not a coincidence, Larissa. How many adoptions do you think the guy did in that year?"

"Honestly, Renee, I have no idea. Maybe a lot? Maybe that was his specialty."

"Nope, I don't think so. Listen, why don't you just call that office yourself. Didn't you say the name on the guy's birth certificate is Laura Miller? Call as her and tell them you found an invoice from them in your mother's stuff. That's true, right? That you found it and you want to know if the child your mother made you surrender, or anyone connected with him, has been in touch. Tell them the search angel stuff and the DNA sites have turned up some interesting possibilities, but you think that finding this invoice might be more important."

"Wow, Renee, don't you think they'd think it a little too coincidental that they get multiple inquiries about an adoption in 1982 in the same week, thirty something years later?"

"Who gives a flying fling if they think it's a coincidence or not? Haven't we all learned there are way too many things we write off as coincidence that are really important, really worth paying attention to? And speaking of coincidence or signs, the message Eric got from Emma about keeping at it even when things are tough? If that's not your little hippie-dippy angel telling you to get your butt in gear on this Everett thing, I don't know what is."

That's my buddy, Renee. Telling me like it is. Or like she thinks it is. She may be a bit much for some people; for me, right now, she gives me the energy boost I need to make the call. She's right about one thing. What do I care if they think it's a weird coincidence? It's everyday business to them. To me, and to Eric, and maybe to my other son, it is our lives, it is our connections. I have nothing to lose, and so much to gain.

The phone number is in one of my email exchanges with Terry. Before I lose that enthusiasm, I dial it up and immediately hear, "Watkins, Smith, and Barbour, Ms. Mitchell speaking. How can I help you?"

Taking a deep breath that brings courage into my lungs, I introduce myself. "Ms. Mitchell, this is Laura Miller." It's easier than I expect to lie, well, to give a name I don't use. Maybe my aunt used it in her correspondence to reference me. I'm hoping so.

Continuing, "I have documentation that suggests this practice provided adoption services for my baby in 1982. I was a teenager, and my aunt lived in a small town nearby. She well, she arranged everything, and I knew nothing. Guess that's how they did it back then. Anyway, I'd like to find out anything that I can from you about this adoption. I've been searching for my son, using a search angel service, and we even have a DNA match to my son and I. The search angel did locate someone but, well, all of the information doesn't necessarily add up yet. I'm hoping you have some details in your records." Time to stop; sometimes more information is not necessarily better, at least when just getting started.

"Hmm, well, Ms. Miller, 1982 is quite some time ago. May I put you on a brief hold and do some checking?"

Not knowing how long "brief" is going to be, I use the sweetest voice I can muster and respond, "Yes, of course, please take whatever time you need."

Ironically, the background music is instrumental versions of rock songs from the same time period we are digging into, the 1980s. How funny. I wonder what the original artists think of these renditions? At least with these tunes playing, I know she hasn't cut me off.

A couple of songs later, so it must have been at least six or seven minutes, she returns. "OK, well, a couple of things to go over, Ms. Miller. First, those records, all hard copy, are usually kept in an attic storage area. We rarely refer to them anymore, but must keep them legally. We also don't get too many requests to go back that far, but weirdly, had another one from that time period recently. The files are in our conference room waiting for one of the administrative assistants to get the time to sort through them. Secondly, I will need to check with Mr. Barbour, if we find the documents, to determine who may gain access to anything we may have in our files. There are many different laws about access to adoption records and they've changed over the years. Can I have your number and get back to you?"

After giving her my contact info and repeating the details of my request, I ask, "Ms. Mitchell, I know this must be a challenge for your office to go back through old records, there's probably not much in it for you. But for me, and for my son who lives with me, this is really important. We recently lost my daughter. Finding the son that I had when I was so very young feels more urgent than I can even describe. And maybe, he needs us as much as we need him. A young man who might be this grown child of mine, responded to the search angel. A few years back, he really wanted to find his biological family, but now because someone important in his current life is ill, he feels it isn't the right time.

But maybe it is; maybe we could support him in whatever he's going through. Please just do whatever you can. When do you think I might hear back from you?" It came out as more of a plea than a question.

Relieved when she speaks, thinking at least I hadn't scared her off, "We are going to try to have our part-time assistant do it when she comes in tomorrow, but I can't promise that. I can promise that we will look, and that I'll get back to you. I just don't know when. And I did hear how much this means to you. I'm going to try."

That's all I can really ask, right?

Going into the kitchen to rustle up some dinner, I notice Eric out on the dock, on the phone. It's like the water is a magnet for him, out there every chance he gets. After I pop dinner in the oven, I pour a glass of wine to go sit on the porch myself. I'm happy the dock is a long one, so I can enjoy this spot and Eric cannot possibly think I'm listening to his conversation. Enjoying the sounds of birds overhead, I'm startled at a loud rapping; it must be someone at our front door. Annoyed, I shuffle my feet into flipflops and go to see who is interrupting the spell, what stranger comes knocking at the dinner hour?

A guy is standing on the landing with a cooler slung over his shoulder. He's dressed in the uniform of the region: shorts, tee shirt, flipflops, and the requisite cap, complete with a fishing tackle logo. I cannot discern his age, maybe thirtyish.

"Ma'am, sorry to bother you, really sorry. I live three houses up, I'm a neighbor, not some weirdo or nothin'."

I'm thinking to myself that even weirdos have neighbors, but keep my thoughts silent as he continues, "I saw you unloading, and uh, is the guy your son? Not bein' nosey, just assuming. Meant to come over sooner, but I've been really busy. Anyway,

I do a lot of fishing and today, well, I caught way more than I can eat. Just wondering if you guys would like some local, super-fresh fish for your dinner? Or, you could freeze it, but it's way better fresh."

Not quite sure what to say, I hear Eric walking up behind me say, "Hey, what's up, man? What's going on?"

"Oh, hey, I just told your mom, I'm a neighbor and wonder if you'd like some fresh fish for dinner. I caught my limit and it's just me tonight. Oh, I forgot, my name is Nate."

No clue what Eric is thinking, but I'm like, this sounds good and all, but I am not a gourmet cook who can whip up fresh fish just because someone brought it to my door. What the heck will I do with it?

Before I can weigh in with any of my hesitations, Eric has invited Nate in, they've each got a beer in hand, Nate is showing him how to season the fish, and Eric is warming up the grill. I guess the potatoes and veggies I'd put in to roast will go perfectly with grilled fish, and the burgers will wait another day.

After setting the table for three, I return to the porch and enjoy hearing the sounds of two young men chatting and laughing while they grill. Dinner is delicious and the conversation fun as the two of them continue the camaraderie that began because of fish. It's noticeably different than all our recent dinners. So nice to hear Eric engaged with a new friend, talking about fishing, talking about today and tomorrow. None of us needing or wanting to talk about the past.

Long after Nate is gone and Eric has gone to bed, I am thankful for this evening. I appreciate and am driven to honor our past and our precious Emma, while also grateful for the opportunity, the chance to create a future. I'm not even going to wish for what that future will entail. It's a moment to cherish the

Wonders in the Waves 159

present and accept that I don't know a blasted thing about what the future will bring. Wishing sets expectations and sometimes, those unmet expectations are exactly what drags us down and stifles the joy in the moment.

20

*When the wild wave meets the calm beach,
when anger reaches tranquility,
anger disappears, serenity triumphs,
the wave experiences enlightenment.*
MEHMET MURAT ILDAN

Walking the beach a couple of mornings later, I'm still enjoying thoughts of the friendship that has budded for Eric. Nate has taken him out fishing, and later will drive Eric to the airport to pick up Hilary. She only has a couple of days, but Eric's excited to show her the island he's been raving about.

Except for the seagulls, it's nearly silent on the beach today. At times in my life, silence was mostly unknown, occurring occasionally in the darkness late at night. Then, it became a curse. Alone, my house was far too quiet without Emma and Eric. Now, on some days, the silence actually speaks louder and more meaningfully than words, even becomes my preferred language. The ocean has calmed down appreciably since my first day out here. The extreme highs and lows have leveled out, and it's nearly as calming as the river. *Serene* describes the last few days of ocean activity, as well as our human activity. I push aside the thought, *calm before a storm.* No need to anticipate the worst, I will enjoy the calm moments.

Ahead of me in the sand are large tracks, like those of tractor tires. Wondering what the heck a tractor would be doing out here, it dawns on me that maybe these are sea turtle tracks. Everyplace you look around here, there are warnings about not disturbing turtle nests, not allowing porch lights to shine out toward the beach, and covering up any holes dug in the sand so that recently hatched turtles don't get stuck in them. Nate had Eric and I hanging on every detail as he described once seeing a mother turtle lay her eggs late at night.

Being careful not to step in the tracks so as to mess them up, I follow the tracks up toward the dunes. Sure enough, here's an area that looks as if it was dug up and then covered over. Nate became so animated as he told us how powerful the turtle's flippers were as she covered the nest. He said it was like she was determined to be sure nothing, no one, knew where those eggs were or could get to them. Her, their, lives depended on that nest being disguised. While I'm staring at the spot, a three-wheeled vehicle comes up next to me, and the young woman wearing an official-looking vest calls to me, "Ma'am, please don't get any closer to that. It's a protected loggerhead's nest. You need to back away, and I need to do my job to mark it and record its location." Her comments are all business, nothing chatty about her presence.

"Oh, right. No, I didn't want to disturb it. I'd never seen one before and when I saw the big tracks coming off the beach, I just wondered if it was a turtle."

"OK, that's fine. I patrol this beach every morning and get a little possessive about these nests. This is one of the first of the season this year. They're mighty precious and need all of us to help protect them."

"Do you mark every single one you find? And then watch for signs they've hatched?"

"You know what, go to our website. It has tons of information. Not to be impolite, but if I stopped to answer everyone's questions, I'd never cover all my assigned territory. I'm happy you're interested, but I need to get going. Quick answers: this year, I mark every eighth nest I find—it's different every year. And yes, while the nesting season just got underway, we are busy for quite a while, all the way through till the hatching of the last ones at the end of the season."

"I'm definitely going to look it up. I appreciate all that you do to help the turtles. Stay well!"

Returning to the shoreline, I find a piece of driftwood with what looks like a seat carved away by the water and wind, and plop myself down on it. Let's hope there's enough cell service out here to find the website. Twenty minutes later, I've read about the turtles, the nesting, and the hatching. Apparently, mothers return to where they were born in order to lay their eggs. What an incredible feat to think that they can find their way back. And their mission is a tough one, not only finding the right place, but then overcoming the barriers that stand in the way of a turtle egg actually hatching and surviving the run to the sea. I'm struck by yet another kind of strength. Strength that endures in spite of tremendously dismal odds of the next generation surviving. Some might say it's just the way of nature. I think it brings perseverance and survival to a remarkable level.

Finding my way back along the beach, the mental images of these turtle mamas pushing their way through the sand in the darkness of night to carry out this essential yet tenuous mission prevail. Human motherhood sometimes feels the same way, like pushing through sand, or even quicksand, in the darkness of night to help our children survive. To help them carry out their own individual missions. It's tiring, and most of the time, worth every ounce of energy that's expended. I need to keep plugging away for Eric, for Everett, even for Emma, who's pushing me forward from afar with her signs and messages of not giving up.

Back on the sidewalk, I feel my phone vibrating in my pocket, but see I've already missed the call. Not a number I know, but I do recognize the 518 area code—it must either be the lawyer's office or someone else that Terry has contacted on my behalf. Just as I shove the phone back in my pocket, the wind whips up and rain begins to pour. Florida rain showers creep up out of nowhere, and so much for the sound of silence. Nothing I can do about it but put my head down and pick up the pace.

Throwing my wet tote bag on a porch chair to dry, I see someone left a voice message. After grabbing a cup of tea, a pad of paper, and positioning myself close to my laptop, I listen.

"Ms. Miller, this is Ralph Barbour calling you about a matter from, uh, several years ago. Can you please call me at your earliest convenience?"

Yup, Mr. Barbour, I sure will. Thanks for the reminder that to you, in my message, I am Ms. Miller.

Once the office assistant puts me on hold, I'm wondering why he, the attorney himself, is calling me back. Is that a good sign or a bad sign, or probably, in spite of my need to overanalyze, no sign at all?

"Hello there, thank you for calling back. We've located some files related to adoptions in the time period that interests you. Can you explain to me again what you are looking for? As you may or may not be aware, these matters are sensitive, and we must hold ourselves to high standards when it comes to people's lives, identities, and so forth."

Now, I'm torn. The other day, after speaking with Renee, I readily took on the fake identity that we're thinking my aunt likely assigned to me. But maybe that's all wrong, maybe there's a real Laura Miller out there who was involved in an adoption around the same time I was, and by being deceptive, I would screw up her life, her kid, as well as my own. One of my dad's favorite sayings was something about tangled webs when we deceive. My life is tangled enough without adding outright misinformation to the mix. The idea of lying to this guy brings on the all-too-familiar signs of panic creeping up on me: fluttering in my gut, hunching shoulders, tightening in my throat, shallow breaths--

"Uh, Miss, are you there? Are you still on the line?"

OK, drop your shoulders and breathe, Larissa. You can do this. "Yes, sir, uh, Mr. Barbour, I am here."

"My assistant gave me a message that you are trying to find a son that was born in 1982 and adopted, is that correct?"

"Yes. My parents sent me to stay with my aunt, Mary Miller, who lived in Whitehall at the time. From the pieces I've put together so far, I think maybe she helped figure out the adoption. That doesn't really matter, I suppose. I'm trying every way I've discovered to try to find my son: online DNA match services, an organization with volunteer search angels, and now you." I proceed to explain my conversations with Terry, the invoices I found, the young man born during that time who reached out to Terry's organization, and the other details recently unearthed. He occasionally provides a "Hmm" or "I see," which feels like encouragement to continue.

"OK, well, one thing in your favor is Terry. She has a fine reputation and has done a lot of good work, all while respecting the boundaries of the law. Did she suggest you call me?"

Definitely time to stick closer to the truth. If he respects Terry, I need to use that to my advantage. "Terry used the letterhead information from invoices I found and left a message at your company to see if you had any other old records. Someone she spoke to indicated your office recently received a letter from a lady who adopted a child in 1982. Terry said she'd let me know when she heard something back. Mr. Barbour, it's just very hard to keep waiting and waiting. So much precious time has been lost already, I thought maybe if I called you myself, rather than Terry, you'd be willing to speak with me. How can a volunteer have as much commitment to getting this done as I have?"

"I can't comment on anyone's commitment. I'm trying to keep all of this straight and not jump to conclusions simply because the last week has brought two inquiries from 1982. There were at least a half dozen adoption matters handled between my father and me in that year. The information you provided and the information in the other inquiry do not match exactly. It's my job to try to figure this out so that no errors are made, no one gets hurt unnecessarily. I understand from my assistant that you've recently, uh, lost another child? A child recently died? Is that part of what's going on here, making this so urgent, Ms. Miller, right?"

Trying to process all that he just offered, I wonder is his question at the end about the urgency or about my name? "Look, Mr. Barbour, we want the same thing. Yes, I had a child die within the last year, actually it will be a year in a couple of weeks. That's not the urgency. But it *is* what made me realize how wrong I was to assume it best to leave Everett alone, not to interrupt his life. I learned that we're not promised anything in this life, not one more hour. If he wants to, I'd like to connect with him and allow him and my other son to be brothers. And my name—it's a little confusing."

"Well, try me. I think I can follow most stories—I sure have heard a lot of them over the years."

"OK, I gave your receptionist my name as *Laura Miller* because I think there's a good chance that might be the name my aunt used back then to protect my, or our family's, identity.

She always messed up my given name and called me *Laura*, and her last name was *Miller*. So, when Terry told me that a young man in their database was born around the time of my son, and that the birth mother was listed as *Laura Miller* on the birth certificate he'd attained as an adult in search of biological parents, it seemed like too much of a coincidence for there to have been another baby adopted that year to someone by that name. I guess I assumed it was probably me and then made it the truth, at least in my mind, when I called your office."

"Interesting. While I can't approve of lying, Miss, um, well, anyway, I'll get to that in a minute. While I don't approve of you making *Laura Miller* your name, I hear the conviction in your voice, and I do have some feelings, you know. I couldn't do this line of work without caring, because believe me, it's a tough part of the law. It can be incredibly rewarding, but when we're trying to put together pieces of puzzles from people's lives, it can be monumentally difficult to sift through. I didn't say it before, but I am sorry that you recently lost your daughter. There is no worse pain, and I respect that you have a unique perspective on the fragility of life." After a few seconds and the sound of papers rustling, he continues, "So, first, I do have some documents in a file labeled *Mary Miller*. These may be of interest to you. But I need to have some way to verify your identity and your relationship before disclosing anything. Can you provide me with a copy of your driver's license and a notary signature indicating that you appeared before them and matched the photo? You can fax or email that to me, and we can talk soon after."

"Yes, sure, yes I can. Is that all you can tell me? I mean, does anything match my story, the dates, anything?"

"I think this can all wait another day or two. And we still didn't get to it—what is your actual name? I want to be looking for it so I respond to you right away."

"Right. It's *Larissa Whitcomb*, and that was my name back then as well. I never, uh, used a married name, for exactly this reason, if my son ever looked for me, I wanted him to be able to find me."

"Wait, wait, say that name again, I got distracted by another call."

I repeat my name and after a deep exhale, he says, "Oh boy, wow. Can you, uh, just get me the identity verification? We definitely have some bits and pieces to try to put together into something that makes sense. I have to get to court now, so tomorrow afternoon is the soonest I can be available again." With that, he ends the conversation. If he wasn't going to court, I'd run to the notary right now, so I could learn more. But no sense in rushing around. I might as well clean myself up and get busy making dinner. Nate, Eric, and Hilary are on their way back from the airport by now and will be expecting the dinner I'd promised.

By the sounds of the voices coming in the front door, the three young folks are getting along as if they've been friends for years. As Eric proudly gives a tour and shows Hilary where to put her things, I hear recounts of some crazy driver on the road, a song on the radio they could not believe was a favorite for each of them, and then, the exclamations as Hilary catches sight of our spectacular view. No silent house now!

Nate excuses himself, sets up a time to meet Eric and Hilary tomorrow, and heads out. The three of us settle into the chairs facing the river to catch up on news back home. School is going well for Hilary, she reports that her dad is super busy, traveling for work, and then says, "Eric told me about the search you guys are trying to do for his brother, uh, your son."

"I figured Eric may have filled you in on the search. I sure talk about it with my friends."

"Well, a weird--no, I guess not weird, just *interesting* thing happened the other night at the siblings' grief group. I learned a lot about another kind of loss. Mind if I share with you?"

"Of course not, Hilary. Let's hear it!"

Hilary sets the stage for her story. "So, I was running late to siblings' group and snuck in the back while someone was already talking. I felt badly about interrupting, but before long, I was wrapped up in the story of the guy who was speaking. I quickly figured out that he was there for a much different reason than the rest of us—or at least what I assumed the reason the rest of us came. This guy came to the sibling loss group because he's adopted. He has a family, and he loves them a ton, but he doesn't know if he has other siblings out there in the world or not. He told us all he feels a loss because there might be siblings somewhere and he misses them. He said he misses the possibility of them. It really got to me when he said, 'I know this might seem weird to all of you, but I wake up every single day feeling like there are people out there who share parents and grandparents with me, yet they are strangers. They should be sharing my life with me; I want them to share my life with me. So, I miss them. You miss your siblings, and I miss mine. I'm hoping you don't mind me coming to this group, and I'm hoping you can help me figure out my feelings. Because they feel like grief. It's not the same as your grief, but it is painful and lonely, and I just wanted to talk to somebody about it. I don't want to hurt my adoptive family; they're good people, but there's a huge hole in my heart that should have other people filling it. I'm sure you know that feeling.'"

By the time she gets to the end of the young man's words, I'm shivering, as if I'm cold, but I'm not. I'm actually sweating, yet shaking and crying at how the young man described his place at that grief group, why he found his way to the meeting, and how he described the shared emotions. Different reason, but shared, nonetheless.

"I can totally see it, I get why he went there. I hope everyone was good to him. He's got a point, and it's kind of what I feel about Everett. He's out there, somewhere. He's my brother, we share a mom, but we've never even been in the same place. It's a loss. It's not the same as Emma, but it hurts." Eric comes to my side and rubs my back while he continues. "We have no clue, Mom, if he has other siblings or not. If he doesn't, I bet he feels awfully lonely and just wants to be around others who might feel the same way. Just one more reason to keep going, right?"

I, too, feel something missing, a placeholder in my heart. "Yes, it's a very good reason to keep going. Sometimes, I'm ashamed that I denied that place in my heart reserved for Everett. No one ever took that place, but I let all of the other important people, you and Emma mostly, occupy my time and my love so that I was not overtaken by a need to find him. Maybe that was right at the time, maybe he had the freedom to enjoy his younger years without the craziness of juggling adoptive and biological families, or figuring out where he belonged. I'm not sure if I was right or wrong in my choices—I've learned right or wrong often don't get cleared up till very late in the game. At least now, he's an adult and can be part of the decision making. We will keep going, keep looking." I fill Eric and Hilary in on most of the conversation with Mr. Barbour, and they agree that my priority in the morning will be to get the identification off to him so we can get some clues about the "bits and pieces" he mentioned as we got off the phone.

While cleaning up from an early dinner, my phone is ringing out on the porch. I ask Eric to pick up, he yells, "Hey it's an unidentified caller, but it's this area code, want me to answer?"

"Yeah, sure, pick it up, I'm coming."

As I walk out to the porch, I hear Eric reply to the caller, "Yeah, sure, Kristy, I remember you, this is Eric. Yeah, it's my mom's phone, but she was in the kitchen. Wait, she's coming now." He hands me the phone, saying, "It's that girl from the bait shop, Kristy. Says she needs to talk to you."

Puzzled, and curious, I take the phone and greet her, "Hello, Kristy. Nice to hear from you so soon." I listen to her ramble on for a few minutes, until she asks if she can just come over and talk to me in person. Glad we'd eaten early, I give her the address and tell her to come on over.

Eric asks, "What was that about?"

"Honestly, I'm not so sure. She was kind of--flustered, I guess I'd call it. She rambled on a bit about her mother and then just blurted out that she had someone to stay with her mom, so could she just come over and talk to me. I didn't see any reason to say no, so I guess she's on her way." Before I go finish with the last kitchen clean-up, I save Kristy's name and number in my contacts.

"OK, so that's weird. I'm going to go show Hilary the beach, but we'll be back in a few. I want to hear what the heck this is all about."

21

*And above all, watch with glittering eyes
the whole world around you
Because the greatest secrets are always hidden
in the most unlikely places.
Those who don't believe in magic will never find it.*
ROALD DAHL

Just as I finish loading the dishwasher, my phone rings again, now showing it's Kristy. I hear a voice, much different than anticipated, say, "Is this Larissa? This is--"

Just then, I hear some background voices, and then, "Larissa, this is Kristy. Sorry, I can't come over tonight. My mother is really agitated, confused, and when she heard me say your name, she waited for me to be out of the room and grabbed my phone. She's acting strangely, and I can't leave her—even with her friend, not tonight. I don't know if I should ask this of you, but any chance you could come here tomorrow? My mother is insistent that she knows you and needs to speak to you. Maybe it's because I told her about those postcards and your parents? She smiled a lot when I told her your parents knew her and Dad. It seems like the past makes more sense to her these days than what's going on right now."

"I have a couple of commitments first thing in the morning, but could probably come by later. If she remembers my parents, I want to meet her as well. After all, that's the connection that brought Eric and me here. Shall I text when I'm free and see if it's a time that works out for you?"

"Sure. I usually get free after twelvish. I like to be open early morning because that's when all the fishermen come for bait, and whatever else they need. That's the most important part of the shop, the cash moneymaker. Text me--I gotta go!"

Anticipating sunset, I walk out the front door to see if Eric and Hilary are on their way back yet. I don't see them but decide to walk around the far side of the house to get back to the porch. I'd not been over here before, and as I turn the corner, I find some stepping stones that are carefully spaced to invite a walker to see the other side of the house. They lead to a secluded area with a white bench, several birdhouses and feeders, with a butterfly-themed clock/thermometer mounted on the side of the house. There are several stepping stones with shells or sea creatures painted on them, and one has a butterfly motif with the saying, "Those we love don't go away, they fly beside us every day." I slowly walk to the bench to take it all in. There is no river view, no road view, just trees, flowers, and many charming garden ornaments scattered tastefully in this tiny, private space. As I sit, the space seems to enclose me and encourage quiet contemplation. Someone put a great deal of thought and heart into this little space. Funny that I didn't see anything about it on the property description. Maybe I'll have morning coffee out here, and evening wine on the porch. Peaceful mornings and peaceful evenings—the perfect bookends to action-filled days.

I continue beyond the secret garden area, out to the porch, to await the young folks and the sunset. Before long, I hear Eric yelling, "Hey, Mom, where are you? Is Kristy here? Or gone already? I didn't see a car. We got caught up in treasure hunting in the sand. Hilary is a magnet for cool beach treasures, wait till you see!"

I greet them at the porch steps. "I'd love to see, and no, Kristy called and can't come. Her mother needed her home tonight. But she asked me to go over there tomorrow. Seems her mother wants to talk to me, talk about old times with Gamma, I think."

"Huh. Well, guess that might be interesting. Look, she found this big conch shell without any broken edges, a sand dollar, and what did you call these bean things?"

Laughing, I reply, "The nickname is hamburger beans—see how the stripe around it looks like a burger between two sides of a roll. I can't remember the real name, but they come from somewhere like Central America, traveling with the currents. The shell and sand dollar are beautiful. Our collection of sea memorabilia is certainly growing!"

I suddenly get a flashback of Eric and Emma walking in from the beach and showing me fistfuls of shells, and an array of other pod-like things I could not identify. We saved them and found a tiny, little kids' guidebook to identifying beach treasures. I don't know if they were more fascinated by the beans themselves or that tiny, little book and its detailed descriptions of items found on the beach and where they came from. Guess that's when we started making a game of finding beach treasures. And it's still fun today!

I share some of that image with them and question, "I wonder if that book is still in print? Maybe in the gift shop at that House of Refuge. They had a lot of guide books. Wouldn't it be fun if it's one that people still enjoy?" As I look at Eric, for just a moment, I see him as he was at about eight or nine years old. Just as quickly, he returns to the young man he is, with a lovely young woman's head right next to his as they survey their finds. I wonder for perhaps the 739th time: *How does the time fly by so quickly?*

I decide to let Eric and Hilary have some peaceful time to themselves on the porch, the dock, or wherever, and retreat to my room. Saying good night, I remind them I will be going to the notary as soon as the bank opens in the morning, although I guess that's not so early. Sharing also that I plan to take an early walk, Eric tells me that Nate is stopping by to pick them up to go to breakfast and then explore some of the beaches south of the House of Refuge. They're local hangouts, with rock and coral formations that he wants to show them.

"OK, well, we'll meet up later in the day. After the notary and sending Mr. Barbour an electronic copy, I'm going to call him and see what's next. I'll probably try to go see Kristy and her mother after that, so who knows when I'll be back."

As I settle into bed, a text comes in from Renee asking when we plan to come home. I tell her there's no plan yet, that I'm thinking I want to stay at least a couple more weeks and get past the date that makes it officially one year since Emma died. She replies with a crying emoji and asks if we'd like company, maybe she'd come to be here on that day. I pick up the phone; it's too hard to text about this sort of thing. Emojis are fine, but they can get pretty tiresome and redundant. A poor substitute for real words.

"I can't text about this stuff, Renee. Anyway, there's nothing, nothing, I will 'like' about that date, but yes, if you want to come see this really unique little getaway, you're welcome. Hilary is visiting now, but only for a couple days. I don't know what I'm going to feel like, or if I'll want to do anything other than lie on the beach and cry that day. Absolutely no clue. If I read one more thing online about just 'getting through' the first of everything after someone dies, I'm going to vomit. But if you want to witness, or be part of that shitshow, come on down. There's plenty of room."

"OK, well, that was the other thing I was going to ask. About space, kinda. Well, have you talked to Steven? He's kind of struggling, Larissa. There's a lot going on with him. I'm not sure he can get away because of Jimmy being so sick and all, but maybe you should think about seeing if he wants to join you guys, too. I'm not trying to tell you what to do, or anything, but . . ."

In spite of the serious topic, I laugh and kid her, "Really, Renee? Since when are you not trying to tell me? So, were you texting for you to come, or was it a thinly disguised attempt to talk to me about Steven? I do feel badly for him. You're right, I haven't talked to him. Eric called him about the DNA match thing, and they talked about Jimmy. But I will definitely call him as well. I've gotten wrapped up trying to convince the lawyer to give me information."

"So did he? Did he tell you anything?"

I give her a brief re-cap of the next steps, tell her again that she can come anytime if she gets time off work, and assure her I'll call Steven, maybe tomorrow after my other call with the lawyer. Maybe I'll have something to share. Then, again, maybe not. Maybe the bits and pieces will not fit together to add up to anything but diddly-squat. I don't know.

The next morning, as I pour coffee, I remember my pledge to enjoy it in that little side garden. Still in my pajamas, I put on my flipflops and start down the front steps, just as Nate pulls up in his jeep, looking all ready for a beach day.

"Oh, hi, Nate. Sorry you caught me in my jammies! I'm just going to sit and contemplate life with my coffee over there," pointing to the front corner that juts out and keeps the little area private and cozy.

He replies, "Oh, you found it, huh? It's a pretty special spot, right?"

More than a little surprised that he knows what I'm talking about, I nod my head and offer, "Yes, very special. I just found it yesterday. How do you know about it?"

"Well, the lady who owns this house and my mom used to be really good friends. I'm not sure how much you know about her?"

"Nothing, really. We just saw the listing online, liked the area, liked the reviews, and emailed her. Never even talked. She just sent me the combination to the front door and ended her email with 'enjoy the magical beauty of my house, many blessings to you and yours.'"

"That sounds like her all right. Well, long story short, the lady and her daughter, who was a single mom, and her little kid, lived here and became good friends with my mom. My mom would help Adele, that's her name, babysit the grandkid sometimes when the daughter was at work. She was pretty young to be a mom. Anyway, Adele was always a little out there—uh, in my opinion. Said she could hear voices of people who died, always said they were angels watching out for her and her family. She built that little sitting area to talk to them and meditate. She brought the grandson in there with her all the time. They'd watch the birds and tell stories. My mom helped her keep it pretty, bought her a couple of those stepping stones."

"It sounds like they were good neighbors. I've kind of been interested in people who can communicate with those who have passed. At one time, I might have said it was 'out there' or strange, too, but my mind has opened up. It's a very peaceful little nook, hidden from everyone else's view, and I'm not surprised that Adele, who clearly designed it thoughtfully, believed in connecting with spirits. That would be the perfect spot to do it."

"I guess, Ms. Whitcomb, but here's the really sad thing. Adele's daughter, well, there was a boating accident out in this channel about five years ago, and she was, uh, killed. Adele, well, you would probably get it because Eric told me about your daughter, but she was devastated. She just fell totally apart. No one could help her. My mom was over here every day, trying to get her motivated to take care of the baby, to maybe get counseling, whatever. But nothing made a difference. Then, one day, she was sitting out in that garden and she heard her daughter talk to her. That's what she told my mom. Her daughter told her to go back to their home where she grew up. To go back to the mountains of Colorado and raise the little boy there. Adele made up her mind that was what she was supposed to do, and just like that, packed up with that little kid and moved to their former hometown. She rents this out, asks my mom and I to watch from afar, nothing official, but just be on the lookout for anyone who might not treat the property right."

I'm stunned by the story of Adele, but can't help but ask, "So, when you came over the other day, you were spying?"

"No, no, no. No spying, no stalking. It's nothing like that. I'd seen you guys and just thought I'd say hi. Then, Eric and I hit it off. I'd bet ninety percent of the renters don't find that little secret retreat. I'm glad you did, though. Looks like you are about to enjoy it, appreciate its unique vibe—no, *aura*—that's the word Adele always used."

"Even more so, now, Nate. It makes so much more sense now with that story. I'm so sad that Adele lost her daughter. Do you think it would be weird if I wrote her, told her I found her hideaway and love sitting there and pondering her little piece of magic?"

"Not weird at all. I think she'd like it. I didn't know her as well as my mom did, but she was always a pretty cool lady. And once her daughter came and told her to go to Colorado, it seems like she was much better. I can't imagine, but if it gives her peace, what the hell, right?"

"Absolutely, Nate. No one can tell you how to get through the crappy parts of life. Most of the time, it's taking tiny, little tiptoe steps forward to see if it feels all right to move in that direction. If it doesn't, you're knocked back on your butt to figure out what you'll try next. If it does feel right, you take a deep breath, say a little mantra of thanks and gratitude, and appreciate making it through another day. Today, that little garden with my coffee is going to start me in the right direction. I feel it."

Surprised at seeing me out here when he comes down the steps, Eric asks, "Why are you out here in your pajamas, Mom? What are you and Nate chatting about?"

"Get in the jeep, dude. You and Hilary jump in and let's get rolling. Leave your mom to her peace and quiet."

Off they go exploring, and off I shuffle into the shady, pleasant shelter of this sanctuary on the side of the house. *Thank you, Adele. May your Colorado mountains guard and protect you, and may your special place bring me good vibes for the day and all I encounter.* It's my version of a prayer, a sincerely felt wish for both of us.

22

*If you have been brutally broken, but still have the
courage to be gentle to others,
Then you deserve a love deeper than the ocean itself.*
NIKITA GILL

I had to go off of the island into town to find a bank with a notary. They gave me a little hassle because I'm not a customer. But when my face crumbled and I started talking about an adoption decades ago and an attorney, the receptionist quickly ushered me over to a private desk and a bank officer with the proper credentials scurried right over. Five minutes later, documents in hand, I looked for an office store that could fax them to Mr. Barbour. Once I had a confirmation from them, I searched for a coffee shop with Wi-Fi to be able to access my laptop and internet in case I need it when I call him.

Of course, the voice at the other end of the phone reports that Mr. Barbour is in court this morning, but I leave as detailed a message as I dare; I just want him to call me back. With it being too early to go visit Kristy and her mother, I look up local parks and find a suitable destination just a short walk from the coffee shop. It's a bright, sunny day, and since I didn't go to the beach to walk this morning, I'm happy for the chance to stretch my legs.

Far more quickly than I expect, my phone is ringing and it's the office number for Mr. Barbour. He comes on the phone announcing, "Well, that case was short and sweet. Not too many like those these days. My office confirmed that you sent a notarized signature document with your photo. Now, can you turn on your video function for a minute so I can compare?"

It didn't occur to me that he might want to do some kind of video chat, but at this point, I really don't care how we get to where he will actually share information. "OK, I'm not sure if we will have a good connection, because I'm not on Wi-Fi right now, but I'll try." A few clicks later, with me adjusting the camera a few times so he can see me without the image being distorted, he is finally satisfied.

After we switch back to voice only, I plead, "So, please, can you share anything with me from your files?"

"I can, but I'm not sure it gets us any further along than you already are." He stops and waits.

"Um, OK, well, can you just tell me what's in the file?"

Clearing his throat one too many times for my patience, he continues, "So, there is a file with documents that correspond with what you found in your mother's belongings. The dates line up, and they could be related. But there are two problems. First, the birth mother's name in our files is Laura Miller. Before you jump in and tell me the story of your aunt and why she might have done that, it really doesn't matter."

"How can it not matter? Because I can't prove I'm her? So, I'm just plain fucked, is that what you're saying? Even though my mother paid you a few thousand dollars—that was a lot for her, you know—because the names don't match, you won't tell me? I'm so damn frustrated I could scream!"

"Screaming and swearing are not going to get us anywhere, Ms. Whitcomb. Please, just listen to me. Yes, the inconsistency in the names is one problem. But because you have the invoices and they match mine, we might be able to figure out a way to get past that. Here's the real problem." He clears his throat yet again, "The invoice was for adoption-related services; things like background checks of the adoptive parents, preparation of documents for both the party surrendering the child and the party adopting the child, etc. So, those services were performed and paid for by someone, seems like your mother. The real issue here is that according to my records, it seems as though the actual adoption didn't ever happen. There are notes scribbled about adoptive parents, and plans for grandparents to meet them because the mother was a minor. But there are no filing records or signed documents consummating the whole matter. It looks like we started work for a Laura Miller, or Mary Miller, or your mother if she paid the bills, but that the adoption never went through to completion."

"What the hell are you saying? Where did the child go? I sure as shit don't have the child. It must have happened. I thought you said you and your father did the work then. Don't you remember what happened?"

"I did say that, ma'am, but I was fresh out of law school. My father handled this. And he is no longer practicing. He died last year. So, there is no memory to tap into either. I am stumped. Now--"

Before he can continue, I continue my rant; I can't help myself. "This is just too damn much. You got my hopes up, you made me go through this ridiculous charade of getting a notarized identification document to you. Are you a freaking torture monger or what? Why the hell did you make me do all that, jump through your legal hoops, just to tell me I'm out of luck?"

"Wait, wait, Larissa, there's something else."

Wait, so now we're friends, now he's calling me Larissa?

"There is something interesting here. Not in the files, but in the letter that Terry told you we received last week. In this letter, the letter from a woman who has a child born in the same month as we've been talking about, she asks if we have any contact information for a woman named Larissa. She says she's not sure what the last name would be now, but that the last time she knew of the woman, her last name was Whittaker, or something similar. She says she's getting 'on in her years' and can't remember exactly. But she wants to know if I can give her contact information. She believes she brought up Larissa's child and wants to contact her."

Now I'm speechless. Part of me wants to hurl my phone as far as I can throw it, and the rest of me is struggling to hang on to any thread of hope that he dangles in front of me. Over the last few months, I've said this is like following breadcrumbs, I've said it was like a tangled ball of yarn, most recently, a tangled web. "So, let me try to get this, this blasted mystery straight here. According to your files, the Miller adoption was planned but never happened, and according to this lady, an adoption from Whittaker occurred, and she contacts your firm. My head is spinning. What now? Can I contact that lady? Is my name close enough?"

"My paralegal is doing some research for me as we speak. We are going to find out as much as we can about this lady through property searches, tax records, etc., and I'm going to write to her. That's the only contact information we have—no email and no phone, because her letter says she can't hear well, and she doesn't want us to contact her family members because this is just between her as the adoptive mother and Larissa as the biological mother."

"Well, if it's just between the mothers, why are you involved? Can't I just write her or go see her or something?"

"We need to be sure this is not some kind of scam, at least rule out anything obvious. It will only take a couple of days to do this screening, and I'm sending the letter by overnight mail today."

The resolve is clear in his voice, and I do not have the energy to push him any further. I need to process the last ten minutes of information. I need to walk the beach, or talk to someone I trust, or something. I need to get out of this park; it feels too public for gathering my thoughts.

I concede defeat for the moment, but let him know I'll be expecting to hear from him, "If I don't hear from you in two days, I'll be back on the phone. I will not be denied this opportunity to see if this letter is about my child or not."

"I don't intend to deny you anything, Larissa. I'm trying to ensure some modicum of security before we jump into correspondence between the two of you. Give me two days, please."

A few minutes later, I'm driving over the bridge to go back to the island. Funny that it already feels like my island escape. The bridge is my connector between the hustle of the real world—places like banks and grocery stores—and the calm sanctuary of the beach, garden, and scenic views of the lagoon. Right now, I gotta get away from the hustle.

Once I'm changed into shorts, tank, and flipflops and halfway down the beach, I remember Kristy and her mother. I was so wrapped up during and after the phone call with the lawyer that I'd totally forgotten. Maybe I'll text her after I get back, maybe not. I don't know if I'm ready to hear someone else's issues right now.

As I walk, I notice several more of the wooden stakes with markers for turtle nests are scattered along the beach. The mamas must have been busy the last few nights. While I was listening to the quiet lapping of the lagoon and sleeping in my cozy bed, those mothers were over here, working like crazy to find safe places to bury their precious eggs. Driven to carry out a mission of survival. It would be so amazing to see them, but I know you're supposed to stay away, give them space. I saw videos on that conservation website of turtles laying eggs, so there must be some legal way of watching. One more thing to investigate.

Feeling the phone ringing in my pocket, I contemplate doing something I rarely do: not answering it. Hesitating, I glance and see that it's Steven. I start to text that I'll call later and then remember all of the times that he has stuck by me. Nope, I'm picking it up.

"Hello, Steven. I'm walking the beach, so if the wind is too loud, I can call you back when I get back to the house."

"No, I hear you all right. And a walk on the beach sounds divine. I'm happy you are able to enjoy it. Is Eric with you?"

"No, he's out exploring with Hilary and a new friend, Nate. He seems pretty happy—and the new activities are keeping him from constantly pressing me about the search for Everett. Not that I blame him, he just has a hard time being patient with processes and wait times."

"Yeah, I know. I experienced that when he called me the other day. About, the um, DNA relationship notice."

"Well, he jumped right in and wrote an email to the young woman. I have no idea if he's heard anything back yet. Like I said, he's been busy. How is Jimmy, anyway, and what's going on with all of that?"

"It's been a rough road. His kidneys aren't working well—you know he's had diabetes for a while. They're considering dialysis, but he might be better off with a transplant. As you might guess, it's kinda controversial for some to think about a transplant for someone with a cognitive disorder like Jimmy. Some question whether he's a good risk or whether he'll follow directions afterwards. I'm making the argument that other than this, he is pretty healthy, young—only in his early thirties—and that he does follow instructions very well. He's probably a better patient than many transplant recipients. Plus, he has care providers. And if that isn't good enough, I've said I'll bring him to live with me. An apartment with his peers was preferable when he turned twenty-one, but if they need me to sign on as his full-time provider, I will. Hell, I'll give him my kidney, too. But I know all of that is jumping the gun. He's holding his own this week. He's in good spirits. Damn, that guy could be an example for a lot of other so-called 'normal' people."

"I hear you, Steven. He's always been a trooper. How about you? You holding up?"

"No choice, right, Larissa? Sometimes all you can do is put one foot in front of the other and keep going. I don't need to tell you." After a brief pause he continues, "Larissa, about that young woman that came up as a match, I think I--"

I interrupt him, "You don't owe me an explanation, Steven. It's your business, and if she's your daughter, it's also Eric's business. You know how he feels about being a brother. But I'm peripheral to this, really."

"Peripheral, my ass, Lissa. We've become a family again through our son. What affects one of us, affects all of us. When Eric called me, I was dumbfounded at first, but I've had some time to think, and might have an idea about this. A couple of years after we divorced, I got pretty serious with someone. She, Pamela, well, we, got pregnant. She wasn't sure if she wanted to have a child in the first place, was a little freaked out by Jimmy, and worried that maybe this baby would have similar problems. No matter what information I gave her, or all the reassurances in the world, she wasn't buying it. We started talking about having testing done so that we would know if the baby had any problems. I agreed with the testing, if it would help her prepare for the possibility, but did not agree to the idea of terminating if the child had Down syndrome like Jimmy—no way. Well, that scared her and one day, she just took off. I tried to find her for weeks, then weeks turned into months. Then, I hoped that maybe when she had the baby, she'd try to find me, but I never heard from her. It's not like I'd be difficult to find—lived my whole life in about a twenty-mile radius. At some point, it dawned on me, she could have taken off to terminate the pregnancy on her own. That made me sick and renewed my attempts for another year or so, but I got absolutely nowhere. That woman knew how to vanish! I ran out of clues or ideas of how to locate her, so I gave up."

Trying to keep up with the story, I ask, "So, you're thinking this match could be that baby? Pamela's and yours?"

"Yeah, that's what occurred to me when I got off the phone and thought about it more. I'm not going to say I never had any other relationships, but let's just say I didn't let myself get too involved with anyone again. After my track record with you and Pamela, I decided to keep my heart on a short leash. It was too much for me to get involved again. Now, the thought that a third child of mine is gone, well, out of my life, just seems inconceivable; for then and for today. Again, I don't need to tell you about that, but it was more than I could handle. I kept busy with work and Jimmy, and was happy for the occasional contacts that you and I had through the work connection. Good enough for me. Now, now, there's Eric. I totally love being that kid's—that young man's—dad, Lissa. Thank you for being willing to figure this all out. Thank you for inviting me into his life."

"Steven, I need to thank you. Your presence these last few months, to help Eric get some semblance of his life back in order, to help me figure out how to help him, has been a real blessing. I'm so grateful. And if this turns out to be the daughter that you and Pamela brought into the world, so be it. We've figured out worse, way worse stuff to get through."

I catch him up on my latest lawyer phone calls. As usual, he is totally in my corner, rooting me on. Once or twice, he sounds like Eric, urging me to push the lawyer, but then he backs off and offers, "Sounds like you're doing everything you can. Keep me posted if I can help. You know, Schenectady isn't that far from here. If I can deliver documents in person or do anything to convince him that you're legit, I'll do it."

We agree to talk again in a couple of days, or sooner if Eric hears anything from the related young woman. I ask him to give my best to Jimmy and confirm what address to use; I want to send him a letter, no, even better, postcards, showing him where Eric and I are hanging out for the time being.

By the time we hang up, I've returned to the beach house. Eric texts me to let me know they're going to lunch and do some more exploring and asks me if everything went OK at the notary. I reply that it's a long story and we'll talk later, but I'm fine. I want him to enjoy his friends and spend time doing fun things with them. Nothing he can do about my conversation with the lawyer except be frustrated along with me—that's a useless way to use up his youthful energy right now.

There's also a missed call from Kristy—somehow I missed that during all of the other correspondence. Remembering that there were several beachy restaurants over in the area of the bait shop, my stomach growls, reminding me I haven't eaten. I'll drive over, grab some lunch, then text her to see if it will work out for me to stop over for a few minutes. That gives her more time after closing the shop to see to whatever her mother might need before having a visitor.

As I'm changing to go back out, the doorbell rings. What the heck? Last time it rang, Nate became Eric's friend. Let's hope it's something as pleasant. Surprise doorbell rings are not always a good thing. *Like when your teenager gets in trouble driving, or there's been an accident, or, geez, Larissa, let's not go there. Not again.*

Hurrying to find the answer to my wandering mind, I fling the door open to see Kristy standing there with a fairly large package. Confused, my mind races to answer questions. *Why is she here? What's in the package? It can't be too heavy because she's holding it casually in one arm while she's checking her phone in her other hand.*

"Hello, Larissa. Sorry I didn't call first, but I was over here on the island running an errand and thought maybe I could talk to you for a minute. Is this an OK time? Oh, and this package was on the steps. Maybe it was just delivered? I saw the UPS truck leaving this access road when I drove in."

Surprised by both Kristy and a package, I don't reply for a moment. I register that neither seems ominous enough for the worry that had started to creep into my consciousness. It feels like I'm always primed, always on the precipice of something happening that will add to the challenges of life, or yet another tragedy. An exaggerated version of waiting for the other shoe to drop.

"Yes, it's fine, Kristy. Actually, I was thinking about driving over to your part of town for lunch and then stopping by. I guess then I would have been the surprise visitor," trying to inject a little humor.

She's having no part of that, she's all business and seems in a hurry. "Oh, OK, then, well, I just want to be sure we find a time for you to meet my mother. Although she is sometimes kind of out of it, ever since your name came up, she's obsessing about talking to you. I tried to get her to tell me what it is, but she shuts right down. I can't figure it out, but I'm convinced she's not going to back off till she talks to you. The, uh, hard part, I know, it's not really your problem, is that her doctor and home aide have been trying to prepare me, they don't think she has long, to be with us. You know what I'm trying to say, don't you? Connecting with you seems so important to her, she won't be at peace until she does. The other problem, again not yours, is that my brother gets back in a few days. When he's around, she's different. She defers to whatever he says. She always says she doesn't want to upset him, that he's had things hard enough. I don't know what else to say, except, can we find a time soon to do this?"

She may be a veritable stranger, but I don't want to keep this woman, who's struggling with her health and her family, from getting whatever it is off her chest. And I am curious! She knew my parents, maybe better than I'd ever realized. I want to know more about that before I lose another opportunity to know what was going on in my parents' lives before I got old enough to care. "Yes, Kristy. I was about to drive over now. Want me to do that?"

"Damn, I do, but she and I both have appointments this afternoon. She has to go to the doctor, and I have a bunch of things to do before my brother gets back into town. Would tomorrow work?"

"I don't see why not. At this moment, I don't have any plans beyond right now."

"Thank you so much. Why don't you text me in the morning and we'll figure out a time?"

We agree to her plan, and off she goes.

23

I am pieces of all the places I have been, and the people I have loved. I've been stitched together by song lyrics, book quotes, adventure, late night conversations, moonlight, and the smell of coffee.
BROOKE HAMPTON

I almost trip over the package. It totally slipped my mind while Kristy and I were talking. I pick it up and head into the kitchen to open it and find something to eat, since my lunch plans changed in that short conversation.

The address is in cheery, bright-purple ink, with Renee's unique, curlicue handwriting, and the package is covered with heart and rainbow stickers. It's bulky, but kind of squishy, like a pillow or fabric or something. What is she up to now?

As I untape the back, I get the unmistakable aroma of patchouli. Emma's scent. Every candle, every oil she bought was patchouli. After she died, I sniffed her clothes daily, craving that aroma. If I smelled her, she couldn't be gone, right? Unwrapping it further, I recognize the bold, tie-dye pattern of purples and yellows swirling around one another, then a floral pattern of blues and greens. What's going on? As the aroma overtakes the room, I'm surrounded by fabrics that are so Emma, it's like she's tumbling out of the wrappings into my lap. Through cloudy, tear-filled eyes, I see a note pinned to one of the squares. A quilt, but how? I can't think straight, I'm overwhelmed by color and smell and the soft, well-worn texture of the fabrics. I'm holding Emma, but I'm not.

OK, what does the note say? *Focus, Larissa.*

Dear Larissa-

Don't be mad, please. We wanted to do something special for you. Something special for the damn "angel-versary" that's coming up. We know you and Eric are doing good so far in Florida, on your little island getaway, but that day is going to suck. So, maybe this quilt, sewn from Emma's things, from her clothes, will encompass you both, bring you her warmth, her presence, and help you get through the suffocating sadness. Please don't be pissed that we just went ahead and took the pieces you'd set aside to get to this someday. We thought this was the day you'd need it most, so found someone who could sew and do this for you. We'll tell you more about her in case you want to do anything else. She was awesome to work with.

And if you want us to come, either to yell at us, or thank us, or to let us give you hugs on that date, we will.

Love you tons, Renee and Isabel (and Valentino may have shed a bit of fur on the quilt while we were trying to get it ready to go; we found him asleep, all curled up on it. He must have been reminded of Emma, too!)

At that, I full-on lose it. My face crumples and the trickling tears become a swelling overflow, salty rivulets down my cheeks, dripping onto the fabric. Her dog curled up on the quilt? Dogs know, don't they? This quilt absolutely feels like Emma is here. She's with me. I unfold it the rest of the way and run my hand over every square. Each one reminds me of the piece of clothing it came from. This brightly colored square with butterflies on it is from a dress we bought Emma while shopping together on her eighteenth birthday. Wow, butterflies. All of those signs from butterflies over the last few months, and I didn't remember until now how much she loved this dress. Another square, from a well-worn tee shirt. Black with green, yellow, and red patterns: a tribute to her favorite reggae musician. And another swirling pattern from loose, flowing pants that we bought on a family trip. I'm so touched by this.

Could I be annoyed that I didn't get the final say in the quilt design, what clothing is featured, and all the rest? Sure, I could. But why? I also might have never actually sent it off to the seamstress because I was afraid of letting go of the clothes—what if they got lost in the mail? Or I might have freaked out about the clothing getting cut up to make the quilt. I might have invented a dozen excuses to delay, and never get to it. My friends did it for me and I'm touched, thankful, and feeling very loved. Memories of Emma to surround me. I'm not sure I'll ever unwrap myself.

Eric and his friends find me sitting on the couch, still wrapped in the quilt, texting Renee and Isabel because I'm not ready to talk yet, but I want them to know that I am anything but mad. Eric is yelling, "Hey, Mom"—until he sees me curled up with a streaky face and the quilt. The fabrics are unmistakably like Emma, and he stops in his tracks to ask, "Are you OK? What's going on?"

I point to the note. As he reads it, his eyes mist over. He comes and sits next to me and strokes his hands across the beautiful Emma squares and says, "Wow, so awesome. This is mint, this is amazing." With quick explanations to his friends, they all sit down and quietly admire this piece of loving artwork.

Hilary shares an observation, "You know, I've always been in awe of this type of sewing. It's so much more than putting fabric together to make something warm. It's all of that, but the way the patterns are arranged to complement one another is true artistry. A real example of the final product being so much more than the sum of its parts. These bits and pieces from all different times and places brought together for so many purposes. Yes, to keep you warm—both physically and emotionally—but also to give the gift of another connection to Emma, to spark memories of her and what she loved to wear and do, to wrap you in love from Emma and your friends who sent it. I want to do one for my dad, with my brother's tee shirts. I thought about it a year or so ago, but never followed through. Definitely on my to-do list when I get home. A gift from David to Dad for Father's Day. Do you think I should?"

Without a second's hesitation, I finally find my voice and reply, "Absolutely, Hilary—do it. Paul, your dad, would love it."

The younger crowd is tired from their day at the beach and decide we should order pizza and watch a movie. They search for a comedy we can all enjoy without the dangers of any emotional triggers that most current hit movies or dramas bring. As the movie ends, I realize I haven't moved from under this quilt in hours, and I'm still not going to. Wrapping it tightly around my shoulders, I say good night and head up to my room for much-needed rest. I toss all the other covers aside and relish the day's comforting connection with Emma for several more hours.

If there wasn't sunlight streaming through the windows, I would have sworn it was only a few minutes later that I hear a soft knock on the bedroom door and Eric half whispers, "Hey, Mom, are you OK? Just checking cuz it's kinda late for you. You good?"

I can't remember Eric waking me ever, or at least not since he was a little kid who wanted attention and cereal in the morning. What is he concerned about? Rolling over, my eyes find the clock, and I'm as surprised as he sounds. Ten in the morning and I'm still asleep? Still wrapped in my new favorite quilt of comfort? Not only did it bring many memories flooding back last night, it must have a sedative effect, more effective than any sleep aid known.

"I'm fine—guess I just overslept. Or maybe, just finally slept *well*. I'll be down in a minute."

Before I can catch Eric up on my day yesterday, I see a text from Kristy. I was hoping for a call from Mr. Barbour, but no such luck. Maybe it's better this way. Clear up whatever it is that is going on with Harriett and Kristy, and get that off my plate. Then, if he calls with the go-ahead for contacting the letter-writing mama, I'll be free to get on it.

"Eric, Kristy wants me to go over and talk to her mother today. There's something on Harriett's mind that she wants me to hear. So, I'm heading over shortly. Do you want to go?"

"How about I drive over that way with you, drop you off, and I'll fish nearby? Hilary goes back later today, but I can bring her along to see Port Salerno. You're not going to be long, right?"

"I sure don't think so. It seems like her health is failing. Kristy wants me to come while her mom's awake, which she thinks will be very soon. Let's just go over and see how it goes."

It's fun telling Hilary all we have learned about the area, and before we know it, we're at my drop-off spot, and Kristy confirms that her mom is up in a chair, having coffee, and anxious to see me. Eric and Hilary head over to a fishing spot Nate told them about, agreeing to watch their phones for when I need a ride back.

Kristy greets me at the front door, "It's nothing fancy in here, nothing like that place you're staying, Larissa. It's what a lot of

Wonders in the Waves 195

people call a 'Florida bungalow,' but it's been a cozy home. My parents moved here well before my brother and I were around, bought it from an old man and his wife along with the bait store. Those folks had run it for a long time. This community's history is mostly all about fishing. Guess that's no surprise to you. Come on in, Mom is waiting for you. Can I get you coffee or water?"

Taking the water she offered, I walk over to the tiny, gray-haired lady sitting in the lounge chair by the window. She has a perfect view of the bait shop and the water beyond. Her terry robe is about three times the size that she needs, but she still pulls the front down to cover her legs more completely, either because she's self-conscious or cold, or maybe both. I offer my hand and introduce myself, "Harriett, I'm Larissa Whitcomb. I think you knew my parents; they came fishing here a few times, and your husband was their guide. Is that right?"

Harriett stares at me for what would usually be an uncomfortably long period of time, but it isn't awkward at all. It's as if she is studying every feature and trying to find a place to store each one in her memory. I continue to hold her tiny, smooth hand while she finds the words she wants to offer.

"Yes, I knew your mother and father—Maggie and Tom—was it Whittaker or Whitman, I can't quite remember. What did you say?"

"Whitcomb. I've kept my original name, never changed it because, well, I just like it well enough, I guess."

"Larissa, your parents were customers who became friends and who kind of, well, like good friends sometimes do, became family. Yes, like family." She stares out the window, as if by staring into space she can bring the memories back into focus. "I've been trying to find you for a while, you know."

"Really? You have? Well, I found some postcards you sent to my mother and became intrigued by the towns and scenery on the postcards. My son and I needed a getaway, and he loves to fish, so we decided it was time to come see this place that his grandparents enjoyed so much."

"Your son? How old is your son, Larissa? Do you have any other children?"

Not at all sure why it matters, I try to answer succinctly, "Harriett, that's all a bit complicated. Crazy that those simple questions are hard. My son Eric is twenty-seven years old. My other children, a daughter and son, are not with me any longer. My daughter, Emma, died almost a year ago, and my other son, well, he's been away from me for a very long time, I actually don't know anything about him. He was adopted." Something about the way she's looking at me, with so much curiosity, makes tears come to my eyes, and I wish that the conversation had not gone in this direction. Why do people always feel the need to start a conversation by talking about children? Part of me loves talking about them, part of me just can't stand going over it all one more time. It doesn't get easier. Changing the subject, I say, "Anyway, that's not why I'm here. Kristy said you wanted to talk to me about something. Is it something about my parents?"

"Your parents? No, it's not. Well, not really. I wasn't sure, cuz my memory isn't always too great, but as soon as I looked at you, well, I'm sure now." She stares back out the window.

"You're sure? Sure of what?"

"I've got a story you need to hear. Kristy knows nothing about it, and my son says he doesn't want to talk about it, but you're my son's real mother, Larissa, like they say nowadays, biological mother."

I stop breathing, the room is spinning. Wait, how come she's still talking when my eyes can't focus?

"Once he got to be twenty-one, we left it up to him to decide if he wanted to know you. He tried to look stuff up once on his own I guess, but ever since I got sick, Junior, I mean, Emery, says no. He says I'm the only mother he needs. He's wrong, though, damn it. It's wrong. I found papers with a lawyer's name on the heading, and wrote to them to see if they knew how to contact you. Since Emery won't do it, I'll do it for him, before I can't. He needs his mother, and I'm not going to be around much longer. No one wants me to say that, but it's true."

Just then, Kristy appears in the doorway, I guess to check on her mother. "What's true, Mom? What are you two talking about so seriously?"

"Kristy, this is my business. You don't need to hover around like a nervous mother hen. Go over and tend the store for a little bit. This young woman isn't going to let anything bad happen to me. And if something does happen, she can call 911 as damn well as you can. Now, skedaddle!"

Kristy looks at me and asks, "That OK with you? I know better than to argue with her, but are you comfortable with this?"

I'm still reeling from Harriett's declaration and the "Junior" startled me even further; as I recall it was on one of the postcards. I want to hear more from her, sooner than later, so agree with the command for Kristy to go and let us talk. Hell, wild horses couldn't get me to go now. "Yeah, sure, we're good, Kristy. I'll text you when we're done and I'm ready to go." As I wonder to myself, *Will I ever be ready to go?*

She walks out shaking her head. Once the door slams, I ask Harriett, "How do you know? I mean what is the story? This is kind of, to say the least, a shock."

"Here's what I remember. May not have all the particulars exactly right, but I do know Emery's your son. One visit, I don't exactly recall when, your mama broke into tears when we ladies were washing up dishes. I was pregnant, and she said it made her think of her daughter. Before I knew it, she was telling me that she sent her pregnant daughter to be with her sister, Mary, until after she—uh, you—had the baby. The sister knew lots of people and somehow was setting up an adoption. Your mama wanted to go back from the fishing trip to be with you, but Mary kept telling her to stay away, to wait till the baby was with its new family. Your aunt was afraid that your mother would stop the whole thing and raise the baby herself. We cried together. Her cuz she was worried about you, and me cuz I told her she was doing a good thing for somebody. I wanted a baby so bad, but Harold and I, well, it just hadn't happened yet. I'd been pregnant a few times before, but it never took—not meant to be. So, anyway, they left and that was that."

"What do you mean, Harriett? What was what?"

"We just cried because wasn't nothing either one of us could do about our sadness, but sit and cry. Made us better friends, though." I watch those tiny hands twist a frilly handkerchief into the tiniest ball, while she sits quietly staring at them.

I don't want to push her, but I still don't know what the story is. Just as I lose patience, she finally continues, "Then something happened. Something didn't go right with the plan. I don't exactly know what, not sure, but not long after they left, I got a phone call from Maggie. Crying again, not making a lot of sense, but said the adoption wasn't going to happen."

Huh. Mr. Barbour said that there was a lot of preliminary adoption work that had been done, but that his records didn't show the adoption ever happening. So how did Harriett...?

"Something came over me, and I started begging. I begged her to let Harold and me have the baby. I hadn't even told Harold yet, but I hadn't felt our baby moving for a few days and was afraid I was losing this one too. I told Maggie it was perfect, because she knew me, she knew I'd take care of him. Told her we'd do anything. We'd come get him. It was the best solution in my mind. She said no way, she didn't think it would work. Three days later, out of the blue, your parents showed up at our door with a beautiful baby boy. They made me a mother that day, just a couple of days after I'd lost another of my own."

What the freakin' hell? Is this real? They showed up at her door?

"After they left, I kept in touch, though not too often. Your mother didn't want anyone, especially you, to find out about this. I thought it was weird, since she'd been using a lawyer before that, and I asked more than once when we'd get the papers, but then I stopped asking her. No one here paid any attention or asked any questions because they'd seen me pregnant again, and this time there was finally a baby. We filed with the state for a birth certificate for a home birth, named him Emery. Emery was our son, and I didn't honestly care anymore about adoption papers, and if I was happy, Harold was happy. A few years later, we had Kristy and we stopped being in touch with Harriett and Harold after they visited one more time. Emery was about three. I think you were off to college, so they came down to see him. Your mama was happy at first to see him, but then said she couldn't do it again, that she couldn't watch him and not want to be with him more. She wasn't going to come back, and I should stop writing to her. She wanted a 'clean break.' I wasn't going to rock that boat."

Silence settles over the room. Harriett is staring out the window again, looking exhausted, and I think I only started breathing again a few seconds ago. Can a person hold their breath that long? No. I was in some type of trance. Harriett's words, everything after proclaiming me to be her son's biological mother, have not registered. They are like word stew, and I've had no time to digest it all.

No time for making sense of it all, the question out of my mouth cuts to the chase—all I really want to know, "Harriett, where is your son, Ev--I mean, Emery?"

"Not really sure. He left about a week ago, saying he had to take care of a few things, but would be back as soon as he can. He'd been here for a few months, but he missed his Beth, and had to attend to his other job. Helping out at the shop doesn't pay all his bills, but he did it to help me, help Kristy. He's a good boy, well, man."

She goes silent again, then starts coughing. She reaches for her water, but tips it over when the coughing becomes even stronger. I run to get more from the kitchen, and as if she sensed something to be not quite right, Kristy comes through the door. Hearing her mother, she hurries into the sitting room. Harriett settles back down, looks toward me, and takes command of the situation. "So, Larissa, I'm glad you came. It was good to talk about your mother. Thank you for letting me know about her last few years, she was a good friend. Maybe you can visit again another day and bring me those postcards. I really don't remember much about them. Maybe Kristy would like to see them?"

Well, I guess I'm being dismissed. There's so much more I want to know, but it's not happening now.

Kristy nods her head toward the kitchen, indicating I should follow her out there.

"Listen, Larissa, I know I practically forced you to come over here, but as you can see, she's had enough. This is a long time for her to have a visit. Did you enjoy talking to her? She can be a character when she gets going, but she wears out quickly."

Enjoy? Well, not the first word that comes to mind, but then, my mind is not really functioning at the moment. I just need to keep this calm and neutral, to honor Harriett's wishes about Kristy knowing nothing, at least for now, till I understand this all better. "Yes, it was a pleasant bit of reminiscing. I'd like to do it again—come over again in a few days? As soon as she's up to it?"

"Sure, I can let you know. It's different day to day. But I think she liked seeing a face other than mine, so that's a good thing. I'll be in touch."

"One other thing, Kristy. She mentioned your brother, and I know you've said a couple of times that he's away. I don't want to intrude on all of you when he first returns. Do you mind me asking when he's coming back?"

"Well, he's not been too sure of his plans. Or, let's just say the plans keep changing. He was pretty torn between being here with Mom and being there with Beth. Not easy splitting his time. I think he wants to come back next week, hopefully, bringing Beth with him, if it works out."

"Sounds like he's got a lot on his own plate and is then trying to juggle someone else's schedule."

"Yeah, well, he's pretty much figured out how to manage his own work, but Beth's schedule is trickier."

"Not everyone's work is flexible. Thankfully my boss is understanding about family stuff and working around it. That's the only reason I'm able to be down here. I hope your brother and his wife can get back down here soon, though. I think your mother's looking forward to that." To say nothing of me; I've got to figure out a way to see him, to talk to him. My hope is that Harriett will encourage him, push him a little harder to contact me, to get in touch, before she, well, before she loses her chance to influence him.

"Wife? No, he isn't married."

"Sorry, I didn't mean to assume. I just hope Beth can come with him, get her work straightened out." With that, I realize I should leave and text Eric to come get me. The more we talk, the more I risk blowing the confidences that Harriett shared with me.

As I wave, say my goodbye, and start to back out of the door. Kristy waves and adds, "Ha-ha—no, Beth is his daughter. She's about to be on school break, so he decided to wait for that before coming back."

24

Sometimes you get what you want. Other times you get a lesson in patience, timing, alignment, empathy, compassion, faith, perseverance, resilience, humility, trust, meaning, awareness, resistance, purpose, clarity, grief, beauty, and life. Either way, you win.
Brianna Wiest

I stumble down the street, trying to walk as fast as I can to a park I saw when we were here last week. I need to get away from the house, just sit and, what, organize my thoughts? What the heck just happened? I walked in that house expecting to hear about my parents' vacations, and walked out with a connection to my son, to Everett, to Emery? And what, Beth? A granddaughter? I'm shaking and grab at the bench so as not to collapse when I sit down. Once seated, I just want to run back there. Run back in the door and ask for more. Ask Harriett and Kristy to tell me all about Everett, all about Beth, where are they? How can I reach him? I need to know. I want to know.

But I don't run back. I close my eyes and envision roots growing out of my thighs. Roots that will wrap themselves around this bench and hold me in place, away from the house filled with details I crave, until my rational brain has time to kick in. I must hold on to this bench, stay put, and reason my way to a plan that has some chance of success. If I let my heart rule, let myself storm back in the house screaming for more information, I may lose any chance of having this go well.

"Mom, Mom, what are you doing sitting here by yourself? Are you OK? Why didn't you text us? We were starting to wonder what was going on. Did you forget I gotta take Hilary to the airport? We need to get back so she can change and pack and, wait... are you OK?" Eric stoops down next to the bench to look into my eyes, then shakes my forearm. "Mom?"

I make eye contact, open my mouth, but then I cover my face with my hands and rub my eyes, then my forehead, pull my hair up off my neck, let it down. I want to tell him everything, and I want to say nothing.

"Let's go, let's get back so you guys can get ready to drive to the airport." I pull myself up off the bench, with all the effort I can muster, and ask, "Where's the car?"

Eric points to the parked car, raises his shoulders as if in question, and then starts walking toward it, with Hilary and me following closely behind.

They each try asking me about the visit, but all I can manage to get out is, "Not now, all right?" Staring out the window as we go over the bridge, dozens of questions bombard me. Most of them are jumping the gun, putting the horse before the cart, getting way too far ahead of myself. Until I find out if and when I can get in touch with Everett, Emery—I need to keep repeating *Emery*—the rest of the questions are useless, a total energy drain.

And what do I do now? Could Harriett be wrong? No, no way. The bits and pieces may not hang together yet in a perfectly concise story, but they definitely line up with Mr. Barbour's bits and pieces. Suppose there was something else going on? What about if the adoption wasn't even legal? Does anybody even care at this point? Ugh—more useless questions.

As we pull in the driveway, Eric tries again, "Mom, what's going on? We have to leave in, like, twenty minutes. Are you OK to be alone, do you want to ride along? We could drop Hilary and then eat somewhere on the way back. Maybe someplace we haven't tried yet?"

"I'm OK, really. I'm exhausted is all and need some time to myself. I'll be fine. I've been fine on my own a lot more than you know." Damn, I wish I could take that back. I don't want to make him feel bad about things in the past; I just want him to be on the road with his friend so that I can, what? What am I going to do?

Trying to lighten things up, I offer, "How about you text after you've dropped Hilary off, and I'll call in an order for takeout that you can pick up?"

We agree on that dinner plan. Hilary thanks me for her time visiting, gives me a hug, and waves as she says, "Take good care of yourself. I know the next couple of weeks will be tough. My family's been through that one-year thing. You and Eric take care of each other."

I keep a smile on my face during the time she's waving and hugging, but then once she's gone, I start to pace back and forth from kitchen to great room to porch. The nervous energy that has built up from the time Harriett started the story until now is unbearable. I need to head out to Adele's secret garden for some time to myself, or to the beach, or out on the dock. Just get outside and breathe. I walk toward her little garden sanctuary, but then even that sweet space feels too contained. I stride right through it, around the back and toward the dock. I pick up a folding chair along the way and carry it out to the very end.

When I get to the end of the dock, I put the chair aside and drop down to sit on the wind-worn wood and dangle my feet in the water. Questions and what-ifs pop up to clutter my thoughts. *What if Emery won't agree to meet me? What if he hates me? What if he agrees to see me, but once he hears what a lousy job I did with Emma, he won't let me near Beth? What if Eric overwhelms him?*

My head starts to pound with the intensity of this. I knew this journey to find Everett would be strewn with rocky detours, but now that I'm so close, it still feels insurmountable. I need to focus on a plan, I need to clear away these toxic thoughts of self-sabotage and see possibility instead of roadblocks. There's much to be grateful for from the conversation with Harriett. Her somewhat vague memories are enough to work with. They are more breadcrumbs leading me to my son, I'm sure of it.

I feel a couple drops of rain but don't want to move. Why do we automatically run inside the second it starts to rain? I look up at the sky to let the raindrops pelt my face. Bring it on. More rain, harder. Pelting raindrops to soothe my pounding head. The fresh rain begins to mix in with my salty tears, diluting them, taking away the stinging. I allow them to splash a refreshing cleansing on a face that has been tense and salt-stained for too many weeks; hell, most of the year.

The act of not running from the rain, of letting myself be drenched by the warm rainwater, is a restorative act. My clothes are soaked and stuck to my body, cooling me slightly as the breeze hits the wet fabric. I sit absorbing the wetness, relishing in the feeling of being cleansed by nature rather than by store-bought, scented soaps.

Rays of sun emerge from behind the clouds, and I wait. I know to the depth of my being what is going to happen next.

On cue, the haziness transforms into the spectacular colors of a rainbow. How is it that something which is always the same—the colors of the rainbow are consistent no matter what—brings such awe and amazement when it happens?

I'm transported to the last time this happened. A time in New York when Renee and Isabel had raced back ahead of me to avoid rain, while I lingered on the trail, set on enjoying as much outdoor time as possible. The rainbow brought me peace then, and I allow it to happen again today. The rainbow reminds me there are souls dancing above, reaching out with arms of beautiful colors to reassure me, to make their presence known, to guide me. The reassurance helps me reframe today's unexpected developments. Rather than allowing myself to churn inside with negative what-ifs, I will gather my resilient spirit and figure out how to navigate the newest of many unknown waters.

Bolstered by my time on the dock under dark rainclouds that, with their own changes, cleansed me of negativity and brought me renewed energy, I go back to the house to make my to-do list and get back on track. No, it's not getting back, it's heading toward a long-wished for destination. First on the list is calling Mr. Barbour.

As I start to provide my personal information to the receptionist, she stops me and says she will put him right on the line.

"Larissa, I was going to get back to you today."

I have no time for his legal formalities. On a mission, I dive right into my story. "Mr. Barbour, I have some more details to share with you. Important details."

Relating the story of Harriett, her relationship to my parents, and my conversation with her, I summarize it all with, "And so, I think your investigation into whether that letter is legit or not should no longer…"

"My dear, I agree, no need to continue on with another of your long stories." I don't know which ticks me off the most—addressing me as "dear" or the "long story" reference—but through my annoyance, it registers with me that he also said he agrees with me.

"You do? OK, so tell me what you're thinking."

"It's me that has some pieces of information that add to your long story. As soon as you said the name Harriett, I was pretty sure this was all coming together. Then, when you added the town, well, this letter in my files is from the same person you were speaking to—no doubt. Well, one of the letters, anyway."

"One? She did say that she'd been trying to find me. I wondered if she meant she had written letters, but then when she told me how my parents brought my son to her, I didn't know if she knew anything about you, or rather, your office. Anyway, you have more than one? Can you help me here?"

"Yes, I think I can clear up a lot. Let's start with Harriett's letter first. I was hesitant to let you count on this being the person connected to your son—first, because it was a Florida address. I had my doubts that your son would have gotten from a tiny, rural town in upstate New York all the way to some little fishing town in Florida. Adoptions between states were pretty rare, and our firm didn't typically do them. Now that you tell me her name, her town, and then her story of your parents showing up with the baby, it's making more sense than it did when I first came upon the letter."

"OK, so now we are on the same page, I think. I have a ton of questions, no clue who can answer them, but maybe they're not important at the moment. She told me that her daughter, who is the one who connected her and me, knows nothing about this, and that Everett, or Emery, once started to search for his parents on his own, but changed his mind when Harriett got sick. But if we're pretty sure it's him, then I'm going to find a way to see him, or speak with him, or something."

"One more thing, Larisssa. There's a second letter from Harriett, and she sent something else with it."

"Like what? I'm not sure I can take any more twists and turns in this saga."

"I wouldn't call it a twist or turn. I'd call it confirmation. It could have been a real problem years ago, but I don't see how it changes anything much at this point, except to give more information. There's another letter she enclosed, told me it is for her son, uh, your son, in case she can't convince him to be in touch with you."

"OK, I'm listening."

"Well, there's a letter addressed to the adopted boy from a nurse. It's technically not yours, and it's fairly lengthy—but, in her note, Harriett asks me to get it to you if circumstances, uh, make that necessary. So, I suppose I can mail it to--"

I can't take this hemming and hawing anymore. "You know what, Mr. Barbour, I'm getting on a plane as soon as I can. I'll be in your office tomorrow. I don't trust the mail, I'm not sure I can tolerate a long reading, I want all of this information in front of me. I need to see it with my own eyes. Please plan on seeing me upon my arrival." And I hang up before he can say another word. I'm not sitting here over a thousand miles away and waiting one more minute.

Opening the airline app on my phone, I find a flight and book it. It leaves Palm Beach in a little over three hours, and I'm going to be on that flight. Throwing a few things in a bag, not really giving a shit about what I have to wear, it dawns on me that Eric has the car. I have no clue where he is in his airport run with Hilary, so call him as I latch my bag up.

"Eric, where are you? Are you on your way back?"

"I just dropped her. Are you getting hungry already? Good—maybe you snapped out of whatever was bugging you?"

"Eric, listen to me. I need to get to the airport as soon as I can. I can't wait for you to get all the way back here. I also need to talk to you, in person. How about if I get a ride from a car service and meet you somewhere about halfway between here and the airport? Like maybe Jupiter? Save your questions; I gotta make the request on my app and get going."

"Um, well, yeah, I guess. This is weird, Mom, but whatever."

He gives me the name of a restaurant we'd been wanting to try in Jupiter, and we agree to meet in the parking lot.

"See you soon, Eric. I love you. Thank you. Drive carefully!"

The app says the driver will be here in thirteen minutes. Not bad, I guess, but it seems like forever. I just want to get to freaking Schenectady; I'm tired of phone calls and letters and emails and waiting for everyone else to make a move. I'm going up there, getting the letters—the whole damn file, cuz who knows what else is hiding in that pile of papers—and getting back here to see Harriett and our shared son.

While I wait, I text Renee, Isabel, and Steven. Just the facts: I'm on my way to Schenectady to see the lawyer; I'll try to send an email while on the flight to tell them more; don't call because I'm rushing; add a series of OXOX so they know we are all right. They are my family of friends and have been along every step of the way, and I want them along now. I'll tell them in the email that I'm only staying a day or two and ask them to come visit next week for the one-year remembrance of Emma. That's what I'm calling it—a remembrance day. I hate every other way I've heard it described. I don't want to have to describe it at all, but that's the best I can do with the situation. And I now know that I want them here if they can make it. I want to be surrounded by their support as I try to expand my family with my son and granddaughter's presence and remember my daughter. I need them all.

The driver is chatty enough to keep me from being a nervous wreck and clock-watching, but not at all obnoxious. Once in the parking lot, I see our car, with Eric waiting at the wheel.

"Geez, Mom, get in and tell me what the hell is going on. Never thought I'd be driving to the airport twice today—especially to take you. And uh, don't faint when you look in the back seat."

What's he talking about? As I open the back door to toss my bag in, an oh, so familiar voice says, "I don't know what the fuck is going on, but you totally ruined my surprise. Where are you going? I thought you were so in love with this place that we'd never see you again—decided I'd better come to you." Renee has her hands out in front of her, palms turned up, to emphasize her question.

Not to be slowed down by anything, I jump in the front seat and tell Eric to head toward the airport and I'll explain.

I launch into a version of the meeting with Harriett. In trying to be concise, I must be missing things because they, especially Renee, stop me at least seven times with questions. Or maybe it's that the story still has some fairly big gaps that we haven't solved yet.

"Listen, guys, there are plenty of details still missing, so let me just get through the rest—like, I thought you'd like to know the reason I'm getting on a plane."

As they nod their heads in synchrony, I explain, "Once Mr. Barbour heard about the meeting with Harriett, he realized there was no reason anymore to wait until he heard back from his inquiry. He revealed that while my story and the one he'd gotten from her letter were very similar and may have matched, he'd still been concerned with the combination of a Florida address and a lady with a fading memory. He's not a bad guy, just cautious and trying to protect everyone as much as he can at this late date with so many people not around any longer. But when he told me about another letter in the file, and a note on that one from Harriett to me, and offered to mail it to me, I just told him I was coming to get it. I don't want to wait for the mail, I don't want it read to me while I wonder if he's leaving things out. I want the file myself, and I want it fast. So, now we're just ten miles from the airport, my flight is on time, and I'm going to get it first thing tomorrow morning."

There is a mile or two of silence. Eric and Renee must be processing all of this. Then, Renee comes up with, "Eric, while there's all of this story dumping going on, I think you'd better tell your mom your news."

Looking as if he'd been shaken out of a deep spell, he offers, "What? Oh, yeah, well, Mom. The girl on the DNA website answered my email. She wants to contact Dad, and she wants to meet us. I'm going to videochat with her tonight. I thought you'd be home so we could do it together, but, well, you gotta do what you gotta do. I'm still going to talk to her. I can't wait! I hear ya when you say you can't keep waiting for the right time or whatever. You go get the scoop on my brother while I meet my sister. How wild is that?"

Wild? Surreal? Serendipity? There are no words.

Renee throws in, "All right, you guys: fast decision. I just checked and there are a couple of seats left on your flight, Larissa. Where do you want me? With you or here with Eric in case he needs, well, I don't know. Do you want me here, Eric?"

"I want everyone all together in the same place. But I know I can't always get what I want. So, I say you go with Mom, keep her company, and then both get back here. I'm OK alone a couple of nights, but I don't want to be alone, on, uh, well, you know. On Emma's day."

"Booked! I don't remember the last time we flew anywhere together, Larissa, but I'm your companion today."

We hug Eric, say our goodbyes and make our way through security with an hour till boarding. Probably the fastest plans I've ever made and executed, and I've still not gotten around to asking Renee anything about her plans.

We walk over to the sign showing the airport amenities, and in silent agreement, head toward the first place that has wine available to fill one another in as much as possible before boarding.

25

*Something very beautiful happens to people
when their world has fallen apart:
A humility, a nobility, a higher intelligence emerges
just at the point when our knees hit the floor.*
MARIANNE WILLIAMSON

"I never got to properly thank you and Isabel for the quilt. It's stunning, quite literally. Every square brought me back to when Emma first got the garment or a special time she wore it. I wrapped it around me and didn't unwrap it for almost twenty-four hours. Thank you, thank you. When I got a chance to call you, I was going to tell you guys to come down, but somehow, I never made that call. I'm sorry, but I'm glad you just made the plan without me and got here. You and Eric plotted to surprise me?"

"We did. And Isabel too. But at the last minute, Bobby got sick and, of course, Hank is out of town. She's so disappointed, but she had no choice. When I let Eric know my flight, it worked out perfectly because his friend—is it Hilary?—had to go to the airport about the same time. He didn't even have to make up some kind of excuse to come get me. And what's the deal with Hilary? Are they, well, involved?"

She's clearly disappointed that I really don't know, and proceeds to ask me more questions. I'm saved by the overhead announcement for our plane to board. I'm relieved, because I'm not sure I could handle any delays or cancellations. I had enough of those the last time I traveled to New York to last me a lifetime!

Thanks to a kind gentleman willing to trade seats, Renee and I settle into our seats. I remembered I'd promised an explanatory email to Steven and Isabel, so I purchase the Wi-Fi to be able to keep my promise. I draft it all and let Renee read it, because who knows if I've explained it clearly?

"Hey, I didn't know that the other letter was from a nurse addressed to Everett. You left that out when you told Eric and me. What's that all about?" Renee never misses a thing.

"I don't know, but that's kinda what put me over the edge on the phone. I don't want Mr. Barbour to be screening these documents and only telling me what he thinks I should know. There's been enough of that already. I'm claiming it all. He may balk, because it's addressed to Everett, but I think my advantage is that the mother, Harriett, also wrote on it that he should get it to me if our son doesn't agree to meet me before she gets the chance to convince him. She thinks the home-care workers are trying to prepare Kristy for her last days. I don't know, though, she seemed pretty good when I saw her."

"Maybe she's rallying to get you all to do what she wants, before she passes on?"

"Yup, you're probably right. Renee, she's set on getting us together, and he's set on not. A battle of the wills. Oh, my gosh, I did leave out something else really important. I'd better add it to the email and fill you in. Emery/Everett has a daughter, Beth.

I guess I'm a grandma." As I utter the name *Beth* to Renee, the realization comes to me: if my granddaughter's name is Beth, more than likely it's Elizabeth. How is this just registering in my muddled brain now? Elizabeth is the name I wanted to give the daughter that Steven and I never had!

The impact of this realization breaks me. I choke, and cry, and put my head in my hands. Renee reaches toward me and pulls my hands close to her. "You got this, Lissa. You're going to get through all of this bullshit and get to your son and granddaughter. I know it. I know it as certainly as the sun will come up in the morning. You will succeed. And if you don't on the first try, I may lose all control and be like a mad dog breaking a short leash with that lawyer. I got your back, my friend."

I silently squeeze her hand three times. Right on cue, she squeezes mine four times. "I felt so privileged when you let me in on the secret of your code." When my kids were little, we made up a hand signal: three squeezes for *I love you* and then four in return, for the message of *I love you too*. I shared it with Renee after Emma died, when I was hoping that Eric would return soon. We hold hands for the rest of the flight.

Searching online while taxiing to the gate, we find a hotel only five miles from the lawyer's office. After quickly changing into our pajamas and ordering room service, we crawl into our beds and re-cap the latest developments once again.

Just as we're about ready to turn off the light, Isabel calls and we put her on speaker phone. "Larissa, I don't know what to say about all of this, except, *wow*, just *wow!* But I'm so glad that Renee made it in time to go with you up to Schenectady. This is all too much to handle on your own. You need another set of ears and eyes on your side. If Bobby was better, I'd give Hank no choice but to have additional time with the kids, and

I'd hop on a plane myself to join you guys. Three of us could be sure that Mr. Barbour doesn't give you any hassle. You've been through enough."

"Well, I think Renee has been plotting against him since the story began, so I appreciate, so very much, that you want to be here, but Bobby needs you. When a kid is sick, it's mama's hugs he needs. You be there, and we'll keep you posted. I plan to be able to tell you sooner rather than later that we got what we came for and we're on our way home!"

A text arrives from Eric just as I'm about ready to turn out the light for the second time. I start to hit the call button, then read his text more carefully. He is reassuring but concise: "Did it. Talked to my sister Nina! It was awesome but too late to tell you about it now. Good luck tomorrow. oxox"

Finally, I'm lying under the covers, hoping that sleep comes soon. I thought I'd have too much on my mind, but I must have drifted off quickly because the next thing I know I'm hearing an obnoxious sound. Totally confused, I squawk, "What the heck is that sound?"

From the bathroom, Renee calls out, "Oh, like my ring tone? It's supposed to be a train—like a choo-choo train whistle."

"Renee, it's a good thing I like you, because I freakin' hate that sound. That awful sound had better not be a curse on our day."

She laughs and replies, "Got you up, didn't it? Let's get rolling. You said you wanted to be at the office when Mr. Barbour got there. Let's go get coffee and get our butts over there."

The lobby has an outside patio, so we wander out to a table to sip and use up a little time until the office opens. As we sit down, something rather shiny on the ground catches my eye, a dime. Bending over to pick it up, I mutter, "I could have used a penny from heaven, Renee. That would be a sign, don't you think? A sign that things are going to go well today."

Before Renee can answer, I turn the coin over to read the date and see it's 1982. The year Everett was born. Showing it to Renee, I suggest, "I guess this is better than a penny from heaven. A dime from my son. Let's go, my friend."

The front desk attendant arranges a cab for us, and we are at Barbour's law office, sitting on a bench in front, when someone arrives to open the main entrance. I offer my name and add, "Mr. Barbour is expecting me." Not entirely sure he is, but it provides the air of authority I want to project.

"Yes, actually, he mentioned someone might be here waiting. I just got a text from him that he's on his way and will be here in ten minutes. Can I get you coffee while you wait?"

She politely shows us to the conference room with a coffee nook where we can fix our own brew to our liking. A lucky dime, a polite reception experience, now all I need is Mr. Barbour to be open to my requests.

As we stir our coffees, Renee says, "I guess I should ask you if you want me in there with you or if you want me to wait in the lobby. It's your son, your life, and I know this isn't easy. I'll do whatever you want."

"Remember our hand squeeze, Renee? I want you in here with me. No doubt about it."

Mr. Barbour arrives at the appointed time, we shake hands, and I introduce Renee. I take a deep breath, clench my fingers under the table, and begin, "I know you have had some reservations about the propriety of all of this, of me seeking documents, but I want, I deserve--"

"Larissa, listen to me. I told you yesterday, maybe you didn't hear me, I agree with you. It's time to clear some of this matter up. My hesitancy all along was to try to discern the veracity of the information that we have, in order to protect everyone involved. And let's face it, there are quite a few players in this scenario. But

I have no intention of making this any more difficult on you than it has been. I've reviewed our files, and since one version or the other of your name is present in the documents, I believe I can legitimately share it all. I may not have answers to the additional questions you might have, but I'll do my best, within the limits of my expertise, to try to help you or steer you to someone who can. OK?"

"Yes, thank you. Unless you have another idea, can you show me this other letter you told me about yesterday? Can we start there?"

"We can. The interesting thing is that the envelope reads 'To: Emery Everett' in Harriett's writing on the outside, and the letter inside the envelope, from the nurse, is addressed: 'To: Everett.' Then, at what is presumably the end of the nurse's letter, in Harriett's writing again, is a note to 'Mr. Barbour or Larissa or Emery Everett.' In her cover letter, Harriett gave me permission to open it all if it helped get the contents to the people she wanted to reach."

I feel, then see, my hand shaking as I take the yellowed papers from him. I scan the pages just to better understand what he has already told me, then return to page one to begin reading it carefully from start to finish.

Dear Everett:

Let me be clear. I should not be doing this. I have been what they call a "baby nurse" for many years and certainly know the privacy rules when a child is going to be placed with adoptive parents shortly after birth. But once I broke (I prefer bent), the first rule and let your mother not only see you, but also touch you, what difference does it make if I go further?

Why did I bend the rule and allow Laura to see you? It was her fear and her sweet face. She was so young, and so alone. I'm sure the woman who dropped her off, I think she was an aunt, meant well, but the girl was too young to be doing this all on her own. I doubted her name was even Laura, but that's all I had in the papers from the lady.

Anyway, Laura was almost silent, stoic during your birth. Immediately after, she could not stop crying. I kept offering her medication for the pain, and she kept telling me her pain was nothing the medicine could help. Kind of strange words for a teenager, but I finally figured out she meant it was emotional pain. She didn't want to give her baby to anyone else. She wanted her baby. She wanted you.

Once the birth was over, the other nurse and doctor walked out to attend to other patients. I was still in the room with you and your mother. She reached toward you and asked me to move you closer. In a weak moment, I saw no harm in just walking over next to her, so she could see. Then an ethereal look came over her face and she begged me to let her touch you. For a moment, I was drawn in and doing what I always do—allowing a mother and child to bond. As she touched you, she whispered, "I love you, little Everett. I always will."

Her words startled me back into my proper role: I shouldn't have let her see you, no less touch you. I put my hand gently on her shoulder, said I'd be right back, and delivered you to the nursery. Another nurse was ready to bathe you and carry on with the standard newborn evaluation. I didn't want to leave your mother alone for long, so went right back in. As I walked in, she said, "Thank you, thank you. My baby is beautiful, isn't he?"

I nodded my head in agreement and choked back my own tears to maintain some shred of professional demeanor. Before I could say anything else, she told me that she looked up baby names and decided you should be Everett, because you would need the strength and bravery that the name carries. Nodding again, I assured her, "And that will always be his name. He may be called others, but he heard that first."

She nodded but then started crying. The doctor had ordered sedatives as needed, and I thought she should have some relief from her agony. She fell fast asleep and I went out to complete the paperwork for a birth certificate. She said "Everett" and that's what I put on the form, along with the name in her chart, Laura Miller.

I never saw the adoptive parents, but when I saw in the chart that it was your discharge day, I decided to take the chance, a stupid chance, and write this letter to tuck in your bag. Whoever found it may be angry and rip it or burn it, or whatever. On the other hand, maybe someone will save it for you. I hope so. You should know that she loved you dearly, she picked a name for you. You are not a child that was adopted because your mother didn't want you. Far from it. You were adopted because someone loved Laura in a way that ruled out her being a young, single mother.

Not signed—of course not. So, it wasn't my imagination running away at the time, or changing things over the years. The nurse did let me hold my son. I hadn't been sure until this moment that my recollection was right, but my memories match this description perfectly. How in the world did this note make it to Harriett? I look up at Mr. Barbour with the question evidently written all over my face.

"Remember to read the part in Harriett's writing, Larissa, it explains some of what you might be wondering." He points to the letter as a gentle reminder that there is more to this piece of history.

To Mr. Barbour, or Larissa, or Emery Everett:

I'm sure you're wondering how I got this note from the nurse that delivered Emery Everett. Truth is, I don't rightly know. I can't answer all of that question because I don't know all of what happened between the time it was written and the time our son arrived at our home.

Here's what I can tell you. Larissa's mother and father showed up at our doorstep with their grandson. They didn't tell us details because they said it was "better for the baby and us not to know." They said the planned adoption didn't work out, and that they thought Harold and I should have you. They were afraid that if too much time went on, they'd change their minds and be tempted to keep the baby. Said that wouldn't be good for their daughter. They felt the best thing for everyone was for the baby to go to us because they knew and trusted us. I'm guessing they just wanted to do it before they lost their nerve.

They brought bags and bags of baby things. They didn't want him to lack for anything. A few days after they left, I found the note from the nurse folded between receiving blankets in the bottom of one of the bags. After Harold and I read it, we were stunned. First, that nurse took a big risk for a reason. She saw something she'd not seen before and was moved. Second, by then, we had named you Emery. We liked the sound of the name, but we'd liked its meaning even more: strong, brave, industrious. How could it be that your teenage mother had named you Everett because of its meaning, and thirteen hundred miles away, a few days later, we'd also found a name with that meaning? That's not just coincidence. From that day forward, you were Emery Everett, sometimes Junior for short.

I saved the letter, not knowing when or if I would ever share it, but it's important now. Emery, you said you don't need any mother but me. You're wrong—you need us both. I don't know how much longer I'll be around, but if there's one thing I want to make sure happens, it's that you and your first mother have the chance to know and love each other. That is my wish. Love, Mom/Harriett

I hand it all to Renee, I've got no words to try to explain the contents to her. I stand up to pace, but my racing heart and the spinning in my head cause me to sit right back down. I feel profuse sweat running down my neck, back, and forehead.

Mr. Barbour strides across the room, quickly, to grab me water. "Here, take this. Just sit still for a minute and breathe deeply. It's a lot, but it's what you're looking for. It's confirmation that the lady you spoke to is the lady who wrote this letter. There are missing details, and we may or may not ever be able to fill in the blanks, but you have the identity figured out. While this record is incomplete, I've made copies for myself, so that you can take the originals. Take the originals, Larissa, and let them guide your next steps. Let the record, your heart, and your brain work together. My work is done."

Renee has just finished reading and exclaims, "Holy shit! We found him, Lissa, we found him!"

I collect myself enough to respond, "Not exactly, Renee. Kristy and Harriett haven't said where he is, but he's supposedly coming back from wherever to Port Salerno sometime very soon. Guess it's time for us to turn around and get back there. Get close as I can possibly be."

We thank the lawyer, check our watches, and agree to go get lunch and figure out return travel. As we enter the lobby, two men stand up and walk toward us. What the heck? Steven? Jimmy?

"Larissa!" Jimmy half runs, half walks over to me with open arms and flings them around me. I've no idea when I saw him last—definitely more than twenty years. I happily hug him in return, and look over his shoulder to see Steven smiling and reaching out to us both.

Renee finds words first and asks, "What the heck are you two doing here? I'm guessing you must be Jimmy," as she holds her hand out to shake his. Then turns to Steven and says, "Long time, no see. Once again: what are you doing here? How did you know we were here?"

"I had an email from Larissa, and texted with Eric. After that, we decided that since Jimmy has been doing well at my house the last few days, we could take a little road trip today and try to find two ladies to take to lunch. What do you think?"

Once Jimmy has released me, Steven comes over, also reaches for a hug, and says quietly into my ear, "You guys look like you survived whatever news was in this guy's files. You OK?"

I nod, return the hug, and say, "Yes, we need lunch, we need to sit down somewhere other than this office, and we need to get flights back to Florida."

"OK, then, it's a plan. Our car is outside, and I looked up restaurants while we were waiting. Let's move on out to somewhere we can talk."

26

Nothing is more important than empathy for another human being's suffering. Nothing. Not a career, not wealth, not intelligence, certainly not status. We have to feel for one another if we're going to survive with dignity.
AUDREY HEPBURN

Small talk prevails in the car and until we place our lunch orders. Steven, with Jimmy chiming in occasionally, fills us in on the health issues and their trip here. Jimmy's been doing much better, and the medical team is still in the process of weighing options. Steven decided getting away for the day would be a good change of pace for them both.

"But more importantly, we figured you two could use some familiar hugs and lunch company, so we got on the road and made great time getting here."

Renee continues the lighthearted chatter by adding in, "Plus, we could really use a couple of chauffeurs about now. This trip wasn't exactly planned down to the level of locking down transportation options." We're still laughing when the food is served, and enthusiastically dig into our meals.

I'm relieved when Renee begins a factual accounting of the meeting and the letter contents. I wouldn't have wanted to fall apart and make Jimmy upset, or make Steven feel it was a mistake to come. Her objectivity saves me from falling face first into any emotional landmines. She concludes with, "So, besides wanting to get back to Eric, back to the sun and surf, she wants to get back to be around when Emery Everett returns, and probably go see Harriett again before he gets there. I'm heading back with her. I already planned to be there for Emma's remembrance day, but now I think ol' Lissa needs friends more than ever, don't you?"

Steven makes eye contact across the table and says, "We all need friends, all the time. Friends keep us going when we think we can't hold up to forces knocking us down. There's been so much going on for Larissa, for Eric, for Jimmy, and now, for another found family member: Nina." He gulps audibly, and we all wait while he pauses, seemingly to gain his composure. I'm guessing he's trying to be nonchalant, at least for Jimmy's sake, if not for his own well-being. "Eric talked with her last night, you probably know, and she and I are going to talk day after tomorrow. She told him she definitely wants to connect with me, but wants time to process their conversation before we talk. Whatever she needs, I'm on board. It's the least I can do, right? Be present for her now. Larissa, I hope more than I can say that Emery Everett will let you be present for him, and uh, for Beth."

I'm nodding in agreement more than I'm speaking today. Words are getting stuck in the back of my throat, stuck in my head, stuck somewhere between my heart and both those places, creating a silence that I've got no desire or power to fill. The nod must be enough for Steven as well. He smiles and reaches across the table to hold my hand. Then, as if on cue, Renee and Jimmy join us in holding hands. It's a circle of friends around the table, silently holding one another up against those forces Steven mentioned. I almost wish I could levitate above the table and preserve this moment with a photo. This moment of silent support and friendship deserves to be preserved and cherished, before the next thing comes along and pushes it to the far recesses of our minds.

It's the server who breaks the spell. Jimmy answers her question about dessert without hesitation, "Yes, chocolate cake, please!"

Renee decides it's time to search for flights and reads the options aloud to us. Discussion of available seats and times reveals that going straight to the airport from here will get us back to Florida late tonight. It's hard to leave our chauffeurs so soon after meeting up, but Steven says it's better for Jimmy to get back anyway; today has been the busiest day they've had in a long while, and while tousling Jimmy's hair, adds, "Hopefully, this guy will get a good nap on the way home in the car." Another round of hugs, and Renee and I are trudging back into the airport less than twenty-four hours since we'd arrived.

Checked in and through security, I have my first chance since I got up this morning to look at my phone. A bunch of texts and a call from Eric. It's only ten minutes till we board, so I text Eric first to let him know our travel schedule and ask if he will pick us up or if we should do a rideshare. He answers back immediately, saying he'll be there and asking if I've been in touch with Kristy. I scroll through the texts and see she's texted me twice, so I let him know I'll do that next and will be happy to see him tonight.

Kristy's second text has an urgency her first one did not, and it's pretty demanding. *I don't know what the hell is going on between you and my mom, but she's told me too many times she wants to see you before Emery gets here. He's coming in three days with his daughter, so can you please answer me and get over here? I'm at my wit's end with this whole mystery you've got goin' on.*

I'm so tempted to tell her. Then, self-talk and reason kick in big time. *Stop, Larissa, you know better. First, text is no way to spill this story. Second, trust your intuition. There've been too many times you didn't. Like, you should've fought back when they took your baby away, but you didn't. You should've insisted Emma stay in rehab longer than the four lousy weeks paid for by insurance. You should've reached out to Eric sooner while he was in Colorado—thank heavens that Renee got fed up with my need to let him have his time. But actually, it was the right thing. He needed to come back without me playing the guilt card, or making him feel like he was obligated to come back. This is kinda the same. Harriett, who's closest to Emery Everett, is still trying to urge him to find me. Her motherly intuition says it's worth letting him take his time. Well, at least she's been thinking that for the last three decades. Maybe the urgency in Kristy's message is Harriett now changing her mind.*

My fingers slowly and carefully type out a response to Kristy, letting her know I'm paying attention, but not revealing anything until I know what Harriett wants. "I'm about to get on a plane back to Florida. Get in late tonight. Will definitely get ahold of you in the morning." Then I add, "Hugs to your mother."

There's one more text, but I don't have time to answer it now. It's Terry, checking in. I'm not even sure what use that will be to me now, but I'll answer her when I have time, just to be polite. She did unearth the connection to Everett before anyone else, so I give her credit for that. And I wasn't exactly easy on her the last time we spoke.

The plane ride gives Renee and me time to rehash the morning meeting and lunch with Steven. She's curious about Nina, but

I have no more information than she does. Maybe Eric will fill us in on the car ride home. Just as I'm ready to tell her I want some quiet time to myself, Renee totally switches gears.

"So, what are we going to do for the Emma remembrance day? I know it's way different than her birthday, but we have to do something appropriate to salute her, right?"

"I haven't thought about it the last few days, Renee. I only just figured out I could better tolerate the thought of the date if I started calling it *remembrance*. I'm really just thinking of hanging out with whoever's here at the rental house. Maybe we can do a walk to pick up litter on the beach—Emma always got pissed off at people leaving their stuff all over where it could harm sea life or take away from the beauty of the beach. Then, maybe we just play her favorite music and watch the sunset. I'm not sure that I can handle much more than that."

"Perfect! I was going to wait to tell you, but when I was talking to Eric about him getting me at the airport, he told me Hilary and maybe Paul are coming down. Guess they found a funky boutique hotel close by. You're going to have your family of friends with you, Larissa. We all love you, Eric, and Emma. And we pray for the chance to love Everett and Beth and whoever else you want to add into the mix."

I'm touched once again by the phrase *family of friends*—that's so appropriate for how I feel. I wish it could include Steven and Jimmy, or even Nina, but that's pushing things. They have their own priorities right now. Keeping that thought to myself, I add, "And Eric might want Nate or Arnie there as well. We can talk with him tonight or in the morning. I'm not gonna say 'the more the merrier,' cuz it's not gonna be anything like merry, but I do know we'll do better if our loved ones are around. It's appropriate, because Emma loved a party. We'll do our best. Maybe she'll be watching." I glance upward, as I always do when thinking about her. "I'm going to close my eyes for a bit, Renee. Doubt I can actually sleep, but I need to rest."

"OK, my dear, you do that." She smiles, pats my leg, and it seems to me she looks relieved not to have to fill the space with conversation. Guess we both need time to reflect on our own.

A delay of our connecting flight brings me anxiety. It reminds me of my trip to New York last fall, and all the crazy twists and turns of that journey. The people I met along the way and while at the lake cottage all turned out to be good ones, ones I'll be grateful about forever, but I don't have time for any delays now. Back then, I felt I had nothing left in my life but time. Now, it's a different story. Quite the different story! I need to get back to see where this chapter is going to take us, to see if the rest of my family can become united.

The delay starts out sounding ominous—"mechanical"—but an announcement twenty minutes later relieves my stress. Whatever it was turns out to be minor and they're saying we'll be on our way shortly. The gate agent thinks they'll make up time in flight, so I text Eric and suggest he watch a flight tracker once we're in the air. I don't want him sitting at the airport half the night for no reason. The thumbs up emoji in return lets me know he got it and will be there. I'm ready to see him. The one day away feels like far more, and the last two days I was in Florida, we were both pulled in many directions. We desperately need to catch up. Wait till he hears he has a niece. There will be no holding him back.

Once off the ground, the second flight is uneventful. We arrive curbside in no time, and Eric is waiting, with Nate along for the ride.

"Good to see you, Nate. Thanks for riding along with Eric. This was a late airport run. This is my friend, Renee. We've been friends almost as long as you guys have been on this planet. She couldn't stay away once she heard Eric and I describe how much we love this place."

"Hey, welcome. Nice to meet you—hope you like it!"

Not only am I happy that Nate was along to keep Eric company, but it keeps the conversation light for the ride home. I want to talk with Eric, I want to hear what Nina said and let him know all we've found out, but not right now. I think morning, when we're all fresh, will be better than this late-night car ride.

Once off the interstate, Eric starts narrating, filling Renee in on the local lore that we've accumulated in our time here. The water views are impressive during the day, but the lighted bridges at night have a splendor all their own. She gasps as they come into view and exclaims, "I love it already. Thank you for letting me come!"

Eric doesn't miss a beat and responds, "Like we could have stopped you?" We all laugh at how well Eric knows Renee. Wild horses wouldn't have stopped her.

The porch light invites us into the beach house as if it has been our home for years instead of a little over a week. After a quick tour of the house, the back porch, and the view of the lagoon, we're back in the kitchen. I suggest, "You guys, there's so much to talk about. I feel like I haven't slept in a month. Can we hold it till morning? Have coffee on the porch and talk, or take a beach walk, or both?"

I expect some pushback, at least from Eric. He surprises me with, "Me too. I slept OK, but I'm exhausted from being on the boat all day, fishing with Nate. He took me to some really cool spots, and we caught our limit. Maybe you two will feel like fresh fish tomorrow, what do you think?"

I put my hand in his elbow, and Renee grabs his other one, so we can walk together toward the bedrooms.

Renee teases him, "I'm all in for fish dinner. Are you cooking?" He laughs, then stops at each bedroom and says his good nights. "I'll cook the fish if you cook the rest."

In unison, Renee and I respond, "You bet."

27

The world is full of magic things,
Patiently waiting for our senses to grow sharper.
W.B. Yeats

I must have forgotten to turn my phone to "do not disturb," because I hear a text break through my dream. In the dream, there's a group of us walking on the beach, looking at turtle tracks and marveling at how those little, bitty creatures make their way out to sea. One little guy makes it to the water's edge, only to be pushed back onto the beach by the next wave. Reminds me of being pushed down by waves of grief, or defeat, over the last months. I'm tempted to help him, yet remember the website warning not to. Eric and I and all our friends watch as the tiny reptile makes progress swimming along on the next wave out, then is seemingly spit back onto the beach. Yet, he perseveres. How relentless are these waves? Can't just one move in such a way as to carry him out where he needs to be? Finally, a wave of mercy embraces him, and he goes off on his own, off into that vast ocean to fend for himself. Nature sure works in mysterious ways.

I might have spent time dreaming about the baby turtle and his wave for far longer if that text hadn't pulled me into consciousness. It's from Kristy. Wow—she isn't wasting any time. Of course, she's probably been up for hours, scooping bait into buckets for the local fishermen. That would kind of distort your perception of what's too early.

I let her know that I made it home, I have a houseguest, and I'm just getting up. I end with, "Promise to get back to you in an hour."

I slide on my flipflops and go toward the stairs quietly, not wanting to wake anyone else. Too late. Renee and Eric's voices waft up from the porch, along with the smell of freshly brewed coffee.

"Morning, you two. How long you been up?"

"Holy shit, Mom. Long enough for Renee to tell me a little bit about the lawyer's office. I got a million questions."

I look over at Renee. I wish she'd waited for me. By the way she shrugs her shoulders and rolls her eyes, it looks like she can read my mind. There's no time for us to have that discussion, though, because Eric just continues on.

"Hold on a minute. I need to pour my coffee and try to catch up with you two. I'm still trying to shake off a dream of baby turtles and crashing waves, to say nothing of answering a text from Kristy already."

"Yeah, what's up with that chick? She texted me last night and again this morning!"

"Well, if Renee told you about the lawyer, you also got the drift of my conversation with her mother, right?"

"Kinda, but why is Kristy all worked up? What's the emergency?"

"The thing is, at least when I left there, Harriett hadn't told Kristy about me being her brother's biological mother. She doesn't want Kristy to know until she first convinces Emery Everett to connect, to agree to meet us. So, Kristy thinks the only reason for us to talk is the friendship between Gamma and Papa and her mother. With Harriett getting more insistent to reach me, the whole thing probably makes no sense to Kristy. I'm sure she's thinking, what's the fuss? It might even make her think her mother is sicker than she is. I don't know. Maybe I need to call her sooner than later and see what's up."

Renee chimes in, "Larissa, you texted her back. Give yourself a little space, here. Give yourself a few minutes with Eric."

"You're right, I will. But just remember, Harriett's also my, our, best connection to Emery Everett right now, so I'm not going to make her wait any longer than necessary."

Eric interrupts with, "Uh, what's with calling him *Emery Everett?* That's kind of a mouthful, isn't it?"

"Short explanation: before Harriett and Harold found out that I had called the baby *Everett*, they had named him *Emery*. Turns out the meaning of both of those names is similar. Anyway, when they found out, they started calling him both names. When they didn't, they called him *Junior*."

"OK, I'm just gonna say 'Double E' for now. Till he's around to tell us what the heck he wants to be called."

After taking a deep breath, Eric continues, "Yikes, this is all crazy, serious stuff we got going on. One of you, please finish catching me up. I feel like I'm ten miles back and you guys are ready to start driving on ahead again. Help me!" Eric dramatizes his exclamation by reaching out and making a fake crying face.

Renee picks up, evidently where she'd left off when I came downstairs. She's doing a decent job, so I just sip, listen, and resist the temptation to stroll out onto the dock and put my feet back in the water. Soon, she runs out of her narrative, and Eric's questions require me to talk about my time with Harriett before we flew off to New York. Every now and then, he interjects another expletive to show his amazement at parts of the saga, like when his grandparents showed up unannounced at the home of Harriett and Harold.

"Geez, this is like episode after episode of some drama series on streaming services. I don't know whether to be excited or be dreading the next episode, Mom. Guess I'm not telling you anything you don't know—you're living this shit." He's got a point.

I glance at the time on my phone and decide we can take a few more minutes for that beach walk and hear about Eric's conversation with Nina. "Hey, you two. I want to call Kristy, and also need to get back to Terry, but I want to hear about Nina first. Let's grab another cup of coffee and walk out there. We can hear the next episode, the one about your chat with Nina last night, OK?"

In a few minutes, we're all staring at the breathtaking view of the ocean. I wonder if it ever stops having this effect? Maybe if you live here full time? I don't know, I kinda doubt I'd ever stop being in awe. Renee and Eric, at the same time, both start to express what's in my head. "Whoa, this is gorgeous!" from Renee, and Eric adds, "Yeah, and look: no one else on the beach as far as you can see. Way cool, right?"

"I'm pretty much mesmerized every time I come out here. I stare at the waves and feel so small and, in a way, insignificant. They've been rolling in and out of this beach forever. Same with these sea turtles, season after season. These tiny, little things are born up there on the beach, and make their way to the water. Against huge odds, some get out there and keep the annual act of survival going. There must be a lesson in that. Until I figure that lesson out, all I can say is that these waves inspire me and bring a lot of comfort. They give me hope that life goes on. Maybe not every single individual life goes on as long as we wish, but life in general, life in this world continues." I hadn't consciously had those thoughts before now. Maybe it was the dream that Kristy interrupted. What was the dream telling me about life, my life, all of life?

"That is so weird, Mom. Last night when I told Nina about where we're staying right now, she said almost the same thing about being near the water. I guess she and her mom lived on one of the Great Lakes for most of her time growing up. She said she loved walking the beach there. Because the lake was so big, she'd pretend she was looking across the ocean to the other side of the world; that maybe her dad was somewhere across the waves, and if she waited long enough, he'd come along. She used the same word you just did about unexpected 'comfort' from staring at the waves."

Such a touching image of a little girl staring out at the water, much the same as I do while I'm here. While there's so much going on at once, these moments on the beach, staring at the waves, are the time for precious contemplation.

"Oh, honey, such a sweet thing for her to share with you. How did the rest of the conversation go? Think you'll meet anytime soon?"

"Yeah, probably. I'm just, well, like you kept telling me when we started this search for Double E, trying not to rush or be pushy. Trying to respect that this connection is sudden for her, for all of us. Then again, like she reminded me a bunch of times, she put her name into the DNA search site for just this reason. She wanted to find out about the rest of her family. She wanted that father to appear in her life."

After stopping to pick up a few shells, Eric continues, "Anyway, she just talked a little about her job and asked me the same. Come to think of it, she asked me a lot of questions. I guess maybe she wants to know what she's getting into? I told her—short version—about actually just finding out myself, a few months ago, that Steven is my father. At first she said something like, 'Uh, so, this guy, Steven, our, uh, Dad, is someone who just went around knocking women up and leaving 'em? Just figured out in the last couple of months that he has two kids?' I had to slow her down and give her details about the three of us. She calmed down, but it took a few minutes. I then told her, 'Listen, he's nothing like that, at least not to me. He's been awesome.' It seems like that's when we kinda turned a corner. I told her how he came to visit us in Georgia, how he helped me write my résumé and supported us both in trying to find my other half sibling. It was a really nice chat. We agreed we'd like to meet some time, sooner than later, and she wants to talk to Dad. I gave her his info, told her he's easy to talk to and excited to hear from her, and she said she's going to call him in a day or two."

"Did she say anything about her mother? How her mother feels about this contact?"

"Yeah, she told her. Said her mother was neither encouraging or discouraging; it was like 'whatever you want to do,' and their conversation was done."

"Well, your dad and Jimmy came to the lawyer's office and waited for Renee and me. He said he'd talked to you about her a little bit and that he's waiting for her to call. I sure hope she does; I think he's counting on it but doesn't want to set his expectations too high. He was also being careful about what he said in front of his brother, because Jimmy can get excited about new people, and he doesn't want him to be disappointed either." I really do hope for Steven's sake that Nina follows through. I know he wants to connect with her.

"That's cool that he drove to meet you guys. He really knows how to support people, you know? Not just sayin' this cuz he's my dad, but he's one of the good guys, for sure."

I catch a smile between Renee and Eric and ask, "What's up with you two? You got some secret? You know I hate secrets."

"We just think that you and Steven could be--"

I stop Renee before she goes any further. "I know what you think, Renee. You don't exactly keep your thoughts to yourself—at least not often. Don't be planting seeds in Eric's head. Steven is an amazing man; after all, I did fall in love with him once, and, well, it was a good thing. And we've got Eric. I'm saying that I don't have any more space in my life for whatever it is that you're thinking right now. Too many people coming and going for me to be thinking about ... whatever!" I'm absolutely serious, and they look at each other and laugh.

"Enough of this conversation. I'm going back to the house to contact Kristy and figure out what's going on with her. What are you two going to do?"

"Whatever you say, boss," is Renee's response. I let the sarcasm in her voice go, no need to acknowledge.

The phone call, not surprisingly, doesn't answer any of the things I want to know at this point. She essentially says the same thing as the other day. Emery Everett will be back to Florida, probably the day after tomorrow, and her mother wants to talk to me again. She seems a little irritated when she says, "I don't know what the big deal is, Larissa, but can you please give me a time so I can tell her when she'll see you again?"

"Maybe you should ask your mother about why she is so anxious to speak. You know, sometimes connections to the past become more important as we get older."

"I've asked her a few times, and she always gives me some line about minding my own business. I feel like a little kid who keeps being told that everything is for grownups, not kids."

Not particularly surprised at her response, I offer, "Well, it was worth a try, I guess. How about later today? I have a couple of things I need to check up on, and then I can come over. Also, I have a friend visiting, so, I'm not sure if I can come alone or not."

"Yeah, this afternoon is fine. Want to drop me a text when you're on your way?"

With that done, I just have one more text to return, to Terry. She responds that she's checking in to see how things are going. Well, that's pretty tough to answer in a text, so I ask if she has a minute to talk.

Within a few seconds, Terry's on the line. "Larissa, how are things? It's been a while since we've spoken, and I try to check in with my clients periodically to see if anything has changed."

To say things have changed is an understatement. "Yes, thanks, Terry. There have been quite a few developments since we last talked." I give her the rundown of meeting with Harriett, of the phone calls with Mr. Barbour, and then the meeting yesterday and the letter that filled in some, but certainly not all, of the gaps.

"There was a letter from a nurse at the hospital? That's, um, quite unusual. And he shared it? Although after all this time . . ." She trails off and I jump in.

"Yeah, it seems like once he heard my stories about Harriett down here in Florida and compared it to what he had in his files, he didn't seem to think there was a problem sharing."

"So, where did you say you are in Florida? I know a little about the east coast. I can't believe that your son ended up there."

"Yes, it's Hutchinson Island, address is Stuart. Harriett and her family business are in a little town nearby, with a long history as a fishing area, Port Salerno, off the beaten path. I came here because my parents used to come here. That's how the connection began."

"I'm going to be praying for you, Larissa. You've put a lot into your search for your son. From the beginning, I could tell from your voice that you love him. It would be so lovely if his mother, his adoptive mother, could help you make your wish come true, by making her own a reality as well. It could be a beautiful story for all involved if it works out. Please keep in touch."

28

We can't change people,
But we can plant seeds
That may one day
Bloom in them.
MARY DAVIS

I amaze myself that I'm able to convince Renee to stay back at the house. She and Eric decide they'll plan and cook the fish dinner while I'm gone. Thank God! It's hard enough navigating the secret-keeping from Kristy without the distraction of Renee along and her desire to be part of it all as well. I love her dearly, but need to do this myself.

Terry's words about a beautiful story swirl around my head as I drive across the bridge. I find myself going over a list of questions in my mind that might help us get to that beautiful story. What's important and what's not? To some degree, I need to let Harriett say her piece, but what else can I find out to make a connection with Emery Everett?

Harriett is waiting for me in a chair on the front porch. Kristy comes out when she hears me call out my greeting, and yells, "Well, Mom, look who's here? Betcha thought she wasn't comin', huh?"

"Nonsense, Kristy. I knew she'd come. Hope she brought those postcards for me to look at. It's been a long time, and I'd like to look 'em over."

Thank heavens I'd remembered at the last minute about the cards being her excuse for seeing me again and had run back into the house to grab them.

"I'm going to go over to the shop and get a few things straightened before Junior gets back here and yells at me for things not bein' in their place. He's hyper about stuff like that, and I don't need to hear his fussin' and cussin'. You two enjoy your walk down memory lane. Larissa, text me if you need anything. I'll come right back over."

As she goes about her business, Harriett and I go in the house. I ask her how she's doing and she gets right to it. "I'm fine. Don't need to talk about me. Emery's coming back this week, so there's not much time to figure out how to get him to meet you."

"OK, well, just so you know, I just got back from New York. A lawyer up there showed me the letter you sent him along with the note from the nurse. How did you ever get that? And how'd you find the lawyer?"

"Not sure how talkin' about that's going to get Emery to do anything, but I s'pose you have questions, too. The nurse's note, like I said in mine, was in with his belongings that your parents brought. I never had the chance to ask Maggie why she put it there. Maybe, like the letter said, she too thought the baby should know he was loved by both his mothers. And for that matter, by his grandmother. She may have given him to us, but she did that out of love for you, Larissa. She was so torn up, and her sister kept telling her what to do. I'm sad for her and you but so happy we had him to be our own—at least for all those years. Now, it's time to share."

She continues, "And about the lawyer. When your parents first brought the baby, I kept asking your mother about official adoption papers. She said she'd talk to her lawyer when she went home. Then before she left, she told me to just make him ours, forget about the papers. She promised she'd never try to take him back. I had to believe her. So, we said he was born at home and filed the forms with the county. I let the lawyer thing go, but many years later, I think maybe Maggie was getting sick, she sent me a letter. Gave me the lawyer's name and said if I ever needed to reach you after she was gone, he'd probably help. I stashed it away; kinda forgot about it. Once Emery said he refused to do anymore searching, I remembered and dug it out."

"Wow, well, you guys sure did your share of letting things go. You know, I've kicked myself over and over this year about not asking my mother the details of my baby's adoption before she died. But now, I'm convinced that even if I'd asked, she'd have made up some story or brushed me off. Makes me sorry she was so ashamed of me being pregnant, sorry I put her through so much agony."

"Larissa, I don't think it was shame that made her do it. It was how young you were. She loved you and didn't want your life ruled by one teenage mistake. But then, and I'm just guessing here, she lost her nerve to give her grandson to a stranger. At least if she gave him to us, she'd have some peace of mind and not wonder the rest of her life if he was OK."

My mother trying to do what we all try to do: the right thing for our kids when "right" is just not so clear. So, do we know what's right for Emery now?

"Larissa, I told Emery when he was in his teens that someone who loved him very much gave him to us because they trusted us to love him. I told him I'd promised not to break the confidence, but that when he reached the legal age, he could do whatever he wanted. I told him I'd be fine with him knowing his "other family." He wasn't too sure, but it changed some when he had Beth. He and his girlfriend raised her together for about a year, but then his girlfriend died in a car accident. He worried about his daughter being raised just by him. It got him thinking more about not knowing your mother, not knowing your blood relatives. I'm thinking that's when he started to search. He used some website that recommended DNA as well as requesting access to an original birth certificate. The one he'd used up until then had our names on it; wouldn't do him any good for finding anyone else. He somehow got the original and put it out there to a search company. I didn't really understand that part. Before he took any more steps, I got sick, and he stopped looking. Like I told you last time, that's when he said he didn't need any other mother. He and Beth would be fine."

"Oh, dear, Harriett, our poor boy lost his girlfriend not so long ago? How awful—way too young, way too young." I'm crying for a girl I'll never know, a son I want to know, and a little girl that I'd love to love.

"It's awful, a damn shame. They were havin' a rocky road when it happened, but nonetheless, it was so sad. Now, he's raisin' that little girl on his own. She sees her other grandmother every so often, but not enough. They're not close. I want him to meet you, but I'm not having much luck. Don't suppose I can force him. I don't know what to do."

"I know you've kept this from Kristy, but maybe she can help you convince him. She seems like a pretty straight shooter, and she wants you to be happy."

"Maybe so. I kept thinkin' that if he doesn't want to find you, I shouldn't share his business with her, but maybe it's time. Maybe we do it so Beth will have a grandmother who can do things with her. You're younger and healthier than I am. Most of the times she's seen me, I've been feelin' poorly."

"Harriett, let's call Kristy in here and get her to help you, help us to help Emery? Sometimes brothers and sisters can communicate what parents can't."

She's looking tired by all of this, but responds, "Guess so. Yeah, call her in here before I change my mind."

Kristy answers that she's just going to lock up the shop and she'll be right over. Harriett puts her head back against her chair and closes her eyes. I really don't have any idea how sick she is, or whether she is more tired than sick. It's tough to tell. Life can drag you down and she's had a lot to deal with in her time.

"What's up with you ladies? Got your postcards all sorted through? Anyone need some tea?"

Harriett's head pops up like she's had a burst of energy jolt through her. "Kristy, sit down. I got something to tell you I should of a long time ago. Just listen and don't interrupt me before I say I'm done."

Now I know for sure where Kristy got her direct, get-to-the-point communication style.

Harriett launches into the story of her lost pregnancies, and a shortened version of Emery coming into their lives. Before she can reveal my connection to all of this, Kristy exclaims, "Holy shit, are you going to break it to me now, at twenty-nine years old, that I'm not your real kid? That I'm adopted? Is that what all this secret stuff is?"

Who'd have anticipated that response?

"No, no, no ... you already know that Emery's the adopted one. You were the miracle baby for your daddy and me. No other baby we'd ever started out to have ever made it, except you. You were our gift from God, and we got Emery as a gift from our dear friends, well, actually from Larissa."

Kristy swings her head around toward me and questions, "Wait, what? From you?"

Addressed to me. Guess I need to find some words. "Uh, yeah, I was pregnant at fifteen, gave birth at sixteen, and my family thought it wouldn't be a good life for me to have a baby so young. So, somehow, and we don't have all the details, they decided that your parents should be my baby's parents. Seems like that's how they decided to solve their problem back in 1982."

Now, even Kristy is quiet. She looks back and forth from her mother to me and finally utters, "Wow." She runs her hands through her hair and just continues to look at us for what seems like a very long time.

Finally, she says, "OK, so why now? And why did you call me in here? What does Emery know?"

Harriett gives her the same accounting of what Emery knows as she gave me and finishes with, "Last time he and I talked about it, he said one more time that I'm the only mother he needs. But I want him to meet Larissa. I want both Beth and him to get to know the rest of their family. As they say, Mama knows best, right?" She winks at me as she finishes talking.

"And I've been looking for Everett, I mean Emery, for the last several months. I want to be part of his life. Eric really wants to meet him, wants to offer Emery the chance to be brothers to one another. What do you think? We, your mom and I, are wondering if you have any ideas how to convince him that the time is right. As right as it will ever be."

"Well, I'm late to this party, but if you're asking me, I think we just tell him what mom said."

29

The most beautiful things in life are not things.
They're people and places and memories and pictures.
They're feelings and moments and smiles and laughter.
                              UNATTRIBUTED

I'm back over the bridge and on the island before I know it. Smells of what promises to be a delicious dinner greet me as I walk in the door, and I'm happy to be back to hang out with Renee and Eric. Without even calling to the busy chefs, I hurry upstairs to change into my favorite tropical loungewear. I'm looking forward to a relaxing evening after the last couple of days.

"It smells wonderful in here, you two! Where are you?"

"Out back, Larissa. Pour yourself something cold and join us."

I find Renee relaxed in the boldly striped hammock overlooking the water and Eric squeezing lemon over foil-encased fish. It's a sight for sore eyes and tired brains.

"Some of the sides are in the oven," Eric says, "and we've been waiting for you to decide when to put this fish on the grill. Nate came over and coached us. He's quite the seafood connoisseur!"

We chat more about the recipe, and Renee reports on a little walking exploration that she did on her own. She found a seaside café for a quick snack around lunchtime and stopped at the Coastal Center to watch their stingray and turtle feeding programs.

As we finish dinner, Eric asks, "So, how'd it go? What else did the old lady, I mean, what's her name, have to say?"

"Harriett. Her name is Harriett. I think she told me everything she can. There's definitely still questions around exactly what happened that led up to Gamma and Papa bringing the baby here, and I'm not sure if we'll ever get all the answers. After we talked, she called Kristy in and told her about the connection to me. We asked Kristy's advice about how to tell Emery Everett--uh, Double E, that I'm here, and she sorta said, 'just do it.' Now, it's time to be patient again. He gets here in a couple of days—let him settle in. After all, he's traveling with his little girl. Then, if I haven't heard from Kristy, I'll get in touch with them at the end of the week. We've got the remembrance day to get through, and I don't know about anyone else, but I'd like a quiet day or two before that. There's been an awful lot going on and I'm exhausted."

"Agreed. Like you've said before, it's waited this long, right? And honestly, Larissa, you've made a ton of progress, considering how little information you had to go on at the start. Deciding to come here really made the difference. If it was coincidence, that's awesome. But you've made me believe over the last few months that sometimes there are other forces at work that we don't understand. The combination of finding Terry and finding the postcards are gifts from somewhere!"

Eric blurts out, "Amen to that, Renee. You rock, Mom. You've had one shitty time of it, but you got us here. This place has been awesome in so many ways. And I'm glad we're gonna be here for April eighth. Let's face it, it will suck no matter what. Might as well be here as hanging around our own house. Don't get me wrong, home is home. But I don't think you need to be in that house on that date."

I totally agree with him. If there, I'll be replaying every step from a year ago, all day long. "As long as we're talking about that lousy date, are we expecting anyone else to come down here?"

"I told Renee the other day that Hilary, and maybe Paul, are coming. But I just found out that Paul had to cancel; he got called away for work. Dad said he'd let us know tomorrow if he's coming. Depends on how Jimmy's doing. I even asked Nina, but I think it's too soon for that. Nate will probably show up at some point."

"I'm fine with any of that. Like I told you, though, let's keep it low-key. I've no idea how I'll feel. I mostly just want to get past it, get the day over with. It's nothing like when I felt compelled to celebrate on her birthday. I may just want to lay low. Maybe pick up trash along the beach like I said before, or just lounge around here. That's it for my effort." I swallow to keep the sick feeling in my stomach from taking over right now. Not sure if I'll hold it together that day, but I'm not going to let it ruin tonight.

"In keeping with low effort, I vote for take-out food; junk food is usually the most comforting anyway, at least for me. I volunteer to do the ordering. Do we need to do anything to prep, with those other folks coming?"

"Honestly, Renee, I don't think so. Maybe just be sure the beds are all made up, towels out. There's plenty of everything in the linen closet." I'm happy she's here. She expects nothing of me, and is always willing to help. "And looking at the skyline, it's about forty-five minutes till sunset. Let's get these dishes out of our way and come back out. Eric, line up the chairs so we can show Renee what a spectacular show Mother Nature puts on around this time."

In no time, we're back out on the deck facing the water, with Eric's most recent playlist of songs about sunshine and water playing softly in the background. Orange and pink hues are creeping in over the sky's crystal-clear, blue daytime vibrance. A few wispy clouds emerge to frame the perimeter of the sun.

I voice my thoughts to the others, "Oh, here it comes: the sky becomes a palette of colors, Renee. I think this is the best night since we first got here—just for you, my friend."

After a long night of star-gazing and wine sipping, no one's up early the next day. We sit around in our pajamas, continuing our chatter about the island.

"Oh, Renee—I need to show you the sweetest, little quiet spot around the side of the house. Nate told me about the lady who owns this house. Adele decorated this garden with some of my favorite symbols, winged ones, like birds and butterflies, as well as ocean-themed ones like shells and sand dollars. She believes in the spirit world and used to take her grandson out there with her to play. It has the best feel to it. Pour yourself another cup of coffee, and let's go sit out there."

Eric calls out that he's going to the bait shop, and says, "Have fun in your secluded meditation space, ladies. I'm going to get serious with my dock fishing today. See you in a while."

"This spot is totally serene, Lissa. She put a lot of love into arranging it all. I can see why you like it."

"Nate told me more about her than I knew from the owner profile. After he told me, I sent her an email to tell her how much I'm enjoying the garden's special aura. Adele's reply was, 'If you feel the aura, then you must have loved ones in the spirit world who are welcoming you to connect with them.' All I can think about is, how did I find online, out of all the places for rent on this island, the house that has this special space, whose owner found the same sort of comfort that I've found?"

Renee is quiet for a moment, then replies, "Because you were supposed to."

"It makes me think about the last time I went to see Marie, before we came down here. Can't remember if I told you or not, but we talked about things I can do to tend my own fire, to take care of myself. Being here, walking on the beach, watching the sunsets, and sitting in this little hidden spot—I've definitely been tending my own fire. It feels good. I'm content here."

After lunch, I log in to my work email for the first time in days and am relieved that there are only one or two customers who need a response right away. I take an hour or so to check that off my list, and when I'm done, find Renee back in the hammock, reading a book she'd found on one of the bookshelves in the house. She's the picture of relaxation. Beyond her, I see Eric casting his line off the dock, true to his earlier proclamation. They're finding ways to tend their own fires, too. It truly is the restful day for all of us that I was seeking.

Days like these, I really enjoy prepping a meal at my own pace, so I decide to leave my companions to their reading and fishing and putter in the kitchen. It's pleasantly satisfying to put together a familiar meal for them, one that I've prepared dozens of times over the years. The dishes are something the same when everything else has changed. Recipes handed down from my mother that she made us lovingly, I can make them for my son and my friend.

A couple of hours later, Renee finds me in the kitchen, wiping the counters down. "What are you doing working in here? I thought you were going to relax as soon as you did your work emails." She pulls out bowls and a tray. "Eric says Nate's on his way over, so I thought I'd get us something to munch on. You stop whatever you're doing and come join us outside—it's beautiful out!"

"I'd love to join you. Just for the record, I *was* relaxing. It felt really good to assemble our meal for later. I made a shrimp dish and salad. They'll go well with the fish. Both recipes that I haven't made in years. It did my soul good to be creative for a change."

"Then, perfect. You fed your soul and later you're going to feed us. I love it! Come on, let's see if that fisherman has caught anything after being at it all afternoon."

Once we heap praise on Eric for all that he's caught, we wait for Nate to come teach him how to filet and get the fish ready to cook. There's enough for tonight as well as fish sandwiches for lunch tomorrow.

I see Steven's name come up on my phone and answer with, "Well, hello from the dock. We're all out here admiring Eric's talents at fishing in brackish waters. Can I put you on speaker phone, so Eric and Renee can talk, too?"

"Yeah, sure. I'm calling to see if the invitation is still on to join you guys. Jimmy's doing OK, so I thought maybe I'd bring him. But he'd rather be close to his doctor, makes him feel more secure. We have a friend who Jimmy knows well who's been certified for respite work, who can come stay with him for a few days if it still works for me to join you. I know you've got mixed feelings about the upcoming date, so thought I'd better check before booking."

Before I can reply, Eric comes over and chimes in, "Hell, yes, please come! I'm outnumbered by these women, and you need to see this place. It's got so much to do. And if you ask me, you could use a little relaxation. We've got all kinds of space."

"Great! I'll do it, then. I'll look into tickets when I get off the phone. But now I have another question, and it's for you and your mom, Eric. I don't want anyone to feel obligated, but I, um, talked to Nina."

"You did? How'd it go? Was she cool with you, Dad, or weird? I mean, not weird. Was it tough? Did you guys get along?"

"Eric, you're doing the twenty questions thing. Give me a second. So, first, it was fine. She definitely hung back in the beginning, kind of stiff-sounding. I think she wanted to hear what I had to offer. Which, I totally get. Who knows what her mom told her about me or how she's felt all these years not knowing her father? What's weird, if you think about it, is that I've got experience figuring out how to bring myself into a child's life later on: I just did it with you! Anyway, we talked quite a while then switched over to video so we could see each other. That did it. When I looked in her eyes, wow! I saw you, I saw me, I saw the connection, and whatever I said or did at that point, I'm not even sure, but she blurted out, 'Can we meet? Like sometime soon?' I was blown away."

I hear the emotion in his voice and say, "Oh, Steven, that's wonderful. Did you plan something?"

"That's my second question to you. She actually lives fairly close to where you are. Other coast of Florida, but that's only three or four hours, right? So, as long as I'm coming down there, I'm thinking . . ."

"Dad, Dad, I want to meet her too. Can she come here? Or Mom? Or, I don't know who to ask, but I want to meet her too."

Steven answers, "I don't want all that on your mother this week, Eric. It's up to her, really. If it doesn't work because of everything else going on, maybe you and I can drive over to see her. There's gotta be a way to make it work. All I told Nina was that I might be coming to Florida soon, and that I'd get back to her as soon as I make a plan."

"This house is open to anyone in our—as you said in Schenectady, Steven—our family of friends. She can stay here at this house if you think she'd be comfortable. She can come to the island and stay at the little hotel a mile down from here. Or if it's awkward for her to come at this strange time, then you guys go. Whatever works. I don't have the energy to make any decisions, but I know that nothing would make me happier than for you two to meet Nina, to be part of her life. There's no way I'm doing anything that would stop that or even slow it down. We're not promised any more time on this planet than we've already gotten. You need to see her as soon as you can." Renee puts her arm around me and just nods her head.

Steven clears his throat and half whispers, "Thank you, Lissa. I love ... um, all of you so much for being ready to welcome Nina."

It strikes me that he was ready to say something else, but I'm just going to let that go. "Steven, we're all bound together now. Nina is as much a part of this group as anyone else, unless she feels otherwise. So, yes, she's welcome."

We speculate on his possible travel options for a few more minutes and he agrees to get back to us as soon as anything gets confirmed.

After dinner, Eric and Nate go into town to have a beer with a couple of Nate's friends, while Renee and I relish the tranquility. Shortly after sunset, we find ourselves stargazing, as we have at home in Georgia, as we have when up in New York last fall. Renee offers her thoughts. "Isn't it amazing that Nina, Steven's daughter, is only four hours away from us right now? So close, and we knew nothing about her until a few short days ago. We've been looking at the same stars as she has since the time she could look up, and we didn't know it, didn't know about her. Makes you wonder, doesn't it? There's just so much we don't know. We go through life so sure of ourselves most days. But when you stare at the big, star-filled sky or miles of waves crashing onto the sand over and over, you realize how little you really know."

"Right? I feel like every day there's less and less that I really know. Other than knowing the people I want to be with, the rest is changing all the time. But even that, how many times in the last year has the configuration of *family* changed? More than I can count. It's more and more clear that the only thing we can do is enjoy the moments we have and be grateful for them. Thank you for being here, Renee. Thank you for sharing the moments."

30

Blessed are they who see beautiful things in humble places where others see nothing.
CAMILLE PISSARO

*F*irst thing in the morning, Steven calls with his travel plans. He's hoping that Nina will drive over a couple of days after he gets here. She's waiting till after the remembrance day. No one blames her for that—it would be a hard way to meet a father you've never known, a sibling, and everyone who comes along with them. That's all overwhelming enough, to say nothing of being introduced on that emotion-laden day.

After a walk on the beach, Renee and I go to the grocery store to stock up on snacks and basic supplies. Putting the groceries away, I confide in Renee. "I'm starting to feel a lot of dread, anxiety. Anticipating tomorrow, that blasted date, is totally nerve-wracking. I don't want it to come, but then, I *do* want it to come so that it's over with. Whenever I look at the clock, I think about what was happening a year ago. What were Emma and I doing on the day before at this time? How was she feeling? Ugh … it's just awful. I wish I could shut down my brain. Stop the scenarios from playing and replaying in my mind."

"Eric doesn't need the car for a while. Let's go do something. A total change of scenery, change of pace: like go to a different beach to explore, or yoga, or something. Get your head out of the dark place it keeps going."

"I don't know. Not yoga. I can't be closed in anywhere. There's a state park south of here with trails I've been wanting to go hike. Might be good to try. But if I start feeling worse, you gotta agree to come back. I don't know what I want from one minute to the next. And I can't drive. I don't trust myself to pay attention. I'm feeling that dizzy/queasy combination that the doctor called *panic*. I don't feel like I can get a full breath, and my ears are pounding. This sucks."

"No worries. You're in charge of when we come and go. Let's grab sneakers and get out. I'll tell Eric while you get your stuff."

Keeping track of our driving directions and following new trails definitely helps me; it's distraction, pure and simple, but welcome. We even see gopher tortoises slowly crossing the trail, and read that they're protected in Florida. The Loxahatchee River runs through the park, giving us an opportunity to kayak and get some much-needed physical exercise before it's time to get the car back.

As soon as we walk in the door, Eric greets us with, "You guys look hot and tired."

"Just what I needed to get my mind off its dismal path. The park has a lot to do. Maybe you can check it out with Hilary or Dad or whoever. Try kayaking and see if you can spot a gator. Can't come to Florida without seeing a gator, right? Anyway, I'm guessing you're ready to get to the airport. Be safe on that crazy I-95 and get your passengers back here safely. We're going to order takeout after we get cleaned up. Like you said, we're hot and tired."

After showering and arranging for the takeout, Renee and I go out on the dock to watch the water and wait for Eric to get back. I'm silently wishing for some kind of sign, something that helps me to know that Emma is near us. Sometimes I just need a sign so damn bad. Today is one of those times. Searching the water for dolphins or manatees, searching the trees for a cardinal, it feels like an interruption when my phone pings with a text. But I can't ignore it. Eric might need something, or a flight might be delayed, or who knows what else?

It's from Kristy. All it says is, "Emery and Beth got here OK a little while ago. Thought you'd want to know."

I was so wrapped up in feeling lousy about the upcoming date that I'd nearly forgotten they were due in anytime. Nearly. Now, my heart is thumping so hard with excitement, I feel it's going to burst out of my chest. Talk about tangled-up emotions! Again. OK, self-talk: *Focus, and follow her lead to keep the communication brief. I can't trust myself to text anything else right now except, "Thank you for letting me know. I appreciate it."*

In the midst of hoping for some kind of sign from Emma, a text comes about Emery. Hmm. Maybe the awaited message from beyond has arrived in the form of Emery and Beth now being safely located only a few miles from me. One step closer to the reality of being able to meet them. Not what I was looking for or expecting today, but since when has the expected brought me what I need? It's been a long while.

Soon, the silence of the last couple of hours is broken by Eric, Steven, and Hilary. A few minutes later comes Nate, and then the food delivery. It's time to keep my head in the present. Wasn't that Steven's wish for me when I left Albany? To be present for the ones I love? Another lesson—finding a fitting way to honor those who are not still physically present in this life, while being sure I'm present for those who need me today, those I can help and support in the here and now. I'm not willing to let either go by the wayside for the other. No matter what date it is on the calendar.

That awareness, that self-imposed mantra, carries me through the rest of the evening. Gathered around the firepit, my loved ones' faces are glowing with the light created by small, flickering flames. The flames bring to mind Marie's phrase to *tend my own fire*, and I'm compelled to say something about what I've been feeling. At the risk of breaking the ease of the moment, I try to capture the essence of what's been going on.

"Hey, guys, I need to say something. I'm grateful, so grateful, that you are here. When Eric and I left Georgia, this day—or rather, tomorrow—seemed far off. We weren't even sure we'd stay this long, or where we would want to be when. We had no specific expectations. I'm grateful for that as well. Far too often, expectations for specific dates or holidays set us up for disappointment. Instead, this gathering with all of you developed, seemingly, all on its own. Thank you for being here, for supporting our ever-evolving family, and for expecting nothing of us except good company and being present for one another.

"For almost the entire year, I've been dreading tomorrow. It's a date of sadness, a date of loss, a date that will never be the same as before. That's as it should be, I guess. I don't think any of us would want it to be the same as before. The energy of a precious soul left this earth, and that's sad. I'd like, though, to remember all the ways we have found Emma's energy to still be with us, to still be cheering us on from afar. Sure, I'll be sad, and you'll be sad tomorrow. Even so, please find ways to smile, to look up and feel Emma, and to be present for one another. And if I forget what I just said, don't be afraid to remind me. With one another, we'll get past April eighth. Once we're past, we've much to look forward to, so many possibilities for love and friendship to enlarge our circle of friends, of family. And speaking of possibility, I'd like to share something with all of you. I'd nearly forgotten that when Renee, Isabel, and I were in New York, I made a pledge to start some sort of memorial to Emma. As I was walking the other day, it struck me what I'd like to do. I'm going to start a scholarship fund in her name for young women of limited means who are trying to complete prerequisites to get into health-related fields like social work or the rehabilitation therapies. I want Emma's legacy to be one of bringing possibility and optimism into the lives of people who think their goals are unattainable." I see each head nod, and feel hands reach out for a squeeze.

Sitting alone on the dock later, I feel the vibration of boards underneath my feet, someone walking toward me.

"Lissa, can I join you for a minute?" Steven asks.

Somewhat distressed at the interruption of the quiet, but not enough to say so, I respond, "Sure, have a seat. The sky is a magnet for me tonight. I can't stop looking at it."

"The sky is beautiful. This whole place is beautiful. Thank you for welcoming me here. You spoke a while ago about all that you're grateful for. It amazes me that in spite of your daughter being gone a year, you're thinking of others and still able to talk about gratitude. My gratitude list is long as well, Lissa, and you're on the list, right up at the top. I've been thinking about this a long time, and I need to tell you that I didn't realize how much I missed having you in--"

"Steven, please stop. I'm not sure what you're about to say, but—and this may sound harsh—but tonight and tomorrow are not the times to talk about you missing me or anything else along those lines. When I spoke earlier, I tried to capture the upbeat part of what I'm feeling, mostly for Eric's sake. But underneath,

I'm actually in a very deep, unfriendly part of an ocean and just barely treading water to keep my head above the surface. It's taking all of my energy to make it through to another day, a day that isn't quite so gut-wrenching to consider. I don't have the stamina for anything else right now."

Looking up at the sky for a couple of minutes before he breaks the silence, Steven says, "OK, I hear you, Lissa. Bad timing on my part. It makes me remember that you told me once last fall that your emotional bank account, as you called it, was depleted. I respect your need to protect the balance. The balance in that bank account, the balance between sadness and joy, the balance between lost and found. So much has been lost, yet we're finding loved ones as well. Though even the finding, even the joy, takes its toll. You're right, I'll drop it for now, but I hope for a time when we can talk about us. Whatever 'us' means."

Not wanting to hurt his feelings, but honoring my own, I continue, "Yeah, not now, Steven. I've no promises to offer. I do know, as I said earlier, that I'm happy we all have one another to navigate both the rough and calm waters. Having someone alongside you helps keep the balance. My wish tonight is to get through the rough of tomorrow and then find ways for you and I to bring our respective children, Nina and Emery, calmly into our lives. That's it for me right now."

Next morning, I'm actually asleep when the morning light hits my face. I feel like I was awake all damn night long, tossing and turning, and seeing Emma's face. I had to lie there with my eyes open, because whenever I shut them, the images were too real, too vivid. Somewhere between dark and first light, my weariness must have succumbed to slumber, at least for a little while. There's a soft knock on my door, waking me and forcing me into consciousness on the day I wanted to skip. Mercy would have been sleeping through it.

Renee tiptoes in, pulls back the covers and crawls in next to me. She reaches to hold my hand and whispers, "Don't worry, I'm not going to say 'good morning.' I know there's not a damn thing good about it. I'm just going to hold your hand till you want to say something. Even if it's all day long. I'm here."

Her words bring a smile to my reluctant face. I told people last night to find ways to smile today, and she just did it for me. A smile and a couple of tears, and I'm ready to utter, "Thank you."

I'm awake now and I can't just lie here. Nope—I gotta do something. If I lie here wallowing in thoughts of what a sucky day it is, it'll be way too many hours until I fall asleep again and have the chance to make the day vanish.

Throwing off the covers that she so gently placed a few minutes ago, I respond, "Let's go. I want to get some coffee in me and then hit the beach with trash bags. Those baby turtles need us to keep that beach clean. Keep crap out of their way. They have a hard enough trek without careless people throwing their junk around."

Two hours later, six of us are spaced out along the beach with large black bags filled to the brim with every possible color of plastic and an array of other random trash. Coming back together, there seems to be a competition for who found the weirdest object. While there are things like single flipflops, toothbrushes, fishing lures offered as possible winners, Nate's report of a set of dentures sends us into fits of laughter.

After the laughter simmers down into giggles, Hilary says, "Look what I found: this isn't weird at all. It's beautiful, don't you think?" She holds out a necklace with a heart medallion. While many of the other items were covered in barnacles or rusted, this looks almost like new, like it hadn't been out here more than a few minutes. In fact, we scan the sand up and down the beach to see if anyone is walking who might have dropped it.

Eric suggests, "It's all yours, Hilary. You found today's treasure. Sweet person deserves a sweet heart!"

Hilary shakes her head and walks toward me. "No, this is for you, Larissa. I'm sure of it. On one side is the symbol of infinity, and look at the other side."

As she hands it to me, she turns the medallion over. "Look, it has the letter E on it. It's definitely for you. On a day about loss, this is a special find."

Instantly, I'm transported back about fifteen years to when Emma first learned the word *infinity*. It was a school vocabulary word, and when she was stumped as to how to use it in a sentence, I told her, "I love you to infinity—that means with no limit or end," and she beamed. From that day forward, she often told me, "Mama, I love YOU to infinity," and we would hug or laugh, or both.

"Let me see it, Mom. Oh, wow. Infinity and an E. Now, there's a sign from Em. From all your E kids. Hang in there. Love you, Mom, to infinity!"

As he hugs me, I feel my breath return to its regular rhythm and depth for the first time in the last twenty-four hours. The love I feel right now will carry me through the rest of the day. I know it will. It must.

31

Traveling through life with curiosity rather than judgement is how one finds the magic in each moment.
ERIN CHATTERS

The anticipation of yesterday was tougher than actually getting through it. Today, I'm proud of myself and thankful to those who stuck by me all day. The younger folks went out in Nate's boat for a bit in the afternoon, but didn't stray very far from the main channel in front of the house. Instinctively, everyone seemed to know I was more comfortable with them nearby. I hadn't said it out loud, but it seemed there was a tacit understanding among my loved ones.

As I dress, I vow to let them all go do whatever they feel like doing today—explore, enjoy the island, and get back to making the most of the time here. Make the most of every day. Heading out my bedroom door, I spot on my dresser the necklace that Hilary found. I grab the gift, a bittersweet reminder of yesterday and of hope for tomorrow, then carefully latch it around my neck.

"Hello, everyone. We did it! We made it past a year. I'm not sure it will be dramatically different, but we're past another milestone, nevertheless. It's time to make today matter. What's everyone want to do?" After the hovering of yesterday, I'm hoping to myself that they'll occupy themselves away from the house for the day. I've a list of to-dos that I'd put on hold while on the countdown to yesterday.

Eric offers to take the others along while he shops for more fishing poles, and my wish for a quiet house quickly becomes a reality. Time to sit down with my laptop and catch up on work. It's oddly satisfying to get through mundane emails and send a summary off to my boss to assure him that I'm keeping current.

A loud knock at the door startles me. I call out, "Just a minute—on my way." Peeking through the hole, there's a woman I don't recognize. Not that I know many people here, but well, maybe it's a neighbor. Maybe it's Nate's mother; I'd been thinking we should meet.

Pulling the door open just a few inches, I offer, "Can I help you?"

"I hope so. Are you Larissa?"

I recognize the voice, but can't place it. Why does she sound familiar? "Yeah, it is. Who's asking, please?"

"My name is Terry. From the, uh, search angel website. Can I talk with you? Can I come in?"

OK, this is weird. How did she get here? And she doesn't look at all how I'd pictured her from the phone calls. I assumed she was maybe my age or younger, but not this woman. She looks to be in her late sixties, maybe seventies. "Yes, come in. I'm confused. How did you know where to find me? You didn't have my address. I thought I only told you Florida, right? East coast?"

"Yes, you told me East coast and named a couple of towns. May I? I'll try to explain."

I still haven't opened the door far enough to let her in. I gather my wits, swing the door open and gesture with my other hand for her to come in. "Of course, please. Come in, Terry. Have a seat." It's strange that for so long I'd looked forward to Terry's phone calls and emails. They were my only connection to my son, a lifeline. Now, it feels odd, almost ominous that she's here. Like she doesn't belong.

"I'm sorry for barging in on you. Suppose it's weird, me coming here unannounced."

All I can think is, "You can say that again."

"As you know, I had the contact information, well, email at least, for the young man who came up in my database search. The one you wrote to, quite sure that it was Everett. When I spoke to him on your behalf, he was still reluctant to meet, even after you wrote the letter. I wasn't sure what else we could do. But when you told me about meeting Harriett, her story matched up with the little bit I'd found out from him already."

"Well, yeah. I just figured at this point, with his mother pushing him to meet me, that your contact with him is no longer necessary. I just don't get--"

"Of course, you don't. But your son and I had continued to correspond. I thought, hoped, that maybe I could help him see why it'd be a good thing to connect with you; I just couldn't let it go. Let's just say, I had a deep interest in the two of you getting to know one another. It doesn't make total sense to you because, until right now, I have known you as-- Oh, for Pete's sake. Larissa, I'm the nurse. I was your nurse when you gave birth to your son. I broke professional protocol back then. Let you see him, hold him, and wrote that note. Now, I've broken it again. Once I realized that you were the sweet young girl that tugged at my heart way back in 1982, I crossed the line again and got way too interested." Terry chokes up at her admission and can't continue speaking.

I should say something to fill her uncomfortable silence. But what? While gathering my thoughts, she pulls herself together and continues, "You touched me back then because you didn't once complain or cry about labor pains. You refused medication to help you with that pain. The only thing that made you cry was when we took him away. Then, you were inconsolable. It broke my heart. I became obsessed with letting him, or his future parents, know how much he was loved. When I saw that he was scheduled to be discharged on my day off, the only thing I could think to do was to leave the anonymous note and hope that someone would save it for him. I also hoped you'd still be there when I came back. You being so young, I figured they'd keep you an extra day, maybe even to be sure that you didn't accidentally encounter the adoptive family in the hallway when leaving. But when I came to work the next day, you were gone as well. I vowed to put it all behind me and never let myself get attached again."

"It may have been against protocol, Terry, but your compassion, well, is a beautiful quality. That note ended up being very special. I bet you made a wonderful nurse."

"Maybe, maybe I did. Nursing took a toll on me. As hard as I tried, I did get too attached, and I did care deeply. I never went as far as writing a letter or violating privacy again, but I did get very burned out. I couldn't stay in the newborn unit. I left hospital nursing, tried being a school nurse for several years. That was hard in a different way. After a few more jobs, I found out about the search angel process. I was close to retirement anyway, so retired and started volunteering for them. I became good at it, and the agency started paying me a small stipend to train others. It's been my passion ever since."

"OK, but I still can't figure out how you got here. And you said you've broken protocol again. How?"

"One more thing I need to say. All of the things about your situation touched me, but it was also about my own story. The passion I developed for the search process was not purely compassion for others. It was selfish. I also reluctantly gave away my own baby once, and even though I had more information about her than you did, I could never find her again. I know too well what it's like to lose a child and not be able to find her." Her voice quivers and trails off, and she holds a hand up in front of her to tell me to wait, not interrupt.

"Uh, anyway, I didn't set out to break protocol. When Emery didn't want to continue on with the search, I sincerely tried to drop it. But whenever I'd speak with you, feelings washed over me. Feelings that brought me right back to the day you had your baby, and back even further, to the day I had mine. Since I couldn't find mine, I wanted you to find him, to be reunited, more than I can explain. I was driven to help you. And remember, I wasn't one hundred percent sure of his identity yet. I checked back with him occasionally. I didn't tell you because I didn't want you to get too discouraged, but I kept hoping I could say something to convince him to get back on board with the search. I wanted you to find what you'd lost. During one of those conversations, he let it slip that he was traveling often to go between caring for his daughter and caring for his mother. He mentioned the eastern coast of Florida. That baffled me. I figured your son would be in the northeast. So, when you also mentioned Florida in the story of meeting his adoptive mother and going to the lawyer, it all came together. I freaked a little when you told me about seeing the note at the lawyer's office, but I realized it probably isn't a big deal now. So, a few days ago, I just came out and asked Emery more about his home, his mother, and asked if I could come meet them both, just to talk. The second time I asked, he surprisingly agreed. So, here I am."

"Yeah, but how did you get here, this house, and find me?"

"I met with all of them yesterday: Harriett, Kristy, Emery, even got a few minutes with his adorable Beth, your--"

"You saw my granddaughter? Oh, my God, this is real, isn't it?" I hear my voice getting louder with each word, and remind myself to take a deep breath, stay calm.

"Yes, only for a minute. She was playing in the yard while the adults talked. She came in the house just as I was getting ready to leave and showed me some stones she'd found in the yard, telling me she liked them because they were pink and white swirled. She thought one was shaped like a heart and one looked like a bug. She was not at all shy! That's when Kristy followed me out to the car and told me where you're staying. She said something like, 'Larissa needed you to search for her son. Now you know all the people and where they are, help her to keep going. Really be an angel.' She's a character, that one—speaks her mind. She's definitely on your side on this one."

"That's good, glad to have both Harriett and Kristy on my side."

"For sure. They pulled out all the stops, including telling him that meeting you is what's best for Beth. Emery talked about things I often hear adopted adults say, like he's afraid you'll be disappointed in him. Since you gave him up once, what's to stop you from walking away again? It's different for the adopted child—although he feels a loss, finding a parent can definitely be scary. What if he becomes attached to the parent he finds, but then it doesn't work out? It's a loss all over again. Worse yet, Beth could become attached, and you don't return the devotion. I think he's actually even more worried about you and Beth meeting than anything. I guess, well, her other grandmother is aloof, keeps them at arm's length so to speak. It's complicated."

"Complicated how? Why is she aloof?"

"The way Emery tells it, Beth reminds the grandmother too much of her daughter, Beth's mother, who was killed in the car crash. And she doesn't like that Beth is, um, mixed race; never liked that her daughter was with Emery, a white man. Somehow,

Emery got it in his head that you might not accept Beth, perhaps for the same reason. Maybe he thinks you, too, will be disappointed, not approve. You'll become involved with Beth and then end up hurting her."

"Oh, my heavens, Terry, all that matters to me is that she's a little girl whose mama is gone, and she needs all the loving she can get. I want a chance to tell him, better yet, show him, reassure him."

"We all kinda went out on a limb and spoke for you on that one. I was pretty sure Beth's skin color wouldn't discourage you. Kristy told him in no uncertain terms that he needs to give you a chance, needs to talk to you and see how it goes. She deserves credit here, for sure."

"Wow, so, what now? How'd you leave it? Does he know you came here?"

"No. I told him that it's totally his call. He can contact me, or since his sister has your information, contact you directly. Kristy followed me outside and gave me your address. I went back to my hotel, had dinner and a glass of wine. I needed rest and quiet time before deciding my next move. This morning, I woke up, looked at the ocean outside the window, and walked. As I walked, I watched the waves roll in and back out again. With each wave that pushed onto shore, I felt encouraged to come tell you the whole story. With each one that retreated, I wasn't so sure. Ultimately, the rhythm of the waves reminded me of the rhythm of life. Life will go on, no matter our decisions. The rhythm of the waves brought me comfort and confidence, and I knew I'd come see you. Here I am. It dawned on me that maybe my letter, written to him the day he was born, would make a difference. You have it, right? The letter from the lawyer? After all, I wrote it to him, for him. Let's give it to him."

"Uh, yes, I have it. Hell, yes, he should have it."

"So, what's the best way to get it to him? I could take it, or, what do you think?"

What I want and what I think are two different things. Willing to give him the time and space he needs—for a little longer, anyway. I tell Terry, "You wrote the letter, I think you should deliver it. Let me know how it goes. I'm ready to go see him the minute he says it's OK. Just so you know, it's taking all my willpower to let this play out. The temptation to drive right over there is testing me, almost past my limit."

"OK. I'll give him some time and call him later. I'm not going to push too hard, but damn, I want to see this through to the best possible outcome for all. Larissa, I've hoped for quite some time that this would work out for you."

"You know, Terry, I've struggled off and on with the idea of hope. Hope has always been something elusive for me. After so much loss, hope comes along like the wind and swirls around me. Then, as soon as I reach for it, hope slips through my hands like the last of a refreshing breeze, leaving emptiness. Its absence is oppressive. These developments are different. They are tangible, they bring a promise of possibility. Possibility is the premise for optimism, a sign or indication that something really good is likely to happen. I'm optimistic that Emery is coming back into my life."

A couple of hours later, I'm walking the beach, wishing it will bring some clarity to my jumbled, conflicting inclinations.

Absorbed in my thoughts, I hear voices calling my name. Four people are walking toward me—a couple holding hands in the middle, and someone on either side of them. Ah—Eric and Hilary have definitely gotten closer, and Renee and Steven are along with them. What a sweet sight; a delightful diversion from the deep questions weighing me down.

Renee calls out, "Did you finish your work? Ready to play? You know what they say about all work and no play? And I say, especially at the beach!"

I'm pretty certain my half-hearted smile gives me away before my words. "No work, and no play. I had a surprise visitor."

Jumping on the surprise immediately, and his hopefulness showing, Eric exclaims, "Whoa, who? Kristy or her, or my, actually our, brother?"

I shake my head and explain about Terry's visit. It's almost a mile walking in the sand before I finish a rundown of the information. "If I were to act on my impulse, I'd hop in the car and go see Emery right now. As I told Terry, I'm using every ounce of willpower to give him some time and space to figure it out on his own. I'm sad that he's worried I'll let him, and his daughter, down. I want to go reassure him in every way I possibly can that I'll be available to them, stand by them."

"What's that old saying, Mom? So close and yet so far? Doesn't it feel like that with Double E? He's closer geographically than he's ever been, but crossing that bridge is a big move. Even though he hasn't decided yet, I know he's going to want to see us, I feel it in my bones. I had a sign today. It was Emma telling us again to keep going, no matter how hard it seems."

"Really? Tell me."

Pointing at the others, he says, "I dropped these three off at a park up aways on the island to go for a walk while I went to get bait and another fishing pole. The place I've gone before was all out of fresh bait, so they sent me to another shop. When I was walking toward the entrance, this older lady waved me to come over to her. I wasn't gonna go at first, I thought she was going to ask me for money, and that always makes me feel so awkward. Then I decided, what the heck? If she needs money, I'm gonna help her. She patted the bench beside her and said, 'I think you need to take a load off, young man.' As soon as I sat, she said, 'Don't you be worried, I'm not gonna bother you. It's just that I see things, like signs and spirits. I just want to tell you that I see a young woman near you, and she's pushing you—pushing you from behind. You need to believe that whatever you're wanting is possible.' Just as she said that, a butterfly landed next to me on the bench and lingered. Like when I was in Colorado, and that woman told me the butterfly was someone close to me trying to send a message. Mom, I never believed this crap till you and Dad told me about your messages from the other side. Now, this stuff keeps happening right when I need it. Emma comes along and gives me a push."

"Eric, I'm glad you sat with that lady. Anything else?"

"She talked a little more. Then she laughed and told me that she knows a lot about needing to take a load off. She just retired from thirty-something years being a cleaner in an airport and moved down here to be with family. Said I looked like I needed reminding that people we love are never really gone—they are always around us if we are open to the possibility."

I smile to myself when Eric says she's a retired cleaner. Of course, she is. It's the same message I got from Clara, who came and sat with me when I spent an overnight waiting for airline delays. Clara, who started me thinking about loved ones being close if only I'd keep my eyes and heart open. I gotta ask, but I already know. Nothing surprises me anymore. Nothing.

"Did she by any chance mention her name, Eric?"

"I don't think so. Oh, wait—it was something like Claudia, no, guess I don't remember."

"Could it have been Clara?"

"Yeah, yeah, it could have been."

"Then, I'm sure the message was from Emma, Eric. Absolutely sure."

32

I do not know what I may appear to the world,
But to myself, I seem to have been only like a
boy playing on the seashore, and diverting myself
in now and then finding a smoother pebble or a
prettier shell than ordinary,
Whilst the great ocean of truth lay
all undiscovered before me.
ISAAC NEWTON

Steven announces that he's heard from Nina, and she's on her way from the other coast of Florida. Both he and Eric are pacing nervously around the house, pretending to help prepare for her arrival, trying to be useful in some way. Renee and Hilary offer them something to eat, to no avail. Finally, Renee shoos them out to the dock to fish, and suggests Hilary should go make sure they don't fall in from being distracted by Nina's impending arrival.

From my bedroom window, I watch Steven and Eric for a few minutes. What a touching scene it is to see my son enjoying a pastime that he loves alongside his father. It's something I never thought I'd see. Oh, at some point early on in my marriage to Roger, I'd hoped for this kind of relationship for Eric, but it became painfully clear it wasn't meant to be, not possible. As soon as Steven came back into our lives, I began to have reason to be optimistic that they might become close. Now, I want the same for Emery and me, Emery and Eric, and hopefully, for Beth. Like Clara told Eric, we need to heed Emma's message and keep trying.

Downstairs after showering, I hear Eric's voice around the side of the house, near the garden. I grab a drink and walk out to see what he's up to. He and Steven are sitting on the bench so lovingly arranged by Adele and chatting quietly. I ask, "Mind if I join you two?"

"Not at all, sit down right here. Eric thought I'd like to see this meditative spot you've been enjoying. He was right—drew me in."

I share the story Nate told me and tell him about Adele's answer to my letter. The three of us are sitting quietly. I wonder out loud to them, "How can a place I've only been for such a short time be so comforting that it feels like home?"

Steven nods his head in obvious agreement, and Eric responds, "I don't know, Mom. It's pretty darn special. The surroundings, the water, the wildlife. Or maybe it's that our people are here? Now, we've even got the chance to add Nina and Double E and Beth? It's kinda like you said about the psychic medium: you don't have to understand it, you just know that it's real."

"You're right, Eric. We don't have to understand at all. Just be open and accept the joy. I can tell you this much: it doesn't seem as if this is a one-time visit."

Suddenly, I hear voices and Renee screaming, "Larissa, Eric, where are you? Hurry up, get in here. Really you guys, I mean it."

Not sure whether to be alarmed, I jump up and call back to her, "We're coming. We're just on the side of the house. What's wrong?"

Half running, half walking up to the front steps, I stop in my tracks. There's a tall, dark-haired, deeply tanned man standing in the doorway in front of Renee. He's not someone I know, but he is. It's my son. It's Everett, Emery Everett. I see a fleeting flashback of the face of the young man I'd been so enchanted with when I was only fifteen, but enhanced with Emma's hazel eyes and Eric's build. There's no doubt, not a single one, who this is.

I sense Steven and Eric right behind me as they round the corner of the house, and my arm shoots out to stop them from bumping into me or racing up the steps. I can't take my eyes off him, can't move, can't speak. A thousand words are racing through my head, words I'd rehearsed for just this moment, but none of them make it to my lips. I want to throw my arms around him, but I'm frozen.

I see his lips are moving as he walks toward me and my ears finally sense the sounds. The words begin to register, "Larissa, I mean, well, I'm Emery, uh, Emery Everett." His arm juts out in front of him, stiffly at first, and then the other one comes forward and I realize he's trying to reach for me. Just as I start to put my arms out, his drop, and he says, "I don't know what to do here. This is so awkward. Can we, uh, sit down inside or something?"

Renee, uncharacteristically silent, finally finds her words and starts talking to everyone all at once. "Yes, yes, everyone get in here and sit down. But wait, no, why don't the rest of us go out on the porch, or the dock, and let you two talk, uh, get acquainted. Eric, can you get your mother and your ... Emery, some water, please? Steven, how about you and Hilary grab the snacks I was working on and bring them outside?"

Eric robotically fills the glasses as directed and sets them down in front of us. He starts to walk outdoors, but then turns to Emery, puts out his hand, and says, "Thanks, man, I knew you'd come. This is all good, you know? Right?"

Emery returns the handshake, smiles, and nods his head once in Eric's direction. My inner voice assures me. The gesture says it all. This is going to be OK, isn't it? It has to be.

Once the others are gone, my brain restarts its connection to my limbs and voice. I walk over close to Emery, put my hand on his shoulder, and say, "I'm so glad you're here. I love you, I've always loved you. I'm so sorry we lived apart. It wasn't my choice." Tears begin to seep out of my eyes. Trying to hold them back only makes it more difficult.

Emery is now the one overtaken by silence. His eyes are looking straight into mine, holding the connection, and then a trickle of tears come down one cheek. As he quickly tries to wipe it away with his shirt, he says, "I don't know what to say, I don't know what to call you."

"Call me anything you wish, I'll answer. I'll always answer. I've been called *Mom, Madre, Mama, Larissa,* and *Lissa*. Probably more than that, but those are a start. I know Harriett raised you, and I don't want to take a thing, not one single thing away from her, not even what she is called. Just wait and see what feels right to you. And for the record, I don't know what to say either. I've been waiting for this day, you'd think I'd have figured out what to say, but I really didn't. The most important thing for you to know is that Eric and I, and all the others in our family of friends, want, more than anything, to have you be part of our lives. You first, your daughter if you'll let her, your mother, sister, and anyone else that might be part of your life. Please. And if there are things you need to ask me, things that will help you decide, I'm here, I'm an open book. There were too many times in the past that information was kept from me, from you, and it's time, past time, to figure out our truth."

"I don't know where to start. This Terry woman, who I guess you know from the search angel place, Kristy, and my mother have all been telling me what they know about our past history. Then, this afternoon, Terry brought over that letter—the one that I guess she wrote to me back in the day—and by the time I got to the last sentence, Kristy was giving me your address over here. But who really pushed me? My mother. She said, 'Junior. I don't know how much longer I got on this earth. But here's what I do know. When my time comes, if you haven't met Larissa and made a relationship with her for you and Beth, I'm never gonna rest peaceful, and I'll be mad at you when I go. Junior, I don't wanna leave this place angry and miserable. I mean it. Now go!' She was yellin' and cussin' and I had no choice. I would've done this sooner or later on my own, when I was ready, but she wasn't havin' it. So Kristy got Beth distracted playing a game and gestured for me to get out, no choice, really. Here I am."

"Like I said a minute ago, I'm glad you're here. I'm beyond grateful to your mother. I know you did try to reach out on your own once before, but she has her mind made up that we need to know one another now. She told you about the friendship between her and my parents?"

"Yeah, I've heard all that from my mom. I've heard what Terry knows. I guess what's missing is your story. I don't even know if I want to hear it, but seems like it's important if we're ever gonna figure things out. It's probably hard to talk about, or private, or whatever, but you did say to ask anything."

"I meant it. I want to share anything I can that will help you understand my perspective, my actions. Or, if not understand, at least hear my version of what I think happened that led up to my parents bringing you to Harriett and Harold.

Even I don't know the whole story, because they kept quite a bit from me."

"OK, well, I know from Terry's letter that you were pretty young, right?"

"Yeah, for sure. I'll just start talking. You can stop me or ask questions. Let's just give it a try and see how far we get."

Emery nods his head, so I start, "When I was fifteen, there was a really handsome exchange student from someplace in South America. I don't even know what country—how ridiculous is that? I had a secret crush on him the whole school year. At the end of the year, at a party, he started paying attention to me. Really talking to me. I was thrilled that he noticed me. Someone snuck alcohol into the party. I didn't even know what it was, but they were mixing it with fruit punch, so when he brought me a cup and another and another, I just drank it. I wanted to be cool, I suppose. Before I knew it, we were, well, making out. I've no clue how much later, I woke up alone, partially dressed in the basement of the house. I was mortified, scared, and just wanted to get out of there. I snuck back home without talking to anyone. A few weeks later it became clear that it was more than making out. He was already back home in whatever country, and I was pregnant. My parents were angry, then ashamed. They shipped me off to my aunt's to have the baby, to have you."

I stop to gather my thoughts and scan my son's face to see if I can determine his reaction. I don't want to upset him, but I'm not going to lie. This is our shared truth and he needs to know it. I'm not going to build a relationship at this late date on half-truths.

He looks straight into my eyes and says, "That's awful. Well, I mean, awful that they shipped you away, but could've been way worse. At least they didn't decide you couldn't even have me. I don't know what to say, except I'm sorry. Were you scared? If something like that happened to my daughter..." His voice trails off and he looks away.

"You have no reason to be sorry. I was scared, embarrassed, confused. My aunt just kept saying things, like 'Girls shouldn't tempt guys that way' or 'She probably asked for it.' My mother mostly cried, and my father left the room whenever we talked about it. And at fifteen, I felt like my body was being taken over. Until I got almost all the way through. Once you started moving, once I could feel a foot or whatever body part, I started to feel different. I didn't know it then, but I was feeling like a mother. I even looked up names and imagined I could change the adults' minds and keep my baby. I wanted to take care of you, but they were in charge, and it didn't happen that way. In the hospital, I remember begging the nurse to let me see you, then hold you. Just like she wrote in the note, she held back at first, but once the others were out of the room, she let me, just for a minute. I looked at your face against my skin, and I didn't want to let go. After that, I cried and cried. They must have given me something to knock me out, to stop my crying. The next thing I knew, I was back at my aunt's house. I wanted to go home to my parents, but she didn't let me, not for another week. I guess that's when they brought you to Florida. No one ever told me a thing."

"Wow, just wow. That's so crazy. I don't know whether to hate or be grateful to your parents, uh, my grandparents, I guess."

"I guess you have good reason for both. I can tell you that they were decent people, kind. I think they just had no clue how to handle the situation, and when they became unsure, my bossy aunt stepped right in. At some point, I'm not sure when, although from Terry's letter, it sounds like the day or the day after you were born, they decided they couldn't give you to strangers. If they weren't going to raise you themselves, they'd be sure you were raised by someone they knew and cared about. That says something."

"But you didn't know that back then, right? You had no idea where I went?"

"Right. They told me you went to a good family, and that I should forget about it all and enjoy the rest of high school. As I got older, it bothered me that I'd never know where you were. I felt an emptiness, but I covered it up, stuffed it away so that I could function. I bought into their explanation that I was too young and you were better off. I think they meant well, but it didn't always feel that way to me. After a year or so, the shame took over, and I tried to forget. Tried, but there were always reminders. Later, when I was married and pregnant, the body changes were so familiar, so bittersweet. I made up my mind that I would be the best mother ever. When that pregnancy didn't last, it was like losing you all over again. I became convinced I'd never be a mother." I stop to give us both a chance to decide how much more of this we can do. I don't want to overwhelm him, scare him off.

Looking grateful for the break, Emery finally says, "Man, you didn't have it easy, either, did you?"

"You know, things are rarely easy. People all tend to hide the tough stuff and answer 'fine' when asked how things are. There's always a burden behind the smile and that rote response. Once I had Eric, then Emma, my life rolled along fairly calmly for quite a while. I divorced, but honestly, that took away a stressor that I didn't need in my life. He was never close to Eric or even his own daughter, and that was very hard to live with. Things were OK until Emma started to struggle with health problems that we could never figure out how to address in a way that made a difference. She became overcome with her struggles, and well, it impacted us all. It's another long story, but she is no longer with us on this earth. In fact, it was just a year ago that she passed over."

"Oh, wow, that's awful." Emery comes over and kneels in front of me, then reaches for my hands and just holds them. We both cry, unified in emotions that we don't totally understand, just together in the moment.

I pat his hand and search for some words. Do we need to keep going right now? Do we take a break? How do I know what is right?

He reaches behind me and pulls the Emma quilt off the back of the sofa. He strokes it gently and says, "This is beautiful. Did someone make it for you?"

Sometime later, I've told him about the quilt, about Emma, about Eric disappearing and returning, and even about Steven, me, and Eric. He has listened, responded, and listened more. We've held hands, we've paced to separate corners of the room, and we've had silences.

"Emery, all I've done is talk. I want to know about you, about Beth, about your life, but I'm guessing you need to get back soon. I don't know how long we've been sitting here. I don't want to break this spell, but ..." Part of me cannot stand the thought of him walking out the door—what if he decides not to come back? But part of me knows this has been a lot, and his daughter and mother need him as well.

Checking his phone for the time, he says, "Oh, yeah, you're right. It's almost time for Beth to get ready for bed. She's not too great about anyone else putting her to bed. It's hard to go, though. There's so much more to say, that I do want to tell you, really."

Those words reassure me and help a suggestion pop into my head. "How about if you just quickly meet the others, so you know who I'm talking about? It's amazing they've waited outside so patiently—not exactly like either Eric or my friend Renee to wait when they're excited. I'll make it clear we're not going to do more than quick intros right now. Do you think you and I can get together, uh, sometime soon?" I try to pick my words carefully so as not to be pushy.

He pauses, looks down at his hands and says, "Yeah, we can get together sometime. We'll figure something out."

The mention of a next time to meet seemed to have reined in his enthusiasm. I ignore his apparent ambivalence and move toward the porch door. "So, now, can we do the intros quick, so you can get going?"

Explaining more about who everyone is as we walk through the house to the porch, I also see Nate and a young woman I don't recognize. Geez—this is a lot to ask of Emery. Oh well, here goes!

"Hey, everyone, Emery Everett needs to get home to put Beth to bed. He's just going to say a quick hello and then we need to let him go."

I get through all of them I know, and then look for help introducing the young woman. Eric and Steven step forward and gesture toward her, then to Emery and me, and Eric says, "OK, well, Double E—that's what I've been calling you since that Emery-Everett thing got confusing—and Mom, this is Nina. My sister."

I'm stunned. I forgot she was coming.

"Dad texted her that she should just come around the back of the house when she got here. That was a while ago—you guys sure gave us plenty of time to get acquainted."

Emery recovers more quickly than I do. "I have no clue what that makes you and me, Nina, but pleased to meet you. And Eric, I don't really care what you call me. I've had a lot of names, kinda like what your mom said to me: call me whatever you want. I'll answer."

There are a lot of hugs, a lot of handshakes, and a few tears, mostly mine and Renee's. Steven's daughter and my son all in one day? Too much to comprehend.

I shake my head and gesture toward Emery. "OK, everyone, this man has got to go see his little girl. I'm going to walk him to the car. When I get back, can someone have a dinner plan, cuz I'm starving?"

As we get to his car, I reach up to put my hands on Emery's shoulders. "This has been quite the day. Thank you so much for coming here, for listening. I'm hopeful that we can continue this whenever you feel ready."

"Can I ask you one more thing?"

"Of course, I don't want to rush you--"

"No, you're right, I gotta get home, but just this one thing before I go. I need to know. Do you have regrets about having me? Are you angry—like about the way you, uh, got pregnant? Or at the adults and how they handled it? I mean, it seems like you didn't really know what was happening at any point."

Wow, I didn't expect that. Gathering my thoughts, I reply, "I certainly wish I could say that things happened differently than they did, but I was never really angry at the guy, your father. We were both stupid kids: drunk, carried away, however you want to say it. Was I ashamed? Everyone told me I should be. Was I taken advantage of? Definitely. I can't remember a thing about it after the flirting. My regret is that I didn't stand up for myself and you, not at the time and not later. I was angry at my parents and my aunt for a long time. But you know what? Anger did nothing to help the situation. That anger paralyzed me. It kept me from asking the questions I should have asked. Anger blocked my ability to act on my own behalf. If I'd given up the anger sooner and asked questions, I'm sure the search would have been easier. Maybe we'd have had decades together by now. That's what I regret: the lost time. Anger caused more harm than good. My counselor helped me figure out how to forgive my younger self and think about her with the compassion I'd give any fifteen- or sixteen-year-old girl. She compared it to my ability to forgive Emma for her foibles and give her the unconditional love she deserved. Forgiveness and love for both Emma and for myself. When I finally forgave myself, I was ready to start the search for you. Way too late, but I'm happy I finally did it. Happy that the anger is long gone, and I can love unconditionally. I want to show you and Beth that kind of love, if you'll let me."

Emery replies, "I'm gonna try. This is an awful lot right now, but I'll try."

33

A friend is one that knows you as you are,
Understands where you have been,
Accepts what you have become,
And still, gently allows you to grow.
   WILLIAM SHAKESPEARE

I watch the car pull out of the driveway and look upward. Please, please, please let this be the first of many conversations like this. I'll have as many talks as it takes to get my son and me to a shared, meaningful relationship.

My ability to pray has been so limited over the years. Yet, as I now look upward to put my plea out into the universe, to appeal to a higher power to help me, help us—I feel a connection. If given this chance, this family of friends that has encircled Eric and me can continue to grow in a way to support us all. It would be such a privilege to be there to lift one another up.

"Hey, Lissa, you OK?"

I'm startled, yet comforted by Renee's voice as she walks toward me in the driveway.

"What are you doing out here by yourself? Come here." She reaches her open arms out and pulls me in. It feels so good to be held.

I lay my head on her shoulder and relish this moment. I read somewhere once that a hug of twenty seconds or more releases hormones that reduce stress. I'm going to hold on to Renee as long as I can; until she gives up.

Renee pats my back and holds on as well. After at least a minute, I slowly release my arms and offer, "I *am* OK. I'm so relieved that we've started, that Emery came here, and we might have the beginning of building something. Let's go assure everyone else. I know how you all are about waiting for information."

She laughs and we walk slowly toward the house. It's as if we've made a mutual agreement to give me a few more seconds to gather my composure and be ready for an onslaught of questions.

It doesn't unfold quite that way. I walk out onto the porch and see Steven pointing to the water. Everyone turns just in time to see three dolphins surface between the end of the dock and the shore.

Nina is the first to break the silence with, "Oh, wow! They're so close! How many are there, anyway?"

Nate jumps up and says, "There's a bunch. At least a half dozen, maybe more. They're putting on a show tonight!"

Everyone is quiet while these graceful creatures spend their evening frolicking right in front of us, moving along with the gently rolling waves. The sight is both invigorating and calming at the same time. It's exciting to share something so unique with people I care about, yet calming because it returns me to that feeling of appreciating the everyday miracles that are present when we watch, when we take the time to enjoy the world around us.

Once the dolphins move on down the river, there's a lively debate about whether they were playing or feeding. The four younger folks are trying to find answers by searching their phones, while Steven, Renee, and I watch them with smiles on our faces.

I quietly observe them and share, "Nina's beautiful, Steven."

Nodding his head, Steven replies, "She is. I still can't believe that she's here, that this is really happening. I'm afraid it's a dream, and I don't want to wake up."

"I think I know the feeling. So happy, but so afraid that it's too good to be true."

Renee interjects, "She's been lovely. She's mostly stayed with Eric and his friends, chatting about beaches and weather, and now dolphins. Want to tell us how it went with Ev--Emery before they finish dolphin research and begin demanding dinner?"

"Sure. You know Eric is also going to ask me as soon as he can break away from them, but the best word I can think of is what I said in the driveway: *OK*. It went OK. I don't know what else I can expect, right? We talked, well, honestly, mostly I talked. I started by telling him he could ask anything, and launched into the story. He rarely interrupted. Either he was dumbfounded, or he's an excellent listener. I want to think I could read compassion in his eyes. But when I finally realized how long we'd been talking, it dawned on me that I'd learned nothing about him, or about Beth. I'm not sure if that's good or bad or normal or what. Maybe I can ask Terry when she gets back in touch. She's seen a lot of adoptive families come together, and maybe some that don't."

Steven gently asks, "Well, OK is a decent start, Lissa. How did you guys leave it?"

"How we left it? Kinda tough to tell. I suggested we try to get together again soon. He didn't respond to that with much certainty, but then asked me if I had any regrets or anger about him or the circumstances that led to me giving birth to him. When I shared my feelings, I shared that I'd learned to give up on anger when I recognized that it stopped me from taking action. I said that giving up anger allowed me to love unconditionally, and that I wanted to give that kind of love to him and Beth, if he'd let me. His answer was that he'd try. I respect his honesty; I guess I wanted more, though. Maybe I expected too much."

Steven reaches over for my hand and reminds me, "Lissa, you told us all before that expectations can set us up for disappointment, stifle the joy that's right in front of us because we anticipate more. Maybe take your own advice? He came to see you, he listened, he asked a tough question, and you answered candidly. He didn't rush off. He came out to meet us all. Compared to your hopes and expectations, that may not seem like enough, but those are giant steps."

As usual, Eric catches the last part of a conversation and jumps right on it. "Liking the sound of that—giant steps! Tell us, Mom."

Renee takes charge. "How about we leave Larissa and Eric out here to take a dock walk? She's been in the house while we've been out here. I could use help in the kitchen, and Nina hasn't had a chance to freshen up from her road trip. Let's go."

I thank her with my eyes, and Steven gives me a thumbs-up as he heads inside. They are the best.

Eric and I stroll out on the dock and sit staring for a few minutes at the space where the dolphins popped up. Eric asks, "So—what's the deal? How'd it go with Double E?"

I recount our conversation in a fair amount of detail. I conclude with, "I just hope that we're getting together again soon."

"Hope? When I heard Dad say 'giant steps,' I thought there was some major agreement or something. Geez—didn't you, like, set up a time or whatever?"

"No, not yet. I talked an awful lot and he listened. He didn't say much of anything. I might have scared him. It was a lot, Eric. How were things with you guys and Nina? That's a lot, too."

"She's cool. She hung with Nate, Hilary, and me most of the time. When she first got here, she went over and kinda hugged Dad. I think he was crying, and when she started to as well, I went over. I guess like you said, it felt like a lot. And she said she's staying a few days, so we've got time."

We sit and watch the sun dip below the horizon until we are called to dinner. Renee's shout "to come and get it" feels a bit like a sudden interruption of a much-needed meditation, but we're hungry and ready to rejoin the group.

As we sit down, Steven suggests a toast. "Here's to family and friends—those with us from the beginning and those who come along to bring light and love to our table. Each and every one is a blessing."

Raised glasses and "cheers" are offered all around the table.

34

You can't force raging water to be calm.
You have to leave it alone and let it return
to its natural flow.
Emotions are the same way.
UNATTRIBUTED

Sunlight comes through my window bright and early, and my anxious anticipation of hearing from Emery immediately starts the wheels in my brain spinning. I jump out of bed to take a solo walk on the beach. I need to distract myself from thinking about why I haven't heard anything yet from Emery, about little Beth, and wondering if all will be well with Steven and Nina. Halfway down the beach, I see several new turtle nests dotting the sand. I calculate the sixty days or so from the first nest I saw and ponder whether I might stay down here for a longer time, to try to catch the spectacle of hatchlings making their way out to the sea. *Who are you kidding? Stay longer to see the turtles or to be with your son and his daughter? Wishful thinking! One step at a time.*

Strolls alone on the beach haven't helped much the last two days. The rehabilitative walks of the preceding days have washed back out to sea. Now, each splash of a wave against my lower leg startles me. And the crashing against the beach that sounded cleansing last week just irritates me now. I'm too on edge for this to be restorative. I turn around and head to the beach crossover. Maybe I can convince someone to do something with me to get my mind off Emery.

Back at the house, the rest of the crowd rises slowly, each grabbing coffee and wandering to a preferred spot to gradually make their way into the day. I glance at my phone every so often, wishing for something from Emery or Kristy, or whomever might give me a signal that we can connect. I know that wishing to hear from him today is probably setting me up for more disappointment, but hey, maybe it can happen.

Steven joins me out on the porch. "Lissa, you've been pretty quiet, yet the tension is written all over your face. Want to talk?"

Ready to refuse the latest attempt from one of my loved ones to get me to talk about all that's weighing me down, I'm surprised at my own reply, "He's not going to call. I scared him off with my story of being drunk and out of it. What kid wants to hear that a lot of liquor is the reason he exists? Or that I don't even know what country his father is from and never even mentioned his name when we talked? Was I out of my mind not to soften it a little? At least I didn't say it was forced or violent. Because it wasn't. I told the truth. The encounter wasn't wanted, and my parents thought it shameful. But once I gained some maturity and perspective, I knew I wanted to be in my child's life and have him in ours. There's plenty of room for him and Beth in our hearts. How can I be sure he knows I mean it?"

"I don't know, Lissa. There's no guidebook on how to do this stuff. You were honest, he's gotta at least respect that. I've not got any words of wisdom. I think you just need to give it some time."

"I'm not great at giving things time. I've had too much experience that tells me I never know if time is on my side or if it's going to kick me in the butt. He and Beth are like five miles away, but no closer than when they were a thousand miles away, or when I didn't even know where they were."

"Now, you know that's not really true. You know that you've made a lot of progress. You've already--"

I hear my voice intensify. "Stop! Just stop! I've already what? Stunned him with too much information too fast? What I know and what I feel are two different things. So different that I feel absolutely schizophrenic! I know all the facts, but they do not help."

Steven's head has dropped. Renee pushes open the back door and says, "Whoa, what's going on out here? Larissa, what's up? Are you OK?"

Steven slowly stands, shakes his head, looks at me briefly, then continues back through the door. He seems to be slinking away, hoping I don't continue my tirade.

"Well, I guess you saved Steven. I have no more patience, Renee. I know I'm driving you all nuts with my fidgeting and obsession with checking my phone for texts. But, damn it, this means a lot to me. My son and his daughter are five miles away. But the distance across that bridge is insurmountable right now. I'm going crazy, wondering when he will be ready. Or maybe I don't wait till he's ready? Maybe I just go over there."

"I'm no expert, but maybe Emery just needs--"

Is she really going to say the same thing? "Renee, don't you dare tell me he needs more time! That's what Steven just said. I'm so tired of this. I know it's only been a few days, I know it's a lot for him to process. But what I feel is desperate. I feel compelled to connect. I want to fulfill Harriett's wish for Emery to have someone else in his life to be a mother, to be an active, fun grandmother for Beth. I may have been passive all those years ago and gone along with my parents, but that Larissa—that young, scared girl called *Laura*—is long gone. Finally. I'm ready to step up and be those things for them. Too much time has gone by already, way too much."

"No, sorry, Larissa, I was not going to say Emery just needs time, give me a chance. I was going to say that maybe he needs more reassurance that Beth won't get hurt in all of this. Think about the way you fiercely protect your kids, always have. Maybe he's kinda the same. What I was actually going to say, is maybe give Terry a call and see if she has any advice about that part of this whole thing. Then, how about if we show Nina, and Steven if he wants, some of the other sights on the island that you and Eric enjoyed so much? Maybe that House of Refuge place or the rocky beaches down at the end of the island? Maybe a picnic?"

I place my hands on my hips, hoping my posture conveys my response, just in case my words do not. "Really? You're really suggesting a damn picnic with Steven and his newly discovered daughter? Like that's going to help me?" I walk away from Renee toward the dock. *Now she's trying to calm me with a picnic? I need space from everyone. I can't listen to any more ideas about what I should or shouldn't do.*

After pacing the length of the dock at least three or four times, I wander back toward the house. It's strangely quiet. Guess I scared them all off. Fine. I stroll around the other side to the little sanctuary created by Adele. I wonder what she's doing now? I wonder about her and her grandson. I've never met them, wouldn't know them if I bumped into them, yet I'm living in their space, and comforted by these surroundings: the garden she created, the river on one side, and usually, by the ocean on the other side. *Why didn't the ocean comfort me yesterday and today? What was different? Help me Adele, I need another mother's perspective.*

Looking upward as I silently mouth "help me," I notice fluffy, bright clouds over on the ocean side, while dark ones are here, moving up the river. The brightness draws me back across to the ocean. I'm going to give it another try.

As I step onto the warm sand, I stop to focus on my feet. I push all four corners of my feet down into the sand, and reach my arms upward. Before I know it, I'm in a tree pose—the yoga pose that has always served to ground me while elevating me, literally and figuratively. As my standing leg helps me root into the sand, my uplifted arms make my heart open to the sky. After a few deep breaths in the pose, I unconsciously shift to begin the alternating stride and arm swing of a slow, deliberate walk, with my senses attuned to the rhythm of waves. Their rhythm matches that of my arm swing. I'm in concert with the sounds of the ocean, and my breathing finally joins in. I was fighting it all earlier today. I was forcing my feet through the water, stomping the sand, rather than allowing them to move in a cadence that aligns with what Mother Nature brings during a beach walk. *Hmm. Trying to force it?* Is that what I'm trying to do with Emery and Beth? Force them to engage, rather than offer them the quiet acceptance that Mother Earth provides to all her living things. Why do the turtles always come back? They're not forced. They're enticed by the warm sand to come back. They're enticed by a combination of light and dark that humans are still trying to understand. There is no guarantee the sand will nurture them enough to make it back to sea, but they return nonetheless.

Of course, I know that the love of a human mother and the act of laying eggs by a turtle are vastly different, but I also know that nature has sent me many wise messages when I'm open to receiving them. The lesson that is making its way to my soul right now is to stop trying to force a decision from Emery. Besides, it's not either/or. I need to give the whole thing enough space to evolve, to be comprised of a give and take that builds trust and commitment slowly. *Duh, Larissa.*

It occurs to me that maybe Renee and Steven were trying to speak to something like this, but they didn't really get a chance before I leapt all over them. Just as this thought registers, I feel the vibration of my phone in my pocket. A message from Renee; "Where are you? Not trying to suffocate you or anything, but we're kinda worried." I reply with a brief "On my way," and turn around to make it true. They all mean well, and I sure don't want to get anyone all worried about me. There's too much worry already.

Slapping the last of the sand off my sandals, I call out, "I'm back. And good news: I left Miss Grump-ass on the beach. Hopefully, the ocean will wear down her rough edges before spitting her back out."

"What did you say?"

"Never mind, Steven, it's my lame attempt at a humorous apology."

Eric comes around the corner and chimes in, "What are you apologizing for, Mom? Who's a grump-ass?"

"OK, everyone, I was a little--no, a lot testy with Renee and Steven earlier. I know you're all on edge because I'm on edge. I've been so anxious about hearing back from Emery that I'm tough to be around. I'm sorry, and I'm going to try to do better. No promises, but I did a little 'wave therapy' out there on the beach and think my attitude is better. Someone mentioned a picnic earlier. Is that invitation still on?"

"You happen to have lucked out. Steven, Nina, and I just got back from the grocery store and were about to make sandwiches and go. If you were any later, you'd have missed the fun. Want to help?"

"Let me rinse off, and I'll be right back down."

Upstairs, I resolve to go about this whole thing in a way that is true to my desire to leave the door open for Emery but doesn't force anything, and doesn't alienate my tribe completely. I text a simple message, to both Kristy and him, saying, "Hope to see you guys soon. You're welcome to come over anytime for a cookout. Bring Harriett or Beth or whoever." Casual but inviting.

A couple hours later, we've toured the House of Refuge, taken a long beach walk to the end of the public beaches at Bathtub Reef, and are deciding on the best spot to picnic. As Nina and I are working on the pop-up sun shade, she remarks, "I like this little historical landmark in the middle of a beach area. Really gives you an idea of how many ships must have become wrecks from the storms. Even the name is cool: a place to take refuge. Such a pristine spot. I've been in Florida a long while and not seen an area quite like this. Definitely a place to take refuge from whatever. How long are you and Eric going to stay?"

"I'm not sure, Nina. The original plan was to stay through the anniversary of when Emma died. Things have changed since the original plan. We never thought we'd find Emery here—or you, for that matter! When I rented the house, she let me do it month to month since she had no interest for spring or summer. So, we can probably rent it longer if we want. Eric and I just haven't even had a chance to talk it over. We'll see over the next week or so. Last I checked with Adele, it's still free."

"Mom? Mom!" Eric's intensity jolts me to look up.

"Hey, keep your cool and act casual." He points at a couple of people slowly walking toward us. His voice lowers to a whisper. "Hilary and I came across Double E and, uh, Beth playing in the sand. As soon as I waved and said hello, he brought his finger up to his mouth, like telling me to 'Shh'. So, I let him take the lead. He told Beth I was a guy who came into the bait shop this week, and I played along. Then I invited them over to have a drink and sit under the umbrella. I mighta put him on the spot without meaning to. Anyway, they're walking over, but I think you need to just chill and follow his lead, right? We're acquaintances."

Oh, sure, I just talked myself down from being a bundle of nerves about Beth, and now they're bringing her right in front of me? Am I being tested somehow? You can't make this shit up!

Emery walks toward us, holding the hand of a little girl with long, wavy hair that's blowing behind her as she looks up at her daddy, talking nonstop. Her lavender dress with an embroidered mermaid unfurls behind her in the same way, making her look as if she could fly off at any moment. *And Larissa, she definitely could. Or, he could scoop her up and carry her away. So, chill out. Oh, and try not to cry.*

As I glance back up, I see Emma. I have double vision. Is Emma walking next to her, or is she surrounding her with an aura? An aura of love and protection is clearly around this precious child. I can do this. I can follow Emery's lead. I can give them the space they need. Emma is guiding me, and Eric is coaching me. I got this. I hope.

Emery waves, then gives me the same signal he gave Eric. "Beth, these are some nice people I met this week at the bait shop. This lady, Ms. Larissa, well her mommy and daddy knew Grammy Harriett and Grandpa Henry. Say hello."

She has moved closer to her daddy, looks up at him, then says, "Hello, Ms. Lissa, pleased to meet you."

Oh, my gosh, she stumbles over a syllable and mispronounces Larissa in the best way possible, then becomes so formal. He's taught her good manners.

"Pleased to meet you as well, Beth. What are you guys doing today?"

"This is daddy's favorite beach. Even though we live on the river, he says this beach is his happy place. First beach he remembers playing at. So, now it's my favorite beach too. Better than Bathtub Reef down the road. That's for babies." Definitely no shyness from her.

Fighting the urge to jump up and hug her, I reply, "And you're certainly not a baby. Are you thirsty, want a lemonade or water?"

I find her preferred drink and ask, "So, what's in your bucket? Find any beach treasures?"

"Only a couple of shells today, but look, I found a sand dollar. It's almost whole. Daddy and I have a rule that if you can see all five petals on top then it's whole, even if some pieces are broken off. When we get home, we shake them to see if we can find the pieces that come out. They're like little doves, but we call them *angel wings*. When we find one with wings, it's like my mommy's here watching out for me."

I feel my breath catch, like I'm going to cry. *Do not cry.* "I'm sure they will be there when you get home, Beth. I can tell that one is special."

Emery gives me a half smile over her head. "Thank you so much for the lemonade and snack. We gotta get back home or Aunt Kristy will chew me out. We were supposed to be back almost an hour ago. She isn't too patient."

"Bye, Ms. Lissa, bye Mr. Eric and everyone. Thank you!"

Just as they slowly strolled over to meet us, they slowly stroll away, hand in hand. I watch and wait. Yup, both turn around and give me, us, a wave. I wave, and see Emma next to Beth once again. Her hair, her essence.

Steven quietly breaks the silence first. "Well, how about that?"

"Yeah, how about that? Remember the postcard I showed you guys of the House of Refuge? Harriett wrote that they brought Junior out to this beach. That's one of the postcards that made us come to this place. I feel like Harriett is working with my mother and Emma and whatever other power is up there to make this happen. Not on my timeline, not when I think it should, but when they think it should. I surrender. I didn't like it when you all told me this morning to give it time, but I'm getting the message. This is going to roll along as powers greater than I want it to. It's gonna be like the waves: coming a little closer with each surge, going back a bit, then coming closer again. I'm hearing the message and surrendering to it."

35

And if, when it is all over.
I am asked, what I did with my life?
I want to be able to say—"I offered love."
TERRI ST. CLOUD

We're all worn out after our picnic and settle in for a quiet evening. We've split into generations: older folks are watching the sunset, while the younger four (Nate is back as well) find a science-fiction movie to entertain themselves. A ping on my phone interrupts my hypnotic gaze at the horizon. From Kristy: "Hey, yeah, thanks for invite. Not so sure we should bring Mom or leave her alone, but thanks anyway."

That response would have broken my spirit a few hours ago, but I'm content to let it be for now. There is only so much I can expect. We have a connection, and I will cherish what I have for now. I still may call Terry tomorrow. Her insight could bolster my resolve if I begin to falter. She knows far more about this than I do, and has proven herself to be invested, both in me and Emery.

Standing, I say good night to the others and go inside. As I walk by Eric, his sister, and his friends, he calls out, "Hey, Mom, wait up."

I stop at the base of the stairs and wait as he comes over, lowering his voice. "I gotta ask you something, Mom. Not to sound weird, but don't you think Beth looks like Emma? I mean not exactly—her skin is a little darker—but that hair and her eyes, like wow, right?"

"I sure did, honey. Not only does she resemble Emma, I could have sworn I saw Emma walking right next to her, or above her, kind of all around her."

"Oh, man, me too. I didn't want to freak you out by saying that, but I sure did. Emma's telling us again, telling us to keep going even if it doesn't feel like we can. I feel like she's saying it's going to be OK."

I smile, nod my head, and hug him. As he hugs me in return, I feel his hand patting my back. It's going to be OK. Maybe not today or tomorrow, but at some point, it is.

The next morning, I vaguely hear my phone ringing as I squirt shampoo on my hair, but think I'm better off finishing what I'm doing than slipping while rushing to the phone or sounding too anxious. Five minutes won't make a difference.

It's more like twenty by the time I dress and check my phone. Hoping for a voicemail with a long, meaningful message, instead I see Kristy's number and a short message. Hitting the speaker icon, I hear, "Larissa, pick up the phone—where the hell are you? Better yet—get your ass over here—and hurry!"

I call her back, but it goes straight to her voicemail. All right, time to go.

Hurrying down the stairs, I shout out, "Hey, whoever's around—I'm going over to Port Salerno. Kristy left me a message to get over there. No clue what's going on." I grab the keys and run to the car.

The fifteen-minute drive feels like an hour. The majestic tunnel of banyan trees that I usually wish would continue on forever is now interminably long. As I turn off the main road, I hear the eerie sound of a siren behind me and the hair goes up on the back of my neck. What the heck is going on? As it pulls up beside Harriett's house, the air is sucked out of my lungs and I'm not sure I can stand on my legs. Something kicks in and I hurry out of the car as a police car pulls in behind an ambulance already parked out front. Nothing about this looks good. Who . . .?

Just as I spot Kristy by the door, bending over a small child, she waves me toward her. Walking as fast as I can, I hear her say, "Beth, sweetie, remember the nice lady you met at the beach yesterday? She's gonna take you for a little walk. There's too many people in this house right now, and I don't want someone to bump into you."

I slow down a little so as not to scare Beth, and Kristy whispers, "Keep her away from the house—go for a walk. I called the ambulance because Mom, well, it's not good."

I kneel down in front of Beth. I want to touch her long wavy hair, stare into her hazel eyes, and throw my arms around her. Instead, I hold my hand out and say, "Hi, Beth. It was fun meeting you yesterday. Aunt Kristy says we need to go for a walk and play outside."

Beth turns sideways and puts her head down for a minute. Then she puts her own hand out and says, "Daddy says when someone puts out their hand, I should shake it and look right into their eyes. Says I need to show respect and be proud."

Her tiny fingers reach for mine. We shake formally for a moment, then switch to clasp our hands. I tell her, "Your pink nail polish is very pretty. Did Aunt Kristy do that for you?"

"No, Daddy did. When we got home last night, we had dinner, then I was supposed to go to bed, but I didn't want to. Daddy told me I had a half hour for him to do whatever I wanted. So, I asked him to polish my nails and he did." She's beaming as she holds her hands out in front to admire the polish. I'm also staring at those precious little pink-tipped hands.

Tightness in the back of my throat tells me tears are on their way, so I change the subject. "There's a park a little way from here that I went to the other day. Want to walk over there?"

She looks unsure and asks, "Are there swings at that park?"

"Yes, I think so. And a slide."

After three or four steps, she takes my hand again and we start walking. I'm torn because I think I should stay close by the house, in case there's something else I can do, some other way to help. But it's way more important to do as Kristy asked. To keep Beth away and distracted.

When she spots the swings, she runs ahead and yells to me, "Hey, can you push me? High?"

Pushing this beloved child, I'm taken back to countless days pushing Eric or Emma in the park near our house. Wonderful memories of simple times. Times when every day was full of little hands in my big ones, of demands to be pushed higher, of begging for popsicles, of the biggest decision being whether to swing more or move to the slide. Times when optimism and joy were taken for granted. Today, it's anything but lighthearted; I certainly don't assume this to be the way it always will be. Out of some kind of as yet unknown-to-me tragedy two blocks away, Beth and I are given more time together, which I will treasure as long as I live.

Beth interrupts my musings with, "Hey, uh, Miss, uh, Lissa, can we go over there?" The little finger pointing toward the water has a braided ring on it. As I look closer, it looks like the infinity symbol is an integral part of the design. Not believing what I see, I answer her, "Yes, we can. But first, can I see your pretty ring?"

She proudly sticks her finger so close to my face that I almost can't focus on it. I laugh and ask, "This is very special, Beth. Where did you get it?"

"My daddy gave it to me. Said it means he loves me to 'finity'—that means a very long time—forever."

"You are a lucky girl, Beth. My little girl and I used to say the same thing: love you to infinity!"

"You have a little girl? Where is she? Can we play?"

I swear I hear Emma's voice in my ear. I swear I hear, "Always here, here to infinity."

"She's close by, Beth. She has special powers and sometimes she disappears, sometimes she looks like a bird or a butterfly. But she's always out there somewhere."

Beth tilts her head at me as if trying to make sense of what I said, and then says, "OK, well, let's look for her while we walk over to that dock. Sometimes there's fish swimming around there. My daddy taught me how to spot a snook."

I grab her hand and ask, "Maybe you can teach me?"

A couple of hours later, after Beth and I go get a lemonade and come back, I see Kristy and Emery walking toward us. They're walking hand in hand, heads down, shoulders rounded. As they get closer, Kristy yells our names and waves.

Emery walks straight to Beth and kneels down in front of her. "Hey, little missy. I need to talk to our friend here for a few minutes. Auntie Kristy wants to take you with her to pick up some dinner for us. Says you can pick out dessert from the big glass case at the restaurant, OK?"

"Can I pick out two kinds?"

A smile breaks out over his sullen face and he replies, "Only if one is chocolate for me." She nods and runs to her aunt.

As soon as she's out of earshot, Emery says, "My mom, she's, she slipped away. Slipped away right in front of our eyes." His tears spill out, and he reaches for me. We stay that way and cry together.

Finally, he says, "Damn it. She's gonna be mad anyway. Even though I came and saw you, and we talked like she wanted, she's still gonna be mad." He swipes his hand across his face to get rid of the tears.

"Why? What do you mean?"

"We started talking last night after I put Beth to bed. Mom was so relieved I'd gone to see you, and glad I said hello on the beach. She smiled and told me she could finally rest easy, now that you and I were making connections. She even made me promise to bring Beth to see you again, today or tomorrow. I didn't get the chance to do that, because everything happened, and then you got here. Thank you, by the way, for watching Beth, bringing her to the park. No one wanted her to see her grandma at the end, to see her leave when they took her out. Thank you. You came at just the right moment."

"No thanks necessary. I'd do anything for the two of you, or your mom, or your sister. Family is family—and sometimes friends are family. But why do you think your mother will still be mad? I don't get it. She loved you more than anything, Emery. More than her own life. That's why she was waiting. She's been sick for a while, yet she held on until she saw you through her final lesson to you."

"She'll be mad cuz she made me promise not to cry, and I keep crying. She proclaimed there was nothing sad about her going now. Said she was happy I'd done the right thing by contacting you, it brought her great comfort, and that she just wanted to go be with Daddy. She said crying now would be wasting valuable time to be happy. Told me to get Beth to see you, to hang out with my brother, and to make the most of every day I'm given. Then she said something I'm not sure I get."

"What was that?"

"She said it makes no sense to cry, that she'll always be here, no matter what. And just because I can't see her anymore, well, that it means nothing. Sure as hell, it means a lot. It means I can't hug her, can't take care of her. I knew she was waiting for me to connect with you. That's what held me back from doing it. Damn it—by connecting with you, it's like I gave her permission to go, gave her the wish she wanted, and now she's gone. She was the best."

"Yes, Emery, she was and is the best. You don't need to use the past tense. I'm grateful to Harriett, I feel blessed that my parents chose her for you, if it couldn't be me. She's been your mom your whole life, given you and Kristy everything she possibly could. She got tired and wanted peace. Now she wants me to give you the things, the memories, that she can't anymore. But that doesn't mean she's gone. She'll be watching you from wherever."

"I don't understand--"

"Of course you don't. We think we learn so much as we grow older, but there's so much more that we don't understand than we admit. The last year and a half brought me a great deal of sorrow, but it taught me more than all those fifty years before. One thing I know—I don't understand, but I *know*—is that love like what you and your mom had, or Emma and me, does not die when a person isn't taking their breaths here any longer. Love lingers in our memories and in the signs our loved ones send us."

"Like what kind of signs?"

"So many—but here's one: When Emma was a little girl, she and I practiced her weekly vocabulary words, and I always made her use them in a sentence. The word *infinity* became one of our favorites, and we'd always say, 'Love you to infinity.' This week, when it was one year since Emma passed over, Eric's friend Hilary found a necklace on the beach and handed it to me. The medallion was a heart with an infinity symbol. When I turned it over, it had an E on it."

He starts to interrupt me, but I stop him.

"Wait, that's not all. So today, I notice Beth's ring and ask her about it. She tells me that you gave it to her. It's beautiful. I told her that my little girl and I always said the same thing about loving to infinity. You and I each gave our daughters jewelry with an infinity symbol. Do you think that's just chance? When Beth asked me where my little girl was, I told her she disappears sometimes, and then has the power to appear like a butterfly or a bird; that although I can't see her, she's always around. I choose to believe those are signs, Emery. Believing in signs has brought me tremendous comfort, maybe they'd do the same for you. We are connected to our loved ones in so many ways we will never understand. But then, we don't need to. We just need to be open, and we will see them."

He's shaking his head. Does he not believe me still? But then he says, "You're right, that's not all. Did Beth show you the inside of that ring?"

"No, why?"

"When she was born, when Beth, Elizabeth, was born, I gave her mama the infinity ring, with the initial E inside. I wanted her mama to know I'd love them both always. When she died, I had it resized for Beth's finger. And I'll have it resized again and again, so she will know she's loved, no matter where her mama and daddy are."

"Exactly. Love for our children does not die. That's your mother's final lesson, Emery. Let her show you the way."

"What about you, what about us? My mom wants us to be together, you want us to be together. You both are so certain, so determined. I want to do the right thing for all of us, especially Beth, but I'm not sure what that is."

"The right thing often seems unclear, but maybe it's because we overthink it. Maybe we need to pay attention to the signs right in front of us. Besides the infinity symbol, you just told me the ring is inscribed with an E. All of my children, including a baby that I was unable to carry to full term, have names beginning with E—is that coincidence or is it a sign? For me, I believe it's another sign of our connection. Beth also told me that you and she shake out the little dovelike pieces from the sand dollars and say they are angels from her mother. Emma and I used to make crafts from the same bits. And when Eric saw a medium just before we came here, Emma communicated that he needs to keep going, keep trying, even when things seem insurmountable. Could her message be in reference to finding you, then forging a relationship?"

"I guess so. My mother sure kept going until she helped me and you find one another. She was definitely determined. But me, not really sure. I was so mixed up yesterday; that's why I went to the beach with Beth. I hoped being outside, walking in the waves with her, would bring me clarity or inspiration or something. Never expected to run into you guys. But, when we did, it actually felt OK."

"When we encountered you out on the beach yesterday, Beth told me it was your happy place, since you were a very little boy. And I always brought Eric and Emma to the beach. It was a happy place for them as well, and it gave me the chance to restore myself while they played. So many forces came together to bring Eric and me to this very island, just a bridge away from you and your family."

Emery stares out at the little bay. He seems to be contemplating all that has happened, all that we've said. I wonder if the water, whether it's calm over here or rough over on the ocean, brings him the insight that it always seems to deliver to me.

Before I have a chance to ask him, he builds on my last musings about the bridge and our connection, "You know, it is amazing. From New York to Florida and apart for decades. Now, you're just a bridge away from where I spent all of my time growing up, and a mile away from where my parents took me to play in the sand. My mom was persistent. I need to respect her wishes and figure this out—for Beth."

I smile and gently place my hand over his. "So many life events, signs from our loved ones, postcards, and letters. We came here expecting a getaway, a break from all that had happened in the last year. We got all of that and so much more. We made new friends, we were comforted by the surroundings of this beautiful place, and somehow, we found you. We found Beth. And Steven and Eric found Nina. I'm not always sure what is right, Emery, but how could this *not* be right?"

Dear Readers

I hope that you have enjoyed *Wonders in the Waves*. It would be wonderful to hear from you – you can send messages to me by email to:

        Wordsinthewingspress2021@gmail.com

    Reviews are always appreciated; please consider posting one on Amazon or Goodreads. Also, check out my website: wordsinthewingspress.com; my Facebook page: Words in the Wings Press, Inc; or Instagram: Words in the Wings.

    I thoroughly enjoy attending book club discussions, am open to in-person events, and available to connect virtually. I have also facilitated meetings of grief groups; I find that talking about a book really helps people to open up about their own feelings. Let me know if your group would like to hear more about arranging an event.

    Thank you for reading and sharing!

Jennifer

Questions for Discussion

1. Larissa often finds it restorative to be near water, although occasionally the waves overwhelm her. How do you feel when near water? How are your senses and state of mind affected?

2. Steven and Larissa share so much and are close in so many ways, yet Larissa prefers to keep some distance. What do you think of this?

3. What are some examples of the "wonders" found in the waves? What wonders have you found when near water?

4. Eric and Larissa share some important discussions and feelings while taking their road trip to Florida. Have you had similar experiences while driving with family or friends?

5. Terry admits that she violated rules during her time as Larissa's nurse. How did those violations make you feel about what is the right thing to do in such situations?

6. What did you think of the first meeting between Emery and Larissa? Was it what you expected? Why or why not?

7. Emery also contemplates what is right about developing a relationship with Larissa. What are his worries and fears?

8. Much of the time, Larissa presents a calm, yet determined demeanor. A couple of times, however, she loses her cool. Were those surprising to you? What do you think of the ways those around her reacted to those times?

9. What signs from loved ones did you find particularly moving or powerful? Have you found signs to be comforting or disturbing or something else?

10. In *Comfort in the Wings*, Larissa travels to the Finger Lakes, and in *Wonders in the Waves*, she comes to the ocean. Do you think these choices are connected to where she was emotionally in her grief? In what ways?

About the Author

Jennifer Collins, PT, EdD, MPA, is a retired physical therapist and college professor whose career spanned more than forty years. She held many titles during those years, but "Mom" was the one that brought her the most joy and pride. While working in her profession, her close-knit family was the center of her universe.

Her debut novel, *Comfort in the Wings*, emerged from the author's own devastating experiences with loss of immediate family members. Overcome, she found herself in awe at the outpouring of stories from others who had lost loved ones. A drive to incorporate all of those emotions into fiction stories has become a compelling force for writing. Encouraged by readers' responses to *Comfort in the Wings*, she is excited to continue the story of Larissa Whitcomb and her loved ones with *Wonders in the Waves*.

Collins now spends her time writing and running a family business alongside her eldest son. She does both from two residences: her longtime family home in upstate New York and Hutchinson Island in Florida.

CPSIA information can be obtained
at www.ICGtesting.com
Printed in the USA
BVHW091530300922
648383BV00011B/1473